Praise for Steven Womack and his Harry James Denton mysteries

DEAD FOLKS' BLUES

"A deft, atmosphere-rich novel: smart, funny, and filled with a sense of wry heartbreak. Steven Womack's Nashville stands out—it is a beautifully drawn backdrop."
> —JAMES ELLROY,
> *New York Times* bestselling author of
> *L.A. Confidential*

"*Dead Folks' Blues* is a virtuoso performance."
> —The Virginian-Pilot and Ledger-Star

TORCH TOWN BOOGIE

"A sure winner . . . Many critics . . . have lauded Womack's sense of setting. In *Torch Town Boogie*, his rendering of Nashville is almost palpable."
> —The Tennessean

*Please turn the page
for more reviews. . . .*

CHAIN OF FOOLS

"*Chain of Fools* is the fourth, most tightly written, and best novel yet in the Denton series."
—*Nashville Life*

"If you're looking for hardboiled, you need look no further than Steven Womack's latest, *Chain of Fools*. . . . A memorable mean-streets tale."
—*Alfred Hitchcock Mystery Magazine*

"Womack's books feature strong, believable characters, fast-paced multifaceted plots, a well-defined Nashville setting, and humorous insights galore. *Chain of Fools* is the latest and best in the Harry James Denton saga, a great series by an extraordinarily talented writer."
—*The Armchair Detective*

By Steven Womack

The Harry James Denton Books
DEAD FOLKS' BLUES*
TORCH TOWN BOOGIE*
WAY PAST DEAD*
CHAIN OF FOOLS*
MURDER MANUAL*

The Jack Lynch Trilogy
MURPHY'S FAULT
SMASH CUT
THE SOFTWARE BOMB

Published by Ballantine Books

MURDER MANUAL

Steven Womack

BALLANTINE BOOKS • NEW YORK

A Ballantine Book
Published by The Ballantine Publishing Group
Copyright © 1998 by Steven Womack

All rights reserved under International and Pan-American Copyright Conventions. Published in the United States by The Ballantine Publishing Group, a division of Random House, Inc., New York, and simultaneously in Canada by Random House of Canada Limited, Toronto.

http://www.randomhouse.com

Library of Congress Catalog Card Number: 97-94455

ISBN 0-345-41447-0

Manufactured in the United States of America

First Edition: June 1998

10 9 8 7 6 5 4 3 2 1

for Tom C. Armstrong,
the humble poet laureate of Music Row

Was mich nicht umbringt, macht mich stärker.
(That which does not kill me, makes me stronger.)
—FRIEDRICH NIETZSCHE, *Twilight of the Idols*

Acknowledgments

I'm deeply grateful to the folks who helped me with research and with many patient readings of the book in manuscript. Jim Veatch and Justine Honeyman have given me insightful and perceptive readings now for four books, and I'm very grateful to them. R. B. Quinn, late of the Freedom Forum First Amendment Center, did a thorough and discerning reading of the book as well, as did Mike Price, who left Nashville for Reno and talked me into setting my next book there so I could visit him. I'm on my way, buddy.

Stacy Miller, attorney-at-law and tennis court terror, gave me insights into estate law and how wills work in Tennessee. I'm grateful to her.

The Nashville Writers Alliance gave me feedback and support during the writing of this book. I hope they know how much I owe them and how much esteem and affection I have for them.

Speaking of esteem and affection, Nancy Yost and Joe Blades once again have kept me in the game. Thanks, guys.

Finally, I'm beholden and grateful to Sharyn McCrumb, my literary godmother, for her metaphor of The Claw, among many other things. Her friendship is a gift in my life.

Prologue

I'd heard of the book. I mean, who hadn't?

It had been on the *New York Times* bestseller list for over a year. *60 Minutes* did a feature segment on the author. Every woman celebrity anchor and interviewer from Diane Sawyer to Oprah to Sally Jessy to half a dozen others I'd never heard of had fawned over him on camera. I opened the Sunday paper a month or so ago, and there he was in the slick magazine insert: Robert Jefferson Reed surrounded by his wife and three fresh-faced teenage children, all beaming, looking like they'd just come in from an afternoon on the slopes. His book was everywhere; you couldn't swing a dead cat in the Wal-Mart without hitting a copy.

But who would have ever guessed that a book called *Life's Little Maintenance Manual* would have been such a runaway smash hit? Or that the author would be from Nashville, Tennessee?

C'mon, give me a break—it's not even really a book. I picked it up at the Inglewood Kroger about six months ago while I waited in line—my Budget Gourmets dripping through the basket—behind some wild-eyed elderly lady who was raving at the cashier. Something about the price of bacon or her food stamps being late or some such crap. I tried not to listen. You know how it is, when something really unpleasant is happening in a public place and you don't even want to watch, but you're stuck there, so you do anything to divert your attention, right?

Anyway, here I am with this lady screaming in front of me,

so I reach down on the rack and pick up this $9.95 paperback and flip through it. It's an odd size, ornate, very thin, and divided into four parts, each devoted to keeping one area of your life in tip-top shape. Part One tells you how to keep the physical side of your life humming. I opened to the first page of that part, and there in bold type about a half-inch tall was the admonition:

EAT YOUR VEGETABLES

And that's it. That's the only thing on the page. There's a cute border around the edge and a couple of swatches of color, but that's it. Eat your vegetables.

So I turn the page:

DRINK PLENTY OF WATER

Jesus, I'm thinking, a tree had to die for this? So I flip to the second part, which is all about how to keep your marriage perking along.

NEVER LET A DAY GO BY WITHOUT
TELLING YOUR SPOUSE YOU LOVE HIM (HER)

Now, mind you, I'm not even Jewish, but expressions like *oi, vey* are beginning to run through my head. Meanwhile, the lady in front of me in the checkout line breaks into a continuous stream of obscenities, like a Subic Bay sailor having a psychotic break in the middle of shore leave.

I open to page two of the section on marriage:

NEVER GO TO BED ANGRY

Or at least not without your lithium, I thought, just as the screaming lady slams down a carton of eggs on the conveyor belt. The cashier picks up the white phone by her register and calls for help, then starts wiping up yellow slime with a nasty rag as the old lady rants on.

Part Three was on the care and feeding of children. I turned the page:

PATIENCE WILL CARRY YOU THROUGH ANYTHING

The guy who wrote that ought to be standing in this freaking checkout line.

Part Four covered the maintenance schedule for one's career:

GIVE A LITTLE EXTRA EACH DAY

Oh, puh-leeze, I'm thinking, somebody get me some insulin.

By this time, a security guard is trying to escort the old lady out as quickly and quietly as possible, only now she's having what looks like a heart attack. She shrieks and clutches at her chest, then paws at the security guard's face as she slumps to the floor. The manager comes over, rolls his eyes; apparently he's been through this before.

I flip through *Life's Little Maintenance Manual* one last time. On the last page of the part about keeping your body in one piece is the exhortation:

TREAT YOURSELF TO DINNER OUT EVERY ONCE IN A WHILE

I take this as divine guidance. I set my by-now flaccid frozen-food boxes on the conveyor belt and step around the scrum of people hovering over the old lady. Then I get back in my car, ease out of the parking lot, and head to Mrs. Lee's for Szechuan chicken. That was the last I thought of Robert Jefferson Reed, his well-scrubbed family, and his thin little bestseller.

That is, of course, until the day his wife knocked on my office door.

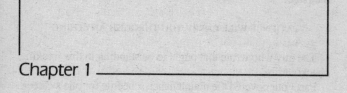

Chapter 1

I've never bought into Nietzsche's notion about what doesn't kill you making you stronger. My experience has been what doesn't kill you *nearly* kills you, beats the crap out of you, and leaves you bleeding by the side of the road.

Take the last few months, for instance. If Nietzsche had been right, I'd be making Arnold Schwarzenegger look like Pee-Wee Herman right about now. And it all started four long months ago.

Four months ago, when I killed a man.

Shot him stone cold, point-blank, more times than I can remember. It was a me-or-him situation and there were other people involved. If I hadn't done what I did, the body count would've been even higher. As a result, I got dragged before the police, then the grand jury, and grilled like Elisha Cook Jr. sweating under a hot lamp. In the end, I was cut loose. Justifiable homicide. Self-defense.

It didn't matter. I'd taken a life. There's a point-of-no-return concept involved here. Unlike virtually every other act of human existence, killing is irrevocable. The weight of it sat on me like a bad winter.

All systems shut down. For months I barely left my tiny attic apartment above Mrs. Hawkins's house in East Nashville. Phone calls went unreturned. When I bothered to go in to my office, the mail—most of it junk—was piled up on the floor like the makings of a good campfire. The days went by in a blur, an endless mire of sleep—sometimes sixteen or more hours a day—interspersed with moments of wakefulness that were so foggy and sleep-logged they seemed as if a dream.

I remember paperbacks, lots of paperbacks. Sometimes I'd wake up, still in my clothes, with piles of them scattered haphazardly across the rumpled bedsheets wadded up next to me. And jazz; the small clock radio by my bed stayed tuned to the all-jazz public radio station outside Nashville and played softly day and night, night and day.

During a rare venture into the outside world, I managed to impregnate the woman with whom I'd been involved for several years. She had her own problems; this was her way of dealing with them. For a while, it seemed as if the prospect of parenthood in my forties would put a spark back. But it didn't.

Ultimately, I had to come out of it.

I thought I'd walk away from it, just chuck it all and start over. But that's easier said when you're twenty or even thirty than when you're in a staring contest with forty-five and you sense that forty-five ain't going to blink first.

In the end, it was the money—or lack of it—that drove me back to work. I'd borrowed a couple of grand from my parents, who are retired now in Hawaii, but I couldn't face going back to that well again.

So I went back out in the world. It was just like starting over again, just like six years ago when I first hung out my shingle as a private investigator. The couple of clients who fed me regular work—fraudulent workers' comp claims and the like— had moved on to other people when I disappeared. The few calls I'd gotten through my tiny ad in the yellow pages never called back when they couldn't find me.

It didn't take long to realize that the hole I'd dug myself into was deeper than I first thought. Bills were piling up fast. My office rent was a month behind. The phone was going to be cut off if I didn't get a check off to BellSouth in the next few days. I sat in my office all morning that first Monday after my momentous decision, balancing the books, going through stacks of checkless mail piled next to a silent phone. As Mary Chapin Carpenter sang: "The stars might lie, but the numbers never do." I took the coldest, hardest look I could, without any sense of panic or desperation, then took the only alternative left.

I called Lonnie.

* * *

I met Lonnie about a hundred years and another life ago,
back when I was a newspaperman. This was when I was writing features for the newspaper, even before I got transferred to
the state capitol beat. I was doing a piece for the Living section
on people who'd come to Nashville to make it big in country
music and then been forced to take other jobs when the record
companies didn't pile dump-truckloads of money on their front
porches. Lonnie'd come to Music City from Brooklyn. I'd heard
him sing; he should've stayed home. But you can't tell these
people anything. They all think they're the next Wynonna or
Shania or Clint or Garth or one of those other odd-sounding
names.

After a couple of years scraping by on Lower Broad, tend-
ing bar part-time and playing open-mike nights, Lonnie decided there had to be something better. A buddy of his said he
knew a guy who repossessed cars and would pay upwards of
fifty bucks a pop for help. Guy could make a quick two hundred a night if he worked at it, paid in cash at the end of the
shift. Lonnie jumped on it, repossessing about four hundred
cars over the next six months before it occurred to him he
could make even better dough doing it himself.

He bought an old junkyard off Gallatin Road on a tiny side
street behind what used to be the Inglewood Theatre back in
the Fifties but was now a salvage store. There was a rusted mobile home on the lot and it was surrounded by a ten-foot-high
chain-link fence. Lonnie and his guard dog, a timber shepherd
bitch whom he'd aptly named Shadow, moved in.

Over the years, Lonnie did real well, branching out into
bounty hunting, industrial counterespionage and security, electronic surveillance, and a few other spook hustles when he got
bored. He was mostly a loner and shut down in front of others.
I knew him for years before I learned he'd once been married
back in Brooklyn and that his wife had been murdered. I never
knew him to date, at least not seriously, and there were very
few people he was comfortable around.

When my career as a hotshot political reporter crashed and
burned and I decided to try private investigating, I turned to

him for some insights. Next thing I knew, I was padding across a dew-soaked backyard in East Tennessee in the middle of a crisp, moonless autumn night, stalking an elusive 1989 Ford Explorer, and hoping the guy who'd been hiding it from us didn't have good hearing and a twelve-gauge by the bed.

Lonnie and I had seen each other through some interesting times in the last few years. We had developed that easygoing, smartassed way of dealing with each other that men adopt when they don't know any other way to show affection. It had been nearly four months since I'd had any contact with him, the longest time that had passed since we became friends. I was looking forward to seeing him—something I took as further evidence that I was almost alive again—but felt almost guilty that after so much silence, I was tracking him down because I needed something from him.

I got over that real quick, though. There was a phone number, one that only a few close associates were given. It was among several lines running into the mobile home and the only one he always answered. If he was out, he even forwarded that number to his cell phone.

I dialed the number. The phone rang about twenty times without an answer.

I didn't think much of it. The next best approach was to hoof it back across the bridge to East Nashville and track him down. I left my shabby office building, which was looking more and more run-down all the time compared to the new construction in downtown Nashville, and walked two blocks up Seventh, to where I'd found a parking space on the street. I used to have a contract space in a parking garage, but the developers tore it down two months ago, paved it over as a parking lot, then jacked up the rates so high, I couldn't afford them anymore.

Progress.

It was late afternoon by the time I found myself weaving through the traffic on Gallatin Road toward Lonnie's junkyard. I made the turn off the main drag, circled back around the Inglewood Theatre, and parked in front of the gate. The sky above was darkening and the wind had picked up, like one of those early spring thunderstorms guaranteed to pop up out of nowhere just as rush hour begins.

I pulled out my key ring and fumbled for the right key. Before unlocking the padlock, though, I rattled the chain-link gate for a few seconds. That was the drill if you didn't want Shadow tearing your arm off. The past couple of years, her sight's been going and she doesn't hear as well as she used to. The hip dysplasia had gotten bad enough that she had trouble walking. But if she didn't recognize you, she'd reach somewhere way deep inside herself and find the strength and agility for one more good lunge at your throat. And there was nothing wrong with her jaws.

I rattled the gate again, whistling this time. I pulled my coat tighter, the wind chilling me. From the north, darker clouds rolled in, heavy and threatening.

"Shadow!" I called. Nothing. I unlocked the gate and eased into the junkyard lot, then crossed a minefield of car parts, discarded tires, puddles of grease and grime, and gravel packed into mud. Perhaps twenty years of classic junkyard stretched in front of me before I reached the faded, pastel green trailer with the rust streaks down the side. I stepped up onto the cinderblock step and rapped on the metal door. The noise rang, tinny and hollow, reverberating through the trailer. I'd wondered at first if anyone was even there; now I began to wonder if the place had been cleared out.

I stepped down, over to a window left of the door, and peered in through a crack between the yellowed shade and the edge of the window.

The place had been trashed.

The couch was over on its back, the coffee table overturned next to it. The place had always been full of an odd mix of junk, car parts, exotic electronic devices, radios, computers, and stuff I didn't understand, some of which would blow you to hell if you touched it the wrong way. Everything was scattered piecemeal on the floor, as if the gear had been thrown about in a rage. Dirty beer bottles littered the floor, with loose pages from books and manuals ripped from their bindings and strewn about.

I jumped back over to the door and pounded hard this time.

"Lonnie!" I yelled. "Hey, man, you in there?"

From my right, from somewhere inside the far end of the trailer, a board creaked.

"Lonnie," I said, my voice not quite as loud this time. I put my hand on the door. Another creak, this one closer. Then another, each one coming nearer the door. I felt the vibrations as the footsteps approached.

"Yeah," a muffled voice inside said. It sounded like Lonnie, but somewhat different.

"Lonnie, you okay?"

The knob turned and rattled as he unlocked the door. I backed away as he opened it, shocked.

Lonnie stood in the doorway, staring down at me. He'd lost maybe fifteen pounds and had neither shaved nor bathed in days. He wore oil-slicked faded jeans and a grimy T-shirt. There were great dark circles under his eyes and the hollows of his cheeks had deepened, the shadow of his beard accentuating the sharp curve of bone beneath skin.

He stared at me blankly for a few moments.

"You okay, man?" I asked. "You look like hell."

He turned and walked back inside. "C'mon in," he said.

I followed him in, my mind jumping from one flash of fantasy to another: he'd been jumped and beaten up by robbers—there had been, after all, a huge run on home invasions lately. Maybe one of his screwy experiments had gone wrong and he'd nearly blown the place up. Perhaps he'd just gone psychotic on me.

Suddenly, he whipped around just as I closed the door, his eyes dark and searing as he pointed a dirty finger at me.

"Okay," he barked. "You're a cartoon character!"

"I'm a *what*?" My voice cracked, a dry squeak that sounded embarrassingly wimpy.

"A cartoon character!" he snapped. "Now listen up, if you're—"

"Which?" I interrupted.

"Which what?"

"Which cartoon character?"

"Damn it, Harry, how the hell am I supposed to know which cartoon character? Any goddamn cartoon character you want to be."

He ran his hands through his hair and squeezed the sides of his head, as if attempting to relieve some horrible internal pressure. He paced back and forth in front of me, his eyes fixed on the floor.

"So you're a cartoon character—"

"Popeye," I said.

"What?"

"Popeye. I want to be Popeye." And I'm thinking to myself that of all my imagined options of what had happened to Lonnie, psychosis was emerging to the forefront.

He threw his head back, furious at me. "All right, damn it, you're Popeye the goddamn sailor man! Now shut up and listen!"

I nodded, afraid to say anything.

He put his hands on his hips and glared at me for a moment, daring me to speak.

"You're a cartoon character," he continued. "Now—and this is very important—who would you rather do, Betty Boop or Aunt Fritzi?"

My mouth hung open slightly. "What?" I whispered after a moment.

"Harry, this is important! This is very revealing."

I stood there a moment pondering, and part of me was thinking that I can't believe I'm standing here seriously trying to come up with an intelligent answer to that question.

Then, of course, I remembered I was supposed to be Popeye.

"What about Olive Oyl?" I asked.

Lonnie exploded, throwing his hands in the air, whirling around and karate-kicking the overturned sofa.

"Olive Oyl!" he roared. "Olive Oyl! That codependent, whiny, anorexic bitch! One minute she's flirting with Bluto, the next she's screaming for Popeye to come save her bony ass *one . . . more . . . time*!"

He stomped the floor, planted his hands on his hips again. I took a step backward, toward the trailer door.

"Jesus, Harry, I don't see how you can even bring Olive Oyl into the equation here. . . ."

I thought for a moment. "Okay," I said. "Okay. Lemme see. Aunt Fritzi's looking pretty good these days. You know, she's got that new guy drawing her. But she's still got that awful Nancy living with her."

"Oh, yeah," Lonnie sputtered. "Yeah, I hate that little fat pig Nancy. I'd like to see Sluggo really lay into her, you know what I mean?"

I didn't know what he meant but suspected now was not the time to ask. My eyes flitted from side to side as I tried to figure out what to say next.

"Jeez, Lonnie I guess I don't know . . . I guess Betty Boop'd be a lot of fun."

Lonnie let loose with a deep sigh of relief as his tightly wound body seemed to unravel and spread a bit. He leaned against the overturned couch and let it take part of his weight.

"Thanks, Harry," he whispered. "I knew I could count on you."

I stepped closer to him, but very carefully, uncertain what would make him explode next.

"Why the sudden interest in cartoon characters?"

He looked up at me, exhaustion in his eyes. "It's very revealing," he repeated. "Passion or responsibility, a life fully lived or a slave to convention. Betty Boop or Aunt Fritzi. When's the last time you saw Aunt Fritzi have a date?"

"I see your point," I lied.

His shoulders sagged and his chin drooped toward his chest. From the inside corner of one eye, a single tear ran down to the end of his nose.

"What is it, Lonnie?" I said, my voice as soft and soothing as I could make it. "What's wrong?"

He raised his head and I saw a pain in his face that I'd never seen before. He looked completely and horribly alone, and suddenly I knew what had happened even before he spoke.

"Shadow died," he said.

Chapter 2

Why is it that when the brain goes to shock, the knees go to mush? The floor seemed to sway beneath me.

"When?" I whispered after what felt like a long time.

He stared, exhausted, into space. "Last night."

"Jesus, Lonnie, I'm incredibly sorry."

His gaze remained fixed midair on something I couldn't see.

"It started a week ago," he said, his voice a low, shocked monotone. "She got weak all of a sudden, couldn't hold her water or her bowels anymore. I couldn't get her to eat. I don't think she was hurting. It was like the fire went out of her."

Then he was silent for a few moments.

"I took her to the vet," he continued. "Doc said she'd had a series of small strokes, said she needed to be put to sleep. Put to sleep. I hate that. He meant sign the papers so he could kill her."

"Lonnie, don't," I said. "This isn't—"

"I couldn't let him do that, Harry. Couldn't let him put my girl down like that."

His head moved up slowly and his eyes met mine. "She was all I had, man."

"You have friends," I said. "You got me. Why didn't you call?"

He shook his head and made a kind of spewing noise. "Shit, Harry, last time I saw you, you looked like an extra out of *Night of the Living Dead.* Besides, what were you going to do? She was dying. Nobody could change that."

All the same, I felt like pond scum for not being there for him, for Shadow.

I realized I'd been standing in one position so long, my legs were going to sleep and my back was starting to hurt. I shifted my weight, took a step over to him, then straightened an overturned folding chair and sat down.

"You didn't have to go through it by yourself," I said. "I'da come, man."

He put his elbows on his knees and rested his head in his hands, face toward the floor, hands rubbing his scalp.

"I'm sorry. I'm just so damn tired. Haven't slept in days. She never seemed like she was hurting, never whimpered, complained, any of that. I sat up with her, held her until she—"

"Where is she now?" I said.

"I buried her out back this morning, just as the sun was coming up." He stopped, looked around at the wreckage of the trailer.

"Guess I went kind of ape shit," he muttered.

I thought for a moment of the times I'd seen her prowling the junkyard, protecting the fenced boundaries like a military outpost. That space was her life, her own private queendom. Somehow it seemed right that he'd buried her there. This sharp pain shot through my gut when I realized I wish I'd had the chance to say goodbye to her.

"Man, this ain't gonna help much," I finally said, after forcing myself to focus on anything but that pain. "But she died at home, peacefully, in the arms of somebody who cared for her and loved her, and she's buried in a place she loved. If you gotta go, that ain't a bad way to do it."

He straightened and raised his head again. I sensed somehow that he hadn't really thought of it that way.

"So what are you doing here, anyway? Haven't seen you in months."

I shrugged. "It's been too long. I'm sorry, especially given the circumstances."

"You didn't answer my question."

I felt shitty enough to begin with without telling him I had tracked him down because I needed work. But it was the straight truth and there was no point in trying to dodge it.

"Things have gotten kind of rough lately on the biz front," I said. "Thought maybe—"

"Thought maybe you'd pick up a few bucks with ol' Lonnie again." His voice trailed off and he shook his head, disgusted. "Jesus, Harry. You disappear for months and then you pop up out of nowhere."

I stood up. I didn't feel like having this discussion right now. "Listen, it's a bad time. Why don't I take off? You give me a call when you feel like getting together, okay?"

I stepped over toward him, stuck out my hand. He watched me, stone-faced, and made no move. I pulled my hand back, stuck it in my pocket.

"You need anything, you give me a call," I said. "I'll see you around, okay?"

I waited a few moments, and when he said nothing I turned and went to the door. As my hand hit the doorknob, he spoke.

"I'm supposed to meet this guy around six," Lonnie said, his voice still that low, numb monotone. "Offered me two bills to cover his ass while he nails a bond jumper."

I turned back to him. He stood up, thumbs in the side pockets of his jeans.

"You want to come along," he said, "we'll split fifty-fifty."

I smiled at him weakly and nodded my head. We didn't go into it any further, but I knew he'd forgiven me.

"She was good people, Lonnie," I said. "I'm going to miss her."

Lonnie squealed the old F-150 through the curve onto the Ellington Parkway entrance ramp. I was on the front seat beside him, a pair of handcuffs folded into my back pocket, a slapjack slipped into my inside coat pocket, a can of pepper spray in my front pants pocket, and a stinger disguised as a beeper on a hook on my belt. I've got a carry permit, but I don't like guns; like them even less now than I used to.

Lonnie had a different take on the evening. He wore a nine millimeter in a nylon-and-Velcro shoulder holster underneath his surplus fatigue jacket and a tiny Airweight .38 in an ankle holster. This was in addition to the slapjack, pepper spray, handcuffs, Taser, and a variety of other toys he carried.

I'd not done a lot of bounty hunting with Lonnie, just enough to know I didn't like it. Under case law dating back to the nineteenth century—*Taylor v. Taynter,* I believe—when a bail bondsman posts bond for you, you essentially become his property. You post bond for a guy and he jumps bail, you can do anything to get him back. You don't need a search warrant to go into his house after him. You don't need an arrest warrant. You don't have to Mirandize him. None of this due process shit; you find him, he's yours. You can go anywhere, any jurisdiction, cross any state, county, or city border. Doesn't matter; if you've got a certified copy of the bond and a warrant for "Failure to Appear," he's the game and you're the hunter. Anything goes.

This also means the jumper hasn't got a lot to lose. Sometimes we'd go after guys who realized what they were up against and were so tired of running, they were almost relieved to be going back to jail. Once or twice, though, it'd been like cornering a rabid dog. I hated bounty hunting the same way street cops hate domestic calls. You just don't know what you'll run into.

"So where we going?" I asked over the roar of the Ford as Lonnie hit eighty on the parkway.

"Hickory Hollow area," he said. "Some Mexican restaurant."

"Why a Mexican restaurant?"

Lonnie turned to me, one hand lightly on the wheel. He'd shaved, showered, changed into some clean clothes while I straightened up what I could of the trailer. Other than the circles under his bloodshot eyes, he looked almost normal.

"Jumper's a Mexican, an illegal up here working construction. Got popped Saturday night for aggravated assault, D and D, and somehow the system got all screwed up and he managed to find a bondsman before anybody realized he didn't have a green card."

"And of course the motherthumper rabbited as soon as he hit the sidewalk."

"Wouldn't you?" Lonnie asked.

The traffic at the cityside end of the Ellington Parkway thickened and slowed as we approached I-65. Lonnie maneuvered around a fender bender, cut in front of a Roadway semi, went partway up on the shoulder, and managed to squeeze around the bottleneck. Then we crossed the river and headed out toward the I-24 split.

We were on our way to the southeast quadrant of the city, which was the fastest-growing part of a town that was already in the biggest population boom in anyone's memory. The city's growth was straining the infrastructure something fierce. Property values were skyrocketing, mainly from people moving in from the northeast and L.A. who were delighted to find that the money they spent in a one-bedroom efficiency in Manhattan would pay the mortgage here on a four-bedroom house on an acre lot in the burbs. The natives were starting to sport bumper stickers with sentiments like WELCOME TO NASHVILLE! NOW Y'ALL GO HOME.

"I still don't get it," I said. "Why's the guy going to be in a Mexican restaurant? Isn't that a little visible?"

Lonnie grinned. "Man's gotta eat, ain't he?"

"Smartass." I propped my feet up on the dashboard and stared out the window at the endless line of cars all around us.

"The restaurant's in a tacky motel just off the interstate. Lot of immigrant construction workers rent by the week, then move on to the next job site."

"So he's hiding out with the brothers."

"Yeah, only thing is, Jerry speaks Spanish, knew where to ask and how to ask. Tracked the jumper down a couple days ago. Jerry was a Ranger, spent a lot of time down in Central America."

"Jerry's the bondsman?"

"No," Lonnie said, grinning. "Jerry's the bounty hunter. You never met him?"

I shook my head.

"He's a trip. A real wild man. Jerry the Drill."

Lonnie swerved to avoid an Oldsmobile that had inexplicably stopped in the middle of the freeway. Tires squealed, the engine whined as he downshifted. My heart raced as we skidded through a herd of stampeding metal. I grabbed the door handle in a death grip as we veered back across the freeway to the far left and slipped seamlessly into the fast lane, the engine screaming as Lonnie shifted back up to ninety.

I cleared my throat, tried to breathe. "Jerry the Drill, huh?"

We were silent the rest of the way. I wondered what life without Shadow would be like for Lonnie. Despite my protestations, he really didn't have anyone else. On the other hand, Lonnie was already beginning to seem like his old self. I'm not sure the same could be said of me.

Twenty minutes later, we turned off the freeway onto Bell Road and into an area of strip malls, car dealerships, a Target, and a couple of motels, one of which advertised in glowing pink neon: HOT TUB AND FRIG IN EVERY ROOM.

Lonnie pointed, laughed. "Hey, my kind of place."

"Think they meant *fridge*?" I asked.

To our right, up a slight hill, an older multistoried motel was painted a fading pink over fake stucco. Blinking Christmas tree lights wound around the windows and along the gutters. The sign above the door, in hand-painted letters several feet high, read CASA FAJITA.

"Party time," Lonnie said, his voice stronger now. I could feel the oncoming adrenaline surge myself.

Up the hill in a crowded parking lot, a tall guy in a black leather sportcoat leaned against the hood of a vintage Cadillac, a huge early Seventies land yacht. You don't park a car like that; you dock it, and I figured Jerry the Drill must be doing pretty well to afford to put gas in it.

Lonnie backed the truck into a spot opposite the Cadillac, so they faced each other nose-to-nose across the asphalt. We climbed down out of the Ford and crossed the blacktop.

"Yo' dude," Lonnie called.

"Yo' ya'self, amigo," the guy in the coat said. He was tall, maybe six-five, about my age, slight roll around the belt line. His arms were crossed and he wore aviator bifocals. Altogether, he looked like a relatively well-off middle-aged guy who'd discovered he had a deep and abiding affection for

BarcaLoungers and multiple ESPN channels. He was not the kind of guy I'd look at and think *bounty hunter*.

We stopped in front of the Caddy. "Harry James Denton," Lonnie said, "meet Jerry the Drill."

I offered my hand. "Glad to meet you, Mr. Drill."

Jerry the Drill swung his head back and howled with laughter. His voice boomed from deep down within, a healthy uninhibited laugh. He took my hand and pumped it solidly.

"Keck," he said. "Jerry Keck. That Jerry the Drill stuff is just Lonnie's idea of a joke."

"Yeah, he's a funny guy," I said.

"So, Harry, how long you known this crazy man?"

I glanced over at Lonnie. "Forever. Taught me everything I know, which is a really sad commentary when you think about it."

"So where's the skip?" Lonnie asked, looking up the flight of chipped concrete steps to the Casa Fajita entrance.

"Sheba's watching him," Jerry said. "Being this is Friday and payday, he and his buddies are in the bar swilling down Tecates."

"Sheba?" I asked.

"Yeah, who's Sheba?" Lonnie echoed.

"My assistant. Every once in a while she likes to join in the fun."

"So what's the drill, so to speak?" Lonnie asked.

"His name's Hector Rodriguez, and he'll pretend he doesn't speak any English, but truth is, his *inglés* is not bad. He's a big guy, 'bout my size plus fifty pounds or so, all muscle. Looks like he's got some Indian in him or something. He's supposed to be real mean, too."

"What'd he get nailed for?" I asked.

"Aggravated assault charge was for beating a guy half to death over a card-game dispute. Broke a bottle of Crown Royal over the guy's head. Picked up a D and D and a resisting arrest when the cops came."

"Jesus," Lonnie said.

"The guy he slammed'll be okay, I heard, except he can't make a fist and drools a lot."

"So how we going to do this?" I asked.

"We'll go into the bar, get a table, order a round, scope out the situation. Basically, I'll take the guy. You step in if his buddies try to pile on. I don't think that's going to happen though."

"Wish I was so sure," Lonnie said, but the tone of his voice was flip rather than anxious.

"One other thing," Jerry said. "You guys carrying?"

"Hell, yeah," Lonnie said.

"Leave 'em in the truck. It's against the law to carry anywhere alcohol is served and I'm not going to mess with that."

"You're crazy," Lonnie said, pointing toward the door. "You think that's going to stop *them* from carrying?"

"I'm not going to get in a situation where we have a gunfight in a crowded restaurant. Guy wants to jump bail that bad, let him. We'll figure another way to nail his ass."

Lonnie shrugged. "Your call, babe. Just don't look for a big red *S* on my chest."

Jerry the Drill looked at me. "You?"

I shook my head, smiled. "I don't like guns. They scare me."

"Good for you, brother. You'll live to be a very old man with that attitude."

We started up the stairs as Lonnie slammed and locked the door of the truck.

"You like frozen margaritas?" Jerry asked. "This place is the best. Frozen margs to die for."

"Works for me," I said. "Hey, I got to ask. Where'd Jerry the Drill come from?"

He laughed. "I've got my license, but I'm not really a private detective. And I'm sure not a bounty hunter by trade."

"Yeah, so what do you do?"

He held the glass door to Casa Fajita open for me. I stepped through into the noise and the aroma of frying Mexican food.

"I'm a dentist," he said.

Chapter 3

The Friday-night crowd inside Casa Fajita jostled for space in the tiny entryway. Bullfighting posters sandwiched in between gaily colored swatches of fabric fanned out in chaotic patterns on beige stucco walls.

"So how does a dentist become a part-time bounty hunter?" I asked over the din.

"Boredom," he said. "I always thought about being a detective."

"Funny you should say that," I said as Lonnie came through the front door behind us. "I been thinking about pulling some teeth."

"Where to?" Lonnie asked, as he maneuvered his way through the crowd. A slender young woman with striking black hair, teeth white as pearls, worked her way over to us.

"Smokeen oh no-smokeen?"

"We're already on the list," Jerry said, pointing at her clipboard. "We'll wait in the bar."

We turned and muscled our way past a pair of beefy guys in line to pay their check, then wound our way into the bar. Mariachi music blared from huge speakers that hung from chains in the corners of the room. The light was lower in here, the air thick with cigarette smoke. A huge machine behind the bar with a plastic cage on top swirled mounds of green slush. A heavyset bartender in a pair of jeans and a white T-shirt held a pitcher under the machine's spout and pulled a handle, releasing a gooey stream of syrupy frozen sludge.

Jerry turned, spotted a table in the corner, and waved. My

eyes followed, then stopped so hard that if my eyelids had brakes, they would have squealed.

At the table, her back to the corner, sat the tallest, most striking honey-blonde I'd ever seen. Her hair was long, thick, and straight, down to her shoulders like a mane, with skin as clear and nearly alabaster as anything I'd ever seen. She was medium in frame, fit, curvy. Brilliant blue eyes seemed to shine from the corner of the room and the edges of her mouth went up in a smile that would rip your heart out by the roots. She wore a blue silk blouse and a pair of white pants, with only the faintest traces of makeup. She was bite-through-your-lower-lip-drop-dead gorgeous.

Ordinarily, women that stunning transform me from a relatively grounded, stable guy into a mouth-breathing dribbler. This one was no exception.

I followed Jerry over to the table as we wove our way through the herd of revelers. The chatter seemed especially loud, chaotic, almost frenzied as folks kicked off the weekend by slurping down frozen margaritas and chugging brown bottles of Dos Equis.

Jerry stopped at the table as Lonnie and I worked our way around him.

"Guys, meet Sheba," Jerry said. "Sheba, this is Lonnie and Harry. They'll be joining us for the evening's fun."

"Hi, guys," she said, her voice barely audible over the din.

She stuck out her hand. I stared at it a moment, with the sense that I had this pasted-on goofy grin spreading across my face, then realized I was supposed to react.

"Hi," I stammered, taking her hand. "Harry Denton. Glad to meet you."

Her palm was cool, dry. "Glad to meet you, Harry. And you must be Lonnie."

I released her hand and she held it out for Lonnie. It hung there a moment, unmoving and unshaken. After a couple of beats, I turned.

Lonnie was staring at her, his gaze fixed on her face, his mouth half-open.

"Yo," I said, nudging him with my elbow. "Earth to Lonnie."

He shook his head as if awakening from a dream. "Uh, oh yeah, hi. How are you?"

He shook her hand for just a moment. "Let's relax, gentlemen," Jerry said, taking the chair to Sheba's right. Lonnie shunted in ahead of me and took the chair to her left. I sat down next to him.

"There they are," Jerry said, motioning across the room with his head.

On the far side of the room, next to the bar, a long table was set up in the corner. I counted eight guys sitting at the table, all Latino, all apparently construction workers, all looking as rough as a cob. They were so loud, we could hear them all the way over here, their outbursts of laughter punctuating a continuous stream of rapid-fire Spanish. The table was littered with cigarette packs, plates scraped clean, bowls of chips, and piles of crumpled Tecate cans.

"Which one's ours?" I asked.

"Back row, against the wall, center guy. Look, he's facing us now. Don't stare."

I turned my head away and looked at Jerry. "Jesus," I said. "Kinda big, ain't he?"

I shifted my gaze. Lonnie was still gazing straight into Sheba's eyes. She looked back at him, a faint smile on her face, but nothing to indicate she was as uncomfortable as she must have been with this bozo yutz undressing her mentally.

"Hey," I whispered. "Pay attention to business."

He turned, gave me a look that told me not to push him, then shook his head again as if to clear it.

"So," he said to Jerry. "How you want it to go down?"

Jerry thought for a moment. "I didn't think it was going to be this crowded in here. That causes problems. If there was some way to get next to him, away from his buddies, then I could take him down, get him out quick."

"Maybe he'll go to the john," I said. "We could grab him with his pants down."

Jerry snickered. "Wouldn't that be an ignominious way to go?"

"I got a feeling Hector don't even know what ignominious means," I said.

"Hell, I'm not sure I do either," Lonnie offered. Sheba giggled.

"Any way it happens," Jerry said, "it'll be me on the take-down. You guys hang back, keep those other gorillas off me."

"What about her?" Lonnie asked, motioning toward Sheba with a nod of his head.

"Hey, the name is Sheba," she snapped. "And I can take care of myself."

Something in her voice made me believe her.

"Sorry," Lonnie apologized. "Didn't mean anything by it."

"What's the deal after we nail the skip?" I asked.

"We go out through the front door, Hector goes in the back of the Cadillac. He'll be cuffed, Sheba'll keep an eye on him. You guys just follow me downtown in case his buddies decide to come after us."

"You got it," Lonnie said.

"So," I said, turning to Sheba to make what sounded like idiotic small talk the moment I opened my mouth. "Sheba's an interesting name. How'd you come by it?"

"It's just a nickname," she said, smiling. "Dad worked the circus one summer when he was in school. Mom never cut my hair as a kid and he said it looked like a lion's mane."

"He a lion tamer?" Lonnie asked, unable once again to take his eyes off her.

"Actually, he cleaned out the cages."

I marveled at the miracle of a guy who once spent a summer shoveling lion shit making something as beautiful as this woman.

"Hey, check it out," Jerry said suddenly. I followed his eyes across the room.

Hector stood up from the table, his massive hands pushing his weight up slowly, a boozy smile on his face. He wavered for a moment, unsure of his footing after God knows how many *cervezas*. He laughed, then let loose with a loud belch that caused the whole table to detonate. Guys slapped and yelled and slammed cans down on the table as he twisted himself past his seated buds and staggered over to the bar.

We watched to see where he was headed. I figured he was off to the john, but then he stopped, found an open space at the bar, and leaned into it. He shouted something in Spanish at the bartender and pointed to a rack of cigarettes.

"Showtime," Jerry said. He faced us quickly. "I'll go up to the bar like we got tired of waiting for the waitress. One of you guys follow me, hang just behind."

I looked over at Lonnie, then back at Jerry.

"I'll go," I said.

Jerry nodded, stood up, quickly wove through the tables over to the bar. He wedged in next to Hector, leaned into the bar, both elbows on the wood. I stood a pace or two behind and to his left, trying to look inconspicuous.

Jerry the Drill was no wimp, but Hector towered over him a full head and had him by maybe seventy-five pounds rather than Jerry's fifty-pound estimate. My gut churned, figuring we were going to really be in it in a couple of seconds. I discreetly dropped my hand to my back pocket and felt for the slapjack.

"Hey, brother," Jerry said to Hector as the two stood there. "How you doing today?" He smiled a wide, goofy, toothy grin. Hector looked at him, squinted his eyes to focus, then stood up. He looked even bigger completely vertical.

"Hey, dood, da's a nice coat," Hector slurred in heavily accented English. "Da's real led-hur, eh?"

"Yeah, it's real leather. Glad you like it."

"Where you get it?" Hector demanded. His tone was surly, arrogant, like he figured he'd take the jacket but it was probably too small for him. He might want to go steal one on his own sometime.

"It's a present," Jerry said.

"Yeah?" Hector asked, his nose and lip curling up in a sneer. "Da's a nice present. Who give it do you?"

Jerry raised himself up to his full height, looked Hector in the eye, held his gaze for a couple of beats, then smiled.

"Guy I used to fuck in prison," he said.

Oh, hell. . . . . I thought. *Party time, battalion-style.*

Hector's eyes darkened and he suddenly looked as sober as an MTV star in rehab.

"You t'ink you wan bad muddah?" he snarled.

"No," Jerry mimicked in a terrible imitation of a Spanish accent, "me t'ink you wan big pooh-see. . . ."

After that, I swear to God it was like one of those slo-mo special effects out of a Jackie Chan film. Hector grabbed the left lapel of Jerry's leather coat with his huge right fist. Before I could even go for the slapjack, Jerry brought his right hand up, planted it on top of Hector's.

Then he pivoted, set himself, and jerked Hector's hand toward the ceiling, pulling the coat up with it. Jerry's left hand shot up out of nowhere, grabbed the other side of Hector's fist, then turned again.

Hector let loose the coat and cocked his left fist, aiming it straight for Jerry the Drill's face. People scrambled around us, frantically trying to get out of the way. I heard a feminine, high-pitched scream somewhere behind me. Out of the corner of my eye, I saw the bartender grab a phone and punch in 911.

Before Hector could even get set for his punch, Jerry spun around, bent his elbows, twisted Hector away from him, and brought both hands down with a twist and a quick jerk.

Hector howled and spun around, his hyperextended right arm now behind him, bent at the wrist at a painfully odd angle with the thumb turned inward and toward the ceiling.

Chairs clattered to the floor as people yelled and scrambled for the exits. At the table where Hector'd been sitting, his buddies all jumped up, too stunned for just a moment to move in.

Jerry moved his hands in a downward motion a fraction of an inch, but it was just the right fraction. Hector bellowed in agony and dropped to his right knee, then all the way to the floor. Jerry planted a foot in the small of his back and let go with his left hand, fished inside his coat pocket, and came out with a black leather badge case.

He flipped the case open and waved it about as he announced loudly: "Police officers! Please don't be alarmed! This man is under arrest. Everyone be cool and we'll be out of here in a minute."

He jammed the case back in his pocket, rotated Hector's hand behind him, and in a split second had the other hand back there and a pair of cuffs on him. I watched the seven dark, burly construction workers as they stood at the table, eyeing Jerry and wondering just how far they could go.

Jerry raised Hector's head, grabbed a handful of hair, and pulled him up onto his knees. Hector wailed again, chattered something in Spanish. One of his bros took a step toward us.

"Siéntese!" Jerry barked. It was not a request. *"Ahora!"*

The guy stopped, but he didn't sit down. Neither did any of the others. I figured we didn't have long before they'd want a closer look at that badge.

Jerry pulled Hector to his feet with amazing ease, given that the Mexican was leaning toward being deadweight at that point. I stepped behind him, then noticed Lonnie was right by me.

"You okay, boys?" Jerry said, turning to me.

"Yeah, but let's split," I suggested.

"Excellent idea," he said, backing toward me, with Hector between us and the table full of Hector's buddies.

"Folks, we're sorry to disrupt your evening, but everything's over. You can all go back to having fun now," Jerry yelled as we backed toward the door.

There was a burst of gibberish all around us, almost all of it unintelligible. But in the racket, I heard a voice with a Spanish accent say something with the words *no esta policía* in there somewhere.

Sheba led the way, with Lonnie behind her, then me and Jerry. We pulled Hector out through the lobby and into the chilly evening. We stopped on the landing in front of the steps that led down to our cars.

Hector muttered something in Spanish that I think made an impolite reference to body parts, or something like that. Jerry had his right hand on Hector's cuffs and his left hand knotted in Hector's hair at the back of his scalp. He didn't have to move much to steer Hector where he wanted him to go.

"Let's haul ass," I said. "I saw the bartender dial 911, and something tells me those guys are going to figure out pretty quick that we ain't real Metros."

"Yeah, let's boogie," Sheba said.

Once down the stairs, Jerry shoved Hector headfirst and facedown onto the backseat. Lonnie and I ran over to the truck.

"Holy shit," I said as we climbed in. At the top of the landing, the crowd of Hector's buddies had pulled themselves together. They stopped, looked around, spotted us, and started down the stairs. One of them held a Louisville slugger, locked and loaded in the pissed-off position.

Lonnie gunned the truck but waited until Jerry got the Caddy started. The huge car jerked forward as Jerry put the coal to it, with Sheba on her knees in the front seat, her back to us, holding something on Hector.

The Caddy's tires squealed as Jerry peeled out of the parking lot, with us right behind him. The guy with the baseball bat slung it at us as we pulled away. I watched out the back window as the bat hit the asphalt and clattered harmlessly.

"Well," I said, as we jerked out onto Bell Road and raced for the interstate. "That beat the hell out of sitting home watching reruns of *Gilligan's Island*." My heart rate was on that long downslide to almost normal again.

Lonnie stared ahead as we cut onto I-24 and followed Jerry's Cadillac toward downtown.

"You're awfully quiet all of a sudden," I said. "What's eating you?"

Lonnie turned to me. There was a look on his face I'd never seen before.

"What a woman," he said.

Chapter 4

That Friday night I went back out into the world. The weight finally began to lift. The sharp, cool night air pumping through my lungs as we ran down the steps with a bar full of enraged Mexican construction workers a half flight behind us was the jolt I needed. My heart beat fast; I was alive again.

Lonnie wasn't the only person whose life I'd dropped out of. It had been weeks since I'd last seen or talked to Marsha, maybe the longest time that had passed in the four years we've been together. It wasn't entirely my doing, though. The last few months had been as horrible for her as they were numb for me, and the last few times we saw each other, we were both strained and awkward.

You'd think a doctor—especially one who cuts up dead people for a living—would have been prepared for the rigors of pregnancy, but apparently that's something you simply can't anticipate. I'd been moved to tears the morning her pregnancy test came back positive. In the middle of all the crap I'd been through, the thought that there could still be new life out there was powerful.

I imagined Marsha blooming like a rose, filled with an inner glow, all those gushy warm and fuzzy images from television commercials. I wanted to marry her immediately, to move in and start painting the baby's room. Next stop: the white picket fence in the burbs and a big shaggy dog and barbecues on Saturdays with the kids romping in the backyard.

Yeah, right. . . . The first thing Dr. Marsha Helms did was instruct me to disabuse myself of any notions in that direction. Marriage was not in the cards for her; love, yes, participatory parenting, yes. But not marriage. She'd been independent, alone, and in control all her adult life and she sure as hell wasn't about to change that now.

The rosy glow didn't happen either. Instead of slowly blossoming into Botticellian bloom, my darling significant other immediately lost five pounds, developed circles the color of eggplant under her eyes, began throwing up everything that went past her lips, and periodically turned into the ice queen from hell. I'd heard dark murmurings of the hormonal roller coaster that pregnant women climbed onto, those same primordial tales Neanderthal men must have grunted to one another over a smoldering fire after they'd been tossed out of the cave.

So far, I'd managed to avoid being thrown out of anybody's cave. But there had been pained silences between us after angry outbursts, moments of forced conviviality, long stretches of awkward small talk. I got the sense that there was something eating away at her, something more than just a fetus.

After we got Hector downtown, Lonnie gave me my hundred bucks in cash, then dropped me off at the junkyard to pick up my car. I drove back to my apartment around seven-thirty, thought what the hell, and dialed her number.

Marsha's phone rang four times and the answering machine picked up, but before the outgoing message ended, I heard the clicking noise as she picked up the phone.

"Hold on," she said loudly, over the tape. I could hear her fumbling with the answering machine as she found the switch to turn it off.

"I'm sorry," she said, her voice hassled, stressed.

"Hi," I said.

A beat or two of silence followed, then her voice, more subdued now: "Oh, hi."

"How are you?"

"Okay." Another pause. "You?"

"Strangely enough," I said, "I'm doing okay. Haven't talked to you in a while. Just thought I'd call and catch up."

"It's, uh . . . it's good to hear your voice, Harry."

"Yours, too. How're you feeling these days? I mean, the baby and all."

"Tired, mostly. I just got in from work. Just as the phone rang, in fact."

"It's late," I said. "I thought you were going to cut back."

"It's been a rough week. Dr. Henry's been out of town at a conference and we seem to have a sudden uptick in business."

Dr. Henry Krohlmeyer had been chief medical examiner in Nashville for as long as anyone could remember. Brilliant, but eccentric and a bit challenged in the people-skills department, he was Marsha's mentor and hero.

"Not only that, Joyce Harrison quit."

"Joyce Harrison?"

"Yeah, the second assistant examiner."

"Oh, I remember. Jeez, she's only been there about six months, right?"

"Not even that long."

"How come she quit?"

"It's a long story. Too long to go into now."

"So there's just you and Doc Henry?"

"You got it." I heard her rustling something on the counter next to the phone.

"Marsha, that's too much. Don't you think you should—"

"I'm all right," she interrupted. "Don't hover."

I gritted my teeth. "I wasn't hovering, Marsha. I'm just concerned."

She sighed into the phone. "I'm sorry, babe. I'm just tired. I've got to get off my feet."

"Have you had dinner?" I asked.

"No, but I'm way too tired to go out."

"Look, I went back to work, made a few bucks today."

Her voice perked up. "You did?"

"Yeah." I cradled the phone in my neck and nervously spun the five twenties into a roll. Eighty-something of it was owed to BellSouth first thing Monday morning. A guy's gotta eat, though, right?

"I decided it was time I got out of this funk," I continued. "I went into the office this morning, balanced the books, figured out how much trouble I was in, then put together the beginnings of a plan."

"Yeah?"

"Yeah. Called Lonnie, picked up a little work this evening."

"Oh." Her voice dropped. "Lonnie. Another repo job, huh?"

"Not this time. Helped a guy grab a bail jumper."

"You know, you could make a decent living at this if you'd just give it a chance and stop messing around with—"

"I know, I know." It was my turn to interrupt. "I've been in a slump lately, but it's over. Why don't I pick up some dinner, bring it by your place."

"I'm awful tired, Harry."

I held the phone away from my ear for a second or two, thinking. Finally, I just said it.

"Look, we need to talk. I don't know what's going on with us anymore, but I don't like it. Let me get some takeout or something, bring it over. We'll spend a little time together. Catch up, reconnect. No strings attached, okay?"

She was silent for a moment.

"C'mon, babe," I said. "I want to see if you're starting to show."

She snorted a laugh into the phone. "Oh, don't worry. I'm showing. And it's not a pretty sight."

"Why don't you let me make that call?"

She was silent for a moment, then sighed again. "No MSG, okay?"

I skittered down the rickety metal steps from my second-floor apartment and jumped in the car. As I passed her back door, I saw that Mrs. Hawkins, my seventysomething landlady, had already turned the lights out on the first floor. I hadn't seen her except in passing for several weeks now and I'd noticed that she seemed to be retiring earlier and earlier these days. She'd not been out as much lately either. When I first met her and became her tenant nearly five years ago, she always had a project going—gardening, painting, redecorating. Nowadays, whenever I passed her window, I noticed she was mostly settled into an easy chair, staring at a television that—with her near to-tal deafness—she almost certainly couldn't hear.

Oh, hell, I thought, as I pumped the accelerator and hoped the old Mustang would start, another person to catch up with.

The Friday-night traffic on Gallatin Road was amazingly light. The air was thick and heavy with the cold, the kind of late winter wet Nashville chill that eats through you so hard you think your pilot light's gone out. The harsh streetlights re-flected off the thin sheen of moisture on the asphalt in blinding sparkles. I cranked the heat up, but it didn't help much.

When you're looking for hot, cheap, and good, there's only one place in this part of town that'll do. I pulled into the park-ing lot of Lee's Szechuan Palace on Gallatin Road, just across the street from the old Earl Scheib Body Shop. Mr. and Mrs. Lee opened their restaurant probably ten or twelve years ago and had turned it into one of the great hidden treasures in East Nashville. That was the problem; as a hidden treasure it had made them enough to live on and educate Mary, their daughter, but not enough to hire help and avoid the seventy-hour weeks that would probably wind up killing them.

The dinner rush was over by the time I pulled into the park-ing lot. Mrs. Lee was wiping down tables as her husband leaned into the opening between the kitchen and the counter, cigarette hanging from his lips, exhaustion on his face. There were only a couple of tables occupied.

Mrs. Lee spotted me coming up the walk and scowled. I grinned back at her and nodded my head as I pushed the heavy plate-glass door open.

"Thought you moved away," she snapped. It was the first time I'd seen her in a month, maybe longer.

"Just laying low," I said. "Too late to grab a couple of takeouts?"

She walked past me, rolling up the wet counter cloth into a tight bundle. "Where you been, Harry? Mary ask about you alla time."

Mary Lee was my buddy, a second-semester freshman at Harvard, a math whiz, and the only woman who ever made me wish I were young again.

I leaned against the counter as Mrs. Lee walked behind it. Loose strands of salt-and-pepper hair hung down her forehead almost to the great purple circles under her eyes. Mr. Lee smiled, sort of, and nodded his head to me. Mr. Lee rarely spoke, and when he did, it was not English—at least not any English I could understand.

"Sorry I haven't been by," I said. "I had kind of a rough couple of months. How's Mary?"

Mrs. Lee came about as close to cracking a smile as I'd ever seen. "She make dean's list her first semester. Bring home all A's at Christmas."

She grabbed a pad and a worn Bic pen. "She call last night upset. Make a B-plus on a test. You think a whole world fall in."

I smiled. "She's just like her mom," I said. "Pushing herself too hard."

Mrs. Lee held up the pad, pen poised. "That not a problem you have, Harry. What you want tonight?"

"I'm taking a late dinner over to Marsha's. Better give me one hot, one regular." I scanned the menu. "Kung pao beef, cashew chicken. That way I've got all the bases covered. Oh, and no MSG."

Mrs. Lee's face torqued into a scowl. "You insult me, Harry. We not use MSG heah!"

"Sorry," I said as she scribbled some Chinese on the pad, ripped off the ticket, and handed it to Mr. Lee with a burst of Chinese. She turned back and punched up the bill on the cash register as I pulled a twenty out of my pocket.

"How Doctah Mahsha doing?" she asked.

"Tired, but I think she's okay."

"How fah along is she?" I handed her the bill.

"About four months, I think."

"Ah," Mrs. Lee said. "Worst of moaning sickness ovah. She start to feel bettah for a while, then much, much worse."

She shook her head as she handed me my change. "Harry, you ought marry dat girl."

I held out my hands, palms forward, automatically going into defensive mode. "Hey, I asked her! She doesn't want to get married. Why? Beats me. . . ."

Mr. Lee put two Styrofoam boxes in the window and barked something to his wife. She turned, grabbed the boxes, slid them onto the counter.

"Modahn women," she muttered, her voice lowering both in tone and volume. "Not undahstand . . . . modahn women."

Modahn women. To have admitted to Mrs. Lee that I also didn't understand what was going on would have been an understatement of classically clichéd proportions.

The aroma of Chinese food filled the car as I started the trek out to Green Hills, the fashionable, upscale part of town where Marsha'd bought a six-figure condo back before the real-estate boom started. No telling what it was worth now.

I'd be less than honest if I didn't admit—at least to myself— that Marsha's success was part of her appeal. I'd always been drawn to intelligent, ambitious women. And as the circumstances in my own professional life continued to deteriorate, there was part of me that wanted to say to her: *Let me be house-hubby, please! I can change diapers, dust away the bunnies, and have dinner ready by six as good as the next guy!*

Why not? I'd been wearied by my own struggles of the past few years. I'd had some good times and some bad times, but all in all, I'd trade it in a New York minute to be a kept man. It's not that I wasn't offering anything in return. It seemed logical to me that having a parent at home was better than paying a nanny or dropping the kid off at daycare, to be cared for by strangers and infected by a lot of other snotty-nosed little curtain crawlers.

Yeah, I thought as I pulled off I-440 onto Hillsboro Road, we need to talk. I had some rights here, didn't I? I wasn't just the sperm donor. I was the father of something that was growing inside a woman whom I still, despite all our difficulty of the past few months, very much loved. Surely she could see that. If I just made my case to her in the right way, she'd understand. She'd have to.

I pulled into the condo development and drove through the

parking lot. There was an empty space next to Marsha's black Porsche, the one with her vanity plate: DED FLKS.

I pulled the paper bag with the two Styrofoam boxes off the floor and locked the car behind me. I noticed for the first time a FOR SALE sign on the dashboard of the Porsche. I stared a moment, shocked. She loves that car; it was her one big yuppie indulgence.

"The times, they are a-changin'," I whispered. I hit the walk and was at her door in a few steps. I rang the buzzer and stepped back. Through the curtained window inset in the door, I saw her form coming closer.

The door handle clicked and shook as she unlocked it. Then the door opened and there, backlit by the hallway light, was the tall figure of Dr. Marsha Helms, the woman with whom I'd had an interior mental argument all the way from East Nashville, the woman I hoped to convince to spend the rest of her life with me.

Only problem was, I hardly recognized her.

Chapter 5

Marsha had always been lean and tall, a good head above me, with straight, thick, full-bodied black hair that hung down to her shoulders. Her skin had always glistened with a clear sheen of health, energy, vitality. She'd always seemed aglow with life, enthusiasm, stamina.

The woman who stood before me now, shoulders drooping, head hanging, was an overgrown version of one of those Sally Struthers kids on late-night cable that can be fed and clothed for pennies a day. Her hair was stringy, unwashed, thinner than I'd remembered. Even in the dim backlighting, her skin was splotchy, loose, with a gray pallor. Her nose was red, chapped, swollen. Her eyes were bloodshot and hooded by dark circles. She seemed thinner everywhere, except for the silhouette of her rounded tummy visible beneath a man's white oxford-cloth shirt that was several sizes too large for her.

"Hi," I said, after the split second it took me to hide my surprise at her appearance. "How are you?"

I stepped into the door frame and wrapped my arms around her, being careful not to bounce the sack of food off her.

"Hi," she said softly as I hugged her. Then she made a sound like an *ooof.* "Not too hard. My back's killing me."

I pulled away. "Sorry."

We stepped in and I closed the door behind us. She moved into better light, which didn't help much.

"You look great," I lied.

"Stop lying," she said, her voice flat, tired.

I was embarrassed. "Okay, pretty feeble attempt on my part. But I am glad to see you."

I put my arm around her shoulders and we walked into the kitchen.

"Thanks for bringing dinner over," she said as I put the bag up on the counter. "I realized after you called I was too tired to even cook."

"No problem, babe. I brought over one high-test, one regular."

"I'll let you have the spicy," she said. "I've had heartburn from hell lately."

I pulled out the boxes. "You sit down," I said. "Let me pull this together."

She nodded wearily, gingerly walked over, and sat down real easy. I pulled out plates, opened the boxes, and tested the food. I piled the rice and cashew chicken onto a plate for Marsha, then popped it in the microwave.

"You okay?" I said as the microwave whirred. "You look like you've got a cold."

"It's not a cold. This is all courtesy of estrogen and progesterone."

"Which?"

"Hormones. Pregnancy elevates hormone levels in the blood, which causes nasal mucosa to soften and swell. It's real pleasant."

"Poor baby," I said.

"Add three months of dry heat in the wintertime courtesy of Nashville Gas, followed by spring and allergy season, and you've got a good case of nasal misery."

She reached into the front shirt pocket, extracted a wadded hunk of tissue, and sniffled into it. "I think I've single-handedly caused a boom in Kimberly-Clark stock."

I chuckled as I pulled her plate out. "I'll remember that the next time my broker calls."

"Oh, you don't know the half of it," she said, groaning. "My back hurts all the time. I'm short of breath. I don't sleep for shit. My hair's falling out, my gums bleed when I brush my teeth."

"Sounds like fun. Tell me again why you wanted to do this," I said as I slid the plate in front of her. "Hold on, I'll get you some silverware."

"On top of that, for the first time in my life I'm constipated as hell and I've got hemorrhoids."

"Well," I said, pulling out forks and grabbing a couple of napkins, "as Uma Thurman said in *Pulp Fiction*, that was more information than I needed."

I set the utensils on the table and patted her on the shoulder. "What can I get you to drink?"

"Milk, please."

I wrinkled my nose. Chinese food with a nice big glass of milk. I suddenly flashed on the *I Love Lucy* episode where Ricky had to go out in the middle of the night to pick up vanilla ice cream, chocolate sauce, and anchovies for Lucy.

"What about you?" she said.

"Go ahead and start," I said, going for the milk carton. Her refrigerator was about as bare as my checking account. "I'm right behind you."

I got her squared away, then shoveled my own food onto a plate. As the microwave worked its magic, I leaned against the counter and watched her. She picked at the food, speared a couple of pieces of chicken, stared at them for a moment, then slid them into her mouth. Two seconds later she blanched. With a gagging sound, she slapped the napkin to her face.

"I'm sorry," she gasped.

"Mrs. Lee would be offended," I said. "C'mon, I thought you were supposed to be eating for two."

Her eyes teared up and she set the fork back down on the plate, then pushed the whole mess a couple of inches away from her.

"Jesus, Harry, what have I gotten myself into?"

The microwave beeped, but I suddenly didn't have much appetite myself. I picked her plate up and took it over to the counter by the sink. No point in torturing the poor woman.

"Is there anything that sounds appealing?" I asked.

"There's a cup of yogurt in the fridge," she said. "Maybe I could pick at that."

"Sure." The only occupant of the second shelf was a container of lemon nonfat Dannon. I picked it up; the sell-by date was about ten days ago.

"This is past its prime," I said, opening it. It was half-eaten already, with a thin layer of yellowish liquid on top. "Yuck."

"It's okay," she said. "Bring it over."

"What if it's spoiled?"

"Harry, it's yogurt. By definition, it's spoiled."

I got her a clean spoon. She stirred the glop a couple of times, then spooned a lump of it into her mouth. This time, it stayed.

I watched her as she ate, genuinely concerned. It'd been weeks since I'd last seen her. She'd been tired and she hadn't been able to eat much. But nothing like this. Something was wrong; she couldn't take five more months of this.

"Have you seen your doctor?" I asked.

"My five-month checkup's in two weeks," she answered.

"Look, I'm not trying to hover or be overprotective, whatever, but, honey, there's no beating around the bush here. You don't look so hot."

She sighed and set the spoon down on the table next to the empty yogurt cup. "You just caught me on a bad day. I'm not always like this. It's been a rough week."

I carried my plate over to the table. "Will it bother you if I eat?"

She smiled. "Not if I don't watch."

I sat down, the steaming plate in front of me. Even nuked, the kung pao beef was wonderful.

"Why's it been such a rough week?" I asked with my mouth half-full.

She picked the yogurt cup back up and scraped the spoon around inside it a few more times. She stared into the cup, as if somehow expecting to find something there that hadn't been there a moment before.

"Just stuff," she said.

"Stuff?"

She set the spoon and cup back down, planted her elbows on the table, and rested her head in her hands wearily. "With Joyce leaving, the workload's been off the wall lately. We're getting the bodies processed, but the paperwork's killing all of us."

"I thought that was Kay's area," I said. Kay Delacorte

had been the administrative guru and head den mother at the morgue since before Marsha started.

She rubbed her eyes. "There's just been stuff going on."

"Well," I said, chuckling, "you don't have to get specific or anything."

She stood up and stretched. "It'll work itself out," she said, yawning. "It always does."

Marsha walked behind me, over to the counter, and fished around in her plate of cashew chicken. She picked up a mushy cashew and popped it into her mouth. Her jaw moved slowly as she stared down at the plate. I pushed my plate aside, scooted the chair away from the table, and leaned way back. She was standing there in front of me, but she was a million miles away. Suddenly, my own gut knotted up and food lost its appeal.

"What's going on, Marsha?"

She looked up. "What?"

"C'mon, talk to me."

Her voice was suddenly tense, borderline angry. "What do you mean?"

I stared down at the floor for a few seconds, noticing the pattern, the tiles, the swirls of color overlaid on the squares.

"We don't talk anymore," I said finally.

"Oh, great," she said, almost spewing the words. "All of a sudden, you're the Great Communicator. What happened, Harry? The Prozac kick in?"

"That's cruel, Marsha," I said. "Not like you."

She crossed her arms, resting them on the top of her curved belly and around her swollen breasts. "I'm sorry, but damn it, you disappear out of my life for huge chunks at a time. I don't hear from you. I don't know where you are, what you're doing—"

"Now wait a minute," I interrupted. "That's only been the last few months or so and only because of all the—"

"I don't need any explanations, Harry! That's not the issue here. You don't need to apologize and you don't have to defend yourself."

I sprang to my feet. "Then what is the issue here?"

Her lips pursed as she stared at me. "I've been doing a lot of thinking, Harry. Things have been crazy at work. So stressful, with the baby coming and everything. I don't even know how long I can stay there anymore. Maybe it's time for me to move on."

The thought of Marsha not being at the medical examiner's office shocked me. Her work had always been her main focus, even ahead of me or any other part of her life. Those were the ground rules from the beginning; I'd always been willing to live with them.

"And my family's not here," she continued. "So they can't help. The few friends I have are all connected with work. I can't ask them for anything, not really. I just—it's just that I don't have any support system."

"You've got me," I said. "I know it's been rough lately, but I've been thinking a lot about all this. Okay, so you don't want to get married. That's fine. But why don't I move in here with you? At least so I can help with the baby, take care of the house. I can be here for you."

"Oh, yeah, right, Harry. Until Lonnie calls up with another repo job out of town, or some client needs you to park out in front of a sleazy motel all night with a videocamera hoping to spy on a cheating spouse."

"I can change all that," I said. "I can stop taking those cases. Maybe I'll just get out of that line of work altogether."

Her head drooped and she turned her dark eyes up to glare at me. "That'll be great because there's tons of places out there just waiting to get your résumé."

I felt my voice tense and my eyes narrow. "Just what the hell is that supposed to mean?"

"Harry," she said, exasperated, "when I first met you, you had a great future. You were a fine reporter, one of the best. I imagined you going to bigger places, bigger papers, or if you got tired of journalism, then into some other field entirely. But, Jesus, *this*! I've watched you over the past three or four years. It's not just the work. Security and investigation can be great professions. There's nothing wrong with that.

"But you . . . I don't understand you anymore. You're different. Something's changed. There's something dark. Something that scares me." She paused, staring down at the floor.

I felt like my face had gone numb. "It's him, isn't it?"

"Who?" She looked up.

"Mousy. Mousy Caramello."

"This doesn't have anything to do with that man you killed. This started a long time before that. I've watched you spiral down for years. More and more, you're living on the fringes, Harry. You're running around with people who live in trailers and have untraceable phone numbers and do all this spook stuff. You're living in an attic yourself. It's not the money, Harry. I don't care how much money you make."

She paused, her eyes glistening.

"It's not what you do," she said. "It's how you do it—and who you do it with. You get yourself in these terrible situations and it affects you so much. You're not built for this, Harry. You're not made this way. Something's wrong and I can't seem to get your attention sometimes. And I don't think I can live with it."

She blinked and a single tear ran down her right cheek. "And I think about the baby, and what kind of a parent I want to be, and what kind of a man I want to raise this baby with."

I took the three or four steps across the breakfast nook over to the counter without even realizing I'd done it. The more this conversation progressed, the less real it seemed.

I stood face-to-face with her, my voice calm, almost a monotone. "So what are you trying to tell me, Marsha? You got something to say, you ought to say it."

She looked down, stared at the middle of my chest for a moment. "What I'm trying to say is that I've been thinking a lot lately about the kind of man I want to spend the rest of my life with, and the kind of man I want to be a father to my child. And over and over, I keep coming up with the same conclusion."

She raised her head, met my eyes, looked squarely into them.

"It's not you, Harry. It's just not you."

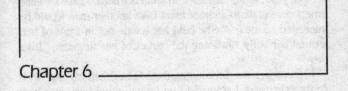

Chapter 6

Well, I thought, *other than that, Mrs. Lincoln, how was the play?*

So whatever Marsha Helms wanted, I wasn't it. In the few seconds I stood there staring blankly at her, before I was able to speak, about a gigabyte's worth of thoughts raced through my head.

Where'd this come from?

How can I fix it?

She's just having a bad day, she'll calm down soon, be okay. Be the Marsha I know, not this . . .

"Marsha, I . . ." I stammered after a few seconds. "I mean, where's this coming from? I mean, I can't . . . This is so weird."

She sighed, backed away from me, turned, and faced the other side of the kitchen.

"I'm sorry," she said. "It's not that I don't have feelings for you. It's just that, well, with the baby and all."

The baby.

"Yeah," I muttered. "The baby. Our baby."

She turned back around quickly, flaring.

"Wait!" I held up a finger. "No matter what you say, that's *our* baby. You and me, babe. No getting around it. My end of the gene pool may be a bit muddy, but you dipped into it and nothing's going to change that."

"And I wouldn't want to change that, Harry! I'm glad that we made this together. Sometimes it's the only thing keeping me going in the middle of . . . of—" She hesitated, struggling for words. "All this mess."

I glared at her. "Is there somebody else?"

"Oh, yeah, right," she said, shaking her head. "Like I've had time to even talk to another man. Like another man would be interested in me . . ." She held her hands out in front of her, around her belly, outlining the curves of her stomach. "Like *this*."

I leaned against the counter, the edge against my hip. Suddenly exhausted, I wanted to go home, crawl back into bed, and never get out.

"So I guess I should go," I said blankly.

"No, don't."

I looked up. "What do you mean, don't? You just said it. You're dumping me."

She groaned loudly. "Oh, Harry, I'm not dumping you. I have feelings for you. I want you in my life. I just want you to understand where I'm coming from. I want you to listen to me, to really hear me."

"Yeah, I really hear you," I shot back. "I hear you say I'm not the guy you're going to spend the rest of your life with."

"Did you want to be that guy?" she asked. "Up until I wanted to get pregnant, you never said anything."

"We never talked about it," I said defensively. "I always figured we were serious. It's not like I assumed anything, but jeez, it's not like I didn't want to either."

She stood there silently, shifting her weight.

"I don't know what to say, Harry."

"Don't say anything, please. You've said enough."

"Maybe we can—"

"I need to go," I said. "This conversation just hit a brick wall. There's nothing either of us can do to fix anything right now. Maybe it can't be fixed."

"Will you call me?"

I made a sound that surprised even me, sort of an ugly snort. "Doesn't sound like you want me to."

She walked over to me, put her arms on my shoulders. "Of course I want you to. I didn't want to hurt you. That was never my intention. But with everything coming down like it is, I've got to get some things straight in my life. I've got to plan, to think ahead, to think of the baby now."

"What is it that's coming down in your life?" I asked, exasperated. "What is it that's got you feeling so scrambled?"

"Oh, Harry, I don't know," she said. "This is crazy. I can't explain it to you. You just have to understand."

"I swear," I said, "I can't figure you." I put my arms around her and hugged her—loosely. Then I pulled away.

"Call me," she said, as I walked to the front door. I turned, took one last look at her, then walked into the brisk night air.

What had happened?

I hit the freeway and headed around to I-65, then headed north and got off at the Ellington Parkway. I felt like taking the long way home, driving with the radio on without listening to it.

What had happened?

I got home around ten, stripped off my clothes, and took a long, hot shower. I was aware of a collage of smells coming from me: adrenaline-enriched sweat from the encounter at the Mexican restaurant, frying Mexican food, Chinese food, even a hint of old yogurt that for some reason or other kept coming back. I scrubbed until it was all off, then dried and settled into bed. Sleep was a long time coming, and when it did, it was restless and unsatisfying, filled with uneasy dreams and vague, unseen anxieties.

What had happened?

Next morning, I threw on enough clothes to pass for legal and stumbled down the steps to grab the morning paper while the coffee maker did its thing. There was no sign of light or activity in Mrs. Hawkins's part of the house. I made a mental note to say hello to her later.

I poured a cup of coffee, sat down at the kitchen table, and pulled the newspaper out of its plastic sleeve. And there in front of me was the headline that went a long way toward explaining everything.

Her line was busy, so I threw on the rest of my clothes, ran a comb through my hair, then jumped in the car and headed back across town. It was one of those times when I was oblivious to time passing and to the other cars around me. The Saturday-morning traffic at Hillsboro Road and Woodmont Boulevard moved at its usual sludgelike pace, but I was still in a stunned state where commonplace things didn't bother me.

I held up traffic for a couple of minutes while attempting a left turn into the parking lot of Marsha's condo development. Finally, some kind soul stopped and let me through. I pulled into the parking lot and around to Marsha's building, then parked in an empty slot directly across the pavement from her Porsche. I sat there for a few moments, unfolding the newspaper, reading the headline and the first few paragraphs one last time.

"Jeez," I whispered.

I looked up as her front door opened. Marsha stepped out, overcoat buttoned tightly in the wind. I opened the door of my nearly thirty-year-old Mustang, its characteristic door squeal alerting her to my presence. She stopped halfway down the walk, alarmed when she saw my expression.

"Harry, what are you—"

"When were you going to tell me about this?" I demanded as I strode up the walk to her.

"About what?" she asked, concerned. I unfolded the newspaper, with the headline:

GRAND JURY PROBE
OF M.E.'S OFFICE WIDENS

splashed across the front page in bold sixty-point black type.

Her face paled and for a moment I thought she was going to faint, but I pressed on anyway.

" 'The Davidson County Grand Jury's probe,' " I read, " 'of irregularities in the medical examiner's office has widened to cover accusations of sexual misconduct, improper handling of bodies, misuse of funds, and potentially criminal misconduct.' "

"Oh, my God," she whispered.

" 'Sources inside the grand jury,' " I continued, " 'reveal

that among other allegations reported are claims of sexual harassment of female employees by Nashville Medical Examiner Dr. Henry Krohlmeyer. One unidentified female ex-employee testified that Dr. Krohlmeyer routinely orders female employees to accompany him on out-of-town trips for purposes of inappropriate sexual conduct. . . .' "

I looked up at Marsha, recalling those trips she and Dr. Henry had taken over the years to conferences and seminars and professional-association meetings, and how they always seemed to be in exotic, romantic places like Lake Tahoe or Barbados.

"Harry, that's Joyce Hamilton. You can't believe—"

"Here's a good one, Marsh," I said, turning back to the paper. " 'Allegations of misappropriation of funds include claims that Dr. Krohlmeyer and his staff may have forged purchase orders and invoices in order to claim payment for equipment never received and for reimbursement of expenses never incurred.' "

"Harry, can we go inside and do this? I can't stand out here. I'm a little dizzy."

"Yeah," I said. "I'm feeling wobbly myself."

"Well, come inside, damn it."

I followed her up the steps into the apartment. She took off her coat, then stopped in the hallway to raise the thermostat. She stepped down into the living room and settled uncomfortably into the sofa, and I sat across from her.

"I know that whatever the hell is going on with this, you didn't do anything wrong. I believe that with every part of me."

She looked up. "Thanks for that much, anyway."

"But why the hell didn't you tell me?"

She wrung her hands, then cleared her throat awkwardly. "I kept hoping it would all go away. I certainly never thought it would get into the papers. Besides, what good would it have done to dump on you? You were absent and unaccounted for."

"It was naïve of you to think the papers wouldn't pick up on this," I said, a coldness in my voice that I hadn't intended. "How bad is it?"

She looked at me a moment, then said, "I've retained counsel."

"That bad?"

"Possibly. I've been subpoenaed."

My mouth dropped. "When?"

"Tuesday morning."

"What are you going to do?" I asked.

"What can I do? Answer the subpoena."

"Do you know what they're going to ask you?"

She sighed. "I have some ideas."

"Do you know what you're going to say?"

"Not yet. My attorney has advised me to take the Fifth."

I leaned over, put my elbows on my knees, and cradled my head in my hands. "What can you tell me about all this?" I asked, looking back up at her. "It won't go any further than this room."

"Dr. Henry's a brilliant pathologist and physician," she said, her voice strained. "I've got the greatest respect for his skills and his integrity. But he's a lousy administrator and he doesn't have the most refined people skills in the world."

"That's a very diplomatic redefinition of sexual harassment," I offered.

"Dr. Henry's never sexually harassed anyone," she said. "At least not that I've noticed. Maybe I wasn't paying attention, though. When Louise left him in '94, he kind of went off the deep end. I think some of his actions were subject to misinterpretation."

"I remember you telling me about the divorce."

"It was awful," she continued. "They'd been married almost twenty years. After the divorce, he was so depressed half the time he couldn't get anything done—and the other half he was dating all these bizarre women."

"Middle-aged crazies," I said.

She nodded her head. "Paperwork went to hell. Books got scrambled. We started having trouble in court cases because Dr. Henry'd go to testify and he'd have forgotten to take the files with him. Or couldn't remember. Stuff like that."

"Marsha, could there be any truth to this . . . these sexual harassment charges?"

"He never hit on me," Marsha said, "if that's what you're asking. But when Joyce came on board, he was . . . Well, maybe he was a little too friendly. She's just in her early thirties, barely out of medical school. Young, pretty. She didn't understand the way the office worked, didn't fit in. It's like a fortress down there, Harry, and there's a certain siege mentality, a kind of camaraderie taken to extremes."

The Nashville morgue—technically known as the T. E. Simpkins Forensic Science Center—was, in fact, built like a fortress: thick walls, armor-plated doors, thin slit windows of bulletproof glass. *Fortress* was an apt description, and sometimes fortresses were subject to siege.

I stood up, crossed over, and sat next to her on the sofa. "And then . . ." Marsha leaned against me, resting her head. I put my arms around her, ran my fingers through her hair. She felt like deadweight leaning against me, as if she would fall at any moment. "We were processing more bodies than ever before, but the budget got cut. We couldn't hire help. Kay got overwhelmed; she couldn't handle everything. Purchase orders and invoices got all screwed up, bills didn't get paid. Dr. Henry dumped more and more of the day-to-day operation on me, but I was so overwhelmed I know it didn't get done right. Hell, I'm a pathologist, not an administrator.

"We got complaints from suppliers, who then went to the city budget office. Suddenly we're getting calls from the comptroller, and then, when they got wind of what was going on, they scheduled an audit."

She pulled her head up, leaned back, looked into my eyes. "That was two months ago."

"That's when it hit the fan?"

"Dr. Henry went nuts one day, started yelling at the auditors, essentially threw them out of the place. About that time Joyce quit. With no notice. All at once we're getting calls from the EEOC, the National Labor Relations Board, the mayor's office."

"And then the grand jury," I said.

She nodded again. "That started about a month ago. Dr. Henry was subpoenaed last week. Mine came a couple days later."

We sat silently for a bit. I fell back on reporter-think, trying to figure out which way a good digger would go next. I know what I'd do in a story like this; I'd be looking around for a source, a mole in the ME's office who could dish me the straight dirt.

"You had anybody from the media call you?"

"Tons of them. But Dr. Henry's issued dead-on instructions. Nobody talks."

"Moron," I said. "Stonewalling's the worst. Just about assures that somebody—probably some lower-level drone who's pissed about his raise last year—will do a Deep Throat number."

"Oh, perfect," Marsha said. "Autopsygate."

I smiled. "Stiffgate."

She smiled, too, for the first time in a long time.

"Marsha, I don't believe anywhere inside me that you'd consciously or intentionally do anything wrong. But is there anything that could be . . . well, let's say subject to misinterpretation?"

She lowered her eyes, her eyelids settling down like hoods, as if she were dropping off to sleep. "Maybe in the chaos I cut some corners," she whispered. "I don't know what they're after. They're fishing and I don't know what they'll find."

"What do you think's going to happen?"

Marsha wrapped her arms around herself, pulling in on her shoulders, trying to squeeze the tension out.

"I don't know," she said. "We're in a lot of trouble. Expensive trouble. The lawyers demanded a ten-thousand-dollar retainer from me. That's just to get started."

I eyed her, trying to get a feel for just how freaked she was by all this. If her lawyers took that much up front, they must anticipate a long, dragged-out affair. As a reporter, I'd seen this process before. Once the course is set and the agony begins, it erodes your life, eats away at your energies, until—even if you're vindicated—there's nothing left.

"Just answer this," I said. "Is there any chance they're going to take you away?"

I half expected her to look at me like I'd lost my mind, but she didn't. She took it calmly, as if the same question had been preying on her mind.

"I don't know, Harry," she said after a moment. "I don't know."

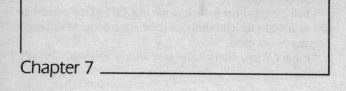

Chapter 7

A few minutes later, I stood there as she pulled away in the Porsche. Saturday was just another workday for Marsha, although she did allow herself the luxury of going in late. She'd been on her way to the morgue when I pulled into the parking lot.

I sat in my own car, gazing out into the parking lot and wishing for a brief moment that I smoked. There's something about smoking and pensiveness that seemed to go hand in hand. But my one experience with tobacco as a child had rendered me so helplessly and violently ill that I'd never touched the awful stuff again.

I was adrift, ready to get back into the world after my long hibernation, but still estranged from it. With little else to do, I drove downtown to my small office on the top floor of the shabby building that was almost doomed to fall to the developers. It was only a matter of when, not if.

My mind ran in circles. The thought of Marsha being in real trouble was something so foreign to me that it was ungraspable, like going to the doctor for a routine checkup and being told you have six months to live.

I always figured it'd be me, not her. Marsha was right, of course. Without even really being aware of it, I'd begun skirting the fringes of polite society years ago. As one by one the connections to my yuppie past life disappeared, a more urban-frontier quality to my life had emerged. The people I'd only written about as an ostensibly objective journalist years before were now integral parts of my life: small-time hustlers, repo men, bounty hunters, massage parlor employees, table dancers, struggling country music wannabes, kooks, wackos, and lunatics. I was no longer an observer.

I was one of them.

That must have seemed quite strange to someone like Marsha, with the Green Hills condo and the Porsche and the designer clothes and the credit cards. I hadn't realized we'd become so different.

I looked around my office, at the dark, dull paneling, the peeling linoleum floor, the window that looked out on a back alley and a rusty fire escape. There was a musty, mildewed smell about the place. The overhead lighting was harsh, unforgiving.

I could leave it all behind, I thought. There were still a few connections I could get to. I could get a haircut, charge a new suit, type up a résumé, probably have a job in PR or as a corporate flack in a matter of days. Maybe thirty, forty grand a year, with health insurance and vacation days. I could rent a nicer apartment, pop for some new wheels. Start living like a middle-class American again. Or that guy who wanted to hire me as an investigator for the insurance company—what's his name? The one who promised a company car, a nice office with carpet and stuff, and a twentysomething secretary to screen my calls and get my coffee.

Hell, it doesn't matter. I can't go back. Wouldn't even if I could. Once you've had a taste of shitting in the woods and howling at the moon, it's hard to go back to being somebody's house pet.

So I jogged the bills into a neat stack, then organized them by temperature. Hottest fires get put out first. I had just figured out that if I held off on the electric bill another few days, I could pay the phone bill and my month's back rent. Which meant I was only, technically, about ten days behind on my office. I'd also heard that if you put a check in the mail, but "forgot" to sign it, that'd buy you a few days as well. They wouldn't cut your power. But if they sent the check through and the bank took it, it'd bounce higher than Bill Gates's tax bracket.

I was pondering the profound ethical implications of going

for it, when all of a sudden there was a knock at my door. I looked up, confused.

Now you have to understand, I don't get a whole lot of drop-in business at my one-man agency. Some detective agencies are high profile, practically a walk-in clinic for people with cheating spouses or bosses whose employees are ripping them off. You got a cold, you go to a doc-in-the-box; you need pictures of your husband with his mistress, you stop by the dick-in-a-box.

That's not my style, though. So when a knock comes to my door, it generally takes me by surprise. I wondered if it was the landlord, coming by to dun me for the back rent. So what, I thought. I'd decided to mail him a check anyway. I eased out of my chair and opened the door.

A tall woman with a face full of tastefully done makeup stood in front of me. I pegged her at midforties, a couple of years older than me, although I'm not always good at guessing ages. She wore an expensive dress with a designer shoulder bag draped over a thin, yet not too thin, right shoulder. Her hair was jet black, precisely coiffed, and her eyes were so brilliantly blue they had to be tinted contacts.

"Is *this* the Denton Agency?" she asked, like she'd expected something more. Her voice seemed anxious, but that's to be expected. First visits to a private detective were frequently anxiety-producing.

"Yes, I'm Harry Denton," I said, staring at her and trying to remember where I'd seen her face. "Please, come in."

There was a stack of file folders on my visitor's chair, but I managed to shuffle it over to my desk and offered her a seat.

"I'm Victoria Reed," she said.

"Pleased to meet you, Ms. Reed. Can I offer you something? Herbal tea?" I asked as she sat down. I had a coffee maker with hot water perking on top of my filing cabinet. "I've got, let's see, some—"

"No, thank you," she said. She fidgeted with her shoulder bag, trying to find a comfortable place on her lap.

"How can I help you?" I asked as I sat down across from

her. I reached for my pen and a legal pad, then wrote the date, time, and her name at the top.

She wrapped her hands together in a ball and wrung them. Her hands were thin, the bones almost visible beneath her pale skin. "This is a little difficult," she said.

"I understand. My clients wouldn't need me if they weren't in some kind of distress."

She smiled. "That's very kind of you, Mr. Denton."

"Please, call me Harry."

"Okay, Harry. This is still difficult. And I would never have come here if I weren't sure that my husband was cheating on me."

My heart sank. Bloody hell!

One thing, though: These cases do pay the bills. And I had plenty of those. My mind raced as I thought of how badly I needed the money, but also of how distracted I was.

"Tell me all about it," I said.

"I got your name from my friend, Barbara Monroe. You helped her out last year. She went through a painful divorce. Her husband ran off with his administrative assistant, a twenty-two-year-old blonde. Anyway, Barbara said I could trust you."

I remembered the case, but barely. No big deal, really, but then you can never convince clients of that and probably shouldn't try. It had taken about six hours to track the husband and his bimbette to a chalet in Gatlinburg. I figure the pictures of them together in the hot tub—sans bathing suits—had gotten Barbara about another fifty grand in the settlement.

"Yes, I remember Ms. Monroe. Of course, I can't talk about her case, you know."

That seemed to reassure her. "My husband is Robert Jefferson Reed," she said after a moment. "Perhaps you've heard of him."

I thought for a couple of seconds. Yeah, it did ring a bell, but where had I . . . ? Then I remembered back a few days: the old lady in the Kroger checkout line, and how I came to see the book.

I snapped my fingers. *Life's Little Maintenance Manual!* I

thought you looked familiar. You guys were in the Sunday magazine supplement a couple weeks ago."

"Yes." She nodded her head sadly. "The happy family with the devoted husband and father who makes a fortune dishing out family-values-based wisdom."

I made a note, then looked back at her. "I gather the reality is somewhat different."

Her eyes filmed over. "Maybe if this were the only time, it wouldn't be so bad."

Her head fell forward. "Mrs. Reed," I said, my voice low, soothing. "Can you tell me who it is your husband is seeing?"

She snuffled, then nodded her head. But when she tried to speak, her voice caught. I reached across my desk and grabbed a box of tissues. She snatched a couple and held them to her nose.

"A year ago he had to hire a secretary. When the book came out, the phone calls and the correspondence were so bad, he could have spent the rest of his life just typing letters and returning calls."

"I can imagine," I said. "Sudden fame, all that attention."

She raised her head back up. "It's not what people imagine. The life is very stressful, although in a good way, if that's what you want."

"So your husband had to have some help?"

"He put an ad in the paper, and this . . . this *girl* answered it. She was a college student, had just graduated from Vanderbilt. Twenty-two or so—maybe a little older. I don't really know."

"What's her name?"

Victoria Reed curled her lip, as if she were being forced to repeat a vulgarity. "Margot," she sniffed. "Margot Horowitz."

I scribbled the name down. "Go on."

"Anyway, it's almost textbook from then on. My husband moved his office to our farm in Williamson County. Claimed it was quieter there and he just couldn't get any work done at home. So the two of them were out there working. Alone."

"He worked at home before then?" I asked.

"After he was fired from the stockbrokerage."

"Your husband was a stockbroker before he became a writer?"

"Oh, a stockbroker, an investment planner, an officer for a mortgage company. R.J.'s bounced from one job to another his whole adult life. He's never gone without work for very long, and he's always made a decent living. It's just that no matter where he was, he thought he was too good to be there.

"I suppose that's even true of our marriage," she added as an afterthought.

I felt for her, maybe because I'd had a marriage go under. It's no damn fun.

"May I ask a very personal question, Victoria?"

She shifted uncomfortably. "I suppose so."

"Do you still love your husband?"

She stared at me as if I'd burst out with a string of Aramaic. "I—yes, I—of course I love my husband."

"And you want the marriage to survive?"

She shrugged her shoulders. "I guess so."

I set the legal pad down on my desk. "Then go home," I said, thinking, *You dumb ass, this is a paying customer!* "Go home and forget about this. Try to get him into counseling if you want. Go see a marriage and family therapist. Confront him if you have to. But don't sic me on him. It'll only cause you more pain."

She thought for a moment. "No, I have to know. I have to know."

"Okay," I said, resigned. "If that's the way you want it. You seem like a nice lady. But if you want me to do this, I will. There is one stipulation."

"Yes?"

"There is the possibility this could get quite expensive, in addition to painful. I charge seventy-five dollars an hour plus expenses. If I have to travel outside the city overnight, I get a minimum twelve-hour day."

She reached into her shoulder bag and pulled out her checkbook. "That's no problem. How much of a retainer do you require?"

Damn, I'm thinking, isn't there any way I can dissuade this lady?

"My usual is ten hours, plus two-fifty for expenses. An even thousand. It'll be credited to your account with any unused part returned."

"Fair enough." She wrote out a check and handed it to me.

"I don't suppose I'll need a picture of your husband," I said. "I can check any drugstore paperback rack. But it would help to have a picture of this Horowitz woman."

She reached into her shoulder bag and pulled out a crumpled snapshot. "This was taken at our summer party last year at the farm," she explained.

In the picture, a group of people in T-shirts and shorts hovered around a Jacuzzi, next to a keg of beer in a washtub, wet plastic glasses cocked in salute. In the center, Robert Jefferson Reed stood with his arms around two women. He looked a bit like Robert Redford, only more windblown and with a slight paunch. On his right, Victoria Reed looked cramped and uncomfortable in the crook of his arm. But if the young woman on his left were pressed in any closer to him, they'd have to surgically separate the two of them.

Margot Horowitz was tanned and dark, short and compact, with a close-trimmed bob of a haircut. She was painfully young, and he was glaringly middle-aged.

And if a camera can capture lust in a casual snapshot, this one did.

"I'll need your home address," I said, sliding the photograph onto my desk, "as well as the address for the farm. Do you own any other homes?"

"There's the apartment in Manhattan. They were there last week. He did the *Today* show and took her along."

She dictated the addresses to me. Their home was in Brentwood, a fashionable and expensive area. The farm was farther out from town, in a part of the county that was equally well-off, just more rural. Both were located in Williamson County, which has the highest per capita income in the state and one of the highest in the country.

"Where is he now?" I asked. "Still out of town?"

"No, they got back Thursday. He told me he was going to be working down at the farm for a few days and that I shouldn't bother him. Last night I called the farm around ten and didn't get an answer. On a hunch, I called Margot's apartment."

"And?"

"No answer there either. I think they're down at the farm," she said, her lips tight as she spoke. "My guess is they were either in the pool or—"

She hesitated. "Already in bed."

I scribbled another note. This was shaping up as a no-brainer, quick down-and-dirty money. And, I thought, the very reason Marsha wanted me out of her life. She didn't want her child to be raised by a guy who took pictures of people having illicit sex.

"Just one last question," I said. She raised an eyebrow. "If your husband has done this before—been unfaithful, I mean—then why now? Why are you just now coming to see a private investigator?"

"Two reasons," she offered. "First, until my husband wrote this book, there was never anything worth going after. If I divorce him now, there's enough there to make sure I won't wind up working in the typing pool."

"I appreciate your honesty," I said. "What's the second reason?"

Her lower lip curled inward and she caught an edge of it on an incisor. Then her mouth opened.

"R.J.'s had affairs before, but this is the first time I've ever thought he might actually leave me."

"So you want to strike first, right?"

She nodded.

"You're sure you want to go through with this?" I asked.

"Yes."

"Okay, I'll get back to you in a few days. I assume you want the usual pictures, videotape, whatever."

"Whatever it takes," she said, then sighed deeply.

"There's always the chance you'll be wrong," I said.

Her hands tightened around the shoulder bag and then she

stood up. "Anything's possible, but my husband's infidelities are legion among our close friends. I wouldn't put this, or much of anything else, past him."

"Okay," I said. "I'll draw up a contract and have it ready for you Monday. It's standard boilerplate, just outlining the terms I've already explained."

"Fine. When can you get on this, Harry?"

"Quickly," I answered. "If they're together at the farm this weekend, then this is probably the best opportunity to get what we need. But I still hope you're wrong. I'm always happy to get paid for proving people *aren't* cheating on their spouses."

I didn't bother to tell her that in all my attempts, that had never happened.

"I hope you're right," she said. She reached into her purse and pulled out a small brown envelope about the size of a cigarette pack. "Just in case, here's a spare key to the house and the code to the burglar alarm."

After she left, I pocketed the envelope and sat back down at my desk, fervently fingering the check, which had only Victoria's name on it. I figured it came from a private account. I lived cheaply; the thousand dollars would just about get me caught up. Might even leave a little left over for a movie—or dinner somewhere besides Mrs. Lee's.

I studied the snapshot. Everyone so happy, so well-off, so healthy. So much ugly subtext. All this from a guy who wrote things like: "Never let a day go by without telling your spouse you love him (her)."

"Oh, well," I said out loud. "At least it'll be over quick." Simple adultery trackdowns, complete with pics and film at eleven, rarely take more than a few days. Just another simple case of a man out screwing around on his wife, complicated only by the fact that a considerable amount of money and fame was involved. Still simple, though. In and out quickly, then back to the more immediate problem in my life: damage control.

Boy, was I wrong. Some damage control.

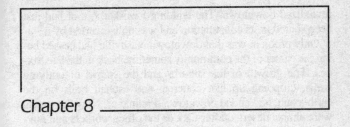

Chapter 8

My hot Saturday night in Music City was shaping up to look like a drive down to a farm in south Williamson County, then parking out in front of some guy's house with a zoom lens on the Canon L-2 that I'd have to borrow from Lonnie. The L-2 shot on High-8 videotape, which meant much better resolution than a regular video camera, and it transferred well to VHS. That way the customer could take home his or her very own personal copy of his or her spouse doing the dirty with somebody he or she wasn't supposed to be doing it with.

The money spent hiring me would be justified. The lawyers and the aggrieved spouse would be satisfied, if not outright happy, and the cheating spouse would learn exactly what the wages of sin really were. Everything would come to a morally proper and fitting end. The only real loser would be the marriage. The only question left would be whether it had all been worth it.

I typed up a contract for Victoria Reed, then dialed Lonnie's number at the trailer. No answer. It was getting close to lunchtime and I was a little too antsy to sit around the office. The sun had struggled through the gray clouds of a typical late winter/early spring day in Nashville and had, over the past hour or two, managed to make some headway. I threw my jacket back on and left my office. I walked up Seventh Avenue and turned onto Church Street, went another half block, then turned into the Church Street Centre. The Church Street Centre had been somebody's idea of a classy urban mall—hence the affected spelling of *center*—that would be the focus of a new, revitalized downtown. The building I worked out of had just been spared in its construction and was now dwarfed by it.

Only problem was that downtown Nashville had ceased being the center of the community sometime back in the late Sixties. The growth of the suburbs and the sprawl of outlying malls, cropping up like concrete and asphalt boils on the earth's butt, had ended downtown dominance. Now the streets were almost deserted after dark as the office workers and government employees headed for the freeways at five-thirty. The only people left after dark in this part of downtown were the predators, street people, and tourists who'd wandered too far afield from Second Avenue.

This had doomed Church Street Centre from the start and there was some talk that the city would buy it when it finally went under and turn it into a new downtown library. For now, though, a few shops and a mall food court remained open. It was a cheap place to get a quick lunch. I rode the escalator up to the top floor and walked about a quarter-mile to a Waldenbooks. There were only a few customers in the bookstore: two obvious tourists, a young black couple, and three or four teenagers wearing starter jackets.

"I'm looking for a copy of *Life's Little Maintenance Manual*," I said to the bored clerk reading a tattered copy of *Entertainment Weekly*.

He looked up, rolled his eyes. "Over there, down that aisle. There's a cardboard dump full of them."

He went back to the magazine, dismissing me with what felt amazingly like contempt.

I wandered over to the aisle, at least half of which was devoted to *Life's Little Maintenance Manual*. There was the trade paperback itself. Then you had your *Life's Little Maintenance Manual* page-a-day desktop calendar, the *Life's Little Maintenance Manual* wall calendar, the *Life's Little Maintenance Manual* Day-Timer, the *Life's Little Maintenance Manual* spiritual twelve-step workbook, and the *Life's Little Maintenance Manual* screen saver—in DOS, Mac, and Windows versions. A ten-foot-long rack displayed *Life's Little Maintenance Manual* greeting cards, with blister packs of *Life's Little Main-*

tenance Manual refrigerator magnets on the wall above. And, of course, the large-print, audio, Spanish, and abridged versions of *Life's Little Maintenance Manual*.

Abridged? How the hell do you abridge something that only takes about twenty minutes to read in the first place? I mean, who doesn't have time to read the whole goddamn opus?

I picked up a copy of the slim paperback and turned it over. Robert Jefferson Reed's black-and-white glossy photo filled half the back cover, with words of appreciation from other distinguished literary figures—Oprah Winfrey, Ann Landers, Rod McKuen, Robert James Waller, Dr. Joyce Brothers—filling the other half. In the photo the author was kneeling down, with his arm around a golden retriever that was almost grinning with delight. Reed looked smug, self-assured, well tended, and like everybody's idea of what a Nineties kind of dad ought to be.

Only I knew his secret. America's Nineties Kind of Dad was getting a little Nineties kind of something on the side.

I paid for the book, eliciting another sneer of disdain from the clerk, and rode the escalator down a floor to the food court. Since I'd last been here, three more counters had closed, leaving only a choice between corn dogs and pizza. I sprung for a three-buck super slice and a Coke, then sat down and started reading.

The more I read, the worse the pizza tasted. *Good God,* I thought, *people actually pay genuine American dollars for this crap.*

" 'Love may not conquer all,' " I read out loud. " 'But it's a good place to start.' "

Several tables away, two young women—one dressed entirely in black leather and chrome body piercings, the other in ripped jeans and an army field jacket—turned my way and glared. The one in black leaned in to her friend and mouthed the word *asshole*.

I smiled at them, then squinted, stuck out my tongue, and slowly licked my upper lip. Can't help it; it's the devil in me. They turned away, thoroughly revulsed, and I turned back to Reed's masterpiece.

His next nugget of wisdom was:

CALL YOUR MOTHER ON MOTHER'S DAY.

"Duh," I whispered.

LET A SMILE START YOUR DAY.

Jeez, I thought a smile was supposed to be your umbrella.
C'mon, damn it, make up your mind—umbrella or day starter.
You can't have it both ways.

DON'T JUST BE NICE TO EVERYONE;
BE <u>REAL</u> NICE TO EVERYONE.

Okay, that's it. I'm going to start blowing mozzarella chunks
all over the place.

BRING A LITTLE BIT OF CHRISTMAS TO EVERY DAY.

I knew there was a reason I hated Christmas.

This was truly sickening, and yet here it was, a *New York
Times* bestseller, and the cornerstone of a merchandising em-
pire that was probably bigger than the combined gross national
products of half the countries in South America.

I shook my head, unable to fathom the phenomenon. Were
people that freaking stupid? On the other hand, Robert Jefferson Reed had at least three homes I knew of, a wife, three kids,
a girlfriend half his age, and the adoration of millions of fans
who'd thrown bushels of money at him.

And what did I have? Let's see: hmmmm, corn dogs or
pizza?

I turned to the copyright page and scanned it. A row of numbers at the bottom of the page read from thirty-two to forty,
which I took to mean that this was the thirty-second printing of
the book with eight more anticipated. And at the top of the
page, the words SPEARHEAD PRESS and an address.

An address in Nashville.

I scarfed down the last of the super slice and headed back to
my office.

* * *

The phone was ringing as I fumbled with the lock. I got the key in just as the machine was taking the call. Halfway through the message, I yanked the phone up.

"Don't hang up!" I yelled. I hit the button on the answering machine to turn it off.

"Hey," Lonnie said. "You called?"

"Yeah, hold on." I held the phone in the crook of my neck as I pulled the jacket off. I threw it on the corner of my desk and settled into my chair.

"How'd you know I called?" I asked. "The machine didn't pick up. I couldn't leave a message."

"I know everything," he announced. "There are no secrets from the Lon-man."

"Yeah, right, as long as the Caller ID box works."

"Okay, you exposed me. Now what can I do you for?"

I put my feet up on the desk and stretched, then stifled a long yawn without much success. "I think this is a never-mind situation. I got offered a gig this morning, but I don't think I'm going to take it."

"What, you're turning away business now?" Lonnie sounded incredulous.

"C'mon, I'm not that much of a bottom feeder. There are cases even I won't take."

"Yeah, gimme a for-instance."

"This lady comes in. Husband screwing around. She wants tapes to play for the judge."

"What's your point? Easy money."

"With one small complication," I offered.

"Yeah?"

"The husband's rich, well connected, famous. A very high profile. I've seen enough of my own name in the newspapers lately."

"Sounds juicy. Who is it?"

"You know I can't tell you that."

"Hey, you're not going to take the gig, the lady hasn't paid you, you got no connection. No confidentiality."

"That's just it. She did pay me. But I think I'm going to send the check back."

"You don't mind my asking, what kind of retainer'd she give you?"

"Grand."

"*A grand!*" he yelled. "You're going to give back a thousand dollars? What're you, J. D. fucking Rockefeller? Jesus, the last time you saw a thousand dollars at one time, George Bush was still bombing Iraq."

"C'mon, Lonnie, it's not that much."

"Not for most people. But you, Harry, you're different. You're broke."

"This guy is famous," I said. "I don't need this kind of aggravation."

"Look, man, take a word here, dig? You gonna stay in this business, you gotta do what it takes to survive. You gotta do whatever's necessary. Okay, so this is distasteful. But you get drawn into it, then you do so by the hour and the meter's always running."

I leaned back and let loose with a long, deep sigh. "I need a vacation."

Lonnie howled. "Hell, you just went back to work."

"All right," I said after a few moments. "I need the L-2, okay?"

"Sure, when?"

"I don't know. The guy's out in Williamson County somewhere. They own a farm in addition to the house in Brentwood and the apartment in New York. Thought maybe I'd head out late afternoon, try to catch him with his babe having drinks in the hot tub."

"Cool. Works for me."

"Say, want to grab an early dinner? I can pick up the camera then."

"Actually, Harry," he said, hesitating, "I, uh, I got plans tonight. And I got to get over to my place, clean up, you know."

"Yeah, sure," I said, intrigued, but knowing better than to push it. "So when can we get together?"

"Let's see." He was silent for a few moments. "How's this? You know the movie house up in Rivergate?"

"Not the one under the freeway?"

"No, the one next to the mall."

"Yeah, sure."

"I'll be in the parking lot at four-thirty. I won't be in the truck, though. You park as close to the entrance as you can. I'll find you."

I chuckled. "Yeah, cool, but why all the cloak-and-dagger?"

"Just be there, ya' bozo." He hung up.

I dropped by a photo store, wrote a check that I'd have to cover Monday for a couple of High-8 tapes, then drove back to my apartment. I tried Marsha at the morgue, but she'd already left. I called her apartment, but got the machine. I left a message, asked her to call me at home, then decided to see if I couldn't nod off for a couple hours. If I was going to be on stakeout—gee, I love that kind of talk—then there was no telling how late I'd be up. I set the alarm for three-thirty.

One of the ways in which I knew that I was coming out of my bad time was that I'd started to dream again. When I was in the worst of it, in the darkest, blackest places of all, I didn't dream. It wasn't even that I was dreaming and couldn't remember it; there really were no dreams. That was a bit unsettling at times, this notion of sleep being like falling into a big vat of black paint. Only it never felt like drowning, like I didn't need to breathe or eat or anything. It was all there for me, safe and comforting.

God, no wonder all I wanted to do was sleep.

But that was over. The dreams were back, and they were busy dreams, frenetic dreams, with flashing images of Marsha getting more and more pregnant, bigger and bigger, until she was like a blimp. A yogurt-eating blimp. And then finally she exploded.

Thank God the phone rang.

I grabbed for it, dropped it, yanked the cord up as the handset bounced off the floor a few times.

"Sorry," I mumbled, still half asleep. "Hello . . ."

"Hi," Marsha said.

"Oh, I was just dreaming about you."

"Erotic dream?"

"Something like that."

"I woke you up. Sorry."

I sat up on the side of the bed and rubbed my eyes. "No problem. I need to get up anyway. I'm working tonight, got a new client. Stakeout."

If I expected her to express disappointment at not seeing me on a Saturday night, it didn't come.

"Oh," she said. "Congratulations. I know that'll help."

"Yeah," I said. "How are you?"

"Tired. I think I'll lie down, take a nap myself."

"If it's not too late when I finish up tonight, maybe I could stop by."

"Uh, okay," she said. "I'll be in tonight. But I might go to bed early. I'm so tired. Call first, okay? If I'm asleep, I'll just let the machine pick up."

"Yeah," I said, feeling awkward. All our conversations had been like this lately: strained, full of cumbersome pauses. "Sure, I'll call first."

"When you called earlier, was there something you wanted?"

"No," I answered. "I just wanted to say hi, see how you were."

"I'm fine. Really. I'm going to lie down now."

"Yeah, take care. I'll talk to you later."

"Okay, Harry. Bye."

She hung up and I held the phone out, staring at it until the dial tone started again, and then the computer voice told me if I wanted to make a call, hang up and dial again. And if I needed assistance, hang up and dial the operator.

"I would, but I don't think it would help," I said.

I rinsed off my face and threw together a couple of sandwiches and a quart of iced tea, then gathered the rest of my gear. I had a pair of binoculars, the High-8 tapes, my old Nikon with the 70–210 zoom, extra film. As an afterthought, I threw the copy of *Life's Little Maintenance Manual* in the bag.

Hell, I thought, maybe I'll get it autographed.

I loaded everything into the car along with a blanket and an extra jacket and headed out. The traffic was fairly light going north to Rivergate Mall. I made it in about twenty minutes.

The movie crowd was filing out after the afternoon matinee. I got lucky and found a spot right in front of the entrance and backed in. I got out, feeling the warming afternoon sun on my shoulders, and leaned against the fender, scanning the area, looking for Lonnie.

I stood there maybe two minutes when a silver BMW pulled into the lot and turned toward me. The windows were tinted nearly black, which if memory served me was now illegal in Music City. The Beamer crossed the road and into the lot from my right and pulled up in front of me. The window dropped a couple of inches and Lonnie looked out.

"Yo, Harry!" he called.

I grinned, walked over. "Hey, where'd you get this thing?" I bent down. There was somebody in the car with him, but Lonnie's head was blocking my view.

"Picked it up in Arkansas last week, decided to buy it from the loan company. Got a good deal."

"Yeah, I'll bet." Lonnie always had a line on good car deals.

He leaned over, picked up a camera bag, and held it up to the window.

"Here you go," he said. "Sorry to have to take off, man."

The bag wouldn't go through the window. "Hey, man, don't push it," I said. "Let the window down."

"It'll fit," he said, jamming it against the glass.

"You're going to bust it," I said. "Just lower the friggin' window. What's the matter with you?"

"He's shy," a voice inside the car said.

"Damn it," Lonnie muttered, rolling the window down.

I leaned in and looked across Lonnie.

"Hi, Harry," Sheba said. "How are you?" Her hand rested on Lonnie's right leg.

"Well, I'll be dipped." I looked at Lonnie and grinned.

He scowled back at me. "Just take the damn camera, okay?"

Chapter 9

I laughed out loud as the BMW pulled away. Hell, he had probably shaved and put on a clean shirt.

Amazing.

I shielded my eyes from the setting sun as Lonnie and Sheba rode off into it, so to speak. Then I hauled the camera bag over to the hood of the Mustang and unzipped it, although it occurred to me that if Lonnie'd forgotten anything, it was too late to fix it now.

Camera body, lens, mike, cords, four battery packs—it was all there. Lonnie was his usual paradigm of efficiency. I unzipped the side pocket to make sure the instruction manual was in there as well. I'd only used the L-2 a couple of times; the documentation would come in handy.

The address Victoria Reed had given me was on the other side of the county, a good hour's drive away. I slid the camera bag into the floor space between the passenger's seat and the glove box, then walked around and climbed behind the wheel. At least I'd be driving away from the sun.

The radio was tuned to the jazz FM station in Murfreesboro. The jock announced the next cut, a 1939 Decca recording of Louis Armstrong and his orchestra doing the Doc Dougherty hit "I'm Confessin' That I Love You."

"I'm confessin' that I love you, darlin', do you love me too?" Louis warbled, his sweet, wonderful voice like a velvet-lined coffee can full of gravel.

I broke out laughing. Lonnie and Sheba—what a concept.

* * *

Now maybe it's just me, but I always figured whenever you give your house a name, it meant either you had one hell of a lot of money or you wanted everybody to think you had one hell of a lot of money. I've named dogs, cats, horses. My first car, nearly thirty years ago, was an old powder-blue '64 Ford Galaxy that I called the Blue Goose.

But, I swear, I have *never* named a house.

Yet here I was, leaving the traffic of Green Hills behind me and heading out Hillsboro Road into Forest Hills, a city-within-a-city where it seemed that every house had a sign out front announcing its appellation. They were all mutated combinations of England and antebellum South: Cumberland Hall, The Jumpers, and the inevitable Dixie Land. Maybe it's some kind of local ordinance.

The sun had almost completely set now, but there was still enough ambient light to see that every place I passed was surrounded by brick or wrought-iron fences, massive gates, long cobblestone or aggregate driveways. Maybe I was just tuned into noticing this because I can't make my office rent this month and the four hundred a month I pay Mrs. Hawkins for my attic apartment was quickly becoming problematic as well.

I left Forest Hills behind. Hillsboro Road had long since narrowed down to two lanes through the rolling hills that surround Nashville, where the land was quickly being bought up by country music stars. Alan Jackson had a huge new place out here somewhere, and I seemed to remember Amy Grant lived out this way as well.

It seemed I was constantly upshifting and downshifting to account for the terrain. I topped one ridge only to find another one in front of me, a roller-coaster effect that made the driving almost pleasant in the fading twilight.

I had an address for the Reeds' farm, but I wasn't sure how to find it. Somewhere out here, there was an intersection where you turn right off Hillsboro Road onto Old Hillsboro Road. I wasn't sure where, but I knew I had to take that turn, then follow that road out several miles until I came to Old Natchez Trace.

I crested one hill and let the car coast down and through an intersection. There was another light maybe a few hundred yards farther on. As I approached it, I squinted to focus.

"Gotcha," I said, and made the turn.

Old Hillsboro Road was even narrower and more winding. The area was a curious mix of horse farms, old farmhouses, trendy new mid-six-figure homes, and grand antebellum mansions. Most of this land, some twelve thousand acres in all, had once been owned by a fellow named Bigbee Perkins, a Tennessee lawyer who in the early 1800s had helped capture Aaron Burr.

Now it was home to old money, new money, and as the occasional run-down farmhouse revealed, little money. My guess is the old places that have been passed down from generation to generation will eventually be bulldozed over so a bunch of health-care executives can put up six- and seven-figure faux-French châteaus.

The moon was rising over a line of trees to my right as I drove on, with the silvery light glittering off the banks of the Harpeth River to my left. The river was swollen with the early spring rains and was already out of its banks. I could just barely glimpse whitecaps in the fading light as the normally slow and placid water raged past in torrents.

I approached an intersection and slowed to read the street sign, which read Old Natchez Trace. I stopped in the middle of the road and checked my notebook for the directions. The road was deserted, incredibly quiet. Somewhere in the distance I heard a lonesome bovine moan echoing over the rolling hills and pastures.

"Okay," I muttered. "Almost there."

I turned onto Old Natchez Trace and drove on until the road made a ninety-degree dogleg to the right next to the polo field; then I started checking numbers on mailboxes. This definitely looked high rent, with breeding farms and stables reminiscent of the bluegrass country dotting the landscape. To my left, the Montpier mansion loomed in the moonlight like something out of *Gone with the Wind*.

About a half mile on, I rounded a turn and there it was. Wooden horse fencing painted black snaked like ribbons suspended midair around the perimeter of the Reeds' farm. The house itself sat back from the road maybe a hundred, perhaps a hundred and fifty yards. I slowed, doused the headlights on the Mustang, and pulled over to the side of the road to scope out the area.

A high gate was swung to at the street, closing off the long driveway that led to a sprawling ranch-style house. Behind the house and up the hill to the left, the dark outline of a barn loomed. To the right were a pair of tennis courts surrounded by a high chain-link fence. There were a few lights on in the house, and from behind the house, the ambient glow of soft outside lights.

I sat there, engine idling at a low purr, as I considered how to approach the place. I had Victoria Reed's permission to be on the property, so technically I wasn't trespassing. I reached into my pocket and pulled out the tiny envelope with the spare key and the burglar-alarm code.

I opened the camera bag and slipped a battery pack into the L-2, then attached the lens. I powered it up and opened the back of the camera, then popped in a blank tape. I looked through the viewfinder and zoomed in as tight as I could get on the house. The light was low, barely enough to register, but enough so that I could see there was no one out front.

The car was another question. I didn't want to risk driving up to the gate and seeing if I could get into the driveway. On the other hand, leaving the car parked out front was not the best idea either. I turned the videocamera back off, put the Mustang in gear, and slowly pulled away.

Maybe fifty yards farther on, the shoulder of the road widened just a bit. I pulled off to the right, the tires crunching gravel as I braked to a stop. I jammed extra battery packs and an extra High-8 tape into my pockets, then zipped up my leather jacket tightly. I hung the binoculars from my neck and strapped the L-2 across my right shoulder. Then I got out and locked the car.

Behind me, up a slight hill, sounds of music and laughter came from another dwelling that looked like somebody's idea of a French country house. Just another Saturday-night party that I hadn't been invited to.

The air was damp and chilly, so it felt good to keep moving. I walked up the road and approached the Reeds' property as it appeared to my left. I stopped before I got to the gate, figuring there might be some kind of security or sensing device. I stepped off the road into some high grass, crossed a shallow, narrow ditch, and got to the wooden fence. I put a foot on the lowest board, then hoisted myself up with little effort, straddled the top of the fence, then hopped down the other side. I leaned down low, listening for any sign of alarms, dogs barking, horses neighing—whatever. I let out a long breath after a moment, relieved, then stood up. Just then, headlights danced on the road as a car approached.

I ducked in close to the fence and stooped down as low as I could, then tucked my head to cover the white of my face. The headlights flickered around me as the car passed without stopping.

I realized that the sooner I got away from the street, the better off I'd be. I stood up and walked through the soft, wet grass as quickly as possible, all the while being careful of gopher holes or sudden dips in the ground. No sense in blowing an ankle on a job like this.

The house was silent as I approached. No music or blaring television, no talking, no panting with passion. Behind me, the moon bathed the landscape in an eerie silver. I looked behind me, smiling. It was almost full. That would help. If someone spotted me, I'd be backlit. No one could see my face.

This was the part of my job that, so help me, I had discovered I liked the most. I felt that rush of artery-clearing adrenaline yet again, just like at the Mexican restaurant, just as I'd felt when Lonnie and I were creeping through some deadbeat's backyard to grab whatever vehicle he hadn't been making payments on.

I was at the house now, right in front of the perfectly manicured hedges and shrubbery that lined the front. Like most people, Reed had let his hedges get too high. People don't understand how much cover shrubbery gives to burglars and intruders. You want to stop daylight break-ins; cut your damn hedges back.

He'd figure it out, I supposed, when he saw the videotape.

The window right next to me was illuminated from within. I edged in between the house and a tall bush on the left. I made sure I was covered as much as possible, then moved my head around to where I could just glance through the sheers and check for movement. If I saw anything, it would be a problem because the L-2 wasn't going to catch much through the curtains. But at least I'd know someone was there.

Nothing.

I worked my way down the house, past the entrance portico, and down every other window. The dark windows revealed nothing, and what I could see through the lit ones didn't help. The window on the far right looked into what was apparently Reed's office. The furniture was all leather, masculine, with a huge desk in the corner and a computer monitor on top. Built-in oak bookcases lined one wall, highlighted against the hunter-green walls on the other three sides.

Damn, I thought. *Where are they? Victoria said they'd be here.*

At least there wasn't a second floor to worry about. I thought about working my way around to the back of the house, but I was on the side next to the driveway. If anybody was out back, that'd be the side they'd automatically look to if they sensed anyone was coming. No, best to backtrack across the front of the house and approach from the side nearest the woods and barn. They'd never expect to see anyone coming from that side in the night.

I quickly padded back across the front lawn, ready to duck behind shrubs at the slightest movement. I came to the corner of the house, rounded it, and stopped to catch my breath and reconnoiter.

Off on the distant ridge that loomed behind the barn, a coyote howled. I'd heard they were back in this part of the state. They'd likely not come this close to a house, but all the same, the hair on the nape of my neck tingled.

As I skulked down the darkest side of the house, toward the

back, I became aware of the sound of water gurgling. I ducked down low, all the way on my stomach, brought the L-2 up in front of me, then switched it on. I heard the whirring of the gears and the slightest click as the heads engaged, but knew the camera was quiet enough not to be heard from more than a foot or two away.

I inched forward on my belly, my elbows and knees propelling me forward slowly. I came to the sharp line of light that went from around the back of the house. I stayed in the shadow, working my way forward until I was at the very corner of the house.

I pushed the record button and brought the eyepiece up to my eyes. I figured if there was anybody back there doing something they shouldn't be, I'd have them on tape even if they spotted me.

The L-2's lens rubbed against the bricks as I poked it around the corner. Through the viewfinder, I saw a swimming pool, a large one with a tall slide at the end nearest me. Steam rose in thick clouds off the water, which led me to assume the pool was heated. The whole backyard was laid out like a courtyard, with the pool at the center. The brick was all distressed, antique, the kind that costs a bundle. A carefully landscaped garden lined the outer edges, with flowers just beginning to come into bloom.

It was all beautiful, and totally empty.

I kept the camera running and carefully raised up on my knees. Still looking through the viewfinder, I leaned against the brick wall and slowly slid up. My jacket against the brick made a scraping sound, but I didn't figure there was anybody there anyway. I was just trying to get higher to get a better view.

The pool was kidney-shaped and lit aqua blue from lights built into the walls below the water. It was incredibly romantic, gorgeous, secluded enough for skinny-dipping and luxurious enough to just sit outside and bask.

The closest I ever came to something like this was a hot shower.

As I stood and got a better view of the area, I realized that beyond the pool, a few feet from the shallow end, another small pool was bubbling and smoking.

Jacuzzi, I thought. *Damn, I got to write me one of them little books.*

No one there, though, so I stood up, lowered the camera, and flicked the power switch. The L-2 nestled silently in the palm of my hand.

I stepped out into the light.

All was silent. I edged up close to the large plate-glass window that looked out onto the courtyard from what was probably a big family room. A large-screen television dominated one end, with a genuine Wurlitzer jukebox blinking a rainbow of color against the wall opposite.

New money; expensive toys.

If Robert Jefferson Reed and Margot Horowitz were anywhere around, they were being awfully quiet. I checked my watch. It wasn't even eight yet. Maybe they'd gone out for dinner. I figured I could go move the Mustang to within binocular range of the house and sit there all night waiting for them to get back. But that was a hell of a way to spend my Saturday, I thought, and probably a waste of Victoria Reed's money.

I scowled, trying to figure out what to do. I took a couple of steps past the large window and gazed out over the backyard.

That's when I spotted it.

I squinted, staring into the churning white froth of the Jacuzzi.

Wait a minute, you don't run a Jacuzzi round the clock. You turn it on when you're going to use it, then off when you're done. But there was no one there. Was it on a timer?

I stepped closer, and with each step, my heart rate went up. There was something dark silhouetted in the bubbling water of the Jacuzzi, something large and dark bobbing up and down in the brilliant white foam.

"Jesus," I whispered. I set the camera and the binoculars down on a large glass-topped table with a patio umbrella sticking up through the middle.

I took the twenty feet or so over to the Jacuzzi in rapid steps.

At the edge I stopped, sucked in a deep breath and let it loose, then leaned down. The sharp smell of chlorine filled my nostrils.

"Oh, my God," I said out loud. I reached over and touched it. It was soft, squishy, wet, and slick. And it had hair coming out of it.

I gritted my teeth, fought back the urge to hurl, grabbed a handful of hair, and pulled it up.

It was Robert Jefferson Reed—at least I think it was—face-down in the whirling foam. His brilliant blue eyes were open, staring, flushed with water. His mouth was open, his tongue swollen, hanging out. Liquid ran out of his mouth, cascading down his face, disappearing into the bubbles.

He was naked, pasty white, and he looked dead as hell.

I let out a sound like a forced, choked squeal and dropped him. Horrified, I thought, *What if he isn't dead?* I pushed my sleeve up, reached in, and grabbed him again, hoping there was still some life left in him and praying I wouldn't have to give him mouth-to-mouth to jump-start it.

In one of those totally inappropriate flashes of memory, my mind went back to page 37 of *Life's Little Maintenance Manual*: NOTHING ENDS A DAY LIKE A GOOD LONG HOT SOAK.

Wonder if this is what the old boy had in mind?

"Goddamn it," I whispered. "Breathe. . . ."

That's when I heard the crunch of gravel behind me. While leaning down over the edge of the Jacuzzi, with a knotted hank of Robert Jefferson Reed's slick wet hair in my hand, I turned.

A tall guy in a dark blue uniform, pistol in a two-handed military stance, looked out over the weapon and sighted right in on my forehead.

"Freeze," he barked. Just like in the movies.

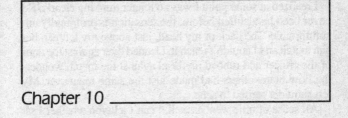

Chapter 10

You want to know the difference between a criminal and a civilian? Okay, here it is: you put a pair of handcuffs on a criminal and he stays in reality. Civilians disassociate; the moment the metal clicks shut, the civilians are in another world. This ain't real. This isn't happening. I'll wake up in just a moment and this will all have been a terrible dream.

I learned something very important about myself that night: I'm a civilian.

From the moment the Williamson County Sheriff's Department patrolman frisked me down, cuffed my hands behind me, and shoved me in the backseat of his cruiser, it was like there was a Harry Denton somewhere else watching Harry Denton sit there with a blank look on his face.

And the lights. Good God, flashing blue lights, harsh headlights, flashing reds and yellows, then the popping white strobes of photographers. Squad cars, paramedics, then guys in ill-fitting suits and polyester ties. Over the front seat of the cruiser and out over the dashboard, I watched the crowd grow. Then above us the *whop-whop-whop* of a helicopter overhead. I leaned out the window, straining to see if it was a police helicopter or a news crew. I couldn't see, and I remember wondering at one point if this much fuss was made over every murder in Williamson County.

Then I remembered who the victim was. Robert Jefferson Reed wasn't just some guy on the street who got popped in a random holdup or a drug deal gone sour. He was rich and he was famous and he was naked and dead in a Jacuzzi on some very expensive real estate.

I realized at some point I was no longer thinking clearly. I'd never been handcuffed before; the sensation is profoundly uncomfortable. The back of my head, just above my left ear, began to itch and I couldn't reach it. I leaned over against the door of the cruiser and rubbed my head against the metal, wondering how many others had made just the same maneuver. My left shoulder started to ache.

All sense of time went as well. I can't tell you whether I sat there for thirty minutes or two hours before somebody finally came over and talked to me. All of a sudden, the car door to my right opened and a brown-haired man in a crisp suit eased into the car next to me, holding the door open with his right knee.

"I'm Lieutenant D'Angelo, Williamson County Sheriff's Department CID," he said. He spoke slowly, his Southern accent rolling off his tongue in a lazy, relaxed fashion. "I'll be handling the investigation."

"Great, Lieutenant. I'll be glad to cooperate in any way I'm able. But unless I'm a suspect, would you mind removing these bracelets? I'm getting kind of sore."

I shifted to my left and turned. D'Angelo sighed, as if he hadn't noticed my hands were tethered.

"Sorry about that. Tommy Grishom's one of our new kids." He turned and looked out the open door. "Hey, Tommy, let me have your keys. I think we can uncuff this gentleman."

I felt a pair of hands pull me around a bit, then the click of metal and the tingle of blood rushing back into my hands.

"Thanks," I said, bringing my hands in front of me and rubbing them. There were ugly red circles around my arms just up from the wrist joint. Yeah, Officer Grishom was a newbie all right, and he liked slamming metal on people. Bad combination.

"So, why don't you tell me how you came to be here and how all this happened?" D'Angelo said.

I rubbed my wrists harder as my hands felt like they were being dragged across the bottom side of a pincushion. Now that the cuffs were off, I was beginning to feel a little less dispirited. Along with that came a surge of anger.

"Before we do that, you got to tell me if I'm a suspect in this. If I am, Mirandize me and let me call my lawyer."

"Relax, you're just a material witness. No need to get tense."

"Then how come that yutz out there slams the cuffs on me and tosses me in the backseat?"

"Try to put yourself in his place. He was the only one here. He investigates a call on a suspected prowler, finds your car down the road, sneaks up on the house, and finds you holding a dead guy in a whirlpool by his hair. Until he got some help here, he needed to make sure everything was under control."

"Tell him if he takes his bullet out of his shirt pocket and puts it in his pistol, he won't have to worry." This voice inside my head said, *Watch it, dude. This guy's laid-back, but he can be pushed too far.*

I looked over to where the crowd of cops and paramedics were wrapping up the crime scene. Two guys in orange were placing a dark body bag onto a gurney.

"If any of my gear's damaged or missing," I said, "I'll be submitting an invoice to your department."

"Why don't we start over again," he said, pulling a notebook out of his pocket and clicking a cheap ballpoint. "You could begin by telling me who you are."

I reached into my jacket and pulled out my license and badge, then flipped the case open and handed it to him.

"Name's Harry James Denton," I said. "I'm a private investigator from Nashville."

He examined the license, then scribbled the information into his notebook.

"Who you work for?" he asked without looking up.

"Myself. Got my own shingle."

"Want to tell me what you were doing out here?"

I thought for a moment. I could push it, claim confidentiality, but I'd already smarted off enough to this guy and, what the hell, he was going to find out anyway.

"Yeah. His wife hired me to take pictures of him and his girlfriend."

D'Angelo looked up. In the dim glow of the car's dome light, he looked my age, maybe a little older. But there was an animated, energized air about him, like a kid watching a cartoon.

"We don't have a positive ID on the victim yet. Can you help us there?"

"Yeah, he's Robert Jefferson Reed. You mean you guys didn't know who he was?"

"On the computer, this house is owned by a corporation. No individual owner listed."

"I didn't know that," I said. "But you know who Reed is, don't you?"

D'Angelo shrugged. "Yeah, but why don't you tell me anyway."

I stared at him for a moment, wondering if this was some cop ploy to find out how truthful I could be. "Well, right now he's the number one bestselling author in America. *Life's Little Maintenance Manual*, you know?"

D'Angelo thought for a couple of beats, then: "Yeah, my wife bought a copy. She loves that crap. Bought some kind of poster, tried to hang it in the kids' room, but they wouldn't have any of it."

"Your kids have taste. The rest of the country doesn't. And you've got a *Lifestyles of the Rich and Famous* dead guy on your hands."

"That explains all the television news crews."

"The TV guys are here?" I asked, wondering how I was going to get past them.

"Yeah, but we're keeping them at the street, off the property. So tell me how you came to be here."

It only took a couple of minutes to describe the whole evening. It was all relatively straightforward; I sneak around a house and find a body in the Jacuzzi. End of story.

"Did you see or hear anybody else?"

"Nothing," I said as D'Angelo took more notes. "I was here maybe ten minutes before Deputy Fife over there decided I was John Dillinger."

D'Angelo looked up at me, clearly irritated. "Officer Grishom was just doing his job."

"Sorry. It's been a long day. So what's the next step?"

"The next step is for you to tell me the girlfriend's name."

Again there was no reason I should tell him, but he was going to find out eventually. If I didn't tell him, he could probably watch it on the ten o'clock news tomorrow night. This kind of juicy stuff doesn't stay quiet for long.

"Her name's Margot," I said. "Margot Horowitz. She was his assistant. Secretary. Whatever."

"With the wife figuring it leaned toward *whatever*."

"That's about it. She just hired me this morning. I figured it would be quick and simple."

"Guess you figured wrong, didn't you?" he said, flipping the notebook shut.

I leaned back on the vinyl seat, stretching my arms out in front of me, trying to unlock a cramp in my left shoulder.

"Yeah. Was he murdered? There's always a chance the guy stroked out, had the water turned up too high. Maybe he fell asleep and drowned."

"Doc says he found ligature marks on the throat and petechial hemorrhaging. But it'll take an autopsy to be sure."

Petechial hemorrhaging, I knew, involved ruptured blood vessels in the whites of the eyes. It was almost always found in strangulation cases.

So Reed was murdered.

"How long will it take the doc to find out for sure?" I asked.

"The coroner here just pronounces death and does the paperwork. We don't do autopsies in Williamson County. They all go into the state ME's office."

That meant Dr. Henry Krohlmeyer's office, since the Metro Nashville Medical Examiner doubled as the state ME. And since Dr. Henry was out of town, that meant the autopsy on Robert Jefferson Reed would probably be performed by Marsha. That elicited a silent *oh, shit* from my interior voice. This time I managed to short-circuit before my regular voice said anything.

"I'm going to have this typed up Monday morning and there may be some questions for you. I'll need you to come in and sign it. And I want your office and home addresses and all your phone numbers."

I pulled a business card out of my license case. "Let me borrow your pen, okay?"

I wrote down my home address and phone number on the back of the card and handed it to him. "Can I go now? I need to pack up my gear and get out of here."

"Yeah," D'Angelo said. "You call me Monday morning."

"Oh, wait," I said. "My car's down the road. How am I going to get past the news crews? I don't want my name in the papers or my face on TV."

D'Angelo smiled. "Got something to hide?"

"Just the nature of my business."

"C'mon, I'll drive you down there."

He climbed out of the car, leaving me room to scoot over and follow him. I turned and looked over the hood of the squad car.

"Thanks," I said. "I appreciate it."

"S'okay," he answered. "Truth is, I'd just as soon keep you under wraps as well."

I walked over, got the videocamera and my binoculars, then followed him over to his white Chevy and eased in next to him. I was still sore and my wrists were stiffening up.

He started the car, looked out over his right shoulder to turn around in the driveway. Over by the patio, two other officers were hauling away the last of their equipment under the yellow crime-scene tape. Another officer was pulling the back door to after wrapping up the search of the inside of the house.

"You know, we haven't had a homicide in Williamson County since 1995," D'Angelo said as we drove slowly down the long driveway. At the end of the drive, behind the gate, about a dozen cars and vans jammed the street. From the top of one of the vans, a tower with a dish on the end of it pointed to the sky, and next to it a floodlight lit a TV reporter doing a live remote.

"I knew it was too good to last," he added. "Say, you wouldn't mind letting me have the videotape you shot, would you?"

I leaned back against the seat and thought for a moment. It was my tape; I didn't want to give it to D'Angelo. There was nothing on it, at least nothing that I thought would do anyone any good. Still, it was *mine*. But then I realized if I tried to hold back on him, it was only going to make him dig his heels in. In the end, he probably had the right.

I hit the eject button on the L-2 and handed him the tape. "No problem," I said. "But there's nothing on it. I didn't see anything."

"Yeah," he said, pulling a manila envelope marked EVIDENCE out of a briefcase between us and slipping the tape into it. "I'm sure there isn't, but we'll take a close look anyway."

As we approached the end of the driveway, a uniformed officer hit a button on a control panel and the gate swung slowly open in front of us. There was a flurry of movement as uniforms held back bodies with microphones and portable TV cameras. I ducked my head as we drove through the gauntlet and tried to look invisible.

It was nearly eleven by the time I started the car and pulled away, easing my way past the news crews and the emergency vehicles. I came back into town by Hillsboro Road, which would take me right past Marsha's condo. I thought of stopping by without calling first, but figured that given how tired she was, not to mention the circumstances of the evening, that might not be such a good idea. I stopped at a BP station and called from a pay phone. Her number rang until the machine picked up.

"Just me," I said. "Wondering if you were still up. I'm close by, thought I'd drop in. You there?"

The tape ran on. "Okay, I'll call you tomorrow." I hung up, bought a Coke from the night man at the gas station, then headed for East Nashville. It was Saturday night, late, and I felt very much alone.

Next morning, I woke up exhausted, as if I'd never even fallen asleep. My wrists were bruised a slight shade of purple and brown now from the handcuffs and my left shoulder was sore, like I'd pitched a hard game the day before.

I tried not to think about Robert Jefferson Reed and what he felt like when I pulled his head up out of the water. At least he hadn't been there a long time. Early in my newspaper days I'd covered the retrieval of a floater, a guy who'd been pulled out of the Cumberland River after being missing for about ten days. What was left of him hadn't been pretty. Yeah, floaters are definitely the worst.

So I had something to be thankful for, I guess. I draped a steaming washcloth over my face as the coffee brewed and let it hang there for as long as I could stand it. Then I threw on a T-shirt and a pair of pants and went downstairs to get the Sunday paper.

Mrs. Hawkins normally gets the papers and lays one at the foot of the steps to my apartment, but I guess she was sleeping in as well. I grabbed both our papers, then left hers at her kitchen door and went back upstairs.

I was eager to read what the Sunday *Tennessean* had to say about Reed's death. Like most Sunday papers, though, you have to wade through about three hundred pages of slicks and coupons to get to the front page. I poured a cup of coffee, yanked the six-inch-thick roll out of its plastic sleeve, and started separating the paper from the junk.

I unfolded section A and spread it out on the table.

"Goddamn it!" I yelped.

BESTSELLING AUTHOR REED FOUND MURDERED

the banner headline read, and below that:

LOCAL PRIVATE INVESTIGATOR DISCOVERS BODY

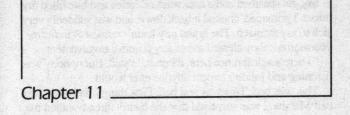

Chapter 11 _____

I scanned the front page, then flipped to the jump. At least they hadn't published my picture. I turned back to the front and speed-read the story:

> The Nashville-born author of *Life's Little Maintenance Manual*, who rose from obscurity to bestsellerdom spinning homespun family-values wisdom, was found murdered last night at his Williamson County farm.
>
> A spokesman for the Williamson County Sheriff's Department said preliminary findings indicate Robert Jefferson Reed had been strangled, but that the cause of death would be determined by autopsy. Reed's wife, Victoria, and family rushed to the Williamson County Medical Center upon learning of Reed's death. A spokesman for the family said Ms. Reed would have no comment on her husband's death.

Three paragraphs down, there I was:

> Police refused to disclose the identity of the person who discovered the body. A source within the Williamson County Sheriff's Department revealed, however, that the body was found by Nashville private investigator Harry Denton. Denton, a former investigative reporter, was implicated last year in the shooting death of Angelo M. "Mousy" Caramello, who was allegedly involved in the local adult-entertainment industry. The grand jury refused to indict Denton in that case. Attempts to contact him for comment have been unsuccessful.

My gut spasmed and a backwash of coffee and bile filled my throat. I grimaced, choked it back down, and was suddenly very sick to my stomach. The grand jury hadn't *refused to indict me*, you morons; they cleared me of any criminal involvement.

"There's a difference here, damn it," I said. But nobody was listening and I didn't expect anyone ever would.

This was bad. This was real bad. First thing I had to do was call Marsha. I was surprised that she hadn't already called me. In fact, I was surprised the phone wasn't ringing off the hook. My phone number was unlisted, which explained why the reporters couldn't find me, but what about Lonnie? What about Marsha? What about . . . I have other friends, too. Somewhere. I'm sure of it.

I stepped over to the kitchen wall phone and picked it up, punched in Marsha's number, and stood there. Nothing. Must've misdialed. I hung up the phone, waited a couple of seconds, picked it up again.

Nothing.

I shook the phone and slapped the back of the handset, just like every dumb shit who thinks that'll help fix a dead phone. Still nothing. I hung up, walked into the bedroom to put the bedroom phone back on the hook. I must have knocked it off last night without realizing it.

I stopped at the foot of the bed. The phone was on the hook.

"What the hell?" I walked over, picked up the bedroom phone, held it to my ear. Dead as a rock.

Great, some jerk's cut a wire somewhere. Go to Plan B, whatever that is. I stood there a moment, thinking. Had I forgotten—

"Aw, shit," I muttered, shaking my head. I turned, stepped over to the small desk next to my reading chair, flipped through a stack of envelopes. The one from BellSouth was unopened, but it didn't look like a bill, so I hadn't paid any attention. I tore open the envelope.

Notice of discontinuation of service, the form read. If I didn't get my account current by the tenth, my phone would be cut off and it would cost me my firstborn child to get it turned back on again.

Today was the twelfth.

"I've got to get to a phone," I mumbled. I threw on a regular shirt over my T-shirt, then ran down the flight of stairs to Mrs. Hawkins's back stoop. The newspaper was still at the door where I'd left it. I hated to wake up the old lady, but this was an emergency.

I opened the storm door and pounded on the wooden door, hard and loud. If she was in the back of the house or still in bed, I'd be lucky if she'd hear anything.

I stood there. Nothing. I banged again, then yelled her name. I sighed loudly in frustration.

"C'mon, Mrs. Hawkins, get up," I growled. I pounded on the door again. "Mrs. Hawkins! Rise and shine!"

I pressed my face to the glass and peered into the kitchen. There was no sign of her and the lights were all out. Where was she? Usually, if she's going anywhere, she tells me or leaves me a note. I house-sit, water the plants, and make sure her herd of neighborhood stray cats gets fed.

Somewhere in one of my kitchen drawers, I had a key to her house. I paused for a second. I didn't want to scare her or anything, but I needed her phone and—

What if there was something wrong with her? I thought of the commercial, the one where the old lady has fallen and can't get up.

I took the stairs to my kitchen three at a time. It took fumbling through four separate drawers, but I finally found the key and raced back downstairs, metal stairs clanging against the house. I opened the door and stepped into the kitchen.

"Mrs. Hawkins!" I yelled. "Mrs. Hawkins!"

I shut the door behind me and looked around. The dishes were washed and neatly stacked in the drainer, like always. The place was clean and orderly, like always. No sign of a break-in. Nothing out of order.

I walked out of the kitchen, into the hallway, down the hall, and to the open door of her bedroom. The covers were pulled back and there was a hardcover book opened, facedown, on the bed. A Grisham novel . . .

My heart thumped a couple times real hard in the middle of my chest. I was starting to get a queasy feeling.

"C'mon, Esther," I whispered. "Where the hell are you?"

I backed out of the bedroom and noticed the door to the bathroom, which was set in a little alcove. A light shone from beneath the closed door.

Great, I thought, the old lady's on the can and I fling the door open and give her a heart attack. How am I going to handle this one?

I stepped over and knocked gently on the door so as not to startle her.

"Mrs. Hawkins? Mrs. Hawkins, you okay?" My voice became louder with each word. *C'mon, Esther, talk to me!*

"Aw, damn it," I said, then turned the handle and pushed open the door.

I'd need that phone for real now. Esther Hawkins lay curled up on the floor in her flowered old-lady nightgown, on her side in the fetal position, already well into rigor.

I sat on a metal step halfway up the flight of stairs to my apartment, a coat thrown over my shoulders, my head in my hands. I could only intermittently watch as the cops, orange-coated paramedics, and guys in suits traipsed in and out of Mrs. Hawkins's house. She'd have hated the way they were tracking up the place.

Jack Maples, one of Dr. Henry's forensic investigators, stepped out of the kitchen, the sleeves of his white shirt rolled halfway up, a clipboard cradled in the crook of his hairy arm.

"Hey, Jack," I said. "How ya doing?"

He turned. "Harry? Harry Denton, how the hell are you? You live up there?" He motioned up toward my apartment.

"Yeah," I said. "I rent it from Mrs. Hawkins. At least I did."

"Yeah, too bad about the old lady."

"How long has she been dead?" I asked.

He shrugged his shoulders. "Rigor's about the shittiest, most overrated way I know of to figure time of death. Body temp's not always much better given she was lying on a cold tile floor. Postmortem lividity was fixed, though. Best SWAG? Twelve, maybe fourteen hours."

I sighed, shook my head from side to side. "Damn, I hate this."

"She was in a nightgown," he continued, "and the bed was turned down, book open next to her. I imagine she got out of bed maybe midnight or so, went in, sat down on the can, and *pow*, the heart goes and she's outta here."

I looked into his eyes. "Think she suffered?"

He shook his head. "Prob'ly never knew what hit her." He laughed, his jowls shaking. "Maybe it was the friggin' Grisham novel."

"Tacky, Jack. Very tacky. . . ."

He held the clipboard out in front of him as he rolled his shirtsleeves back down.

"In any case, there's shittier ways to die," he said. "Trust me on this."

He buttoned his sleeves, then looked around as if he'd forgotten something.

I looked over his shoulder, across the five-foot-high box hedges that ran along Mrs. Hawkins's driveway. In the window of the house next door, Mrs. Hawkins's neighbor, Gladys, stared wide-eyed at the goings-on. Mrs. Hawkins once warned me not to talk to her; she was a nervous, gossipy woman who liked to make trouble in the neighborhood because she didn't have anything else to do. Esther called her Crazy Gladys.

My eyes met Gladys's and we both looked away simultaneously. "What's next?" I asked Jack. "I mean, what's procedure?"

"I see no reason to think this is anything other than a natural-causes situation. Police chaplain can notify next of kin, or you can do it. Then it's up to the family where to take her. You know her people?"

"No, but she talked about a grown boy from time to time. Preacher, I think she said. Got a church up in Goodlettesville."

Behind him, two paramedics wheeled a gurney out with a zippered black body bag strapped to it. I winced, looked away. I would miss the old girl. She was kind and she was good to me. I regretted not spending more time with her and not telling her more plainly what I thought of her. Maybe everybody feels that way when somebody he likes dies.

"Hey, Ray," Jack called. "I leave my jacket in there?"

The guy at the back of the gurney turned and glanced inside the house. "Yeah, it's in the kitchen."

"Great," he said, then turned back to me. "Hey, big guy. I opened my Sunday paper this morning and saw your name in the lead story. You're not careful, you're going to get famous."

"Great, just what I need. I got to tell you, Jack, the last couple of days have—in a word—sucked."

He chuckled. "Look, Harry, I gotta go. But I want to ask you something." He leaned in close to me, lowered his voice, and raised his eyebrows like we were some kind of close buddies in a conspiracy or something. "There's a rumor going around the office," he said.

Oh, hell, I thought, he's going to ask me about Marsha and the grand jury. Get ready.

"Some people are saying that Doc Marsha is maybe, just possibly, might could sort of be just the littlest bit, uh . . . knocked up. . . . Any truth to that?" He leered like a fat twelve-year-old telling a dirty joke as if the world had never heard one before.

I gave him the blankest stare and the straightest screw-you monotone I could muster. "You're right, Jack. You gotta go."

The place seemed uncomfortably empty and painfully silent after everybody cleared out. I wandered from room to room, trying to find where she kept her papers, her bills, her private directory of telephone numbers.

In the living room, there was a table next to the sofa, with an old-fashioned dial telephone resting on top. I pulled the drawer out and found a plastic spiral-bound directory. The shiny cover was imprinted with a photograph of brightly colored flowers. Mrs. Hawkins always had a thing about flowers.

I remembered she told me once her son's name was Brian. I opened the directory to the *H* section and there he was. I took a deep breath, held it a few moments, then let it out slowly. May as well get it over with.

The phone rang three or four times before a female voice answered.

"Hello."

"Brian Hawkins, please."

"He's not here. May I take a message?"

I hesitated. "Is this Mrs. Hawkins?"

"Yes, this is Brian's wife. Who's calling?"

"Well, this is Harry Denton. I'm Mrs. Hawkins's tenant at her house in Nashville. I'm afraid I've got some bad news."

I paused just a moment, just long enough for her voice to tense as she said, "What is it?"

"I'm sorry, but Mrs. Hawkins died—"

"Oh, no!"

"Yes, last night. I knocked on her door this morning and when there was no answer, I used the key she'd given me to get in. I called 911, but they said she'd been gone at least twelve hours."

The voice on the other end was brittle, strained. "Where is she now?"

"The paramedics took her to the morgue here in Nashville. She'll be there until you decide . . . you know, which funeral home you want her to go to."

There was another silence on the line, this time an uncomfortably long one. "I'm sorry," I said finally. "She was a very nice lady."

"Yes, of course," the daughter-in-law said. "Brian's at the hospital, doing visitations after church. Will you be there for a while?"

"I'll be here for a bit. I may have to run out later."

"Where can you be reached?"

"My phone's out of order right now. I'm actually downstairs at the house using Mrs. Hawkins's phone."

"I expect him back within a half hour."

"Okay, I'll stick around."

The phone clicked loudly as she hung up. I tried to read her, without much success. I looked around the house. Lots of chintz and a hodgepodge of decorations, old furniture, odd sorts of things to keep.

Then I remembered I hadn't yet reached Marsha. I dialed her number and got the answering machine on the fourth ring.

"Hi, it's me," I said. "I'm sort of having a rough day. I'll try you at the office."

I dialed the morgue and as usual on a weekend, it rang about ten times before anyone answered.

"Simpkins Center," a male voice answered. I recognized the voice: Jack Maples. He'd returned to the office quicker than I would have expected. I didn't want him to know I was calling Marsha right after he'd tried to find out from me if she was pregnant.

"Simpkins Center," he said again.

I hung up.

Damn. The day was shaping up as a real loser. I leaned back in Mrs. Hawkins's overstuffed chair and tried to figure out what to do next. I needed to check in at my office, where I feared the answering machine would be jammed with incoming messages. But with the dial phone, I couldn't retrieve my messages remotely. I needed to get cleaned up, out of this house. I wanted to see Marsha, Lonnie, anybody.

I considered bringing my phone downstairs and plugging it in. Somehow, it didn't seem quite proper, my being in her space so soon after her death.

I walked outside, around the side of the house to the gray plastic box with BELLSOUTH imprinted on it. I unscrewed the lid of the entrance bridge with my pocketknife and examined the insides. One cable led into the bottom, then plug-in connectors ran to each side of the box, and two cables out. One cable ran up the side of the house to my apartment, the other through the bricks and into Mrs. Hawkins's.

I unplugged each connector and swapped them. If I'd done it right, her phone would ring in my apartment. With my Touch-Tone phone, I could call my office, check for messages, see how much damage control was going to be called for over the next few days.

I closed the lid on the entrance bridge and screwed it down tight. I stood up and turned to head for my apartment.

Crazy Gladys was at the window again just across the driveway and the hedge, her tangled salt-and-pepper hair piled crazily on top of her head like a bird's nest. Her eyes met mine for one dark second, then she jerked her head away and pulled the curtains to.

Chapter 12

Amazingly enough, my tampering with the telephone box worked. I picked up the kitchen phone, got a dial tone, and immediately dialed my office.

I punched in the remote code just as the message started. A few clicks, pauses, and then a computer voice said: *Hell-o, you have—twenty-three—messages.*

"Crap," I muttered, scrambling in a drawer for a pad and pencil.

The first seven messages were from a guy I used to know at the newspaper, Randy Tucker. Randy did an internship the year I got fired. He had the longest hair of anybody who'd ever worked there, given that the editor-in-chief was a conservative Neanderthal, but he was just enough of a hotshot J-school maniac to get away with it. After graduating, he'd come back and managed to get hired with a minimum of sartorial damage.

"Harry, Randy again," the last message said. "C'mon, call me, man! For old times' sake."

"Yeah, right," I grumbled. "Old buddies just catching up."

Truth is, I was surprised to hear from him. He'd gone to work for the business section and had brought a life to it that had never been there before. But why would the business section be interested in a murder?

The next bunch of calls were from two of the three local network stations, one all-news radio station, a newspaper up in Clarksville, an AP reporter I had a passing acquaintance with from years past, blah blah blah. I didn't even write them down. I had no intention of saying word one publicly about any of this. I'd gone to ground and was by God going to stay there.

Message sixteen was from Marsha: "Harry, call me. It's just before ten Sunday morning. I'll be at the center till late. Okay? Please, I want to talk. And hey, what's the matter with your home phone?"

Next was Victoria Reed, who sounded as if she'd been crying: "I would have thought you'd have tried to call me by now."

I gritted my teeth. She's right. I should have.

Three more reporters I didn't know, followed by an anonymous sobbing female voice who said that a wonderful and wise man had had his light prematurely extinguished and if I had anything to do with it, God would see that I was punished.

"Maybe I should just let my office phone go under, too," I said.

Next up was Lonnie: "Hey, dude. Tried to call your house and your phone's been disconnected. What's up? Listen, sorry I was so weird last night. It's just that, well, it's the first date I've had in a while. Kinda nervous. You know how it is. Or maybe you don't. Anyway, I'll be over at the yard working this afternoon. Drop by, give me a call. Whatever."

So he didn't know, at least not yet.

The last message was the worst. In Hawaii, my dad had watched the early Sunday-morning news just about the time the paramedics were hauling Mrs. Hawkins away.

"Son, I tried to call your apartment and couldn't get through. Nashville made CNN this morning. Did you hear? That guy who wrote that stupid little book got killed. Give us a call. Mom sends her love."

Over the years, I'd developed a keen ability to sense subtext in the tone of my father's voice, like all sons who could instantly read what kind of a mood Dad was in when he came home from work. Clearly, my name had not been mentioned, at least not by CNN. I was off the hook for now, but I better not let too much time go by without calling him.

There was one last cup of thick, aging coffee left in the pot, so I poured it into a mug and splashed enough milk in to at least thin it out a bit. I sat down at the kitchen table and tallied up the score. Of the important people in my life, one knew of Reed's murder and my involvement, one knew of the murder but not my involvement, and one knew nothing. Nobody knew about Mrs. Hawkins yet.

Of the unimportant people in my life; well, hell, there were a whole slew of them. And they all wanted a piece of me.

To hell with them.

I leaned back and gazed out the kitchen window for a few moments. Mrs. Hawkins's death hadn't quite hit me yet. She was a sweet old lady; patient, nonjudgmental, kind of like my own grandmother. She never intruded into my life, never pried. Never asked questions when I came home in the middle of the night after being gone for three days.

Never threw me out after an attempt on my life a few years ago backfired and ended in the death of a man she loved. . . .

I couldn't think about that now. It was all in the past and nothing could change any of that. Death is messy, but life's even messier. Right now, I had to figure out just how big a mess my life had become.

I'd taken a shower, shaved, cleaned up, and was about to give up on the Reverend Brian Hawkins when his silver Lincoln Town Car pulled into the driveway and parked in the back next to the garage. I was standing at my kitchen window, looking out at a gray late-winter Nashville day.

He was a big man in a black polyester suit, with a wide regimental tie clipped down over his white-shirted belly. He walked around the back of the car and opened the passenger's-side door. A late-middle-aged thin woman in a stiff blue dress climbed out of the car and pulled a fur jacket around her to ward off the damp cold. Her hair was starched into a beehive, the original Sixties rendition of Big Hair, and even from the window of my apartment, I could sense a certain tightness about her. She was thin-lipped and thin-hipped, and looked like if she cracked a smile, her face would shatter.

I threw my jacket on and stepped out on the landing. The noise caught their attention. They looked up; I nodded and went down the stairs and onto the porch.

"Reverend Hawkins," I said somberly, holding out my hand as they stepped up. "I'm Harry Denton. Sorry to have to meet you under these circumstances."

He shook my hand. His hand was soft and fat, his grip squishy like kneading warm bread dough. "Mr. Denton," he said, "thank you for calling us. This is my wife, Mrs. Hawkins."

I nodded. "Mrs. Hawkins," I said, being careful to use the two-syllable traditional pronunciation of the word and not the more contemporary *Miz*.

"Mr. Denton," she said. Her voice was brittle, dry. I tried to figure out what mistake of nature had put these two in the same family with the warm sweet old lady I'd known the past few years.

"Well, I guess we should go on in." I turned to the door and fished the key out of my pocket. "Have you had a chance to call the—"

"I've already made the arrangements," he said. "The funeral director is on his way to the morgue now."

"Good," I said, unlocking the door.

We walked into the kitchen and I switched the overhead light on. I'd turned the heat down and the place had quickly become damp and cold.

"When will the service be?" I asked. "I'd like to be there."

"She'll be at Holt and Chandler up in Goodlettesville," Mrs. Hawkins's son said flatly. He looked around the room, sizing the place up like he hadn't been here in a while.

"Hasn't changed much," he commented.

"Nothing ever did," she said.

I looked at the two of them. "Why don't I leave you two alone down here? I'm sure there are things you want to take care of."

I started for the door. "Where did you find her?" he asked.

"In the bathroom. She was on the floor. For what it's worth, it looks like her heart gave out and she went quickly. They said she didn't suffer."

"The Lord calls us in His own way and His own time," the Reverend said. I didn't know what the hell that had to do with anything, but I nodded my head in agreement anyway.

"I'll be upstairs for about another half hour," I said, "then I have some errands to take care of myself. If you need me for anything, that is. And by the way, I'm happy to keep an eye on the place until you, you know, decide what you're going to do and all."

"Actually, Mr. Denton, that won't be necessary," the wife said. "We'll take care of everything from here on out. In fact, there won't be any need for you to have a key. So if you don't mind . . ."

She held out a gloved hand.

"Sure," I said. I reached into my pocket, laid the key in her hand.

I stood there a moment, strangely awkward. "Thank you," she said, dismissing me.

I started out the door. "Oh," I said, "I, uh, had switched the phone lines so her phone would ring in my apartment. Just in case you or anybody else called. I'll just switch them back."

The two stared at me without moving, damn near without blinking. I could understand about her; when you smear on makeup with a butter knife, you don't want to move those facial muscles and risk cracking anything. But I didn't understand that attitude in the son of a woman like Mrs. Hawkins. I turned and exited.

Outside, under the ever-watchful eye of Crazy Gladys, I rewired the phones and shut the entrance bridge. Then I went upstairs, gathered my stuff, and got the hell out of there. All the time I couldn't help but wonder what they would do with the house and how much longer I'd have a roof over my head.

Maybe, I speculated, Lonnie had a spare room in the trailer.

The phone was ringing in my office as I got the door opened. I reached for it, then stopped. What if it was another reporter?

I wished I had Caller ID, but, hell, I can't even pay for regular phone service, let alone the extras. I let the answering machine pick it up.

After the beep, Marsha's voice started. "Harry, it's me again and I—"

"Hi," I said, jerking the phone up and switching off the machine. "I'm so glad it's you."

"Where have you been?" she demanded. "You know your home phone's not working?"

"There's nothing wrong with it. It's just been disconnected."

"Disconnected?" Her voice rose.

"I forgot to pay the bill. I feel like a dumb ass."

"Forgot or didn't have the money?"

"No, really forgot. I mean, I don't have the money and if I thought of it, I still wouldn't have paid it. But I didn't even think of it."

She sighed. "Harry, let me loan you some cash. This is ridiculous."

"No, I'm okay. Really. I've made a little money. I'll pay off the phone company," I said. "Are you at the office?"

"Yes, and I'm exhausted. I'm on my way home."

"I tried to call you last night about Robert Jefferson Reed. Have you . . . done him yet?"

"Finished the paperwork an hour ago. We bumped him up to the head of the line. Famous people get special service here. Why do you ask?"

My God, I thought, she doesn't know.

"Marsha, have you not read the paper today?"

"Of course not. Who's got time?"

"And you haven't talked to Jack Maples?"

"Jack was in and out, but—" She stopped for a beat. I could hear her breathing. "Harry, what are you talking about?"

"Sweetheart, Robert Jefferson Reed was the person I'd been hired to follow. His wife thought he was cheating on her. I was out at their farm in Williamson County last night. I'm the one who found him dead."

She gasped. "Oh, my God, you're kidding!"

"I wish I were. And somebody in the Williamson County Sheriff's Department ran his big mouth and told the papers. I'm front page this morning, darling."

She moaned into the phone. "Good heavens," she said. "Has anyone questioned you?"

"Well, yeah, I got questioned by the homicide detective in Williamson County. I gave a statement, they let me go."

"No, Harry, I meant the papers, the TV stations."

"I'm dodging them."

"You better keep dodging them. Reed was murdered."

"So I figured. He drown?"

"Yes and no," she said. "We won't have the tox-screen results back for a couple weeks, so this isn't final. But he had a fractured hyoid bone, interior tissue damage to the neck, throat, and larynx. Petechial hemorrhaging in the conjunctivae cinched it, I thought."

I knew just enough of the buzz words to know what she was talking about. Reed had been strangled.

"You thought?" I asked.

"Then when we opened him up, he had water in his lungs and I noted the presence of hemorrhagic edema fluid in the mouth and nostrils."

"I don't know what that means, but it sounds impressive."

"He was frothing at the mouth," Marsha said.

"Was there a ligature? I don't think the cops found anything."

"Bruising's wide, unfocused. If a ligature was used, it was most likely something like a towel. And since he was in the water, any fibers might have washed. We did scrapings, didn't find anything under the scope. My guess? A very strong forearm."

"Could it have been a woman?"

"Oh, sure. But it would have to have been a pretty fit woman with some leverage."

I re-created the scene mentally and scanned the area. "He was found in an outside Jacuzzi, in a secluded backyard. The whirlpool motor and the motor jets would have disguised the noise of footsteps."

"Yeah," Marsha said, into it now. "And if somebody came up behind him and had him locked in a choke hold, the bottom of the tub might have been too slippery for Reed to get a foothold. Then they finished the job by jamming him underwater."

"He would have splashed around like a landed fish," I said. "But there wouldn't have been any getting away from it. Great, so now we know how. The only remaining questions are *who* and *why*. How long do you think it took?"

She shrugged. "Several minutes probably. Pretty agonizing way to go."

She was silent for a moment. "Why did you ask about Jack Maples? What's he got to do with this?"

"Oh, yeah, I forgot to tell you. I ran into him a while ago."

"Yeah?"

Then I told her about Mrs. Hawkins. And Shadow.

"You've had a rough couple of days," she said. "Are you all right?"

I reflected a moment. Was I? "Yeah, I guess I'm okay."

"Harry, I apologize for the other night. I'm not sure I even meant what I said. It's just that I've been under an awful lot of strain. And I feel lousy. All the time. I don't know what I want anymore."

"Have you told anyone at the office? About being pregnant, I mean?"

"I haven't even told Kay. That way, it'll stay a secret."

"Not much longer. Jack tried to pump me for information."

"You say anything?"

"Of course not," I said. "I got pretty damn chilly with him, though. Maybe he took that for an answer."

She sighed again. "Doesn't matter. I can't hide it much longer."

"I'd like to see you tonight."

Silence for a beat. "Yeah, I guess we could both use a little company. I'll stop at the Kroger on the way home, pick up some dinner."

"Okay," I said, smiling. "Around six?"

"Sure. We'll watch a movie, crash early."

"Oh, does this mean I should bring a toothbrush?"

"Not necessary. You've already got one at my place."

"Perhaps a change of underwear?"

She snickered. "That's not my area, Harry. I don't monitor these things unless they get to be a problem."

We said a quick goodbye. I was relieved. I'd expected

another tense conversation and this one went okay. Damage control was progressing pretty well.

Now if I could get off so easily with Victoria Reed.

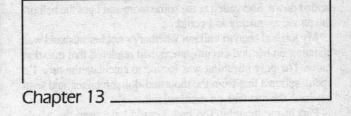

Chapter 13

I didn't.

When I dialed the private unlisted number of the Reed home in Brentwood, it rang about ten times with no answering machine picking up. Finally, a male voice answered. Something told me it was a young voice trying to sound older and more serious.

"Hello."

"Hello. This is Harry Denton calling for Mrs. Reed, if she's available."

"She's not," the voice said, stern and abrupt.

"Who is it?" I heard a voice in the background ask—Victoria Reed's voice.

A hand scraped over the receiver on the other end, but I heard my name in a muffled voice. Then it sounded like the phone was being drop-kicked across the room.

A strained, shrill voice snapped into the phone so loud and hard I had to jerk the handset away from my ear.

"You were supposed to watch him, damn it!" Her voice rose to a scream. "Where were you while someone was murdering my husband?"

I knew then that I was on Victoria Reed's list.

What was I going to say to her? *I'm sorry I wasn't there to stop your husband from being murdered, Mrs. Reed.* Of course I'm sorry I wasn't there. I'm sorry I wasn't in Dealey Plaza to push Kennedy out of the way, either, but that doesn't change anything.

I explained that I'd be back in touch with her when things

settled down. She yelled at me some more and I got the hell off the phone as quickly as I could.

My job had been to find out whether or not her husband was cheating on her and circumstances had rendered that question moot. The only fair thing was for me to calculate the time I'd spent, subtract that from the thousand-dollar retainer, and send her back the rest with an itemized bill.

Part of me thought: Too bad, I could have used the whole grand. But there'd be other jobs. There always had been. I just had to get out there and find them.

I toted up my hours and typed up an invoice. I'd cash her check tomorrow, then put the cash directly in the bank and write her a partial refund. Then I was done with it.

The phone rang again just as I got the paperwork together. The machine picked it up on the fourth ring and the outgoing message played out. I waited a second, thinking it was a hang-up. Then I heard the voice of Lieutenant D'Angelo, calling me from the Williamson County Sheriff's Department.

"Harry Denton, this is D'Angelo from—"

I picked the phone up. "Hello, Lieutenant."

"Mr. Denton?"

"Yeah, it's me. I've been screening my calls. It seems some-one gave my name to the papers."

He cleared his throat. "Yes, I know, and I'm pretty upset about it. I don't like it when this happens."

"I can understand that. What can I do for you?"

"I called your home phone number and couldn't get you."

"I'm having a problem with my phone."

He was silent for a moment. "That's not what the recording said. The recording said your phone had been disconnected."

"Okay, Lieutenant," I said. "I was late paying my bill. First-degree stupidity. Guilty plea offered and accepted. I'll straighten it out Monday morning."

"You can understand my situation, can't you? One of my deputies finds you leaning over a hot tub holding a corpse by the scalp. Next morning I call you and your phone's been disconnected. One could draw some conclusions."

"And those conclusions would be hasty, Lieutenant. As the fact that we're talking together now proves."

"Maybe."

"I didn't have to take the call," I offered.

"That's true," he agreed. "And I could have issued a warrant and had the Metro police pick you up."

"That's true as well. But since we're talking now, why don't you tell me how I can help you?"

"I've had your statement typed up. I'd like you to come down tomorrow morning and review it."

I promised to meet him at eleven and we did our goodbyes. I didn't know what the big hurry was but decided I'd antagonized him as much as I should.

With as little business as I'd been doing lately, it didn't take me long to get my whole working life in order and my office cleaned. The last thing I wanted to do was go back to my apartment. Reverend Hawkins and his warm, fuzzy wife might still be there. Lonnie'd left a message that he was going to be working in the yard today. Maybe I'd go hang with him awhile before I took off across town for Marsha's.

I'd just thrown my jacket on when the phone rang again. Damn, maybe I just ought to leave it off the hook.

"Hey, Harry!" a male voice said after the outgoing message finished. "This is Randy Tucker again. I desperately need to talk to you, guy. C'mon, please call me. I'm at the newspaper."

I stared at the machine as he rattled off the phone number, then hung up. Relays clattered, the tape stopped moving, and all was still.

I didn't need this crap.

Lonnie was leaning against the side of a sexy little red Miata when I pulled up in front of his chain-link fence. The edge of the door barely came to his knee. I pushed the gate open and walked in, dodging a puddle full of water with a thin sheen of oil on top and a ring of fuzzy green foam around the edges.

"Whoa, cowboy," I said. "Where'd you get that one?"

He crossed his arms and his ankles and leaned against the

quarter panel. "Picked her up in Dyersburg last night. Some bozo in a trailer had it hid behind a pickup with a tarp over it."

I walked around him, admiring the tiny elegant beast. I leaned down into the cockpit. That new-car smell hung above the seats, sweeter than a cake baking.

"How far behind was he?"

"Shit!" Lonnie spewed. "Guy leased it three months ago, never made a payment. Me and Carl had to have an attitude-adjustment seminar with him."

"I hate when that happens. When you got to take it back?"

"First thing tomorrow. Want to drive it down to the lot just for kicks? I'll follow you, bring you back."

"Can't," I said. "Got a few fires to put out."

"Yeah?" he drawled, clearing his throat and spitting about six feet in front of him, then giving himself a good long scratch. "What's going on?"

I leaned against the door next to him, crossed my own arms, and put my weight on one hip. "Well, let me see if I can keep it all straight. First, my best canine buddy in the whole world passes away. Then my girlfriend, who by the way is pregnant courtesy of *moi*—"

He laughed. "Yeah. You mentioned that a month or so ago."

"—tells me I'm not the man she wants to spend the rest of her life with. And then I get hired to spy on a rich guy who can't keep it in his pants, and I find him, only he's facedown in a hot tub deader than a box of rocks and some yutz with the Williamson County Sheriff's Department draws down on me."

"This's getting good, Harry. You oughta write a book someday."

"Nobody'd believe it," I said. "Then I go downstairs to borrow my landlady's phone and I find her similarly dead as a box of rocks on the bathroom floor."

Lonnie snapped to at that one. "Mrs. Hawkins?"

I nodded my head.

"Damn, man!" he said, kicking the dirt and stretching the word *damn* into about four syllables. "I hate that. She was a sweet old lady. What'd she have, heart attack?"

"Yeah, and her son, the Reverend Pauly Polyester, and his

wife, who's so stiff she makes the Church Lady look like Tina Turner, show up and look at me like I'm one of those guys standing at an exit ramp with a sign that says 'Will Work for Beer.' So that's been my day."

He stepped away from the car, turned toward me, smiled sheepishly, and nodded his head.

"So tell me, Lonnie," I said. "Just how the fuck are you?"

"Well," he answered. "I miss my baby. I really do. Place ain't the same without her bouncing around here drooling all over me. But I'm gonna make it."

"Yeah?" I said teasingly. "So what else is going on? C'mon, you can tell your old buddy."

He grinned, one of those aw-shucks kinds of grins that would have never made you think he moved here from Brooklyn.

"Hell, Harry. I'm in love."

I grinned back at him. "C'mon, get the fug out of here."

"Naw, man. I'm serious. I think she likes me, too, man. I really do."

"Shit, who's going to fall fo' yo' mangy ass?"

"You know who it is. . . ."

"Sheba?" I said, trying to sound as flabbergasted as possible.

"Yeah, man. Sheba."

"*Shee-yit*, I thought that girl had some sense."

He lowered his voice, doing his best Elvis: "Don't be talking 'bout my woman now, Harry. I doan wanna have to whup yo' ass."

I broke out laughing. "Hell, man, I'm happy for you. I really am. You ain't brought her here yet, have you?"

"Hell, no! I ain't brought her here. But I will tell you one thing—"

"Yeah?"

His voice lowered to a conspiratorial murmur. "I did spend the night at her place last night."

"Whoa!" I hollered. "It was your first date!"

"I know," he said. "It's crazy. It's absolutely insane. But it's magic, man. Ain't nothing like this happened to me in a long time. I'm sorer'n hell, too."

I stopped laughing, gave him a look that was as serious as I could muster. "Well, I don't mean to pee on your Cheerios or anything, but you could give it a week or two before you ask her to marry you."

The grin left him and he looked almost thoughtful for a moment, which is saying something for a guy whose usual modus operandi is *Do something, even if it's wrong*.

"You know something, Harry? For the first time in years, that thought's crossed my mind."

"Hell, buddy," I said. "At least one of us is doing okay in that department."

Marsha looked better that evening. So much better, in fact, that I decided to take it on faith that she was just having a bad day the last time I saw her. She met me at the door, hair pulled back neatly, just a touch of makeup, her eyes clearer and brighter than before. She was almost like the woman I thought I'd known for years now.

We danced around the issues that distanced us, with me not pursuing the what-do-you-mean-I-can't-spend-the-rest-of-my-life-with-you stuff and her not pursuing the when-are-you-going-to-grow-up-and-get-a-real-job thing. We made dinner and opened a bottle of wine, two sips of which she assured me as a doctor would not cause any problems. I had two glasses, which is the legal limit for me. We had the lights down low and the jazz FM public radio station on softly in the background. Eddie Harris played "Harlem Nocturne" as we relaxed on the couch.

She said her back was sore, so I propped pillows on the couch in such a way that she could comfortably lie on her stomach. I eased in on the edge of the couch and started on her shoulders, kneading and twisting and pulling. She moaned and I pulled her hair up off her neck, then worked my way over to the center.

"God, that feels good," she murmured.

I smiled down at her, then rolled my knuckles up and down her spine. She jerked once when I tickled her but said not to stop. This went on another five or ten minutes, then I had this compulsion to lean forward and nuzzle the left side of her neck. She cocked her head to the right, and I opened my mouth slightly, took a small fold of skin gently between my lips, and ran the edges of my teeth up and down.

She shivered and took in a sharp breath, then squirmed on the couch. I dug in a little farther, toward her shoulder, and nibbled some more as my hands continued to rub her shoulders.

She made her *ooof* sound and shuddered again.

"Wait," she gasped. "Wait!"

I sat up, afraid I'd hurt her. She rolled over on her side and looked up at me.

"You okay?"

Her eyes darkened. "You know that old wives' tale about pregnant women being really frisky?"

"Yeah."

Her hand grabbed my wrist, her nails digging in.

"It's true," she said. "C'mon."

It had been so long for both of us that we even managed to overcome the physics of the situation. I found it strangely arousing to make love with a pregnant woman. Her breasts had swollen and the areolae had darkened, enlarged, and become hypersensitive. There was a suddenness to her passion that had never been there before. She pulled me to her and into her almost abruptly; it was a sensation not unlike that of being consumed, taken. And I let myself go in ways I'd never done before, losing myself in her heat and her strength, and feeling deep within a fever that I'd feared had gone out for good.

We sprawled across the bed, exhausted, covered in sweat that cooled us as it dried in the night air. I reached over her to turn the light off and pull the covers up over us.

"Wait," she said, rolling over toward the edge of the bed. "I, of course, have to pee."

She pulled herself up slowly, sat up, then cautiously raised herself onto the floor.

"Legs shaky?" I asked.

She turned. "It's my center of gravity," she answered. "I have to be careful when I get up or I'll wind up on the floor."

"Need me to go with you?"

Marsha turned and smiled. "No, babe. I'm okay."

She waddled forward, and for the first time, I got a side view of her standing up naked. The curve of her stomach was pronounced now, the baby clearly growing rapidly. Something twinged inside me at the thought of something growing in her that was as much me as it was her. I ached to think that I might lose her and what we'd made together. I'd never experienced paternal impulses before, and I'm not sure that was what I was feeling now. I only felt a dull, unsettling throb.

I settled into the pillow and stared up at the ceiling. I'd started to drift off after we made love but was wide awake now. She was gone perhaps three minutes before I heard the toilet flush and water running.

She came back in, stretching her arms above her head, yawning. "I'm exhausted."

"Me, too." She came over and rolled onto the bed, then scooted close to me on her left side, with me curled up against her like a pair of spoons in a drawer. I pulled the comforter over us and she reached to turn off the light.

Her breathing became heavier and I could tell she was sliding off into sleep. I raised myself up on an elbow and looked down at her in the dark. She turned her head slightly toward me.

"What?" she asked.

I thought for a moment. "Look, I know it's late—" I began.

"Very late," she interrupted, her voice heavy and drowsy. "So whatever it is, can it wait until morning?"

"I just have this dilemma. . . ."

"What dilemma?" She cocked her head farther toward me.

"The dilemma is that I love you so much, I don't even know how much I love you."

I saw the outline of her face against the pillow and sensed that she was frowning.

"Harry, what the hell does that mean?"

"Well—it's like diving into a pool where you can't see the bottom and you have to take it on faith that you won't break your neck because it's too shallow or drown because it's too deep."

She shifted her weight, rolled to where she could look directly at me. "So where are you now?"

"Somewhere in the middle," I said. "And I'm afraid. I ain't got much breath left, but I still haven't found the bottom."

"What happens if you get to the bottom?"

"Then I can put my feet down, push off, spring back to the top."

"Yeah? What happens then?" Her voice was slurred with sleep now.

"Then I can know how deep it is and I can go back down anytime, all the way to the bottom, and feel what it's really like. And I'll always know that I can get back to a place where I can breathe."

"Yeah," she mumbled. Then she took a couple of deep, slow breaths and rolled back over, bending slightly at the waist and pushing her bottom into me.

"Ain't love a bitch, Harry?"

I settled down next to her and put my arm around her.

"Yeah," I whispered. "Yeah."

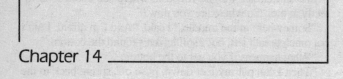

Chapter 14

A late cold snap left me shivering and cussing the ancient Mustang the next morning as I drove down I-65 toward Franklin and Williamson County. Low-hanging, ugly, scudlike clouds pushed a layer of fog down on the freeway that cut visibility to about half of what it ought to be. The car's barely functional heater strained to pump what little warm air it could muster. Something was caught in the intake vent as well, so when the fan motor ran it made that noise that bicycle wheels made when we were kids and clipped baseball cards with clothespins to spin in the spokes.

I hadn't wanted to get up. Marsha radiated heat beneath the covers. We were warm and safe and insulated from the outside world. I never wanted to go anywhere again, and for a while it looked like she didn't either. She turned the alarm off and we fell back asleep, then finally crawled out of bed around nine, which was as late as I'd ever seen her sleep on a workday. She showered as I fixed breakfast and we shared a long, slow meal. Finally, reality hit. She had to get to the ME's office and I had an appointment with Lieutenant D'Angelo. The telephone company could wait for now.

I exited the freeway at Highway 96 and headed into Franklin through the long, wide avenue of strip malls, car dealerships, minimarts, and gas stations. Everywhere I go in this part of the state, I'm amazed at the way what used to be quiet, charming, sleepy little towns are becoming smaller versions of Nashville, complete with Nashville's own far-thinking and wise land-use planning and zoning controls. Soon the entire midstate area will be paved over with Wal-Mart superstores and Mapco Expresses and as long as we can get to a turning lane, life will go on.

I wasn't even sure how to get to the Williamson County Sheriff's Department. All I had was an address and a sense of where it was. I wound around several streets by instinct alone and was surprised to find that I'd made it without getting lost.

There were a few visitor spaces out front, with one left open. I pulled into it, switched off the Mustang, then sat there as the engine continued to run another ten or fifteen seconds like a chicken with its head cut off. This car was old and tired, and forty minutes of freeway driving was about all it could take at one time. Maybe I'd head back into town on Franklin Road and stay off the freeway.

I sat in the car, thinking for a moment. I had a couple of minutes to go before the eleven o'clock appointment. In my memory, I replayed again what had happened Saturday night, with the mental video running back and forth. I replayed it in slow motion, frame-by-frame, trying to figure out if there was anything I'd left out, forgotten. Perhaps something I'd noticed at the time but not given any thought or importance to it.

Nothing.

I'd told D'Angelo everything I knew, everything I'd seen, when I talked to him Saturday night. Now all I had to do was go in, read over the statement, sign it, then get back to my life. Piece of cake.

On impulse, though, I reached into the glove box, pulled out my microcassette recorder, and slipped it into my inside coat pocket.

The front-desk receptionist smiled at me through a small haystack of blonde hair. Her lipstick was ruby red, shiny, and glossy. She logged my name in on a visitors' list, then picked up the phone and chirped into it. Her smile disappeared for just a moment, then flashed back on as she put the phone down.

"Lieutenant D'Angelo asked you to wait over there," she said, pointing.

I took a hard plastic seat next to a cinder-block wall painted pastel lime green. The place smelled of cigarettes and disinfectant, but not the kinds of smells associated with a big city jail.

A stand-up ashtray over in the corner had a pile of butts in it, and tipped over in the center, a nasty crumpled Styrofoam cup with brown tobacco juice stains down the side.

I looked away, watching the receptionist as she juggled phone lines, messages, and visitors with relaxed ease. I wondered how long I'd have to sit here, and wondered, too, if this was some kind of device D'Angelo was using to make me nervous.

I didn't have to wonder long. A minute or so later, a uniformed deputy stepped out through a door and walked over to me.

"Mr. Denton?"

"Yeah," I said. I stood as he approached.

"Lieutenant D'Angelo asked me to take you down to the conference room."

"Let's do it," I said.

I followed him back over to the door and we stood there a second before the receptionist buzzed us in. We entered a long narrow hallway lit with harsh, uncovered fluorescent tubes. The hallway was narrow enough that you had to shift just an inch or so to the right, brushing against the wall, in order to avoid touching anyone.

The deputy stopped at the last door on the left and held it open for me.

"Lieutenant D'Angelo will be right with you."

I nodded and stepped in. The room was short and narrow, windowless, with a rectangular wooden table in the center scarred by penknife graffiti and cigarette burns. A few battered wooden chairs were scattered about, and on the wall to my left, a mirror about two feet high and four feet wide.

Jesus, I thought. *Conference room, my ass. This is an interrogation room.*

I wondered who was on the other side of the mirror.

No point in speculating, I thought. I pulled my baby Swiss Army knife out of my pocket and opened the scissors attachment. Then I stepped over to the other side of the table, put my face an inch or so away from the mirror, cocked my head, peeled back a nostril, and proceeded to trim my nose hair.

On the other side of the wall, I heard the faint rumbling of chairs being shifted. I tried not to smile, probably without much luck.

A moment later I turned as the door to the room rattled, then opened. D'Angelo stepped in, grinning and shaking his head from side to side. He stepped inside and a younger man in a gray suit followed him in.

"Real funny, Denton," D'Angelo said as he closed the door behind him.

I eyed the two men, trying to figure out just what the hell was going on.

I shrugged. "I'm a stickler for personal hygiene," I said.

"I guess we should be happy you weren't checking your pubes."

"That was next."

The younger guy, a close-cropped blond, stared at me like I'd be a good snack for his pit bull. He was probably thirty but looked a few years younger—short but solid, like he worked out. Maybe a racquetball player.

"Sit down, Denton," he snapped. I stood there.

"I said, sit down," he repeated.

I stood there a moment longer, a blank look on my face. Then I shifted my head in D'Angelo's direction.

"Lieutenant," I asked brightly. "Who is this rude motherfucker and why is he here?"

The kid's face flashed bright red; he grunted and moved toward me. D'Angelo held up a hand without looking at him. The kid stopped.

"That was uncalled for, Denton."

"Answer my question," I said. Something inside of me'd gone numb. I ought to be nervous about this, but for some reason or other, it wasn't coming through. Maybe the patron saint of anxiety was failing me.

"You're not here to ask questions, damn it," the kid barked again. "You're here to answer them!"

"Oh, jeez, wait, let me see." I snapped my fingers. "Don't tell me. Uh . . . 1937, Pat O'Brien to Humphrey Bogart, *The Great O'Malley*! Yeah, that's it—"

I turned back to D'Angelo. "—only you couldn't say 'damn it' back then."

The kid curled his lip back. Swear to God, bared his teeth like a dog. Hadn't seen anything like that in a long time. Maybe I really am getting old.

"Stop it, Denton," D'Angelo said.

I turned back to him, raised my voice half an octave. "What? I should let this kid waltz in here and roust me?"

Christ, I thought. *Speaking of bad Bogart movies . . .*

"This is Greg Bransford, assistant DA, Williamson County District Attorney's office."

I shrugged, pulled a chair out, sat down. "So why didn't he say that up front instead of coming in here and busting my chops?"

"Gentlemen, can we start all over again?" D'Angelo asked, pulling a chair away from the table and easing into it across from me. He looked up, motioned to Bransford, who, of course, took the seat at the head of the table.

I looked first at D'Angelo, then at the kid. Neither of them carried any paper, at least not any paper that I could see.

"I thought I was supposed to look over my statement and sign it," I said.

"Well," D'Angelo said slowly, "that's a little problematic right now. We'd like to follow up on a few aspects of your statement if you don't mind."

I eyed the two of them and noticed that the patron saint of anxiety hadn't completely left me.

"Define *problematic*," I said.

"We think you're lying," Bransford said, voice calmer now.

"Well, how about that. . . ."

"But before we get into that," D'Angelo said, "we'd also like for you to know that we're going to be recording this interview for accuracy's sake, if that's all right with you."

I stared at them a moment, time slowing in that way it does when you realize something real bad's about to happen, that the car careening through the intersection really isn't going to stop and that all you can do is brace yourself and wait for the crunch of metal on metal.

Without thinking, I reached inside my coat pocket and pulled out the small gray microcassette recorder, flicked it on, and put it in the center of the table.

"Long as you don't mind if I make my own copy."

Bransford's jaw locked up and the red came back into his cheeks. Kid's got to be a lousy poker player.

D'Angelo turned, looked at Bransford, who forced himself to nod.

"Okay, fair enough," the lieutenant said. "Tape away. Let's get started."

D'Angelo rattled off the date and time, my name, his and Bransford's, then paused. I looked around, wondering where the microphone was. Maybe the ceiling, I thought, and looked up. There was a mirrored ball about the size of a basketball in the corner of the ceiling at the far end opposite me. I hadn't noticed it when I came in.

D'Angelo'd said they were taping the interview. I now knew that meant videotaping it. Great, I'd been a smartass on camera.

I was starting to get a real bad feeling about this. All the bastards had to do now was Mirandize me and I knew I was in deep shit.

"The other thing, Mr. Denton," D'Angelo said, "is that we need to tell you that you are entitled to an attorney during questioning."

Great. . . .

"If you so desire an attorney and cannot afford one, one will be provided for you. You have the right to remain silent. Anything you say during this interview can and will be used against you in a court of law. Do you understand these rights as I have explained them to you?"

Suddenly there was a buzzing in my ears, a hollow kind of buzzing with a slight ringing echo behind it, as if I'd picked up a seashell and held it to my ear, only there was an angry wasp inside trying to get out. And from the edges of my peripheral vision, tingly fields of red began to work their way toward the center. I sat there silent and motionless for I don't know how long.

"Do you understand these rights as I have explained them to you?" D'Angelo repeated.

My voice was quiet this time, a lowered monotone that sounded strange even to me.

"Am I about to be arrested?" I asked.

To D'Angelo's left, Bransford sneered at me. "Not so cocky now, are—"

D'Angelo silenced him with a swift motion of his hand.

"Mr. Denton, do you understand these rights as I have explained them to you?" His voice was stern, louder, but then dropped and became almost soothing. "Harry, we can't go on if you don't answer."

"Are you arresting me?" I asked again.

"That depends in part on what comes out of this interview."

I nodded my head. "Yes," I said slowly, "I understand my rights as you have explained them to me."

"Do you wish to have an attorney present during questioning?"

"Not at this point," I said blankly. "But I reserve the right to call one later."

D'Angelo nodded. "You have that right," he said. "Now let's get started."

Chapter 15

In retrospect, it may not have been the best move in the world to hack off the assistant DA. There was something about the guy I just didn't like, though, and it seems that the older I get, the less able I am to play the game.

They did a number on me, dragging me through the process like a couple of pros. D'Angelo was the older, cooler one, while Bransford was the hotheaded young buck out to make a name for himself by nailing my hide to the side of the barn. They had me recite my tale time and time again, starting in different places, winding me around from one end to the other, twisting and turning, all with the goal of tripping me up and catching me in my own lie. I'd heard cops talk about the drill back when I worked the police beat on the newspaper. The idea is not to whip out some piece of evidence and yell "Aha!" as you confront the suspect. It's much more subtle and insidious than that. The goal is to just follow a path, then retrace your steps, then jump on the path at different places, look forward and backward, to the left and right. If a suspect's lying, sooner or later he'll trip and fall over his own feet. And you just stand over him asking, *Hmmm, want to tell me how that happened?*

After about three hours, I knew my own crashing blood-sugar levels and exhaustion would soon be my worst enemy. Cops don't distinguish between the cold sweat of insulin shock and that of guilty conscience. Eventually, even they got tired of going over the same ground. And I finally realized that they didn't have anything on me; hell, there wasn't anything to have. I wasn't even guilty of trespassing. If Victoria Reed paid me to kill her husband—which I guess is where they hoped to get to—then there were too many missing pieces. I had no history with Reed or his wife, so it was hard to establish a motive outside of money. I thought his book was living proof of P. T. Barnum's dictum, but that was little enough reason to kill him. It's not like the guy was Salman Rushdie or anything.

Finally, they had to hold me or let me go. I stuffed my microcassette recorder, which had long since run out of tape, in my jacket pocket, threw the jacket back on, and took myself and my drenched armpits out to the parking lot. Bransford had given me the stern admonition to keep myself available for questioning and it was all I could do to avoid making matters worse by telling him exactly which part of my anatomy was available for him to kiss.

Outside the clouds had broken up. The sky had erupted into a brilliant clear blue in the wake of a cold front. The temperature had gone up about ten degrees; it was almost warm. Ordinarily, it would have been a gorgeous day. It was hard for me to enjoy it, though. Being named an official murder suspect has that effect on one.

I needed calories and I needed them fast; it almost didn't matter what kind. Three blocks away I pulled into a Wendy's and hit the ninety-nine-cents menu. Biggie fries, biggie drink, bacon cheeseburger. My mother would have had a fit.

As hungry as I'd become, I still wasn't in the mood to eat alone. Reading material might help, I figured, so I shoved three or four fries into my mouth to hold me, walked outside, and pumped fifty cents into the newspaper machine. The early edition of the afternoon daily headlined the latest in an outbreak of fast-food robberies in the Priest Lake area. Whoever was pulling these jobs was determined to leave no witnesses; so far, eight people—all of them kids—had been slaughtered in three robberies. But this time the shooter blew it; a sixteen-year-old Laotian girl who knew just enough English to work the counter survived. She was critical, under heavy guard at Vanderbilt, but she was going to make it.

I got so engrossed in the story, I didn't even taste most of the sandwich. I turned to the jump page, read the rest of the lead story, then folded the paper back to the front. And there it was:

LOST AUTOPSY REPORTS
ENDANGER MURDER CASES

I sighed, rubbed my temples, muttered, "Oh, hell. . . ."

Marsha goes before the grand jury tomorrow, and here was a story about how the district attorney's office was having so much trouble getting timely autopsy reports out of the ME's office that some very bad guys were liable to walk. Just what she needed.

What in hell was going on over there?

I finished lunch with all the enthusiasm of a bored 7-Eleven cashier handing change back to a customer. There was half a cup of soda left, so I kept reading the paper. I opened to section B, the section that carried all the local news that didn't make it into the front. As I expected, the lead story was on the murder of Reed, but it was mostly a recap of what the paper had run Sunday morning. There wasn't much new to report other than a comment from the Williamson County Sheriff's Department that police had questioned a number of Reed's close friends and associates. Strangely, neither story I'd read so far had mentioned Margot Horowitz. And my scarfed-down lunch sat easier when I got to the end of the story without seeing my own name in print again.

Enough reality, I thought. I flipped to the section with the comics, laughed at one, found the rest tepid. I read my horoscope, then turned to the obituary page. The write-up on Mrs. Hawkins was short and to the point. The funeral was set for tomorrow afternoon at the church in Goodlettesville. I tore out the obit and stuffed it in my shirt pocket, then got up.

Outside, the world looked newer. Once fed and stabilized, my senses seemed more acute and I was aware of the smells of frying food and automobile exhaust mixed in with the strange sensation of fresh, cool air. I smiled, felt better, like the shakes had been held off for another few hours and my metabolism was settling down to its normal routine. I was still in an odd kind of shock, though. It isn't every day that a guy in a gray suit decides you're a murderer.

*   *   *

The BellSouth lady took all but six bucks of my cash and promised to have my phone turned back on by tomorrow afternoon. The bank lady cashed Victoria Reed's check and let me deposit it as cash in my account. I wrote Victoria a refund check and dropped it off with the post office lady.

I was a couple of bucks ahead, but barely. As for the upcoming rent . . . can I not think about that now, please?

Back at my office, the answering machine light was going off like a popcorn popper. I growled under my breath and locked the door behind me.

Hell-o, you have—nine—messages.

I grabbed a pen, sat down, punched the button. The first one was the one I dreaded because in the rush of yesterday's crisis du jour, I'd forgotten to call him back.

"Son, this is Dad. Listen, what's going on out there? I kept thinking the phones were all messed up and finally got an operator to check. Your phone's been *disconnected*, boy! What's the story? You moving? Your mom's worried sick. Call us!"

"Oh, hell," I muttered. What can I tell him? Sorry, Dad, but I've been kind of busy lately. Two dead bodies in a sixteen-hour span, my phone turned off for not paying the bill, the Williamson County Sheriff's Department thinks I'm a murderer, and I may get kicked out of my apartment. But don't you guys give it a thought, okay?

"Oh," I continued aloud, "did I mention my girlfriend's pregnant, only she doesn't want to make an honest man out of me?"

Message number two was from the local ABC-affiliate reporter, three was from the morning paper, number four from Marsha, five from Marsha, six and seven from Randy Tucker at the afternoon paper, eight from Lonnie, and nine from some attorney I'd never heard of.

"Crap," I said. I checked my watch: three o'clock here in Nashville. My parents would just be getting in from their pre-lunch nine holes. I punched in the number, hoping to get their answering machine. My luck held out, as Dad picked up on the third ring.

"Hi, Dad," I said.

"Harry!" he yelled before turning away from the phone. "Janet, it's Harry! Hey, son, what's going on down there? We've been worried half to death."

"Life's been a little crazy. But as for the phone, I just forgot to pay the bill and they cut me off. I went down there today, gave them the cash. It should be back on tomorrow."

"That's a relief. Jeez, we were—"

"Harry!" my mother yelled, picking up the extension in the bedroom of their condo.

"Hi, Mom!"

"Are you okay?"

"Yes, ma'am, I'm fine. I was just telling Dad, I forgot to pay my BellSouth bill, so they decided to take away my phone privileges for a few days. It could've been worse; they could have grounded me."

"Oh, good. When are you coming out here, son?"

"Yeah, boy," Dad agreed. "It's been too long."

Suddenly, the thought of hiding out in my parents' spare bedroom was pretty damn appealing. Something told me, however, that the Williamson County DA's office might not appreciate the gesture.

"I'd sure like to, but work's picked up a bit lately. In fact, that's part of the reason I'm calling. You know that guy you called about on Sunday, the writer who got killed?"

"Yes," they both chimed.

"Well." I hesitated. May as well get it over with. Sooner or later one of their friends back home'll tell them if I don't. "I was working that case," I continued. "His wife hired me because she thought he was having an affair with his secretary. Anyway, I went to his house and found him dead."

My mother gasped.

"Jeez, son, that's horrible," Dad said.

"Has your name been in the papers?" Mom demanded.

"Yeah, 'fraid so."

"Harry, you simply have got to find another way to make a living. I will not have you embarrassing yourself and the whole family like this!"

The hair on the back of my neck bristled. "Ma, it wasn't my fault. I didn't kill him."

"No one says you did!" she yelped.

Wanna bet? I thought.

"It's just so . . . so tacky," she protested. "You were raised better than this."

"Leave him be, Janet," Dad said. "The boy's doing what makes him happy."

I was beginning to wonder about that.

"It was supposed to be relatively cut-and-dried," I said weakly. "It wasn't supposed to get complicated like this."

"It sounds just horrible," she said.

"Well, there's more," I said. "My landlady died Sunday."

"Mrs. Hawkins?" they asked in unison, voices higher.

"Yes. Looks like a heart attack. Problem is, I'm not sure what her son's going to do with the house. I may have to move."

"Good heavens," my mother said. "Harry, how can you—"

"You just hush, Janet. Now's not the time to be chewing the boy out. He's had a rough time."

"It's okay, Dad. Really."

"I'm not chewing him out. I'm just worried."

"I know that, Mom."

"All the same, he's a grown boy, Janet. And we're burning his nickels up on this phone call."

"That's okay. Don't worry about that."

"Listen, son, why don't I drop you a check in the mail? Little something to tide you over. You move, you're going to have some expenses."

"No," I said, perhaps a little too sharply. "I still haven't paid you back for the last loan."

"Don't worry about that," she said.

"Mom, I have to pay you back before I borrow any more. I mean it, really."

"You sure, son?"

"Yeah, Dad. I'm sure."

"You'll change your mind if you really need it?"

I sighed. "Yeah, sure. No problem. Listen, I got to go. Just wanted to let you know I was okay."

"We're glad you called. Take care of yourself."

"Yes, Harry," she said. "Be good!"

"Yeah, Mom. 'Bye now."

Be good, she said.

How old do you have to be before you get to be a grownup?

I tried both Marsha and Lonnie. Marsha was in the middle of someone and there was no answer at the trailer. I looked back over my notes from the answering machine. I had no inclination to return the reporters' calls. I didn't want to answer their questions and the easiest way to avoid doing that was not to talk to them at all.

There was one that bothered me, though. The messages from the TV reporters and the morning-paper guy had just been the standard requests for callbacks. But Randy Tucker's second message bothered me. I leaned across the desk, hit the button on the answering machine, and started shuffling through the messages until I got to his.

"Harry, this is Randy Tucker again. Listen, pal, I'm doing you a favor. You really want to talk to me. Read my lips. Return this call. Take it from a buddy. You *really* want to talk to me."

Okay, I thought, why not?

I dialed the newspaper, got shuffled through the operator to Randy's extension and then to his voice mail. I mulled over what to say as his message ran on, then when the beep came, I said: "Randy, Harry Denton here. I'm returning your call. I'll be in my office a while longer. You've got the number."

I hung up and looked down at my list. There was one left to take care of: the attorney. I flipped through the scribbled Post-it notes and found his name—David Merrone—with a telephone number bearing the same exchange as my home phone.

"East Nashville boy," I muttered as I punched in his number.

"Law office," a woman's voice answered.

"Harry Denton, returning Mr. Merrone's call," I said.

"Oh, yes, Mr. Denton, he's expecting you. Please hold."

My curiosity piqued, I drummed a pencil on my desk maybe thirty seconds before the lawyer picked up the phone. His voice was deep, older, a bit gruff.

"Mr. Denton," he said.

"Yes, Mr. Merrone. What can I do for you?"

"I understand you were Mrs. Esther Hawkins's tenant and friend. Is that correct?"

"Yeah," I said. "For about four years now. She was a great lady; I'm going to miss her."

"Are you planning on going to the funeral?"

"I'd intended to," I said. "You don't mind my asking, what's this all about?"

"I was Mrs. Hawkins's attorney and a good friend of both her and her late husband's. I'm handling the details of the estate. This should be a straightforward matter. The funeral's scheduled for two. I wonder if you could come to my office. Say around four-thirty?"

"Yeah," I said, hesitating, confused. "But I still don't get it. Why do I need to be there?"

"Because you're mentioned quite prominently in Mrs. Hawkins's will."

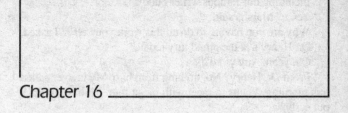

Chapter 16

I leaned back in my chair, stunned, and tried to figure out what to do next. I'd never been mentioned in anyone's will, let alone *prominently* mentioned. Truth is, I was kind of hoping it'd be a while.

Over the years that I'd lived upstairs from Mrs. Hawkins, I guess we'd gotten closer than I figured. Funny thing, though; she'd always seemed quite content to be alone, which is how she spent most of her time. Occasionally we'd cross paths as I was coming in from either a Saturday night at Marsha's or from a stakeout or car pickup. She seemed to enjoy hearing about my work, what little I was able to share with her.

But I never got any sense that she considered me important or special. In a way, it made me even sadder that the old lady had had to die alone like that.

I sighed and rubbed my eyes. The last few days had taken it out of me. There was nothing to do around the office. Maybe I'd go home and take care of some laundry that had been building up for a while.

Just as I was about to blow off the whole day, the phone rang again.

"Denton Agency," I said.

"Hi." Her voice sounded tired as well.

"Hey, how are you?"

"Weary. This's the first chance I've had to sit down all day."

"Busy?"

"Yeah, work's been piling up, so to speak, all weekend. Three homicides, a suicide, one OD, and the out-of-county work."

"Including our famous writer buddy."

"Yeah," Marsha said.

"Why are you having to do all this work yourself?" I asked.

"Dr. Henry's at the grand jury today."

"Oh, yeah. Any word?"

"From Dr. Henry? No, nothing from him. My lawyer called this morning. Wants to meet with me at four. I'll have to duck out early."

"I had my long little talk with the Williamson County Sheriff's Department this morning."

"How'd it go?"

I leaned back and plopped my feet up on my desk. The chair creaked and squealed.

"They think I killed Reed."

"What?" Her voice tightened to a sharp edge.

"Apparently so," I said. "Got this hotheaded young buck assistant DA that tried to beat up on me."

"Harry, what did they want? I mean, what did they say? What did they want from you?"

"They had me go over everything, then grilled me for a couple hours afterward."

"My God, you mean you talked to them?"

"Yeah, what was I going to do?"

"Get a lawyer and keep your mouth shut!" she snapped. "How's that for starters?"

"Look, I do that, I become number one on their top ten list. I know I didn't do it and that they couldn't possibly have anything on me, so I cooperated."

She was angry now. "I thought you had more sense than that! Don't you know how these small-town DAs are? They don't care who they get as long as they get somebody! They didn't put you in a holding cell with anybody, did they? They pull that jailhouse-snitch shit and you're gone. That's it. You're history."

"Look, they didn't hold me. They don't have anything."

"That doesn't mean shit, Harry. I'm really worried about this."

"Don't," I said. "I answered their questions, reserved the right to call in a lawyer at any time—"

"Did they Mirandize you?"

"Yeah, I mean they kind of had—"

"Jesus Christ, Harry!" Her voice broke. "You've got to get an attorney and get one now!"

"Can't afford one, babe. And besides, this isn't going anywhere. Honest. Trust me on this one. They got nothing."

She was quiet for a moment. "Besides," I added, "you've got your own stuff to worry about. You're the one who goes before the grand jury tomorrow."

She groaned. "It's really coming down on us, isn't it?"

"Yeah," I said after a moment. "But it felt awfully good waking up next to you this morning. Not to mention the going-to-bed part last night."

"Silver-tongued devil, you."

"Look, I'm not trying to score points with you. All I'm saying is that there's something between us that's real powerful. And I don't want to let it go. You're going to have a baby we made."

"It's not necessary to remind me of that."

"Sometimes I think it is."

She sighed. I tried to read her silence, wondered what to say, how to say it.

"I wish it were all that easy," she said finally.

"Hey, I never said it was easy."

She laughed, just enough to convince me she was going to be okay for now.

"Can I see you tonight?"

"By the time I get home from the lawyer's, I'll be exhausted, Harry. And I have to get up so early tomorrow, and—"

"Hey, no need to give reasons. You need some time. Take it."

"How about you?"

"I'm doing laundry tonight. I'm going to a funeral tomorrow."

"Oh, babe, I forgot. I'm sorry. Sorry I can't be there with you."

"Sorry I can't be there for you with the grand jury."

"Me, too. Call my office tomorrow, okay? Let me know how to find you."

I was relieved she still wanted to find me. "Sure," I said. "You be careful, okay? Get some rest."

We hung up and I gathered up a pile of mail and a couple of folders. I had some bookkeeping I could do at home while my laundry was running. Mrs. Hawkins had let me use the washing machine in her laundry room; I assumed it'd be okay for me to keep using it, at least until the Reverend Brian Hawkins told me to stop.

I threw my coat on, tucked the files and papers under my arm, and opened the door to my office with my free hand. I stepped into the hallway and locked the door. Just as I pulled the key out, the phone in my office started ringing again.

"Damn it," I growled. I pressed my ear against the door. If it was Marsha or Lonnie, I'd grab it. If it was anybody else, to hell with them.

The outgoing message finished, followed by the beep. A voice started in. I recognized it: Randy Tucker, the afternoon-newspaper guy.

Yeah, to hell with him, I thought. I turned and headed down the dimly lit, dingy hallway to the narrow stairs that would take me outside and then home.

Mrs. Hawkins picked a good day to be buried. I walked out of the church in Goodlettesville and into a warm brilliant blue spring day behind a group of maybe a dozen people. A preacher who didn't know her had eulogized her with as few words as possible. She'd borne one son in her life and a still-born daughter. She'd married a man who worked at a tobacco-distributing company for forty-five years and died from lung cancer only six months after retiring. She'd been a faithful member of the church. No one ever thought ill of her.

Six men who'd never known her but had been furnished by the undertaker served as pallbearers. They loaded her bronze casket into a black hearse. Her son, the preacher, and his wife followed in their silver Lincoln Town Car. I thought the least they could have done was have the funeral at her church in East Nashville.

But then again they didn't ask me.

The funeral procession was only five cars long counting the hearse. We drove north a few miles, out of the town, down a side road away from the main highway and into a cemetery behind a small white-frame church with a soaring steeple. As I got out of my car, I heard one of the women say it was the church where she and her husband had married back in '38 as the Great Depression was about to end and just before the war changed everything forever.

A green canvas tent had been set up in case of rain. The hole was already dug and the green carpet thrown over the pile of dirt to hide it. They buried her beside her husband, who'd died a decade before. I stood at the back of the tent with my head down and my hands folded in front of me, the wind blowing my hair forward and down over my forehead, as the preacher said one last prayer, then went down the line shaking hands with the family. Not once did I see Brian Hawkins or his icy wife shed a tear. They were somber, stiff, their faces frozen in masks. The only other person I knew or recognized was Crazy Gladys, who kept turning around and staring at me as the service progressed.

It was nearly three-thirty by the time they started shoveling the dirt in on top of her. The few mourners were backing away from the tent, chattering low among themselves, as two men in overalls pulled the carpet back over the soil. Their shovels made a *scritch* sound as their blades sliced the brown dirt. The dry clods hit the casket with a dull thump.

I'd not said anything to anyone at the church, just walked in and sat down far enough in the back so that no one would notice me. At the grave I felt as though I really had to try at least to say something to Mrs. Hawkins's son and his wife.

They were both dressed in black. She wore a high starched lace collar atop a white blouse. His wide polyester blue-and-red regimental tie lay dead center down his paunch, held in place with a silver monogrammed tie clip. The two stood next to Crazy Gladys, who wore a tight blue skirt and jacket that looked very Forties and a black hat with a veil pulled down. As I approached them, Gladys looked at me, then turned quickly and walked away like somebody'd jerked her leash.

"Reverend Hawkins," I said, extending my hand. "I just wanted to tell you again how sorry I am about your mother. I was very fond of her and she was very good to me."

"Yes," he said dismissively, taking my hand and giving it a quick dead-fish handshake. "Thank you."

The wife turned, made a face, looked directly into her husband's eyes. "Tell him," she ordered.

Hawkins cleared his throat, a rumble of phlegm rolling around sloppily in his chest. "Yes," he began. "Of course."

Then he turned to me. "As soon as the will is probated, we'll be selling the house. Did you and my mother have a lease arrangement?"

I shrugged. "Not really. I signed a lease for the first couple of years, then we just never got around to doing it again. She pretty well trusted me and I trusted her."

"Well, then," he said, as next to him what almost resembled a smile spread across his wife's pancaked face. "We'll need you to vacate the premises as soon as possible."

My heart felt like it was somewhere below my belt line, although I can't say any of this was surprising. I wondered how I'd like crashing in the back of Lonnie's trailer. Now that Shadow was gone, maybe I could be his guard dog.

I sighed, shrugged again. "When would you like me out?"

"How much time will you need?" she asked.

"Well, if you could give me thirty days, I'd appreciate it. Plus you'd have somebody there to watch the place. Empty houses are a target for vandals."

The wife gritted her teeth, shifted her gaze to her husband for a moment.

"Yes, thirty days will be fine. We'll expect you out by the fifteenth of next month."

"We have to run," he said. "We're due at the lawyer's office in forty-five minutes."

Then I remembered. I was due in the lawyer's office in

forty-five minutes as well. Maybe, I thought, it would be best not to mention that right now.

I was in no hurry to get to the lawyer's office or anywhere else. Maybe Marsha was right, that I had been on a one-way spiral down to the fringes. I'd lost a job and a career, then just as another had started to look promising, I'd gotten myself in a big enough mess to set myself back for months.

And now this. Now I was, technically speaking, facing homelessness. God, I hate technicalities.

"That's it, guy," I said to myself as I threaded my way through the thick four-o'clock traffic on Two Mile Parkway. I'd intended to cut over to Gallatin Road and head back into town against the rush-hour traffic, but on the radio I heard that a flatbed semi overloaded with dirty PortaLets had overturned on the I-65 median just south of Millersville, scattering maroon water closets loaded with dirty blue juice all over hell and back. At last count, sixteen cars had been involved in the pileup. Both the north- and southbound lanes were closed until they could get the toxic-waste team in for cleanup.

And I was trapped, stuck in traffic hell, with the water-temp needle on the Mustang dancing in and out of the red zone.

"Yeah, this is bullshit," I continued, wondering if talking to oneself was a further sign of downward progress on the socio-economic ladder. "Go ahead, borrow the money from Pop for an apartment deposit and some new threads, brush up that résumé, cut that hair, get back into corporate life."

It was my only out.

It took almost half an hour to make it the mile or so to Gallatin Road, but once I got into the southbound lane, the traffic at least moved fast enough to keep the car cool. I made it through Madison and pulled into the lawyer's parking lot only twenty minutes late.

David Merrone's office was a simple, almost shabby brick house in East Nashville, up the road from the old Earl Scheib body shop, and not very far from Mrs. Lee's. I crossed the gravel, hopped up the stairs, and went through the front door.

What had once been someone's living room had been converted into a waiting room, complete with middle-aged receptionist sporting a bouffant of dyed red hair.

"I'm Harry Denton," I said, almost breathless. "Sorry I'm so late. I got caught in the traffic jam up in Rivergate."

She stood up. "I heard on the radio. Can you imagine? Spilled PortaLets on the interstate!"

She crossed in front of me and led me to a closed door on the other side of the entrance foyer.

"Yeah, it's a real mess up there."

She turned, grinned. "They're waiting for you. Go on in."

She held the door open into what I guess had once been the parlor but was now your typical attorney's office: leather furniture, floor-to-ceiling bookcases, desk bigger than the president's.

And in two wood and leather visitor's chairs in front of Merrone's awesome desk—Reverend Hawkins and his wife. Merrone was a large man, old and bulky, with bloodshot yellowed eyes that seemed younger and more energetic than the rest of him. He stood up and moved slowly as the two swiveled in their chairs, a look of horror on their faces.

"Mr. Denton, please come in."

"Sorry I'm late," I said.

The Ice Queen's jaw dropped. On her left, the Reverend Hawkins's jowls bounced back and forth as he sputtered and shook.

"What is *he* doing here?" She spat the words out like she'd just stepped in something unsavory.

"Mr. Denton is the other party mentioned in Mrs. Hawkins's will."

"That's impossible!" the reverend squawked.

"Yes," the Ice Queen agreed. "It's outrageous!"

Merrone motioned with his head toward a third visitor's chair, then stepped out from behind his desk and pulled the chair over to the side. I felt awkward, wishing this would all go away.

"Please sit down," he said.

I moved to the chair, settled into it.

"Sit down nothing," she ordered. "Get him out of here this instant."

Merrone's face never changed, the creases in his face just this side of shar-pei and his thin gray hair held straight back across his dome with a sheen of Vitalis.

"Mrs. Hawkins," Merrone said as he eased back into his own chair, "Mr. Denton is legally entitled to be here. As the executor of Esther Hawkins's estate, I am required to have him here before the will can be read."

I glanced over at the two of them. Almost on cue, the two harrumphed in unison and turned away, refusing to look at me.

"Now," Merrone continued, "shall we get on with it?"

No one said anything for a few moments. I looked down at the worn Oriental carpet and wished I could crawl under his desk.

"Very well then." He pulled open a drawer in the desk and extracted two manila folders.

"I've furnished you each with a certified copy of the legal last will and testament of Esther Hawkins. The original will be filed with the probate court. Barring any unforeseen problems, the probate will be handled by the special master and won't even have to go before a judge. As you can imagine, Mrs. Hawkins's estate is modest and the disposition relatively simple. By modest, I mean that its aggregate value is under the IRS exemption for estates. So there will be no tax liability.

"I won't bother to read the entire will word-for-word. I'll spare you the legalese and the whys and wherefores. If you like, you can go through that on your own. The estate consists of a portfolio of stocks and bonds that Mrs. Hawkins and her husband accumulated over the years and which, by the way, Mrs. Hawkins shepherded quite well. There is the house and its contents, of course. And there is her checking account, savings account, and some short-term CDs with the bank as well."

Merrone reached across and handed me one of the sealed manila envelopes. He handed the other toward the Reverend Hawkins, but the Ice Queen snatched it out of his hand.

I held the envelope loosely in my hand, not wanting to open

it, still uncomfortable with being left anything, and sure as hell not wanting to be around these people any longer than I had to.

"To summarize the contents of the will, the estate is divided in two parts, with the bulk, of course, going to Reverend Hawkins. That part consists of the investment portfolio and the contents of the house. In your envelope, Reverend Hawkins, is the necessary paperwork for transferring all the accounts at the brokerage to your name. If there are any problems, call me. But I don't expect any. As to the contents of the house and Mrs. Hawkins's personal property, you can make arrangements for retrieving that with Mr. Denton at your convenience."

Something in me went numb. I looked up. "What? Why my convenience?"

Merrone stared at me, studying my face for a beat or two. "Yes, that's the other part of the disposition of the will. It was Mrs. Hawkins's wish that Mr. Denton inherit the house and whatever monies were accumulated in the bank accounts and CDs."

Everyone was very quiet for a few moments. Then the Ice Queen stood halfway out of her chair, shrieked, and fell back, apparently in a dead faint.

"Wait a minute," I said. "But I don't under—"

The Reverend Hawkins stood up, his eyes afire, his face red, as he boomed out in his best revival voice: "What kind of *ee-vuhl* hold did you have on my dear, blessed mother?!"

I turned to him. "What the hell are you talking about? I didn't know anything about this!"

Hawkins jumped in place. "It's Satan!" he cried. "Satan at work in my mother's very own home! It's evil and it's the devil!"

He pointed a fat shaky finger at me. "The devil is at work in you."

Next to him, the Ice Queen stirred, shaking her head, moaning and groaning.

I looked at Merrone. His face was absolutely expressionless. "How much?" I asked. "How much is there?"

He sat silent for a moment before answering. His eyes flicked over to the rev and his wife.

"In the checking and savings accounts, just under twenty-five thousand. And there are five ten-thousand-dollar CDs that mature at varying times over the next six months."

My jaw went slack. "She left me the house and seventy-five thousand dollars?"

The Ice Queen stood halfway up, shrieked again, this time even more dramatically, and fell away in a real faint. I could tell because her head went limp, dropped to her shoulder, and she immediately started drooling.

Merrone nodded his head. "The necessary paperwork for transferring the bank accounts into your name, as well as the deed and its transference instrument are in your package. I've set up an administrative account, which I'll keep open for six months. It consists of monies taken equally out of her bank account and the money-market account at the brokerage. That money must remain available for six months in case there are any claims against the estate. But I don't expect any."

"I'll sue!" Hawkins screamed, spit flying out of his mouth as his face reddened to a deep crimson. "I'll take it to court! You defrauded my mother! She was senile! I'll have you thrown in jail! You—you—you—*usurper*, you!"

I looked at Merrone, who rolled his eyes upward just enough for me to notice.

"You are, of course, perfectly entitled to bring suit if you so choose, Mr. Hawkins. Your mother told me you probably would. That is why she instructed me to take special care that everything in her will was precise, legal, and to the spirit and letter of the law. In short, you can file a formal will contest if you want. The result will be that you will lose, much of the estate will be eaten up by attorney's fees and court costs, and your portion of the estate as well as Mr. Denton's will be tied up in court for at least a year. Perhaps several."

He paused and folded his hands together on his desk blotter. "Is that what you really want?"

"But—but—" Hawkins sputtered. "This isn't fair! It isn't right! It's the devil's work!"

Merrone shook his head from side to side slowly.

"It's perfectly fair, Mr. Hawkins. Tell me, how many times did you see your mother in the past year?"

Hawkins's jowls shook as his head vibrated. "Why, what's that got to do—"

"How often did you call her?" Merrone interrupted. "Mrs. Hawkins told me that for the past four years of her life, Mr. Denton has been a good and trusted friend. He may have even saved her life once, when a house . . ."

He looked at me. "I believe it was across the street?"

I nodded. "Yeah."

"Yes, the house across the street caught fire and Mrs. Hawkins couldn't hear the fireman calling because she'd taken her hearing aids out."

I smiled, thinking of how I'd caught her in bed with someone, too, that night. Wonder how the rev would react to that?

"So you see, Mr. Hawkins," Merrone said, "your mother's wishes were clear and legal and distinct, and you should respect that."

The Ice Queen started coming to, moaning and groaning and fumbling in her chair.

"This is your fault!" Hawkins yelled, pointing at me again. "You're responsible for this sacrilege! It's the devil's work and I am the Lord's hand! What do you say to that?"

I thought for a moment, staring at him, trying to figure out what the hell had just transpired. Then it hit me. I stood up, faced the fat reverend and his convulsing wife.

"I say you've got thirty days to get your shit out of my house."

Then I nodded to Merrone and walked out of his office.

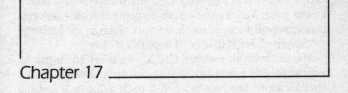

Chapter 17 ⎯⎯⎯⎯⎯⎯⎯⎯

My hands shook as I made the turn onto Greenwood Avenue, missing the worst of the rush-hour traffic by cutting through neighborhoods and taking the side street between Cora Howe Elementary and the old Bailey School.

This changes everything. Suddenly, I've gone from broke and prehomelessness to landed gentry. Like the bumper sticker says: SHIFT HAPPENS.

Mostly I couldn't feel it yet, but what parts of me did couldn't help but register one big hunk of guilt. Here I'd managed to bollix up everything and it took the death of a friend to give me a second chance.

Not exactly the manly way to put one's life back in order. . . .

Maybe I should give it back. After all, I'm not blood kin. I'm just some putz who decided to be nice to an old lady. Maybe her kid deserves it, even if he is a jerk.

On the other hand, in all the time I'd lived in her house, I'd never seen him visit. I rarely heard her mention him. If there were any pictures of him in her house, I'd never seen them. Sometimes close blood relatives are the most distant of all.

I'd give myself some time to ponder, but the chances were good that I was going to consider this a gift from a friend who wanted me to enjoy it and let it go at that.

Right now, I wanted to share this with someone. I drove right past Mrs. Hawkins's—excuse me, *my*—house and headed for the other side of town.

When she came to the door, I held a huge bouquet of fresh flowers I'd picked up at the market, along with two salmon steaks, fresh asparagus, salad makings, and an exotic cheese-cake with swirls of raspberry stuff mixed in. What the hell; it looked good. And to top it off: an icy bottle of some California chardonnay that cost as much as a tank of gas in the Mustang.

"Surprise," I said quietly. "I hope this is okay."

Marsha wore an oversize UNLV sweatshirt and a pair of sweatpants that would have been twice her size under normal circumstances. Her hair was pulled back. What little makeup she wore had been scrubbed off, revealing tired dark circles under weary bloodshot eyes. For a moment, she looked almost angry.

"What are you doing here? I thought we were taking a night off."

"We're celebrating," I said, walking past her into the hall-way with my bags.

"Celebrating?" she asked, shutting the door after me and following me into the kitchen. "This has been one of the worst days of my life. You've buried your landlady. And we're celebrating?"

I set the packages down and handed her the flowers. "I know it's been a killer," I said, cranking the corkscrew into the bottle of wine. "And I want to hear everything. But first there is some good news and we need it more than we need the bad."

Marsha pulled a vase out of the cabinet and jammed the flowers into it, then leaned her hip against the counter. A con-fused look crossed her face as I pulled out two wineglasses and poured a full glass for me, a half inch for her. I handed one to her, then clinked her glass with mine.

"*L'chiam,*" I said. "And to Esther Hawkins."

She raised her glass to her lips, brow furrowed.

"What's going on?" she asked.

I took a great slug of the wine and let it slide down. It was buttery, cold, wonderful. I waited until it hit, then savored the buzz.

I moaned, closed my eyes for a moment, opened them. Marsha was still staring, still waiting.

"She left me the house," I said quietly.

Her eyes widened. "What?"

"The house. And a wheelbarrow full of cash."

She set the wineglass down on the counter, hard, and looked as if a wave of dizziness had come over her.

"Here, sit down," I said, taking her hand, leading her over to the kitchen table.

"My God," she squeaked. "But . . . but why?"

I squatted down in front of her, looked into her eyes. "I guess she just couldn't resist my charm. Either that or she was trying to piss off her obnoxious son and bitchy daughter-in-law."

"I don't believe it."

"Neither do I. But the paperwork's in the car. All signed and ready for filing. It's a done deal."

Marsha squinted her eyes, thinking hard for a second. "If it's not butting in, how much?"

"Seventy-five thousand."

She looked even more stunned.

"I can't retire on it," I said. "But it's breathing room. For the first time in years, I've got a safety net."

"How does it feel?" she asked.

"I'm not sure yet. But I think good."

She smiled, nodded her head. "Yes, yes. I think we should celebrate."

Three hours later, we'd eaten, cleaned up the dishes, made love, and filled the whirlpool bathtub in the master bathroom. She'd set out candles around the edge of the tub and stuck a couple of burning incense sticks in an antique wooden holder. We settled into the hot soapy water, with me trying real hard not to be reminded of what had happened the last time I saw a human body in a whirlpool. I leaned against the back of the tub, my legs spread, her leaning back into me. A Billie Holiday CD played softly in the background—"God Bless the Child."

She'd relaxed finally, and seemed to have gotten over the worst aftereffects of her horrible day.

"It was dreadful," she said, leaning her head back into my chest. Her black hair seemed longer, straighter, when wet and draped across my shoulders like a cool blanket. My hands were wrapped around her, and I was looking down over her breasts, to the V made by her legs. Her belly was becoming more rounded by the day. She wouldn't be able to hide anything much longer. I wondered what she'd do when everybody knew—the few that didn't already—but decided that was best taken up some other time.

I wrapped my hand around a bar of soap floating in the water and swabbed her stomach with it, then moved up the valley between her breasts.

"What kind of stuff did they ask you?"

"They grilled me about every trip I'd ever taken with Doc Henry. They had it all, every one for the last seven years. They wanted to know stuff I couldn't remember. What our room numbers were, were we on the same floor. . . . Mostly they wanted to know if he'd ever hit on me. If we'd ever slept together."

"What'd you tell 'em?" I murmured.

"The truth," she said sternly. "The absolute truth. That he had never behaved improperly toward me. But then they asked if I had ever witnessed his making a sexual advance on anyone else."

"And?"

"No," she said. "Oh, he was touchy-feely sometimes. He liked to pat people on the back, hug them. Sometimes I or Kay or any of the other staffers would be sitting at our desk and suddenly he'd walk up behind you and start massaging your neck or shoulders. But hell, Harry, we liked that."

"You liked it. Maybe others didn't."

"Maybe. But then the DA asked if I thought it was possible that Dr. Henry would commit sexual harassment."

"What'd you say?"

She hesitated, relaxing as she did so. Her body became heavier on mine and she slid down just a bit in the water. "I had to tell him the truth. I don't know. I just don't know."

I leaned back, the hard acrylic edge of the oversize tub rubbing the muscles between my shoulder blades.

"I could handle all that," she said. "I didn't like it, but I could handle it. It was the other that really scared me."

"Other?"

She turned, faced me at an angle. "There's a lot of money no one can account for. Invoices for equipment purchases that no one can find the order for. Paperwork scrambled all over the place. Huge overtime payments for the staff, with no paperwork to back it up."

I stared down at her. "How much of it was yours?"

"A lot."

"But you worked a ton of overtime. Up until recently, you put in more hours than anybody."

"Best I can figure," she said, "I've averaged about sixty hours a week for the past three years. I once worked twenty-seven days straight without a day off."

"Yeah, I remember that. Two summers ago. Jesus, did I miss you."

She giggled, ran her hands down along her sides in the soapy water, and slid them between my legs. "I know what you missed."

"Yeah, that, too. But now they're trying to say you didn't work those hours?"

She moaned, rolled her head around my chest, then leaned up and kissed me.

"No," she said after we pulled apart. "They're saying there's no paperwork. The money's just disappeared down a black hole. You take all the OT for all the staff over the past five years, it runs into hundreds of thousands of dollars. Maybe even seven figures. And that's not counting the equipment, the invoices paid without purchase orders, the money paid to suppliers with no proof of service delivery."

"But it sounds to me like it's not a problem of anybody stealing. It's just that somebody's a lousy administrator."

"Dr. Henry's weakest area is administration," she said.

"What about Kay?"

"Ten years ago, when the ME's office had a fifth the number of bodies to process each year, Kay could handle everything. But have you seen the homicide statistics for Nashville in the past five years?"

I felt her body tense.

"Nashville," she continued, "now has a higher per capita homicide rate than New York and Los Angeles. Harry, this city has become one damn dangerous place to live. And we don't have the resources to deal with it. Kay now has a full-time job just keeping up with the paperwork for the bodies themselves. It's a full-time job just to type up our reports."

"What a mess."

"Everybody's exhausted, completely burnt out. Everything came unglued and nobody had the time or the . . . the foresight to see it coming and prepare for it. It's all coming apart at the seams, Harry. All of it. I've got a real bad feeling about this. You see the news tonight?"

I shook my head.

"The mayor says he's withholding comment until the results of the grand jury investigation are released. But he's not at all unhappy to see the office privatized, if that's what it takes."

"What'll happen to you, to Dr. Henry and the rest?"

"We're out of here. We're history, bud."

I settled back, wrapping my arms around her, feeling her warmth and the slickness of the hot water and soap on her skin. Then I remembered Reed.

"God, I just thought of something."

"What?"

"We're sitting in a Jacuzzi and I'm thinking about some-body who was murdered in a Jacuzzi."

She shivered. "You're terrible."

"You're not. This is wonderful," I whispered.

After a few moments, she said, "What are you going to do with the money she left you?"

I smiled. "I don't know. You hitting me up for a loan?"

"Not yet. But give me time."

"I haven't given it much thought. Pay off my credit cards, get out of debt, pay my dad back. That's first, I guess."

"Smart move. And maybe we could go on a vacation."

"I'd like that," I said.

We were quiet for a few moments. The CD changer shuffled and clicked, then *The Best of Ella Fitzgerald* took over. She was just getting into "Much Too Young for the Blues" when the damn phone rang.

"Hell," I muttered.

"Wonder who that is?" She shifted her weight around, as if readying herself to climb out of the tub.

"Who cares?" I asked. "You're not really going to get that, are you?"

She cocked an ear. The answering machine was across the hall, in the spare bedroom she used for an office.

"At least see who it is. . . ." she said.

Her outgoing message played, then the machine clicked and over the gentle voice of Ella Fitzgerald came the unwelcome voice of Randy Tucker.

"Dr. Helms," he said. "This is Randy Tucker. I hate to bother you at home, but I've left messages for you at your office for two or three days in a row. I don't know whether you're getting them or just not returning them, but I really need to talk to you. I'm up against a deadline and we don't have much time. It's very important that you return my call as quickly as possible. I'll leave my office and home phone numbers. Call me anytime."

As he dictated the numbers into the machine, Marsha turned to me.

"Who the hell *is* he?" she whispered.

"Guy works at the paper, in the business section. I don't get it. He's been calling me, too."

"You?" She sat up slightly.

I shrugged. "Go figure."

"Maybe I should call him back," she said.

I pulled her closer. "Not right now. It's almost bedtime."

She turned sideways and rubbed her body against mine, slipping and sliding in the cooling water.

"Let's rinse off," she said. "I'm beat."

We drained the soapy water, then closed the shower curtain, turned on the spray, and rinsed off the soap. We wrapped up in thick towels and I made some herbal tea. We climbed into bed shortly before eleven, and she drifted off immediately. I thought I was sleepy as well, but as I lay next to her in the dark, feeling her breathe as much as hearing it, I was suddenly wide-awake, staring at the ceiling in the darkness.

Something told me we'd better get back in touch with Randy Tucker, and the quicker, the better.

Chapter 18 _____

For some reason or other, I figured it might be prudent to wear a suit and tie to the bank. So I drove home after morning coffee with Marsha, then showered and changed.

I had no idea what was involved, but the instructions in Merrone's package indicated that I was to talk to a trust officer at the main branch of the bank, which was downtown on Union Street. I went ahead and parked the car near my office, then walked under darkening skies, the cool wind whipping down the canyon of office buildings, and got directions from a security guard in the lobby.

The young bank VP kept me waiting about five minutes, then ushered me into his small office. The procedure was pretty simple. He'd received a letter from Merrone authorizing the disbursement of Mrs. Hawkins's money. Since I had my meager checking account at the same bank, it was all pretty straightforward. I walked in practically a pauper, signed in a couple of dozen places, and walked out with just short of seventy-five grand in my name.

Yeah, shift happens. This was real.

A slow drizzle glittered as it fell, leaving a slick film of oil and water on the asphalt as I walked back up Church Street and turned on Seventh toward my office. The heavy glass doors into the building could use about a quart of Windex. From the smell, I gathered the alcove had been somebody's bedroom/bathroom combination overnight. With the influx of tourists and the "Disneyfication" of Second Avenue, the homeless had been chased away from their riverfront shantytowns and were migrating toward downtown center. One abandoned office building farther down Church had become famous as almost an officially sanctioned flophouse. Most of the time it didn't bother me, but this morning I had to hold my breath as I entered the building.

A couple of the bare bulbs in ceiling fixtures down the narrow hallway had burned out, leaving the interior even creepier and darker than usual. If I decided to stay in this business, it might be a shrewd investment to move into better quarters. At least I could afford something more suitable for the time being.

I climbed the stairs and turned left down the second-floor hallway and opened the door to my office. A pile of mail, mostly junk, had been jammed through the slot and lay scattered all over the floor. I gathered it up and was just sitting down to go through it all—to be followed by a lengthy check-writing session—when I heard steps in the stairwell. There had been a recent exodus of tenants from the building. The only other inhabitants of the second floor were Ray and Slim, the two songwriters who owned a struggling music-publishing company at the other end of the hall. Couldn't be them, though; they were never in before lunch.

The steps paused as they hit the second-floor landing. I sat very still in my chair, waiting to see which way they turned. In a moment, the clicking of heels on linoleum became louder.

I turned to check my door. I've only got a one-room office— no waiting room—so I've taken to locking the door behind me. The footsteps came closer; high heels, I guessed. Then they stopped in front of my office and the door handle jiggled.

A knock followed a second later. I stood up, wondering why I was being so paranoid. Maybe it's the fact that I've seen two dead bodies since Saturday night.

"Who is it?" I called.

"Victoria Reed," a voice said. It was her voice, only calm this time. No trace of hysteria or anguished sobs.

I thought for a moment. *Open the damn door, you idiot. What's she going to do, shoot you?*

Then it occurred to me that might be exactly what she had in mind.

"Hold on," I said. I crossed the room, unlocked the door, and cracked it just a bit.

Her hands were empty, at her side. I opened the door all the way. "Come in, Mrs. Reed," I said.

I held the door open as she came in and sat down, then closed it behind us. I studied her as I crossed to my desk. She wore a pair of black slacks and a white sweater over a white blouse. She crossed her legs primly and stared at me without expression.

"I'm surprised to see you here," I said as I took my seat.

She looked down at the floor, then back at me. "I'm sorry to have spoken to you the way I did. I was upset."

"Understandably," I said. "Don't worry about it."

She knitted her hands together. Her skin was thin, translucent, with a network of blue veins visible on the backs of her hands. I figured that when she was ready, she'd get around to telling me why she was here.

"The police won't tell me anything about their investigation."

"I'm not surprised," I said. "They think you killed your husband."

Her head shot up, eyes erupting. "How? How could they?"

That was a cruel way to say it, but I did it on purpose. I wanted to see her reaction; she'd given me what felt like the right one.

"Tradition. The first suspect is always the spouse."

"That's crazy!" She gritted her teeth, the muscles of her jaw knotting under the skin.

"Is it? Your husband's cheating on you with a younger woman. You think he's going to leave you. You start preparing for a nasty divorce. There's a lot of money involved, lot of property. Maybe you just decide to bypass the legal system, cut out the middleman. Who knows, maybe you figure if you can't have him, nobody can."

Her jaw loosened, her mouth cracking open just wide enough to let a sigh out.

"Makes perfect sense to me," I continued. "And, conveniently, they think you hired me to do it."

Victoria Reed's shoulders sagged and her head relaxed so that her chin almost touched the collar of the sweater.

"My God," she said blankly. "You're not kidding, are you?"

I shook my head.

"They haven't even questioned me yet," she said.

"They will."

"How bad is it?" Her voice dropped to a whisper.

"Not bad yet. They grilled me Monday afternoon for almost three hours. They didn't get anything. That doesn't mean we're off their list."

She raised her head, her eyes darker, the skin of her face taut, brittle.

"Did you kill him?"

I shook my head slowly. "No. Why would I? Doesn't make any sense. There are only two possible motives I'd have for killing him. One, you paid me to do it. And we both know you didn't."

"Yes, we both know that. But do the police?"

"Sooner or later they'll figure it out."

She turned, faced the window at an angle. The light across her nose and chin cast long distinct shadows on the right side of her face and neck.

"What's the second possible motive?" she asked.

"I'm a hard-to-please book critic," I said, smiling.

She almost cracked a smile, but then forced it back down. "I'm scared," she said simply.

"Me, too."

"Want to know the worst part?"

I wasn't sure if I did. "Sure," I said.

Her face tightened again, her eyes filled, and her voice became higher, strained. "I really miss him."

"I know you do," I said soothingly.

Her hands were knotted in front of her, jamming into her crossed right knee.

"The kids miss him."

"I know they do," I said even more soothingly.

She sniffed, choked back a sob. "I called her."

"Her?"

"Margot. Margot Horowitz."

Whoa! I thought. *That's pretty weird.*

"Why'd you do that?" I asked.

"I'm not sure," she said after taking a moment to compose herself. "I guess I wanted to hear her voice, to try to figure out if she was involved with R.J.'s death. But she was completely broken up. I don't think she knows anything."

"What else did she say?" I asked. "Had she been out to the farm that afternoon?"

"I didn't ask. She was crying so loud it was hard to talk to her."

"I can imagine," I offered. I could feel myself being drawn into this almost as an intellectual exercise. Now that I stood back and pondered it a little, Reed's murder didn't make a whole lot of sense.

Okay, so the guy's the king of schmaltz, with his trite little homespun adages. And he'd become damn wealthy and famous. He had a wife and kids who loved him, apparently, despite his lack of what one might call a moral-genital compass.

Maybe it was a random act of violence. Only nothing was taken. A crazed crackhead would have broken into the house and grabbed everything pawnable that wasn't nailed down. Not even a window had been busted.

Maybe it was a wacko fan, a Mark David Chapman of the Hallmark-card arena. Even so, it would take a persistent mother of a stalker to wade through the tangled corporate ownership paper trail to find out Reed even owned the farm in Williamson County where he was murdered. Those kinds of obsessive-compulsive nuts usually devote their energies to movie stars or rock idols.

No, it just didn't make any sense. With the exception of one or two unbalanced paranoiac examples, most book authors simply don't need a whole lot of security.

So it had to be somebody he knew. And if it wasn't his wife or his girlfriend, who in hell was it?

"Victoria," I said, "tell me about your husband."

She sniffed. "What do you mean?"

"Who were his friends? Who were his business associates?

Who'd he play golf with? Who'd he drink beer and play poker with? What made him tick?"

She pulled a tissue out of her purse and wiped her nose. "You mean, you think . . . somebody we knew?"

"Why not? The more I picture this as hit-or-miss chaos, the less sense it makes. Your husband's the first homicide in Williamson County in years. Doesn't that strike you as an odd case of random violence?"

"One of our friends?" she asked incredulously.

"Maybe. Somebody in business. Somebody from his past. That's what we've got to find. Somebody who benefited from your husband's death."

"What are you saying? Are you going to try to find the killer?"

I thought for a moment. "It's not how I'd planned to spend my time. But truth is, the workload around here is kind of light. Also I don't like being called a murderer. It would suit me fine to make that sawed-off little SOB ADA down in Williamson County look like an idiot."

She smiled—just a trace, but still a smile. "If you don't mind my saying so, you're a very strange man."

I squinted at her. "What do you mean?"

"You're obviously a capable, intelligent human being. I'd guess you're pretty well educated. And yet you choose this kind of work, and you do it"—she looked around my office— "here. Very strange. And more than a little eccentric."

I reached for a pen and pad.

"Funny you should say that," I offered. "My girlfriend was just telling me the same thing. Now let's get to work."

It took nearly an hour for Victoria Reed to recount the convoluted saga. Robert Jefferson Reed's story was one of those uniquely American mythic tales of a guy who spends his life looking for One Big Lick and finally gets lucky enough to nail it.

As for literary aspirations, she said he had none. His sole objective seems to have been the realization of his own special brand of narcissism. He set out to become rich, famous, adored, and it didn't particularly matter to him how he did it.

He had the intelligence and the drive to succeed in any of the numerous careers he pursued. But each time he was about to break into the top ranks, something happened.

In the mid-Seventies, it had been "creative differences" with his partner in the ad agency the two started after leaving a larger agency in New York. Reed was only twenty-five, his partner twenty-eight. They were bright, creative, on fire. They landed a couple of huge accounts almost immediately. Then something happened. Victoria Reed was out of the loop; R.J. had no intention of sharing that part of his life with her. Three years after its creation, the agency fell apart, closed its doors, and the two founders never spoke to each other again. A reporter from the trades finally got the "creative differences" comment in a short article announcing the agency's closing.

In the late Seventies and early Eighties, Reed tried running with the big dogs in the stock market. He got his broker's license and put in the brutal hours required of novice stock traders who want to get ahead. The money started rolling in just as, in quick succession, the kids came along. The future was so bright—as the Eighties tune suggested—he had to wear shades.

That's when their marital troubles began. As much time as R.J. put in at the office, it was a testament to his youth and energy and Victoria's patience that they had any kids at all. In the mid-Eighties, they moved to Atlanta, where Reed managed the junk bond and arbitrage department of the largest locally owned stock brokerage in the Southeast. The bucks were rolling in, but R.J. was rarely at home for his wife or kids. Victoria speculated there were other women. She heard rumors about a long-standing affair with another woman at the company, but she didn't confront him. She feared he was drinking too much and even wondered if he'd picked up some nastier habits. At a party one night, she walked in on R.J. and several other young brokers doing a few lines out by the pool. Again, no confrontation. She became the long-suffering, victimized little woman at home with kids.

Then the '87 crash hit. A series of deals turned disastrous. An SEC investigation into some of the junk bond deals Reed had put together eventually cost him his broker's license and a six-figure fine for the company. Reed was fired just at the moment when his personal portfolio was at its lowest. He had to liquidate everything just to pay the bills and hold off creditors until his home could be sold, even at a loss.

The Reeds entered a dark time. Nearly broke, Reed was out of the brokerage industry, out of a job, with few resources and forty staring him in the face. He pulled up stakes and came north to Nashville, where Tennessee's liberal bankruptcy laws made it easier for him to go Chapter 7.

As Victoria Reed portrayed it, though, this was a period when she hoped the marriage might survive. She'd never been attracted to the high-rolling lifestyle in the first place. And R.J.'s fall from the loftier heights actually made him human again, at least for a while. He spent more time with the kids, with her. They moved into a small rental house in Donelson. To help out with the bills, she got a job as a proofreader at Spearhead Press, a local regional publisher of arcane books on the Civil War, Southern history, and cookbooks. R.J. took a succession of jobs as a mortgage broker, Realtor, and finally, selling cars. Each time, however, Reed's inherent narcissism and firm conviction that he knew how to run a business—any business—better than his boss hurt him. With each round of hiring and firing, Reed seemed to spiral downward. Over forty now, he began to suffer bouts of depression and serious self-doubt. What she'd seen as focus, passion, energy, and ambition in the younger man now seemed simply manic.

He became moody, unpredictable. R.J. and Victoria spent their twentieth wedding anniversary barely conversing. Their oldest child, sixteen-year-old R.J. Jr., suffered the most from his demanding, unforgiving father. Victoria had become concerned that her son was inheriting his father's worst traits. The two younger children, fourteen-year-old Beth and thirteen-year-old Jessica, simply avoided their father and seemed none the worse for wear.

A year after moving to Nashville, R.J. was fired from his seventh job in twelve months, selling Fords at a dealership over on Thompson Lane. He spent several months out of work. At the same time, Victoria had been promoted to assistant editor at Spearhead Press. The money was lousy, but she enjoyed the work. The kids were old enough to make extra money baby-sitting or cutting grass in the summertime. They were barely solvent, but in a strange way Victoria Reed was exhilarated by the struggle and, with the exception of her loose-cannon husband, she was about as close to fulfilled as she'd ever been.

It was during this long period of unemployment that R.J. conceived of his guidebook to a life well-lived. Victoria Reed didn't specify this, but I gathered she thought it was the purest definition of egomania that someone who'd managed to screw up every aspect of his life felt entitled to offer instruction to anyone else. He billed the book as his legacy of wisdom and insight to his own and the world's children, and wrote in the introduction that he wished his own father had been able to share these secrets of living with him.

Reed wrote the book in a week. (No surprise.) In manuscript it ran barely fifty pages. In a flurry of bipolar enthusiasm, he'd fired it off over-the-transom to every publisher in New York. The few that bothered to reply promptly sent form rejection slips.

R.J.'s troughs ran as deep as his peaks, and when it became clear that *Life's Little Maintenance Manual* was going nowhere, Victoria feared for her husband's sanity. He took to bed for days at a time; she was afraid to leave him alone for fear she'd find him hanging from a rafter.

Reed had, of course, not bothered to solicit Victoria's opinion of his creation. But one day she pulled a copy out of the trash after it was returned by a publisher and took it to her boss. Spearhead Press at that time was going through a dark period as well, and Victoria Reed wasn't sure how much longer she'd even have her job. Her boss, the cofounder of the company, and his partner spent a couple of weeks arguing over the commercial prospects of the manuscript.

Finally, the two men published the book, more as a favor to Victoria than anything else. No one expected much out of it. The owners of Spearhead Press thought so little of the book that they didn't even offer an advance.

What occurred over the next year became one of those archetypal publishing stories of which legends are made. The book was ignored upon publication, but R.J. in his mania had loaded cases of the book into the family station wagon and begun an odyssey of book promotion that put nearly seventy thousand miles on the car in six months. Gradually word got out. R.J. discovered he knew how to do television, and soon he was working the local noontime talk shows, and then syndication. He had the look that every movie superstar has, the look that's adored by the camera. His voice was resonant, and he picked up the drill quickly.

The big break, of course, came eight months after the pub date, when Oprah's producer called.

That's all it took. Sales started out flat-lined, but in less than a year, *Life's Little Maintenance Manual* went into second, then third, then fourth, fifth, twentieth, then thirtieth printings. Booksellers couldn't shovel the damn things out the door fast enough. It went on to *The New York Times* bestseller list in November a year ago and was still on it. Autographed first editions were going for five grand.

Reed's first royalty check four months after publication had been for $647.56. Victoria and R.J. added two dollars and forty-four cents to it and paid the rent on the house that month.

Six months later the next royalty check came in: $246,333.78. The one after that went just into seven figures. It was, Victoria Reed said, like riding a tidal wave. Robert Jefferson Reed joined the ranks of other marginally talented but highly successful writers by embracing the two criteria even more important than talent: luck and timing.

Robert Jefferson Reed also single-handedly saved Spearhead Press. The company relocated its headquarters from the basement of one of the owners' house just off Lebanon Road to a five-story building in Maryland Farms, one of the more prestigious addresses in prestigious Brentwood. They were eaten up with prestige.

Three months later the company bought the building and Victoria Reed retired from publishing.

R.J. did *Oprah* four times, interspersed with stints for Sally and Rosie and Jerry and Geraldo. The book became a merchandising phenomenon. R.J. had completed the manuscript to *Life's Little Maintenance Manual, Volume II*. It wasn't a matter of millions but of how many.

Then someone murdered him. I'm not exactly sure why, but I decided to find out who.

What the hell, maybe I just needed to keep busy.

Chapter 19

So I went back on Victoria Reed's payroll.

She wrote me another retainer check, went over a list of contacts with me, cried a little more, then wearily left my office. She had much to do. The day after tomorrow she would bury her husband. Then she would get on with her life, raise her children, manage a much larger estate than she had ever envisioned, and eventually wake up one morning and realize that the worst was over. She had survived.

But that day was a long way off.

Before she left, I asked one favor. Would she be willing to set up a meeting between me and the two owners of Spearhead Press?

"Why?" she asked.

"Background, mostly," I said. "Maybe just fishing. But I want to get a sense of what they're going to do now without R.J. Obviously, the book'll get a little bump from the publicity surrounding his murder. But that won't carry them far. Eventually, these two guys will suffer a lot because R.J.'s not around to crank out volumes three through infinity."

"I guess it's possible they'll know something I don't," she said. "Funny, R.J. didn't talk much about money when there was plenty. Only when there wasn't enough."

Her face seemed to hang, like a weight was pulling it down. "I liked it better when he talked about it."

Victoria pulled herself together, made the phone call, and set up a meeting between me, Karl Sykes, and Travis Webber for eleven A.M. I had just enough time to make it.

* * *

The I-65 construction past Old Hickory Boulevard had slowed traffic to a one-lane, ten-mile-an-hour crawl. Fortunately, the jam started past the exit ramp. As I pulled onto the long stretch of concrete that would take me off the freeway, I felt almost sorry for the rest of the herd.

Maryland Farms is a sprawling complex of brick, reflective glass, and shiny chrome office buildings just past Franklin Road. The network of buildings is so extensive that it has its own road system. I turned left off Old Hickory Boulevard and maneuvered around several other buildings before finding the corporate headquarters of Spearhead Press.

It was an impressive building, new and futuristic. It towered five stories over the delicately manicured landscape, with a fountain out front and in the center, with the spray spreading out like a fleur-de-lis around it, a sculptured stone Spearhead Press logo.

A long way from Karl Sykes's basement, I thought.

I parked the Mustang in a slot on the far side of the crowded parking lot and walked in the springtime heat across to the entrance. The doors were polished brass and smoked glass, heavy and cumbersome. The lobby was cold, air-conditioned to the max. The walls of the lobby were poured aggregate concrete, with leather furniture, potted palms, and dozens of framed book covers, portraits, and newspaper articles as decoration.

A receptionist sat behind a desk with a high counter that looked like one of those control panels at a jet propulsion laboratory, as if she could pull a joystick and thirty minutes later a robotic toy on Mars would change directions and sniff a different rock.

"I'm Harry Denton," I said as I approached the huge desk. I looked over the counter and saw a row of built-in security monitors that focused on different entrances and locations throughout the building. On one monitor, three people in corporate uniforms huddled together outside one of the doors smoking.

"I have an eleven o'clock with Mr. Sykes."

She smiled. "Please sign in, Mr. Denton."

I took out my pen and signed the guest log just as she phoned upstairs for clearance. Then she spoke into a microphone and a uniformed security guard stepped around the corner and into view.

"Please follow me, sir," he said.

What is this? I thought. *CIA headquarters?*

I did as I was told, though, and followed the guard around the corner to a bank of elevators. When an elevator came, he held the door and followed me in. He pressed the button and stood silently as we ascended, staring ahead at his own image reflected in the polished metal.

On the fifth floor, we stepped out into a wide hall that ran to either side in front of us. To the left, a glass wall with more smoked-glass doors emblazoned with the corporate logo in gold foil faced us. The guard led us through and into another carpeted lobby with walls covered in framed book covers, awards, pictures.

"Mr. Denton?" another receptionist asked. Only this one was older, more aloof. The girl downstairs had an element of window dressing about her. This woman, I sensed, was pure business.

"Yes, I have an eleven o'clock with—"

"Mr. Sykes and Mr. Webber are in the conference room waiting for you right now," she interrupted, pointing over my left shoulder.

I turned and walked across the lobby, then through a wooden door in the paneled wall that was almost invisible from a distance.

The door opened into a large conference room with a polished mahogany table that could have seated about twenty people. Two men were at the other end of the room. The one at the head of the table was tall, thin to the point of emaciation, with thinning silver hair cropped short and wire-rimmed glasses. He wore a beige wool sweater with no jacket or tie. The man to his right couldn't have looked any different if they'd been from different planets. He wore a brown suit, weighed perhaps two hundred and fifty, and couldn't have been more than five feet six. His thick lips protruded as if he were in an eternal pout. While the wizened guy at the head of the table looked comfortable and self-possessed, his corpulent partner shifted restlessly in the chair next to him, a sheen of nervous sweat across his forehead.

"Mr. Denton," Silver Hair said.

I nodded. "Yes, Harry Denton." I stepped into the conference room and closed the door behind me. "Thanks for taking time to see me."

"Please, sit down." Silver Hair gestured to the chair to his left, the side closest to me.

The carpet was thick and soft beneath my feet. As I turned to take the chair, I noticed on the wall opposite us, behind the door where I'd stepped in, two large portraits of the men I was now sitting next to. Pretty impressive.

"I'm Karl Sykes," Silver Hair said. He spoke with the faintest trace of an accent. I tried to place it but couldn't. "And this is Mr. Webber."

Webber nodded to me, his fingers laced together, his hands across his belly. This thought ran through my mind—*Laurel and Hardy in corporate drag*—and I suppressed a smile.

"Unfortunately, Mr. Denton, we have another meeting to prepare for by eleven-thirty. So if we can get right to business, that would be helpful."

I felt a little burble of nervousness deep in my gut, then looked away for a moment and began.

"As Victoria Reed explained, gentlemen, I've been retained by the family to investigate the circumstances surrounding the death of her husband."

"And I assume," Sykes interrupted, "that you have the proper authority and credentials to conduct such an examination."

So far, Webber hadn't said a word. His eyes flicked away as mine met his. I reached into my pocket and pulled out my license.

"I'm licensed as a private investigator by the state of Tennessee," I said. "And I have authorization from the Reed family. That's all I need."

"I see," Sykes said, giving my license a cursory examination before handing it to his partner. Webber picked it up, held it open, and seemed to be reading every word on it.

"I'm attempting to learn as much as I can about R. J. Reed. Who were his friends and business associates? Who might possibly have had some business dealings with him that had gone sour?"

"Who might have a grudge against him?" Webber commented. His voice was deep, gruff, with just a touch of evangelical fervor behind it.

He slid the license across the polished tabletop to me. It stopped right at the edge. I reached out, slipped it back into my pocket.

"Possibly."

"Well," Sykes said, "I can tell you unequivocally that you won't find that here. From the moment we first began our dealings with R.J., nothing has resulted except more profit and good fortune than any of us could have ever imagined. His loss to us personally and to the company is a great one. We shall all miss him."

"Who actually edited the books?" I asked. "Who worked closest with him?"

"I edited the manuscript initially," Webber said. "In addition to my other duties, I'm editor in chief of Spearhead Press. Everything published by this company is ultimately edited by me."

"Initially," I said. "Someone else took over at some point?"

"One of our senior editors, Erica Benedict, worked with the final edits on the manuscript and oversaw the production process," Sykes said.

"Well," I said, hesitating a moment, "what was it like to work with Reed? Was he difficult?"

Webber pursed his lips. "All authors are difficult," he offered. "If they weren't, they wouldn't be authors. But he was no worse than the rest."

"I understand that he had completed the manuscript to *Life's Little Maintenance Manual, Volume II*."

"Thank heavens," Sykes responded somberly. "Publication will proceed."

"I understand that it was the profits from that first book that enabled you to"—I gestured around the room—"expand the company."

"That's not true," Webber snapped. "Spearhead was doing very well without that book. The product was very profitable, yes, but this company was a success without Reed."

"All the same, I'll bet you had to give him an advance the second time around," I said offhandedly. I looked directly at the two men and smiled.

Neither Sykes nor Webber seemed to find humor in this.

"Of course," Sykes said finally. "The first volume performed spectacularly. It was perfectly appropriate that the company demonstrate its commitment to the second in a concrete fashion."

"Mind sharing with me what the advance was?"

Sykes and Webber glanced at each other, then quickly away.

"That would be inappropriate without the permission of Victoria Reed," Sykes said.

"She won't mind," I speculated.

"Bring us that in writing," Webber said.

"No need to get testy," I said. "But you gentlemen have to understand, everybody I talk to, even the ones whom Reed hurt, all loved him and thought he was a swell guy and the business was all great and everybody was happy and shiny and nothing could be better."

They stared at me for a second.

"What is your point, Mr. Denton?" Sykes asked.

"Well, if Reed was such a great guy and the books were so good and everything was working out so well . . ."

I sat there, just gazing at the two of them.

"Yes?" Sykes said impatiently.

"Then how come somebody murdered him?"

There was some small talk after that, but I was basically ushered out of Spearhead Press like an unwanted salesman. I pulled out onto Old Hickory Boulevard, then pulled into the Shell station to gas up the car and call Lonnie. I was looking for a lunch buddy and hadn't yet told him about inheriting Mrs. Hawkins's house.

"Damn, Harry!" he snapped. "I been trying to call you. You seen the afternoon paper?"

"Not yet. Kind of early, isn't it? Say, you and I got a lot to catch up on. Guess who's the newest homeowner in a fashionably quaint East Nashville neighborhood?"

There was a long silence.

"Lonnie?"

"Look," he said after a moment. "Don't go back to your office. Don't answer your phone. Sheba and I are having lunch at the soda shop. We'll be in the back booth. Meet us there in twenty minutes."

"What's going on, man? Why all the cloak-and-dagger?"

"Just do it, Harry." He hung up.

Lonnie wasn't one to take that tone unless there was a reason. I got this queasy feeling in the pit of my stomach and did as he said.

There are three daily rush hours in Nashville: morning, evening, and that amorphous chunk of time between eleven and one when everybody jumps into a car and drives somewhere else for lunch. The popular lunch places are jammed by twenty after eleven. The Elliston Place Soda Shop, a Fifties-era chrome, glass, and red-vinyl-boothed place down near Baptist Hospital, was one of the most popular. The specialty of the house was the ubiquitous Southern meat 'n' three: three vegetables—usually days in the making—and a meat entrée, either deep-fried or smothered in gravy, your choice.

I got lucky and found a place right in front of Mosko's, just diagonally across the street from the restaurant. I pumped my only change into the meter and hoped that would do; the local traffic cops in their Cushman three-wheelers were notorious for running up and down Elliston Place at lunchtime meeting their quotas.

The soda shop was indeed jammed, with a dozen people or so crowded around the front door waiting for a table. To the right, at the back of the restaurant, Lonnie and Sheba sat huddled together in the last booth facing the door. He looked up and caught my eye as I maneuvered through the crowded tables and motioned me over quickly.

"Hi, Sheba," I said, sliding into the booth facing them.

"Hello, Harry," she said. "I'm so sorry."

"About what?" I said.

"Keep your voice down," Lonnie whispered.

I leaned in toward him. "You want to tell me what the hell is going on?"

The waitress came over, pad and pen in position, ready to go. I scanned the menu quickly as they ordered, then looked up as the waitress stood there tapping her foot.

"Vegetable plate," I said. "Macaroni and cheese, double white beans, cottage cheese."

The waitress scribbled a moment, then walked away. Sheba smiled, shook her head. "You just ordered a vegetable plate that didn't have a single vegetable on it. Congratulations."

I smiled back at her. "What you talking about, woman? Macaroni and cheese *is* a vegetable."

I could get to like Sheba. "So, how you guys doing?" I asked.

"You know a guy named Randy Tucker?" Lonnie asked.

Suddenly, I wasn't so hungry anymore. "Maybe. Why?"

Lonnie pulled a copy of the newspaper out of his lap and unfolded it in front of me.

"He knows you, bud," Lonnie said. "He knows you."

I unfolded the paper. The two-column headline alone made my heart jump in my chest:

REED AUTOPSY PERFORMED
BY SUSPECT'S GIRLFRIEND

And next to the headline, taking two more columns, was the mug shot off my private investigator's license. I felt the blood drain out of my face. Suddenly, the booth started swaying back and forth and I felt cold, shaky all over.

"Hey, man, you okay?" Lonnie asked.

"Oh, shit," I muttered.

The article carried Randy Tucker's byline, and if I'd been double-jointed, I'd have kicked myself in the ass for not calling him back.

The autopsy of bestselling author Robert Jefferson Reed was performed by Metro Assistant Medical Examiner Dr. Marsha Helms, the girlfriend of the man whom police say may have killed him.

Confidential sources within the Williamson County Sheriff's Department confirm that Nashville private investigator Harry James Denton is their chief suspect in the murder of Reed, whose body was found Saturday night at his Williamson County farm.

The autopsy revealed that Reed, who rose from literary obscurity to international fame as the author of *Life's Little Maintenance Manual*, had drowned. Police sources state that Denton was discovered at the scene by Sheriff's Department Deputy Thomas Grishom, who reportedly held Denton at gunpoint until backup officers arrived.

According to one source, Reed was drowned by being held underwater in a hot tub on the grounds of the Williamson County farm. Denton was allegedly standing next to the hot tub holding Reed's body out of the water when Deputy Grishom arrived.

Denton was questioned and later released by authorities. But sources within both the sheriff's department and the Williamson County District Attorney's office confirm that Denton is considered a prime suspect in the murder.

Nashville Medical Examiner Dr. Henry Krohlmeyer issued a written statement last night indicating that Dr. Helms performed the autopsy because he was out of town on official business and no one else was available. When asked if Dr. Helms should have recused herself because of potential conflicts of interest, he refused to comment.

Repeated requests for comment from both Dr. Helms and Denton were ignored. Confidential sources within the medical examiner's office confirmed that Dr. Helms has been involved in a long-term relationship with Denton and is now reputedly pregnant.

This latest revelation of alleged misconduct at the medical examiner's office comes on the heels of a grand jury investigation into the office. An ex-employee has charged Krohlmeyer with sexual harassment. A Metro internal audit has charged the office with sloppy bookkeeping, possible misuse of funds, and lack of supporting records for thousands of dollars in overtime, a large percentage of which was paid to Dr. Helms.

Mayoral spokesperson Tammy McCallister issued the following statement last night: "If the facts surrounding the autopsy of Robert Jefferson Reed reported by the media are accurate, then this represents a serious conflict of interest and breach of public trust. The public must have confidence that the medical examiner's office is operating in a way that meets professional standards and does not jeopardize the resolution of criminal cases. If that confidence and trust is or has been betrayed, then a very serious examination of that office must be conducted."

There was more, but I couldn't read it. I folded the paper in half and tucked it into my lap as the waitress brought over plates of food and slid them onto the table. I pushed mine away. I caught myself staring down at the table, not wanting to look her in the face.

"I feel awful," I said after she went away.

Sheba grimaced. "Poor baby," she whispered.

I raised my head. The world was swimming around me. This was insane. I'd been in some scrapes before, but none that had ever involved Marsha, and none this bad. The early edition of the paper had just hit the stands. Maybe I had time to get to her before anyone else did.

"I've got to make a phone call," I said blankly.

Lonnie nodded his head. "Yeah, I guess you do."

There was a pay phone in the back of the restaurant. I borrowed a quarter from Lonnie and waded through the crowded tables, dodging a hefty waitress with a scowl. Time seemed to have slowed to a crawl and I felt like everyone in the place was staring at me. I ducked my head, not meeting anyone's eyes.

The phone rang about twenty times before a clearly exasperated Kay Delacorte answered the phone. "Simpkins Center," she snapped.

I identified myself.

Her voice dropped to a pressured whisper. "Jesus, Harry, what the hell's going on?"

"You read the afternoon paper?"

"No, but there's about a hundred reporters camped outside trying to get to Dr. Marsha! They got those stupid trucks with the satellite dishes on top!"

"Has she talked to any of them?"

"She's locked in her office, not taking any calls at all. Dr. Henry's not here. We can't even get out!"

I thought for a second. How to play this one?

"What's going on, Harry?" Kay hissed.

"Randy Tucker at the *Banner* somehow found out that Marsha did the autopsy on R. J. Reed, that she and I are an item, and that she's pregnant. The headline on the early edition is how the girlfriend of an alleged murderer did the autopsy on his victim."

There was a moment's silence on the other end of the line, then Kay let out a sound kind of like a rusty door hinge being opened slowly.

"Whatever you do—" I started.

"*Jeezus*, Harry! What are we going to do?"

"Just listen, Kay. Whatever you do, don't let Marsha or anybody else talk to the press. I hate the idea of stonewalling 'em, but it's too late to handle it any other way. This time I got a feeling we're in a world of shit, lady. Let Marsha know what's going on and that I've called. She probably needs to call her attorney."

I thought for a moment. "Maybe it's time for you and me to get one, too," I added. "In the meantime, we've all got to be very quiet until we find out what's going to happen next."

"They really think you killed Reed?" Kay asked, her voice still tight, scared.

"Aw, hell, Kay," I complained. "I don't know anything anymore. Maybe I did kill the son of a bitch."

"You want to talk to Dr. Marsha?"

"I got a feeling neither of us is in the mood for chitchat. Tell her I'm going home, and when she gets someplace safe to call me."

"I'll tell her," Kay said. "And Harry, be careful, okay?"

I looked out across the swarm of noontime diners and wondered how I could get out the front door without drawing any attention to myself. I felt like Harrison-frigging-Ford in *The Fugitive*.

"Look, Kay, there's one other thing."

"Oh, great," she gasped. "What else?"

"Dr. Henry issued a statement last night to the press. Maybe I'm wrong, but I predict that pretty soon it's going to be every man for himself down there. Like I say, I hope I'm wrong."

There was a long silence on Kay's end of the phone. Then her voice went back to normal, professional, almost cold.

"No, Harry. I don't think you're wrong."

I didn't stick around to finish my alleged vegetable plate. I dropped a five on the table, turned down Lonnie's kind offer to use his trailer as a hiding place, then pushed my way out of the Elliston Place Soda Shop. At least a half-dozen people clearly recognized me.

There he is! That guy that killed Robert Jefferson Reed! And to think I got the author to sign a copy for Mama. Wonder if it's worth anything now?

Get a life, I thought to myself. But I didn't push the issue.

I drove down Church Street to the I-40 ramp and got on the freeway headed north toward I-265. I needed to get home quick, and the quickest way was the longest. In twenty minutes, I'd exited the freeway, cut through some side streets in quiet neighborhoods, and crossed Gallatin Road. I was about to turn onto my street when the thought suddenly grabbed me— maybe there's a satellite truck out in front of my house.

I skipped the turn, drove another block, turned, and parked on the street in front of a frame house with a concrete Madonna in the yard. The religious one, not the singer, although there's almost certainly a concrete pop-singing Madonna somewhere in this part of town, probably with an exposed concrete breast.

I locked the car and walked around the corner, a half block or so toward my street, then cut down the alley that ran behind

Mrs. Hawkins's house. I still can't get used to the notion of calling it mine.

East Nashville alleys are creepy, narrow brown gravel pathways barely big enough for one car to get down. Some people have garages that exit onto the alleys. Other people just let their hedges grow until the alley becomes invisible. That's when they're really dangerous.

This particular alley was strewn with amber and green broken glass mixed in with discarded syringes and the occasional waterlogged pornographic magazine cast off by a wayward youth of the male persuasion. I kept an eye out for surprises and stayed toward the center of the alley so as not to surprise anyone else. The thick overhanging branches shut out most of the sun and the air was redolent of garbage.

Mrs. Hawkins's house was the fifth one down on the left. I figured I'd hop the fence that ran along her backyard—what the hell, it was my fence now—and sneak in through the back door. But first I'd have to check out the area and make sure no one was waiting.

I approached from the garage side, figuring I could look over the hedges in Crazy Gladys's backyard and have a clear view of my front yard. I crunched over some broken glass, got to the box hedges, wove my hands carefully into the dense shrubbery, and pulled two chunks of it apart. I had a view of the street in front of my house and the driveway. It was clear: no satellite trucks, no waiting reporters, no Metro squad cars. Nothing.

I breathed a little easier, letting the pressure out of my chest slowly and trying to breathe deeply, to relax. Before backing away from the shrubbery, my eyes scanned the whole area from left to right.

Then I saw it. To my right, parked behind Crazy Gladys's house, was a silver Lincoln Town Car. I didn't connect for a second, then remembered.

It was the Reverend Hawkins's Lincoln in Crazy Gladys's driveway.

So much for that deep-breathing relaxation stuff.

Chapter 20

What in the hell was Mrs. Hawkins's son doing paying a call on Crazy Gladys? Social visit? Old friends reminiscing over a lost loved one, sharing a few treasured memories and a good cry?

Yeah, maybe, except in the years that I was Mrs. Hawkins's tenant, I never saw that silver Lincoln sitting in her driveway. She rarely mentioned her son and apparently seldom saw him. As for Gladys, Mrs. Hawkins had warned me about her, so it was tough to buy into the notion of this being a combination wake and kaffeeklatsch.

The whole idea would have given me the creeps, except it'd have to stand in line with about two dozen other problems giving me the creeps right now. I backed away from the shrubbery and stood, pondering my next move. Then it occurred to me that the neighbors might get suspicious seeing a lone guy loitering in the alley. And suspicion in this part of East Nashville is expressed by a call to the cops—if you're lucky. And a buttful of double-ought buckshot if you're not.

The rickety wooden fence that ran behind the house was chest high on me. I grabbed the top, the green-tinted mildewed wood soft and moist in my hands, and jumped as high as I could. I managed to pull myself up onto the top of the fence, then push off and land in the soft grass of the backyard with a thud. I stood back up, trying to make this appear to be a perfectly normal occurrence—after all, if a guy can't jump over his own fence onto his own damn grass, whose can he?—and strode quickly across the backyard and up the stairs to my apartment.

As I expected, the red light on the answering machine was

firing away like an Uzi knockoff in a drug deal gone sour. I hit the play button, fixed a cup of coffee, changed clothes, drank the coffee, went to the bathroom, and still the damn thing was blathering away. There was a thirty-minute tape in the machine and it was full. I didn't even bother to write any of the messages down, although I did note that I was getting a higher class of call. Even *Hard Copy* and *Entertainment Tonight* wanted an interview.

Great. Just frigging great.

I locked the door and pulled the shades, then sat at the kitchen table drumming my fingers. I could wait for Marsha to call, but if she didn't in the next five minutes, I was going to be scraping paint off the wall with my fingernails.

I opened my notebook and called the switchboard at the paper.

"Randy Tucker, please," I said when the operator answered.

"May I ask who's calling?"

"Tell him it's Mr. Floyd. P. B. Floyd," I instructed.

"Yes, Mr. Floyd. Please hold."

I laughed softly, shook my head. I was on hold for about thirty seconds before Randy came on.

"Yeah," he said, distracted.

"Hey," I said.

For the next several seconds, all I could hear was background office chatter and noises.

"Who is this?" he asked. I had his attention now.

"Who do you think?" I asked quietly.

He made a tongue-clicking sound, then sighed. "You're not pissed at me about this, are you, Harry?"

"Of course not," I said, my voice layered with smartass. "Why should I be angry with you? My life was ruined long before you came along."

"You shoulda called me, asswipe. There might've been some way to keep you out of this. But no, Mr. Hotshot Private Investigator had to play hard to get. . . ."

"You were on my list."

"That's what I'm afraid of. That I'm on your list."

"It's not *that* kind of list," I said.

"Look, Harry, what the fuck's going on?"

"They think I killed Reed and I didn't. There's no motive, no reason for me to have killed him."

"So what were you doing out there?"

"Oh, the Williamson County Sheriff's Department didn't tell you that, did they?"

"Tell me what?"

"This is off the record, okay?"

"Not a chance. You're a principal."

"Bullshit," I snapped. "Somebody else killed Reed and the case against me is so weak, those Keystone Kop bastards never need to see me again! They're just feeding you that line of shit to cover up the fact that they couldn't find their asses with both hands and an operating manual."

"They're blowing smoke at me?" he asked.

"And if I see my name in the newspaper attributed to those fumblebutts again, I'm going to start filing some goddamn lawsuits. I've had it."

"Okay," he said. "I'll work with you here, Harry. We're off the record. Anything you tell me is OTR unless I can find it and verify it somewhere else. That okay?"

"Fair enough."

"Good. Now how did you get involved with this mess?"

"Reed's wife hired me to tail him and get pictures of him with his girlfriend."

"Cool." He laughed. "America's dad. Who's the tootsie?"

"No," I said. "Not from me. Go back to Williamson County for that one."

"All right. Now what about you and Dr. Helms?"

I thought for a moment. Hell, he already knew. "We've been together for years. Not that it's anybody else's goddamn business."

"She pregnant?"

"Yeah."

"Did it ever occur to either of you that it was a lousy idea for her to autopsy a guy you're accused of killing?"

I felt my face redden. "No, damn you, it didn't. First of all, she did the autopsy *before* she knew I was involved. Besides, I didn't kill the son of a bitch in the first place. And second, no one—you understand me, *no one*—has ever questioned the integrity of Marsha Helms. If she'd found a bullet with my name on it inside the guy, it would have been turned over to the cops same as anybody else. If it had sent my sorry ass to Old Sparky, that would've been too bad. She'd have kissed me goodbye and gone on with her life."

"Whoa, cowboy, cool down. What about all the other stuff coming out of the ME's office?"

"Look, I ain't saying they ain't got a shitpot full of problems down there. I'm saying Marsha Helms didn't do anything dishonest. You got that?"

"Yeah, I got it." He was silent for a few moments, then he, surprisingly, did something reporters seldom do. He apologized. And then: "What are you going to do now?"

"Find out who killed R. J. Reed. And when I do, I'm going to give him the world's first intra-anal foot transplant."

Randy Tucker laughed out loud. "Can you notify us in advance so we can have a photographer there?"

"No way," I said. "This is between me and whoever killed him. It's personal now."

Okay, so it's personal now. What the hell does that mean? I'm sitting here practically a prisoner in my own house with my picture plastered across the afternoon paper, and a pretty solid assumption that the morning paper and the TV stations won't be far behind. Not exactly what I had in mind, but it's the hand that was dealt.

So quit moaning and play it.

I opened my notebook to the pages of notes I'd been given by Victoria Reed. The first place to start was the obvious one: Margot Horowitz, the supposed girlfriend. Might not be a bad idea to shake her tree and see what falls out.

I grabbed a clean shirt to go with my jeans and threw a sportcoat on. Just as I was about to head out the door, the phone rang again. I glared at it, wishing once again that I'd had Caller ID put in. That was next on my list.

The answering machine got the call on the fourth ring. The relays clicked and Marsha's voice came on the speaker.

"Harry, are you—"

"Hi," I said, grabbing the phone and switching the machine off. "Where are you?"

"In the office. I just got off the phone with my lawyer."

"What's he say about all this?"

"He's not happy."

"There's a lot of that going around," I said.

She sighed and I could imagine the weariness in her eyes. "I just can't believe I was so stupid. It didn't even occur to me to think I shouldn't perform the autopsy."

"Of course it didn't!" I snapped. "You didn't even know I was involved then!"

"After you called me," she said blankly, "I could have gotten Dr. Henry to sign off on the paperwork. I should have held up the paperwork."

"No, Marsha. If you'd done that, then your integrity would be out the window." I paused, took a long breath, and let it out slowly. "Look, did you follow the same procedures as always? Would another pathologist performing the same autopsy get the same results?"

"It was cut-and-dried, so to speak. A med-school student could have done it."

"Then you didn't do anything wrong."

"I wish Dr. Henry agreed with you," she said.

"Have you talked to him?"

"He called in from Chattanooga. The mayor and he had a chat last night. I'm going to get a badly needed vacation."

Something grabbed me in the middle of my chest. "What?"

"I've been placed on administrative leave with pay pending an investigation."

I had to sit down. "What kind of investigation?"

"I don't know, Harry. Dr. Henry just told me to clean out my desk. I'm putting all my files and reports in his office, then I'm heading home."

I was stunned. "When did this happen?"

"About twenty minutes ago. I'm still trying to take it all in myself."

"My God, Marsha. I'm so sorry. I mean . . . I mean . . . Hell, I don't know what I mean."

"Stop, Harry. It's not your fault. I should have known better."

"Will you be able to get out of there without running a gauntlet?"

"Most of them have gone. I'll go out the back door and sneak around to the side parking lot. Kay called the security folks next door at General. They said they'd send somebody over, but it probably won't do much good."

"When do you think you'll go back to work?"

"Dr. Henry said we'd have a better fix on this in a couple of days. We'll know just how bad it's going to be."

"Jesus, I just can't believe this. Nobody's ever questioned your integrity or your work before. On anything you've ever done before . . . How can they do this?"

"Maybe this is a message from the universe. Maybe this is God's way of keeping us humble, babe."

"Excuse me very much," I said, "but that's a message I don't need right now. I'd appreciate it if the universe could send me another message."

"Look, I've got to run. I've got a few more boxes to pack and I want to get home before rush hour and the five-o'clock news programs. Got to see myself on TV, right?"

"Be careful, Marsha. And hey—"

"Yeah?"

"For what it's worth, I love you."

She made a little rumbling sound in the back of her throat. "It's worth a lot. I love you, too. I just wonder if that's enough anymore."

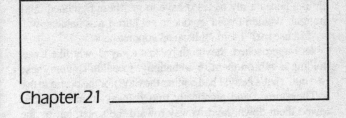

Chapter 21

I loaded up a shoulder bag with a couple of cameras, tape recorder, binoculars, and a pair of cheese sandwiches just in case I wound up sitting in a car half the night. I added an extra sweater to fill the bag out, then stepped out onto the landing.

At the foot of the stairs, peering through the back door into what had been Mrs. Hawkins's kitchen, stood the Reverend Hawkins and his wife.

"Can I help you?" I called from the top of the stairs.

The Ice Queen whirled around like somebody'd popped one in her from behind. He turned, stood ramrod stiff, or as ramrod stiff as you can with about one hundred twenty-five pounds around your waist that shouldn't be there.

"We—we were—" he stammered.

Her eyes got as big as golf balls. "We were just wondering if you were home." She finished his sentence for him, something I'm sure he was quite used to.

I leaned against the railing and crossed one ankle over the other. "I'm still up here," I said. "You'll have to climb the stairs and knock."

"Yes, I understand that. We were just—"

"I haven't removed anything of hers," I said calmly. "And I won't. It's all yours. I'd appreciate it if you'd get movers here to pick it up, but do so at your own convenience. I'm not going to be a jerk about it."

She didn't finish my sentence for me, which if she had would've ended *unlike some people I know*.

I walked down the rickety stairs, the metal creaking and

rattling beneath my feet. I'd have to get these tightened up, I thought. Wouldn't want anyone to get hurt. I was liable now.

"Excuse me," I said. "I have an appointment."

As I approached, they both backed away slowly like I was holding a gun on them or something. I couldn't figure these two out. That's okay; I had neither the time nor the desire to try.

They turned and practically trotted away from me. I followed them down the driveway toward the street, but by the time I'd gotten to the corner of the house they'd already rounded Crazy Gladys's house and headed down her driveway to retrieve the Lincoln.

"Strange ducks," I said out loud, then turned left out of my driveway and began the two-block walk to get my own car.

Call me nosy, but before I went to visit Margot Horowitz, I wanted to check one thing out. I had an address for her, a place out on Otter Creek Road off Granny White Pike. This is a part of town that wasn't exactly Belle Meade, but it was expensive and chic and exclusive. Radnor Lake, which was originally created to provide water for the L&N steam locomotives at Radnor Yard, borders Otter Creek Road and is now one of the finest urban wildlife sanctuaries in the country. It's only been in the last ten years or so that any of the land close to Radnor Lake has been parceled off for development, and the houses that were built there all started in the mid-six figures and went up from there.

The point here is that most young women fresh out of university—even Vanderbilt University—would be hard-pressed to qualify for that kind of mortgage. It might be interesting to pop over to the property tax assessor's office and see just who owns the house on Otter Creek Road.

Only problem was I couldn't get across the river. I cut over to Shelby, figuring I'd cross over I-65 on Shelby Street, cut right, and take the side streets to the Jefferson Street bridge, then cross the river into Germantown. But as I got closer to the freeway entrance, the traffic slowed and finally stopped. In the distance, from across the river, I heard faint sirens growing louder. I sat there, fuming, for about fifteen minutes as the sirens got louder and continuous, then noticed the temp gauge on the Mustang was doing its dance up into the red zone again.

Now this was a challenge. I was between Sixth and Seventh Streets, just up from the Communications Workers of America retirement homes and in the middle of a neighborhood most noted for the many varieties of Dilaudid one could get on almost every street corner. Dilaudid was, of course, just one option available. The pharmaceutical alternatives seemed endless, if that's what I was in the market for.

The problem was that if the Mustang began to seriously overheat, I'd have to kill the engine for a while. And overheated carbureted Mustangs tend to vapor lock and not want to start again. This was not a great neighborhood to break down in.

"Damn," I muttered, pulling the parking brake and stepping out of the car. I stepped up on the doorsill, stretched as tall as I could, and tried to see what was going on.

"Hey, dude!" a voice behind me called. "See anything?"

I turned, shrugged, shook my head.

Two vehicles ahead, a black guy in a T-shirt four sizes too big for him stepped out of a battered green pickup that might have been even older than the Mustang.

"I heard on da' radio they's a truck over on I-65."

I turned to the guy behind me. "Semi's over on I-65," I said.

From behind me, a young gangsta type in oversize jeans hanging so low on his hips that I wondered how he managed to stay legal walked by chanting the word *smoke* over and over again in a kind of singsong fashion. He made eye contact with me for a split second. I shook my head imperceptibly, as ahead of us a cloud of blue-black smoke billowed up from the freeway. The column thickened, looking meaner and uglier by the second as it climbed into the sky. A crowd of kids gathered on the corner in front of the grocery store with the bricked-up windows and began hooting and pointing and dancing. I turned and saw traffic backing up all the way to the top of the hill behind me.

Every once in a while, I begin to wonder if the whole damn city has gone mad or if it's just my perception of it. One thing was clear: This was no way to get across the river.

I climbed back into the Mustang, threw it in reverse, backed up as far as I could without banging the guy behind me, and U-turned into the oncoming lane. I headed out Shelby back to Fourteenth and began weaving in and out of neighborhoods, through side streets, until I made my way to the Ellington Parkway and got on I-65 north, away from the chaos behind me. I crossed into North Nashville at the Jefferson Street bridge, then cut through Germantown and got to the assessor's office a few minutes before it closed. It had taken nearly an hour to get maybe three miles, what a crow might fly if it wasn't caught in another bloody traffic jam.

"I heard it was a tanker truck," one lady said to another as they exited the building just as I walked in. "I'll have to go through town."

"Somebody told me they heard a bomb went off," her companion answered.

I assumed they were talking about the conflagration on the freeway. The half-hourly radio traffic reports during rush hour were the most-listened-to programs in the whole city.

The bank of computer terminals for public use was empty. A few straightforward keypunches will find out who owns any piece of property in the city. I typed in Margot Horowitz's address. I was almost willing to bet the listed owner on the property tax rolls was the same corporation that owned R. J. Reed's farm in Williamson County.

The machine flickered green for a split second after I hit the enter button, and then the name M. J. HOROWITZ flashed onscreen.

The property was assessed at $275,200, which seemed low, but property-tax assessments are usually lower than market value. Just a little way in which the politicians fool us into thinking our taxes aren't as high as we think they are.

Victoria Reed had said Margot was in her mid, maybe late twenties. She'd just graduated a year or so earlier and was working as a secretary, personal assistant, whatever, to R.J.

Unless he paid the hell out of her, she had to have some other resources to be able to afford a place like that.

"Hmmm, maybe I should just go ask her," I murmured.

"Pardon?" said the receptionist at the desk behind the terminals.

"Oh, nothing. Just thinking out loud."

"Yes," she said, smiling. "I do that, too. It's the only way to keep your sanity around here."

I smiled back at her. If she only knew . . .

An hour later I pulled left off Granny White Pike onto Otter Creek Road into a section of new homes that looked like they catered to what the locals called "HMO millionaires," the legions of entrepreneurs who'd moved into Nashville in the last twenty years or so and gotten rich creating the "revolution" in health care. Only this revolution was more like the French Revolution than the American, and with a little luck the ones who started it would wind up on the guillotine just like their forebears.

I checked the numbers as I went by and noted Margot Horowitz's house. I kept going, though, driving into the wildlife sanctuary area and pulling off into a parking lot on the left. The part of Otter Creek Road that actually went through the park had been closed off to traffic. Joggers, bicycle riders, dog walkers, early-evening hikers all moved back and forth on the road in front of me. I checked my watch: 5:45. The park would be crowded with people taking walks or exercise at the end of the day. It had warmed up, was maybe seventy degrees now, with a gorgeous orange and blue sunset settling into a cool, dry night.

I stood there thinking, people-watching, trying to figure out the best way to approach Margot Horowitz. This was the part of the job that always gave me just a twinge of butterflies. Stage fright might be a better word, since there's a certain amount of acting you have to pull off to get people to talk to you when you know and they know it's in their best interests to keep quiet.

It really was staggeringly beautiful out here. If I lived this close to the lake, I know where I'd be every night about this time. I leaned against the car and put the binoculars to my eyes, scanning the area, enjoying the warm sun on my shoulders, the relative quiet. I was a dozen worlds away from Shelby Avenue and the Dilaudid corner.

The road curved up a hill to my left and disappeared into the trees. I focused the binoculars and followed the road down in front of me and to my right, just watching people and killing time more than anything else. I had turned the Margot Horowitz question over to my subconscious, hoping that somewhere down in all the bubbling muck was an answer that would come to me eventually.

In that steady stream of interior monologue that most of us have going on in every waking moment, I was wondering just how long *eventually* would be when the binoculars caught and froze on Margot Horowitz walking up the road in front of me.

It caught me so by surprise that my hands kept moving before my brain could tell them to stop. I jerked, gasped slightly, and snapped the glasses back. I twirled the focus knob. Was it really her?

I got a good look as she approached from maybe twenty or twenty-five yards away. I froze the image like a mental snapshot, then pulled the photo out of my pocket that Victoria Reed had given me, the one taken at the barbecue last summer down on the Williamson County farm.

Yep, it was her.

I smiled. Maybe my luck was changing. I brought the glasses back up and got a closer look at her. She had black hair, cut just above the shoulders, with loose curves that bounced as she walked. Silver-rimmed oval glasses perched on her nose, and there were dimples on her cheeks big enough to spot from this distance. She was maybe five feet five inches and wore a pair of khaki walking shorts and a pullover shirt. She looked like there'd once been a little baby fat on her, but not anymore. She wasn't knockout drop-dead gorgeous, but she was attractive enough in an urban New England kind of way.

Apparently, she was out for her evening constitutional. Margot Horowitz walked with a steady pace that was more than a stroll but less than serious hiking. If she was in mourning, it didn't show. Nobody could have ever guessed she was carrying on with a man who'd just been shoved underwater in a Jacuzzi and held there until he stopped squirming.

Or maybe she wasn't in mourning because she was the one who'd done the shoving.

I had to think fast, and in the end I fell back on the last refuge of those who lack finesse, cunning, and wit: blatant honesty.

I crossed the parking lot and hopped onto the street just as Margot Horowitz was striding past me in the middle of the road.

"Hi, Margot," I said, regular old how-the-hell-are-you conversational tone.

She slowed, a quizzical look on her face. "Hello," she said.

I quickened my pace and caught up with her, a step behind and to her left.

"How ya doing?"

She looked back, still walking. "Do I know you?"

"Not exactly," I said. "I'm an acquaintance of R.J.'s."

She stopped, and faced me with a stern look. "You knew R.J.?"

"Well, we met," I said. "But he might not remember it."

"Who are you?"

"Name's Harry. Harry Denton."

She studied me for a moment. She was young, unlined, attractive in that healthy, vibrant way characteristic of twentysomethings before time and mileage start collecting the toll. Her most distinctive feature was her eyes, which were a deep unsullied brown and large, piercing. As the realization of who she was talking to came to her, though, her eyes narrowed and her lips tightened.

"I know who you are," she said, her voice tense, low. "I saw your picture in the paper. Get away from me."

She stomped away quickly. I kept up with her, right beside her.

"Look, I just want to talk to you."

"I'm going to scream," she said. "I swear, I'll scream."

"Just let me ask you one question," I said. "Please."

She ignored me, kept going. We were headed up the hill now, toward the earthen dam that created the lake.

"Look, if you're afraid to talk to me because of what you've read in the papers . . ."

She stopped midstep, turned with her hands on her hips. "Afraid? I don't think so, buddy. I can handle you just fine."

"I didn't have anything to do with R.J.'s death. I just found him," I said.

"Yeah, and you found him because Victoria hired you to spy on us!" She kept her voice low, her teeth almost gritted, as a pair of lean runners wearing Walkman headphones padded past us on the way up the hill.

"What would you have done if you'd been married to him and you thought he was having an affair?"

Her face reddened. "I don't know what she told you, but we were *not* having an affair!"

That one caught me by surprise. It was my turn to narrow my eyes and squint at her. "You telling me you weren't sleeping with the guy?"

She puffed her cheeks out, looked away from me a second, then spewed a long sigh. "No, no thanks to R.J. Like it's any of your business."

"Look, Margot, Victoria thought he was screwing around and she was just trying to protect herself. People do that when they're threatened. And now that he's dead, believe it or not, she's heartbroken. She's hired me to find out who killed him."

Margot softened, but just for a moment and only a little. "Well," she said gently. "I wish you luck."

"Thanks. I'll need it," I offered.

"What was your question?" she asked.

I stared at her. Okay, I could see what R.J. might have seen in her. "What?"

"Your question. You said you had one question."

"I said one question, but that was just to keep you from screaming. Truth is, I've got lots of questions."

She turned. "Walk with me then. I've got to meet someone for dinner in an hour."

Margot went back to her walking pace, rolling smoothly up the hill with me behind her wondering how long I could keep up without getting short of breath. I hadn't had much exercise lately.

"I just can't buy that his murder was a random act. Whoever killed him had to know him," I said. "If you could just tell me about him, maybe it would help me understand. His wife told me a lot, but maybe her perspective was a little skewed."

She turned to me. "Just a bit."

"The better I know R. J. Reed, the better my chances of figuring out who in his world gained something by his death."

"What makes you think I didn't kill him?" She began pumping her arms in time with her steps, smoothly accelerating to what was beginning to feel like a race walk. We entered the curve that wound around one side of the lake. A fallen tree lay out in the water maybe twenty feet. Two tortoises as big around as large pizzas sunned themselves on the main trunk a few inches above the water.

"Maybe you did," I said, starting to notice my breathing. "But I don't think so. For one thing, R.J. was no delicate little flower. It took somebody with some weight and upper body strength to hold him under."

"Maybe somebody knocked him out."

"No, not a mark on him. The tox screens aren't back yet, so maybe he was toasted. But there were no wineglasses or empty bottles around. No roaches, no evidence of drug usage."

Margot shook her head as she walked. "They won't find anything. R.J. didn't use, and he didn't drink a lot. White wine with dinner, that sort of thing. He told me when he was younger, he did a fair amount of coke, doobie, yuppie shit like that. But he'd given it up a long time ago."

"That's what Victoria told me," I said. "So the only way you could've killed him is if you caught him by surprise and were so incredibly pissed off at him that it put a big red *S* on your chest."

"Don't discount that," she said, eyes intently staring ahead. "I could get pretty mad at him."

"Yeah, maybe," I said, huffing. "But I got a gut feeling you didn't."

We walked on a dozen yards more in silence.

"Did you love him?" I asked.

She turned quickly. "God, you're direct."

"When I have to be . . ."

Her head swiveled back ahead. "I was fond of him, most of the time. He had a crush on me, was always trying to get me interested. But he didn't push, at least not hard. He knew I'd split."

I began pumping my arms as well. Any faster, I was going to have to break into a jog. "What did you do for him? Professionally, I mean."

She smiled. "It was only professional. Anything else he needed he got somewhere else. He sure as hell didn't get it at home."

"Maybe that's another thing I need to examine. Think he had another girlfriend?"

"Maybe, but I doubt it. He'd had them before. But after I'd worked for him a year, I began to be able to read him. Part of the job."

"Which was?"

"Everything. Nobody ever expected The Book to do so well. That's what he always called it—*The Book*. Truth is, he could barely bring himself to say the title out loud."

"So when The Book took off, he was overwhelmed?"

"Completely. His life was a mess. I took over his office, scheduled his appointments, fielded thirty to fifty phone calls a day. Most important, I learned how to say no for him. Once you're on the *Times* bestseller list, you have to start turning down the blue-haired little old ladies and their book clubs or that's all you'll do for the rest of your life."

"That sounds like a problem"—puff-puff—"anybody'd be glad to have."

"Yeah, but I think somewhere in the back of his mind, R.J. had some real literary ambitions. This book was such a fluke, and when Travis and Karl started the marketing, it was like a cloudburst. And it was raining money."

Sweat was beginning to break out on my forehead, but she wasn't even glistening yet.

"They'd never handled anything like this before," she continued. "It made them. All the marketing possibilities. A sequel is already written and in the pipeline."

"I heard," I said, panting. "*Life's Little Maintenance Manual, Volume II.* . . . Is the world ready?"

She turned. "The world was screaming for it. And R.J. got four million for signing the contract."

"Wow! That's getting up there in the realm of serious money. So you guys were busy."

"Pretty soon I was going to need an assistant."

"There's something I still don't understand. Victoria said you just got out of Vanderbilt a couple years ago."

"Yeah, came to Nashville for my master's in English."

"With that kind of background, how come you took what was essentially a secretary's job?"

She smiled again, cocked her head in my direction. "I graduated with a degree in English and honors from Emery as well. You know what having two English degrees from exclusive private Southern universities makes you?"

I shook my head. "No."

"Unemployable."

I laughed.

"At least being the personal assistant to a famous, bestselling author had some cachet to it," she continued. "And if you wanted to work in the book business, it beat the hell out of being a junior editorial assistant sharing a one-bedroom flat in Queens with three other girls."

"Apparently the pay was better, too," I said, fighting off wheezing. Jeez, I didn't want to embarrass myself any more than I had to. "Judging from the house back there. You don't get that kind of mortgage on sixteen grand a year."

She stopped cold in the middle of the street. "You nosy bastard," she said, panting a bit herself now. "How dare you!"

"Property taxes are public record," I said. "All it took was a visit to the assessor's office, M. J. Horowitz."

"As if it's any of your damn business, M. J. Horowitz is my

father. My father started a managed-care company in Atlanta and has done very well, thank you very much. He bought this house as an investment when I came here to do graduate work. He'll sell it at a profit when I leave town. It was cheaper in the long run than paying rent for an apartment."

"Yeah," I said. "Sorry."

"No, I'm glad you snooped around. Now you know that I didn't have a motive for killing R.J. either. I wasn't sleeping with him, wasn't in love with him, needed nothing from him except an insignificantly small paycheck."

"I believe you," I said.

"The only thing I gained from R.J.'s death was unemployment."

"What are you going to do now?" I asked.

A thin film of sweat shimmered on her upper lip in the dying light. "I don't know. Truth is, I could help Victoria straighten out all this stuff if she'd let me."

"Have you talked to her?"

"She called me right after I first heard the news. I was so broken up, I could barely talk. Then later I tried to call her back. She wouldn't take the call. Her son even told me not to come to the funeral." There was genuine sadness in her voice.

"You want me to say something to her? Maybe I can help."

The edges of her lips curled up in the slightest trace of a smile. "No, Mr. White Knight," she said. "This is a piece of my life that I'd just as soon forget. I'll probably go back to Atlanta, maybe live at home for a bit. My parents will give me a place to stay and some space to decompress in. Then I'll get on to whatever's next." She laughed. "Maybe I'll get a Ph.D."

"Okay, Dr. Horowitz," I said. "That'll work. One last question."

"Yes, brave Sir Harry?"

"If you were taking bets, who would you think killed him?"

She thought for a moment. "I don't know. But there was so much money. So much money. More than any of them had ever seen before."

Margot Horowitz looked back into my eyes, hard and deep,

and I did everything I could to keep from having this momentary attraction to her, largely without success.

"I'd follow the money, Harry. Follow the money."

Chapter 22

Follow the money.

She was a smart lady; young, special, and smart. What a combination. With a little luck, she'd go far and do a lot, as long as life didn't beat the hell out of her.

God, I sound old.

While I liked Margot Horowitz and was almost relieved to honestly believe she hadn't killed R. J. Reed, this didn't put me any closer to finding out who had. And while there was clearly a money trail, where did it start? And how did it come to end in the death of R. J. Reed?

I left Margot Horowitz in the parking lot just below Radnor Lake as the sun was setting behind a row of trees. The day was nearly at an end, but I wasn't ready to call it quits. I checked my watch; the worst of the rush hour should be over.

The air was cool, dry as I turned right on Granny White Pike and headed back toward the freeway. I popped onto I-65 and made it back downtown in about twenty minutes. The center had pretty well cleared out by the time I found a parking space in front of the main branch of the public library. I'd taken a chance and gotten lucky: the library was open until nine.

Inside the business-reference section, I sat down in front of a computer terminal and typed in the words *Spearhead Press*. In a couple of seconds, I had a long list of newspaper articles and dates. I routed that list to a printer, then typed in the names of the two principals, Karl Sykes and Travis Webber, and ran a printout of those articles. Finally, just for grins, I typed in R. J. Reed's name and got a list of a dozen or so local newspaper articles. I punched the key to print those, and while they were printing, I got ten dollars worth of quarters out of the dollar-bill changer next to the Xerox machines. It was going to be a long night.

There wasn't time to read the articles. I threaded in microfilm, reeled as quickly as possible to the right day, found each article, then dropped a quarter into the slot to print it. It was monkey work; a high school intern could have done it. Unfortunately, I had neither the intern nor the monkey.

I tried to keep them in chronological order, but invariably the growing pile of paper got scrambled. What the hell, I'd straighten them out later. Truth is, it felt good to be working again, to be in that mode where focus becomes so clear, so intense, that one finally becomes unconscious even of time passing.

I was threading the last reel through the pulleys when a thin woman in glasses tapped me on the shoulder and announced the library was closing in fifteen minutes. I'd dropped almost three hours without realizing it. I also noticed for the first time that I was getting kind of hungry as well.

I put the last microfilm box back on the cart for reshelving, gathered up the three-quarter-inch stack of paper, and headed for the front door. It was nine o'clock, and it had been a long day. A little dinner, perhaps a beer; yeah, that'd work.

I stepped into a phone booth in the lobby by the checkout desk and dialed Marsha's number. She answered the phone half asleep, told me she was already in bed and about ready to drop off. I said good night, told her I'd call her in the morning, and was privately relieved that she didn't want company. Maybe I should've taken that as a warning sign, but I was too glad to have the rest of the night to myself.

I decided to leave the car where it was; I was only a couple of blocks from my office and it was a pleasant enough night to walk. I strolled up the hill in front of the library and around the corner to the Huddle House, a small twenty-four-hour diner attached to a downtown motel that always struck me as a little seedy. I was in the mood for seedy, though, and felt right at home. The place was practically empty, so I took a booth to myself and ordered a cup of decaf and some bacon and eggs.

The waitress had a tattooed rose on one hand and a man's name—P-A-U-L—across the knuckles of the other. She poured the coffee, gave me a dentally challenged smile, then walked over behind the cash register and lit a cigarette while waiting for the cook to finish my order.

I spread the photocopied articles in front of me and decided to start by cross-referencing the duplicates. Once I had the extra copies off to one side, I divided everything up by subject and put them in chronological order. I felt very organized and virtuous and even a bit obsessive-compulsive. Okay, I reasoned, you can't force order on to your life but you can impose order on your stuff.

I had three separate piles by then: one of articles on R. J. Reed and *Life's Little Maintenance Manual*, one that included articles about the publishing house and its two founders, and a third of duplicates.

R.J.'s pile came first. The very first article published in the local media about R. J. Reed was a short little squib on the book page of the afternoon paper. For a town its size, Nashville has the reputation of being a "good book town," and both the dailies carry weekly book pages. The afternoon paper, though, is much better at covering local and unknown writers, so I wasn't terribly surprised to find R.J.'s first piece there.

It was a short review and went pretty easy on him, I thought. The reviewer quoted from one or two of the less saccharine parts of the book and called it a great gift idea.

Not exactly the sort of juice that gets the attention of the Pulitzer Prize committee . . .

That was the only piece on R.J. for almost six months. I surmised this was the time when he was driving around the country hustling every bookstore clerk, wholesaler, and drugstore paperback buyer in the country. Then, about six months after publication, there was a short notice in the weekend section about R.J.'s upcoming appearance on *Oprah*. Apparently, even the TV columnist didn't pick up on what that meant. Two weeks later, though, R.J. was lead feature in the "Living" section, and the story of his breathtaking rise was impressive.

I scanned the feature, having heard most of this stuff from

Victoria and Margot. Nothing new, nothing revealing, just the same old PR crap: R. J. Reed as the emerging nexus of New Age philosophy and family values.

"Yuk," I muttered as the waitress brought the plate of bacon and eggs and slid them in front of me.

"C'mon, you haven't even tried 'em yet."

I looked up, smiled. "Not a comment on the food. It's the reading material."

"Yeah?" she asked, snapping her chewing gum as she talked. "Whatcha reading?"

"Articles about a guy who wrote a book."

"Yeah? Which one?"

Okay, I thought, *I can play along with her.*

"Book called *Life's Little Maintenance Manual.*"

"Oh!" she squealed. "You know, I *never* read books. I mean, *never!* But my sister bought me a copy of that book and I swear, it changed my life! *Really!*"

"I believe you," I said. "Honest."

"Swear to God!"

"I *believe* you."

"You know, the guy that wrote that? He's from Nashville!"

"Yeah, I was just reading about him."

"God, one of these days I'd just love to meet him. He's so handsome and *so wise!*"

"Yeah, well," I offered, "maybe one of these days you will."

She turned, walked away still muttering about how much *Life's Little Maintenance Manual* meant to her. It had changed her life, taught her to live again, given her new insights into what a meaningful life meant.

Is it just me, or has the entire world been dumbed down to imbecility?

Suddenly I was very depressed.

A half hour later, I'd managed to scarf down the greasy bacon and eggs and thin coffee. I walked over to Seventh Avenue and down the darkened streets to my office. The air was heavier, wetter, with the threat of one of those early spring rains that are sometimes lazy, moody drizzles and sometimes full-scale gully washers.

I stepped over a sleeping transient in the entranceway to my building and unlocked the front door, locked it back behind me, then went down the darkened hallway. The building super had taken to turning off all the hall lights at night in a desperate effort to cut expenses enough to stay in business. I felt my way down the hallway, then by memory up the flight of stairs. On the second floor, the dim light of an exit sign provided enough light to keep me from tripping over my own feet.

The second floor was empty. I thought maybe Slim and Ray would be up there, this being the time of night when they often got the most work done, but they must have been off playing a gig somewhere or else down on Second Avenue swilling beers and trying to pick up the tourist babes.

I unlocked my office door and flicked on the light. It had been a long day, like a year had passed since I was in here talking to Victoria about her husband. Before leaving, I'd decided to hell with telephones and unplugged mine. The answering machine sat there blessedly mute. I didn't expect any calls at this time of night but figured that I really should have the answering machine on duty during office hours. Somebody might even call with a paying gig, like I had time to deal with anything else. Right . . .

I cleared away as much empty space on my desk as I could find and spread the photocopied articles out in front of me once again. This time, no tattooed gushing waitresses would interrupt my train of thought. I quickly scanned the articles on R.J. There was nothing new up until the last one, which was dated two months ago. It announced the signing of R.J.'s deal for a sequel to the book, with an unnamed source confirming what Margot Horowitz had told me: four million bucks for a book it probably took him a couple of weeks to write.

"Jeez," I whispered. "I'm in the wrong business."

It's like playing the lottery, I thought. You throw these things out there and if the public bites, then it's a license to print money. Or maybe it's like those machines that I used to play at the state fair when I was a kid, one of those glass cages with all the stuffed animals in the bottom and a metal claw at the top suspended by a cable, and you put in a quarter and turn the wheels and the claw drops and grabs your prize.

Only instead of little stuffed animals, it's a gagillion books in the bottom of the glass cage and the publishers and the reading public pumping in the quarters and dropping the claw. And if the claw grabs you, then you're the prize.

The Claw, by God, grabbed R. J. Reed, grabbed him and took him to the top and dropped him down the chute and made him the prize.

I filed the articles on R.J. in a separate pile. I felt like I knew him about as well as I ever could without having met him, or at least meeting him when he could acknowledge the introduction. I turned to the ones on Spearhead Press, feeling like the effort was probably futile but not knowing what the hell else to do.

The early articles on Spearhead Press and the two men who founded it predated the publication of *Life's Little Maintenance Manual.* The initial article announced the publication of their first book, a history of evangelical fundamentalism during the Civil War. I didn't know there had been any evangelical fundamentalism during the Civil War. The book was entitled *Witnessing to War* and was written by a retired professor from the American Baptist Bible College. Published in hardcover, it sold for thirty-five dollars and was nearly eight hundred pages long.

"Jesus," I muttered, "bet they sold the hell out of that one."

There was a little background on the company in that first article, and later articles filled in the missing pieces. Sykes and Webber had come to Spearhead Press from two different directions. Sykes had worked in Chicago for an academic press that went under in the early Eighties. Webber had worked for one of those TV ministries and left that field about the same time. None of the articles mentioned why he'd left that career. They'd both wound up in Nashville working for a religious marketing company, a distributor of hymnals and Sunday school manuals, leaflets and prayer books.

In the mid-Eighties, after some success with the company, both Sykes and Webber lost their jobs. Again, no mention of

why, although the mid-Eighties marked the beginning of
the corporate downsizing bloodbaths. No jobs were safe,
white-collar middle-management jobs especially. They both
got caught in a corporate tailspin and plowed a big one.

At least that was my guess. I made plenty of notes on
the progress of the company, which was traced in a series of
articles in the business sections of both dailies. When the company hit with *Life's Little Maintenance Manual*, the articles
got bigger, flashier, and were accompanied by color photos
of Sykes and Webber that sometimes were bigger than the
articles themselves.

Last year, Webber's new home in Brentwood was added to
the annual mansion tour, a fund-raising event for the cancer so-
ciety. Sykes had built a new home in Mount Juliet, a suburb out
I-40 toward Knoxville. A reproduction of Twelve Oaks from
Gone with the Wind, it sat in the middle of almost fifty acres in
Wilson County.

Sykes and Webber had come a long way. The company had
started in the basement of Sykes's rented home off Lebanon
Road. And as Victoria Reed had told me, and I'd seen for myself, they now owned their corporate headquarters building in
Maryland Farms.

The Claw had grabbed them, too.

I finished up my notes and collected the highlighted articles
into a file folder. It was well after eleven, and I suddenly felt
exhausted and a bit apprehensive at having to walk four or five
blocks this late at night to get to my car. I gathered everything
up and locked my office behind me. I had solid information
now, enough background to get started. Tomorrow, the real
digging would begin.

I took the stairs slowly as my eyes adjusted to the darkness.
My hand ran down the dust-covered handrail. Down the hall, I
heard a scurrying noise.

"Great," I said out loud, more to hear my own voice than
anything else. "Rodentia. I've got to find another office."

I made my way down the hall and stopped at the glass doors
leading out onto Seventh Avenue. A light drizzle fell through
the sulfurous amber glow of the streetlights. Whoever had been

sleeping in the entrance foyer had wandered off to another sidewalk motel.

What bothered me was the dark sedan parked out front, across Seventh, in a No Parking zone on the street next to a parking lot. It was big, blocky, like an old LTD or a Crown Victoria.

I stopped, studied the car for a moment. The windows were smoked, nearly opaque. I hid in the shadows for a second, then decided I was being silly. I was too tired for this crap.

The key turned in the lock and the heavy plate-glass door went outward as I pushed it. I stepped out, locked the door behind me. As I turned back toward the street, the driver's-side window lowered smoothly, like an electric window. I tucked my head and held the folders in close to me, then started up the street.

"Hello, Harry," a voice called from within the sedan.

I stopped.

"How ya doin'?"

I turned, my stomach tightening. I squinted, tried to see inside the car.

"Who is that?" I said, my voice low, almost as if I didn't want anyone to overhear me.

"A friend. Step over."

I looked both ways, up and down Seventh Avenue. The streets were deserted, deadly quiet, with only the slight misting sound of a falling sprinkle. Cautiously, I stepped into the street, walked about halfway across Seventh, stopped. If whoever inside was coming out after me, I had half a running start on them.

If they had something more effective in mind, like a pistol, I was history anyway.

"Who is it?" I said.

The dome light flicked on inside the car and a hulking man turned to me from behind the wheel.

It was Lieutenant Howard Spellman, head of the Metro police department's homicide squad. I sighed, relieved, and stepped over to the car.

"Howard, you scared the shit out of me."

"How are you, Harry?" His voice was low, careful.

"About ten years older than I was two minutes ago. What are you doing here?"

"I was just cruising around and saw the Mustang parked in front of the library. Figured you might still be working late."

"So you just decided to stop by for a social visit, right? C'mon, Howard, don't bullshit a bullshitter. What's going on?"

"Get in," he said. "I'll drive you to your car."

"Actually, I thought I'd just walk. You got something to say, say it."

"Get in the frigging car, Harry."

I leaned down. "You want to tell me what the—"

"Now, damn it."

All things considered, it didn't sound like a request. I shrugged, thought to myself *What now?*, crossed in front of the car, and climbed in.

Spellman wore the same rumpled suit I always saw him in. Jeez, I thought, real cops really are like the ones on TV. His tie was pulled down and he was starting to get a little rank. Must have been a long day.

"What's up, Howard?"

He started the car, jerked it into gear, pulled a U-turn in the middle of Seventh, and headed up the hill toward the state capitol.

"I been reading about you in the papers, bud."

"Yeah, well, I hate to fall back on clichés, but don't believe everything you read."

He chuckled, brought the car to a stop at the light on Church. "I don't. But sounds like you've gotten yourself in a rack of shit this time."

"I think it's just some wild imaginations down in Williamson County."

"I wouldn't take this too lightly if I were you, Harry. I spent six weeks at the FBI academy with D'Angelo. He's no small-town cop."

I stared out the window, waiting for the light to change. "Yeah, but I'm not sure it's him. There's a smartassed little punk of an assistant DA down there who seems to have a hard-on for me."

I saw Spellman grin in the green glow of the stoplight as it changed. "You do have that effect on people."

We drove up the hill to the next corner and made a left to circle around in front of the library. I sat silently, wondering what was going on. Howard braked to a stop behind the Mustang and killed the engine.

Spellman leaned into the corner made by the door and the edge of the seat and propped his feet up on the transmission hump.

"You look tired, Howard," I said. "What are you doing up this late?"

"It's been a long day," he said. We sat there a moment longer and I began to feel those flickers in my gut again.

"I'm doing it, Harry," he said. "Next month."

I cocked my head toward him, eyebrow raised.

"Bagging it," he continued. "I'm taking my retirement."

I smiled. "Good for you."

"My oldest boy's down in Florida working on a dive boat. He got me interested in it."

"No shit," I said. "Howard the diver."

"Made a deal on a boat down there. We sold the house. The wife's home packing now. Got an apartment outside Key West. We're going to open a dive shop. I drive the boat, the kid'll be divemaster. The wife'll keep the books."

"Every cop's dream," I said. "Retire to Florida."

"Yeah," he said.

"So is this just your way of saying goodbye? Sitting outside my office in the middle of the night?"

He sat there a moment longer, saying nothing and staring out through the windshield.

"Harry, I seen you fuck up before," he said after about thirty seconds of awkward silence. "You'll probably fuck up again. It's not your fault; you can't help it, I guess."

"Thanks, Howard. I appreciate your understanding."

"I'm worried about you this time, though."

"Man, I didn't kill R. J. Reed. There's nothing they can hang on me. They're just blowing smoke 'cause they got nobody else. It'll blow ov—"

"That ain't what I'm talking about," he interrupted.

I tried to study his face, but it was too dark. "Want to tell me what you *are* talking about?"

He drew in a deep breath, then let it out in a long sigh. "Harry, we been getting calls. Calls about your landlady."

Something inside me went numb and I started hearing a lot of wind in my ears, like that familiar old feeling of picking up a conch shell and holding it to the side of your head.

"What kind of calls?"

I saw his tongue catch the light and glisten as he licked his lips nervously. "Some people have been complaining that maybe you had something to do with it."

I could hear my own heartbeat above the wind now.

"What the hell—" I stammered. "I mean, she had a heart attack, died. I wasn't even there. I mean, what's his name, Jack Maples, was there. He said it was natural—"

Then it hit me.

"Goddamn it!" I snapped, slapping the dashboard, suddenly furious.

"What?"

"It's that son-of-a-bitch son of hers, isn't it?" I demanded. "She left me the house and some money and the lawyer told him if he contested the will, it'd tie up everything for years. So he's decided to get it this way."

Howard stared at me.

"Am I right?" I yelled.

"Calm down," Howard said.

"Let the bastard prove it! I'll sue his ass for defamation so bad. . . . If he wants a war, I'll give him one."

"We've got a statement from someone, Harry."

My chest locked up, midbreath. "What statement?"

"A statement from someone who says they saw you tampering with the phone box outside Mrs. Hawkins's house the day before she died. They think you were disabling the phones so she couldn't call for help."

I slid down on the vinyl just a little, my butt forward, my shoulders sagged.

"That's Crazy Gladys next door. She's nuts, Howard. Besides, that was *after* Mrs. Hawkins died. My phone had been turned off because I forgot to pay the bill. I switched the wires at the entrance bridge so I could call out on her line—"

"Save it, Harry. It's not my case. I'm not on this one."

"You mean you guys are taking this seriously?"

"We don't have any choice," he said.

"What's going to happen?" I asked blankly. This can't be happening, I thought. This isn't real.

"The family's pushing for an exhumation. They want an autopsy, which given what's going on in the ME's office, is a bit of a problem. We'll probably have to send the body down to Memphis to the medical school. The farther away from Nashville, the better."

"This is insane," I said. "This is crazy. I don't believe this. You can't believe I killed her."

"I don't. I also don't believe Doc Marsha did anything hinky on the Reed autopsy either. But it's appearances, Harry. When something looks rotten, you gotta check it out."

I turned and faced him. "Just tell me one thing. How bad is it? Do I need a lawyer?"

"The truth?" he answered. "Probably. But if you get one, it's only going to make you look like you've got something to hide."

"Who's handling the case?" I asked. "Who's going to be calling me?"

"Fouch," he said.

"E.D.'s a good man. He'll be fair."

"That's right. Be straight with him and you'll be okay."

"Yeah, right," I said. "And the good guys always win."

"I'm sorry, Harry."

I stared ahead through the windshield. "And this conversation never happened, right?"

Howard nodded. "Dive boat means a lot to me. I ain't going to jeopardize my retirement."

"I understand."

"Good night, Harry. Watch your ass."

"Yeah." I sighed. "Guess I'd better."

I opened the door and stepped out onto the sidewalk. The drizzle had turned into a light but steady rain. I felt it running through my hair onto my scalp and down the sides of my face, but it was like it wasn't really me there.

Like it was somebody else standing there at midnight watching Howard Spellman pull away in the rain.

Chapter 23

I'd stopped dreaming again. I took that as a bad sign.

Sometime in the middle of the night, I finally fell asleep for a little while. About three hours later, I awoke before sunrise, trying to digest what it felt like to be accused of not just one but two murders. In my mind was this image of Mrs. Hawkins on the bathroom tile floor, curled up like a little kid asleep in front of the television. Only it wasn't any sleep she'd ever wake up from.

Damn it, this wasn't right. The old lady deserved to have her rest. For that fat blubbery bastard son of hers and his icy wife to dig her up and subject her to an autopsy, all in the name of defying her wishes and getting back at me, was a travesty of filial love. They should be ashamed of themselves.

There had to be a way of stopping it. But how? I wasn't a blood relative, and the chances of the police or the courts forbidding an autopsy at the request of the person the family says had something to do with the deceased person being dead in the first place. . .

Nah, not a chance.

This one was out of my hands. Let it go. If that's how the Reverend Hawkins wants to respect the memory of his mother, to hell with him. I've got other things to do.

I showered and brushed my teeth, then fixed a pot of coffee and waited for the sun to come up. The newspaper hadn't even arrived yet, so I sat with my copy of *Life's Little Maintenance Manual* and drank several cups of coffee. I hadn't noticed it before, but there was an acknowledgment page. R.J. thanked his wife and his kids for their patience, support, and understanding, *blah-blah-blah*. He thanked his dead father for imparting the wisdom contained herein to him—*oh, yuk*—and he thanked his editor.

"Hmmm," I said out loud. "Editor . . ."

I jotted the name down in my notes: Erica Benedict. Sykes and Webber had mentioned her, but I hadn't thought of her since. She was another person who might be worth tracking down.

I reread the book again, which took all of fifteen minutes, and decided that I'd gleaned about as much out of it as I could. Thank God, I thought, that means I don't have to read it anymore.

I flipped on the television and sat there watching the news without really taking much of it in. It was background noise, chatter, just stuff to fill the silence while my head ran around in circles trying to figure out who could have wanted R. J. Reed dead and why. The only thing I could come up with was that I didn't have enough information to go on.

Whenever someone's murdered, someone else benefits. It's one of the unbreakable rules of murder. That benefit might be a ton of money or power. It might be something as simple as revenge for a perceived slight or wrong, or jealousy and possessiveness. Hell, it could be anything, up to and including the twisted sexual gratification of the serial sex murderer. The world is full of reasons for killing somebody.

The problem is that I can't see any benefit to killing R. J. Reed. Sure, he left insurance to his wife and family—that's why that idiot assistant DA down in Williamson County thinks Victoria hired me to kill him—but he can't possibly have left enough to make up for the millions he was earning as a famous author and celebrity. In fact, even if Victoria Reed was mad enough at R.J. to kill him, she'd be cutting off her nose to spite her face.

Maybe not, I thought. He'd turned in the manuscript to *Life's Little Maintenance Manual, Volume II*. She'd almost certainly get to keep the four mil advance. And in this rather twisted culture of ours, Reed's murder was probably going to create a hell of a sales jump, at least for a while.

"Yeah," I said out loud to the television, chuckling. "It's probably not the first time an author's been murdered as part of a marketing plan."

Then I thought about that for a moment. Maybe I just didn't get enough sleep last night, but why not? Maybe I needed to look at this differently.

" 'Scrazy," I muttered, getting up to get more coffee. Besides, Willard Scott was about to kiss some old lady on her hundred-and-tenth birthday and I wasn't sure I could handle that. Even I have my limits.

Yeah, that's crazy. The book was going to sell like hell anyway, if the first book was a sign of things to come. And whoever killed R. J. Reed had squelched any possibility of bringing to the public the wisdom of *Life's Little Maintenance Manual, Volume III* and beyond. Maybe the screen savers and the refrigerator magnets would keep them afloat, but I doubted it.

This is frustrating. On the other hand, it beats standing around trying to figure out how to convince someone I didn't commit two murders. Innocent until proven guilty works fine, but only up to a point.

I sat down with another cup of coffee just as Willard was segueing into a commercial. I gazed at the screen, again without paying much attention to what was on. Something about some revolutionary new design for sanitary napkins. It looked to me kind of like a flattened space shuttle. You know, I just don't keep up with these things like I used to.

Then the top-of-the-hour news came on and the anchorperson led off with the upcoming funeral of R. J. Reed, one of America's most beloved and celebrated authors. He was to be buried at two P.M. today at, of course, Mount Olivet Cemetery, Nashville's cemetery to the stars. Nearly every prominent member of every prominent family in Nashville history was planted up there off Lebanon Road, on a hill overlooking a company that sells salvaged building supplies.

Victoria Reed had told me about the funeral, had said it was okay if I wanted to attend. I hadn't given it much thought, but I wasn't at all sure that was such a good idea. For one thing,

Lieutenant D'Angelo was almost certain to be there. Investigators often attended funerals of murder victims as part of the investigation, especially if it was someone prominent. I wasn't particularly sure I wanted to run into him.

But he might think it suspicious if I didn't show up.

"Oh, hell," I whispered, as the two women on television shared how the newly designed sanitary napkin brought heretofore unknown levels of joy into their lives.

One thing was for sure. I was tired of having so much attention paid to me. I'd been on television and in the newspapers more in the past week or so than I ever wanted to be or thought possible. If going to R. J. Reed's funeral meant questions from newspaper reporters or cameras shoved in my face, to hell with it.

I was suddenly very tired; three hours sleep has that effect on me sometimes. As I sat there in the overstuffed easy chair in my bedroom, the television droning on, I fell into an uneasy half sleep. It was like sticking your toes in the water, then slowly wading in, but never letting your head go completely under. From time to time, I was cognizant of what the voices coming out of the television were saying, but only in convoluted snippets that ran together in a jumble and never quite made sense.

I let go and slowly found myself drifting along as if on the water now. A dream came slowly to me, a dream where I was a prisoner, locked in a tiny stone room. I tried to recall what I'd done to get in so much trouble, but I couldn't. Couldn't remember what had happened to put me in this place that was so cold. I was naked and it was hard to breathe. And there were noises everywhere, the din of prison, metal clanking on metal, and everywhere the frenetic chatter of imprisoned men.

I sat on the edge of the bunk, the single thin gray blanket scratchy against my bare skin. There was a small barred window at the very top of the wall behind me. I stood on the edge of the bunk and stretched as high as I could to look out. The stone was damp, freezing, sucking the heat out of me. I jumped, grabbed the bars, and hoisted myself up. I was looking down from above on a massive courtyard full of anonymous imprisoned men in gray uniforms. Panic spread over me as I realized this really was prison, and I was here and I didn't know why. I opened my mouth to scream, but nothing came out.

A bell snapped in my head, a ringing that filled my skull and jerked me out of that prison cell. I awoke with a start and yelped like a dog whose tail had been stepped on.

"Damn," I mumbled, "if this is dreaming again, make me stop."

Confused, I looked around. Had I dreamt it, that horrible ringing? Then it went off again. The phone.

"Yeah," I mumbled, pulling the phone to my ear.

"Harry Denton, please."

Oh, shit, I thought. *Another reporter. Should I just hang up?*

"Who's calling, please?" My voice sounded thick and syrupy, as if my tongue was swollen and paralyzed.

"Sergeant E. D. Fouch," the voice said. "Metro police department."

"This is Harry Denton," I said, blinking my eyes and rubbing them, trying to pull myself together. I glanced at the clock: It was five minutes to eight. Hardly a decent hour for phone calls.

"Good morning, Mr. Denton. I hope I didn't wake you up."

"No, I'm already up, sort of. It's okay."

"We understand that your landlady, a Mrs. Esther Hawkins, died recently."

"Yes, just last weekend."

"We've received a report that there may be some unusual circumstances surrounding her death. I wonder if I could ask you a few questions."

"Sure," I said, awake and on point now. "Would you like me to come down there?"

"No, over the phone's fine if that's okay with you."

"Sure."

"First of all, we understand you discovered the body. Is that correct?"

"Yes, I found her Sunday morning."

"About what time?"

"I don't know. Must have been around nine. I went down to

get my Sunday paper and I noticed that her house was dark. She was usually up early. I knocked on her door and couldn't get an answer. That made me kind of nervous, so I went upstairs and got my key."

"You had a key to her apartment?"

"Yes, but it wasn't really an apartment. She had the first floor of the house and I rented a small attic apartment from her."

"I see. When was the last time you saw her alive?"

I thought for a moment. "Well, I didn't see her all day Saturday and didn't see her Saturday night. I was working. So maybe early Friday morning. Lately, she'd been staying in more than usual."

"I see. So it was unusual for her to stay inside so much?"

"Yes," I answered, realizing that Fouch was getting me to talk by repeating the last thing I said. He was sharp. "She was always working in the yard or cleaning or doing something. Whenever I'd come in from work, she'd stop me, want to chat for a while."

"So she liked to chat?"

"Sure, she was very friendly and didn't seem to have a lot of company."

"Hmmm, not a lot of company. Family not come around much?"

"I've lived here for over four years and I never saw them visit. Not once."

There was a moment's silence, then: "Can you tell me where you were Saturday night?"

"I'm a private investigator. I was working on a case. You probably read about it in the paper. I was doing a surveillance job on R. J. Reed. He was dead when I found him."

"Dead, huh?"

"Yes." I was through playing this game with him.

"Isn't it curious that you should come across two dead bodies in the space of a few hours?"

"Just bad luck, Sergeant. Damn bad luck."

"Bad luck . . . I understand Mrs. Hawkins left you some part of her estate."

"She left me some cash and the deed to the house." I wanted

to say, *And that's why her son sicced you on me*, but then remembered I wasn't supposed to know anything about this.

"Hmmm," he mumbled. "Mr. Denton, did you have occasion to work on or tamper with the phone lines at any time before Mrs. Hawkins died?"

"No," I said firmly. "Not before she died. My phone was out of order. After she died, I went down to the entrance bridge and swapped the lines so I could use her line from my apartment until my phone was fixed."

"Interesting," he said. "And did you figure out why your phone was out of order?"

"Because," I said, "I didn't pay my bill on time."

There was another moment of silence before he spoke again. "Been having trouble paying the bills, eh?"

"Just a cash-flow problem. Nothing serious. It's all fixed now."

"Of course it is," he said. "Now that you've inherited all this money."

I decided it was time to turn the direction of this conversation just a bit. "What are you trying to insinuate, Sergeant?"

"Oh, I'm not trying to insinuate anything. I'm just recording my observations."

"I find it very odd that you would be interested in an elderly woman who dies of an apparent heart attack alone in her own home. Aren't you with the homicide squad, Sergeant Fouch?"

"Yes, I am—"

"Is there some reason that you think Mrs. Hawkins's death was anything but natural causes?"

"We're just looking into some circumstances that—"

"What circumstances?"

"Just we've had some reports—"

"Reports from who?"

"Whom."

"What?" I asked.

"Whom. Reports from *whom*. Not *who*."

"Excuse me, Sergeant. I should know better. Is there anything else you need from me?"

"Not right now, Mr. Denton, but if you could make yourself

available for questioning if we need anything else, I'd certainly appreciate it."

"I'll cooperate in any way needed."

"Thank you. Have a nice day."

"Yeah, you, too," I said. I held the phone away from my ear, waiting for the click of him hanging up. Apparently, he was doing the same thing.

I set the handset back down in its cradle. Then I picked it up again, got a dial tone, and punched in a number. I waited for a series of beeps, then punched in my own telephone number. Then I sat back to wait for Lonnie's call.

I'd held them off for now. But time was running out.

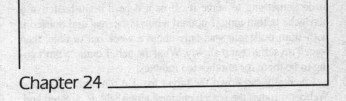

Chapter 24

"You're serious, aren't you?" Lonnie asked.

"As a heart attack," I answered. "I don't care what it costs."

"Well, hell, it won't cost much. That's not the problem. It's just that this kind of a background check's pretty invasive."

"Look, I can do it on my own but it'll take longer. All I've got is a 14.4 modem. You've got the ISDN line and a faster computer.

"Plus," I added after a moment, "you know what you're doing. I don't have time for a learning curve."

"Heat's rising, huh?"

"You got an extra pair of flame-retardant boxers I can borrow?"

He chuckled. "Okay, I'll meet you at the trailer. Only thing is, I gotta meet Sheba for lunch. But you can stay and keep working."

"Jesus, when're you guys moving in together?"

"How'd you know?"

I held the phone for a second. "You're serious, aren't you?"

"As a heart attack. Give me twenty minutes, okay?"

"Hey, I got my own key."

"I installed a new security system."

"Oh, all right," I said, more irritably than I'd intended. "Twenty minutes."

I gathered up my notes and files and threw them in a shoulder bag, then slammed down another cup of coffee. This was either the fourth or fifth—I'd lost count—and I hadn't eaten since sometime last night. Couldn't remember exactly when. I could feel one of those ragged, up-the-spine-and-into-the-skull caffeine tremors rippling through my lower back. I'd have to do something to stave it off or it'd be a brain-buster of a headache before long. I poured a bowl of cereal and doused it with skim milk that was only about a week out of date, then forced myself to eat it slowly. What the hell, Lonnie wasn't going to be there for another ten minutes.

I mentally ran down the target list. I'd run both Sykes and Webber through the search engines, along with R. J. Reed and, for grins, Victoria and Margot Horowitz as well. Then I'd run Spearhead Press and see what came up. Then the editor, Erica Benedict. See what came up on her. There was something else, though. Something nagging at the back of my mind, like a voice coming muffled through a wall. Like when you can hear something, but you can't understand it.

I stared blankly at the opposite kitchen wall as I leaned against the counter munching cereal glop. As a concession to middle age I'd bought fat-free health-food cereal at the store the last time I went shopping. As with most things billed as health food, the package it came in had more taste. I swallowed the last of it, though, just to have something in my gut. I was packing calories; it didn't particularly matter where they came from as long as sugar and caffeine weren't involved.

What was that? I wondered. What little nagging, gnawing, pesky little thought had shot through my brain like the stealth bomber and then disappeared before I could register it and store it?

Something to do with Reed. Reed, the book, the money, the homes, the—

That's it: the house. The house was owned by a corporation. It wasn't in Reed's name. I flipped open my notebook and started thumbing through piles of material. I hadn't realized I'd taken so many notes already. But combined with the stack of photocopied newspaper articles, I was soon going to have to get a thicker file folder.

There it was—the Sirius Corporation.

Okay, something called the Sirius Corporation owned the house where R. J. Reed was murdered. Maybe it was just part of a tax dodge or a way to hide from the public. I'd run that one through the search engines as well.

I opened up a copy of the book again. The copyright was held in Reed's name. It would have been, since before *Life's Little Maintenance Manual* was published, Reed didn't have enough cash to keep a checking account open, let alone the money to incorporate. I made a note to try to find out if he'd signed the rights to the book over to his own corporation.

In desperation and with what I sensed was not much time, I made up my mind to dive headfirst into this and to keep going down until I found the truth. It was out there; all I had to do was find it. And I had one advantage even the police didn't have. As far as Lieutenant D'Angelo was concerned, it was his job that was on the line. It was different for me.

It was my life.

"You're sure you want to do this?" Lonnie asked as he pointed what looked like a car-alarm remote at the house trailer and punched the button.

"What's the downside?" I asked.

"The downside is you're invading people's privacy and digging into shit you don't have any business digging into." A small red dot glowing just above the trailer door went black and Lonnie pushed the gate open.

"Is any of this illegal?"

He shrugged. "Beats me. It's just cheesy, that's all."

"Murder's pretty cheesy, too," I said. "And being blamed for it when you didn't do it is ethically problematic as well."

"No argument there," he offered as we walked across the debris-strewn junkyard. "All I can tell you is, if they arrest you, demand administrative segregation. Tell 'em you're gay or sick or scared or you like little girls and you're afraid someone'll find out, whatever. Just don't let 'em lock you in a holding cell with anybody else."

"Why?" I asked. "What's the big deal?"

I stepped around a puddle of something that looked oily, had a green sheen on top, and was giving off a kind of thin smoke. Ahead of me, Lonnie pulled out a cylindrical Chicago Ace

Lock key and inserted it in a metal plate beside the door to the trailer. I hadn't seen that before. Part of the new security, I guess.

"Because chances are the guy in the cell with you is a snitch who's just cut a deal with the DA to swear you told him just how and why you strangled Reed, then held him underwater just to make sure the job was done right," he said, stepping into the trailer and flicking a wall switch by the door.

"And he'll go before a jury of his own free will," Lonnie continued as we walked down the hall toward the back bedroom that served as his office, "and repeat the story because *it's the right thing to do.* About a month later he'll be off trout fishing and blowing doobie in backwater Montana while you're looking at spending the rest of your life in Riverbend rooming with Bobo the Slack-Jawed Boy."

"C'mon," I said, following him into a room packed floor to ceiling with computers, printers, electronic surveillance devices, all kinds of spook shit. God, Lonnie likes his toys. "Aren't you getting just a little cynical?"

He turned, sneered at me. "Aren't you getting just a little gullible?"

Lonnie had a huge monitor in the center of the small desk crammed into the bedroom amid the shelves of equipment. The screen saver on the monitor displayed a line of letters that read: HI, ERIC STRATTON, RUSH CHAIRMAN, DAMN GLAD TO MEET YOU. . . . HI, ERIC STRATTON, RUSH CHAIRMAN, DAMN GLAD TO MEET YOU. . . . HI, ERIC STRATTON, RUSH CHAIRMAN, DAMN GLAD TO . . . in bright red on black in a continuous stream.

"I always thought your sense of humor was a bit . . ."

"Quirky?" he asked, sitting down in front of the monitor and grabbing the mouse.

"I was going to say sophomoric, but I guess quirky will do."

"I can play 'Louie Louie' through the speakers if you want. Can set it up in a loop so it'll repeat over and over. How's that sound?"

"Like dying and going to hell?" I suggested.

"You're no fun," he said, turning to the monitor.

"That's what they tell me. Fire that sucker up now."

Lonnie launched his Web browser and then I heard the beeping of his modem and a dial tone as the computer connected. I was inexperienced at this sort of thing but had read articles and heard many times from Lonnie about the oceans of information that were available for the adept Web surfer.

"Where should we start?" I asked.

"Give me the list of all the individuals you want traced," he instructed.

I opened my notebook and showed him the list.

"Let's start," he said, "by collecting everybody's social security numbers. That gives us a platform to start the real digging."

"You can do that? I mean, aren't they supposed to be private?" I asked, ripping the page out of my notebook and handing it to him.

"Up until about a year ago," he said, moving the mouse around and double-clicking on a couple of items on the screen, "the frigging government had a site where you could get 'em. The idea was that anybody could go check their earnings and their social security account, so they could see just how much money they were never going to get after they retired."

"And let me guess," I said. "The only problem was that the honor system didn't work."

"Yeah." He smiled. "You weren't supposed to check anybody's account but your own. But lo and behold . . ."

"So how are you going to get all the socials if they shut the Web site down?" I tore several pages out of my notebook and started writing one name at the top of each page.

He turned and grinned just as he finished typing in a row of letters and numbers, then hit the return key.

"Before the feds shut the site down, a couple of guys went in and copied all the records into a mirror site."

"What?" I said, aghast. "You mean all the hundreds of millions of social security records for the whole country?"

"Amazing, ain't it?"

I finished copying the names onto the sheets of paper. I had one blank sheet of paper for each name. Now all we had to do was fill them.

"And how did you find out about this mirror site?"

"Guy in Atlanta I know. A P.I. who makes his entire living from his computer. Never leaves his basement. Charges fifty bucks to find anybody, anywhere. On average, it takes him about ten minutes per name. Makes mid–six figures every year."

"Hey, why don't you do something like that?"

He grimaced. "Can you imagine how boring that must be?"

I sighed. "Yeah, well, I could use a little boring."

"Something tells me you'll find it, Harry," he said blankly, staring at the screen. "You always do."

"So this guy runs the Web site?"

"No, he just found it. The site changes URLs about every forty-eight hours. You have to have encryption to find out where it's moved to."

A screen came up on Lonnie's computer that was just text, no fancy graphics or frames or anything like that. In fact, the words on the screen didn't make sense. It just looked like scrambled gobbledygook. But one of the words was underlined. Lonnie clicked it and a dialogue box came up on the screen asking for his password. His fingers moved so fast, they were a blur as he spurted a series of keystrokes. The screen went blank for a few moments, then filled with code, jumbled line after jumbled line.

Then the screen stopped moving and a display jumped up. SNOOPER'S HOME PAGE the headline read, and below it: KNOWLEDGE IS POWER, AND ALL POWER TO THE PEOPLE with one of those black-and-white silhouetted outlines of a raised fist from the Sixties.

"Amen, brother," Lonnie said. "Give me those names."

In less than two minutes we had everybody's social security numbers. I copied them down as Lonnie pulled them up.

"Okay, who else?"

"That's all," I said.

"Let's move on."

"Wait," I said, putting a hand on his shoulder. "Let's do one more, just for grins."

He turned. "Who?"

"Let's try Gregory Bransford," I said. "I don't have his address, but plug in Franklin, Tennessee, as the address and see what the site comes up with."

"Who's Gregory Bransford?" he asked, typing the name in.

"He's that sawed-off son-of-a-bitch assistant DA down in Williamson County who busted my chops."

Lonnie smiled broadly as he hit the return button. "Oh, you sly old dog, you."

"Hey, knowledge is power," I said.

"And all power to the people!" we chimed in together.

Two hours later Lonnie left for his lunch appointment with Sheba. He gave me a spare key to the new burglar alarm and a remote for the infrared motion sensors he'd installed after Shadow's death.

"They ain't as good as Shadow," he explained, "but they don't hurt as much when they go down."

By the time he took off, I had social security numbers and wage and earning statements, along with dates of birth, home addresses, phone numbers, credit reports, the names of their spouses and children as well as bankruptcy records, any civil lawsuits they were involved in, and, the most staggering of all, NCIC records of arrest histories, outstanding warrants, and convictions. I found Web sites with names like StalkX and BotSnooper and Up-Yerz, all intriguing names with slightly sinister overtones. Hell, I even got marriage and divorce records and college transcripts. I had to type in my credit card number a few times, but hey, it's all a business deduction, right?

"Amazing," I whispered, as I sent another batch to the printer. Try as I might, I couldn't find out if any of them had any outstanding parking tickets. I'm not sure that would have helped anyway. It's not like you can confront a murderer and say *Confess or I'll have your car impounded!* with much hope of success.

As with last night's library search, there wasn't time to read any of this stuff. It was dump the data to Lonnie's printer and go on to the next name or the next Web site or to the next search engine. After a while it began to feel like a game.

After I exhausted all outlets for personal information, I turned to tracking down the Sirius Corporation and the corporation that owned Spearhead Press, which bore the intriguing name of Spearhead Partners II, LLP. I didn't know much about limited liability partnerships, other than that they were privately held partnerships where your liability is limited—*duh.*

I hit several different Web sites, finding nothing and resigning myself to that, when I located a place called Private Securities Finder on a links page. My eyes were starting to blur and my brain was fogging up, but the name caught my attention, so I double-clicked on it.

In a few seconds, I was at a Web site that claimed to have hard-to-find information about privately held companies. Stuff you couldn't find anyplace else. There wasn't much on the Spearhead partnership and only a page or two on the Sirius Corporation. I dumped that information to the printer and was trying to figure out what to do next. I'd been surfing the Web for nearly five hours by then and was getting to the point where I couldn't remember what I'd read thirty seconds ago and was linking to sites I'd already been to. I figured it was a good time to take a break, but as long as I was at Private Securities Finder, just for the sheer absolute joy and delight of it, decided to run searches for R. J. Reed, Travis Webber, and Karl Sykes.

Sykes's name popped up with the Spearhead citation only. I already had that one. Apparently, he wasn't prominent or active in any other corporations.

Reed came up listed with corporate involvement in the Sirius Corporation and another company, the Harvest Moon Corporation.

Okay, I thought, *add that one to the list.*

I typed in Webber's name and waited a couple of seconds.

Then the screen displayed his name, and below that: Spearhead Partners II, LLP, and—

"What the hell?" I said out loud.

—the Harvest Moon Corporation.

"Well," I whispered. "I'll be damned."

Chapter 25 ⎯⎯⎯⎯⎯⎯⎯

So Robert Jefferson Reed, the murdered author of a best-selling collection of homespun family-values wisdom, and Travis Webber, his editor and publisher, were doing some biz together that apparently did not include Karl Sykes, the third person in this little marketing genius ménage à trois.

"Hmmm," I whispered. "Wonder what this means?"

What the hell, it could mean anything. Maybe the two of them bought some fast-food franchises. *Life's Little Mainte-nance Manual* burgers or some such. They had to do something with all that cash. I put the cursor in the field search line and typed in Harvest Moon Corporation and waited. And waited. And waited.

Then two lines appeared:

INCORPORATED 1997, CAYMAN ISLANDS
NO OTHER INFORMATION AVAILABLE

Well, that put a whole different spin on things. Okay, so nobody buys Burger King franchises through the Caymans without a damn good reason. Wonder if Victoria Reed knew anything about this, and if so, why didn't she tell me? She'd given me a rundown of his stock holdings, had even shared the latest statement from his broker listing his entire account and its considerable worth.

Wonder if the Harvest Moon Corporation shows up in the will? Wonder if Victoria Reed's even seen the will, and if so, will she share it with me? And if she won't, wonder what it'll take to get a copy of it?

Damn, too many questions. Too little time.

My head was spinning as I shut down the Web browser and closed the modem connection. The bowl of cereal goop hadn't stayed with me as long as I hoped, either. I needed food and I needed time to think, in that order.

Before leaving Lonnie's fortress-disguised-as-a-mobile-home I decided to call Marsha. I hadn't really talked to her since yesterday afternoon. In a few hours, her life had completely changed. For the first time since I'd known her, and for the first time in her career, she had no place to go and nothing to do.

Maybe it won't be for long, I thought as I dialed her number. The morgue in a city the size of Nashville can't shut down for long; they'll be stacking the bodies like cordwood in a few days.

"Hello." She sounded down, way down.

"Hi," I said, as brightly as I could muster.

"Hi, Harry. How are you?"

"Fine. I'm over at Lonnie's. Been using his computer to do a little digging."

"Oh," she said. She didn't ask any follow-up, so I didn't offer any.

"How are you?"

"Uh, I'm okay, I guess. Just kind of lying around. I woke up about five this morning, couldn't go back to sleep."

"I'm sorry," I said. "I know this has been really hard on you. Have you heard from your lawyer or anybody else down at the office?"

"I talked with him yesterday evening. He was going to have a conference with the district attorney this afternoon."

"Really? About what?"

She sighed. "I don't know the details. But he told me the mayor's office had contacted him, too. I've got a feeling that there's some deal brokering going on here. I spoke with Kay this morning. She said Dr. Henry's not back in town yet. He's not answering his car phone and he hasn't checked in."

"Hmmm, wonder what's going on?"

"I'm sure I'll find out eventually," she said. "In the meantime,

I'm just trying to keep from going nuts. I've got a guy coming over at four-thirty to look at the Porsche."

"Yeah, I saw the sign. How come you're selling it?"

She laughed softly, but there was a bittersweet edge to it. "Another month and I won't be able to get behind the wheel. No, a 911's no car for an expectant mother."

"What're you going to do?"

"Buy something else, I guess."

"You'll need transportation. Somehow I just don't see you standing at a bus stop."

"I've ridden buses before," she snapped. At last, I thought, a spark.

"You know I'll be glad to chauffeur you around anywhere you need to go."

"Thanks, I appreciate that."

There was a long moment of silence on the phone, the kind of awkward reticence that quickly becomes the reflection of a deeper, more profound silence, the silence of distance between two people. I realized that I missed her, and maybe the thing to do was let her know that.

"I'm sorry things have been so tough lately," I said. "I really miss . . ."

It was hard to say.

"Well, I really miss what we used to have."

"Everything changes, Harry."

"I know that. But why does it always seem to change for the worse?"

"It doesn't always."

"Just lately."

"I think that what we're going through has its beginnings way back there," she said.

"What do you mean?"

"I'm not sure we were ever really together. We were both so wrapped up in our work, both carrying so much baggage from past lives, other people. Both so afraid to get any deeper into it."

"Yeah," I said after a moment. "Maybe. But does that mean we can't ever get to where we want to be?"

"Sure, it's just that maybe we don't want to be in the same place."

"We could figure that out," I offered. "Perhaps there's a way to find out. Then if there isn't, at least we tried. At least we gave it a shot."

"I don't know. With the way the rest of our lives is going, now might not be a good time to begin a voyage of self-discovery. The good ship *Lollipop* might turn into the *Titanic*."

"You never know," I said. "Now might be a perfect time. Think about it."

"Okay, I will."

"By the way," I said casually, offhandedly, "the police questioned me about Mrs. Hawkins's death. It seems her son is trying to claim his inheritance by having me declared her murderer."

She gasped. "Jesus, Harry, are there any dead people out there you *didn't* kill?"

"Thinking about changing my name to Lee Harvey. How's that sound? Lee Harvey Denton . . ."

"Almost appropriate, given the circumstances. How serious are they?"

"Fouch asked me a few questions. I tried not to get any smarter with him than I had to. He said the family wants the body exhumed. Hey, maybe you'll be back in the saddle and get to do the autopsy."

She laughed. "Not a chance! I don't even want to be in the building when that one comes up."

"I hate to see it happen," I said. "The old lady deserves better."

Marsha was quiet for a moment, then spoke again, her voice somber. "If I thought an autopsy was a sign of disrespect for the dead, I'd get out of this line of work. Once you're gone, the body's just an empty house."

"I guess there's no point in worrying about it."

"Try not to even think about it."

"Thanks for the advice."

"Anytime, soldier. Call me later. If this guy buys the Porsche, I might need a ride to the store."

I smiled. That meant that, at the very least, I'd get to see her. "You got it, Doc. No problem."

I tried hard to focus on the labyrinth of information I'd gathered in the past two days on the world of R. J. Reed. Part of it was that I was being drawn further and further into this case. But a big part was that this gave me the chance to escape my own world, which seemed to be more and more uncomfortable with each passing tick of the cosmic clock. A man my age should not be living hand-to-mouth and facing a solitary future. I couldn't avoid the feeling that somehow I had managed to screw up just about everything: career, marriage, relationships, money. The only reason I even had a roof over my head was because somebody else died and, through whatever misguided sensibilities, left me that roof.

And now it looked like even that might be coming down around me.

"Stop that," I said out loud, pulling into the parking lot of Mrs. Lee's. "You're just feeling sorry for yourself and there's too damn much work to do."

I slung my bag full of paper over my shoulder and walked into the restaurant. It was a little before twelve, but there were only about a dozen people in the place and nobody in line at the counter.

"What's going on?" I asked Mrs. Lee as I walked up to the register.

She scowled at me. "What? You not see TV last night?"

"No, what are you talking about?"

"Dat damn channah foah," she complained. "We on dat t'ing dey do evah week on restaurants."

"What?" I asked. She was upset. When Mrs. Lee gets upset, her accent thickens and she's hard to understand.

"You know. Dat 'eat, dwink, be wahey.' "

"Oh," I said. "Eat, drink, and be wary."

The local NBC outlet, Channel 4, has a weekly news segment where they report the health department's sanitation scores on local restaurants. They pick the top three scores and the bottom three. It's always fun to see the really expensive places get nailed.

"What did you do to piss off the health department?" I asked. Jeez, seems like everybody's having a tough time.

"We have bad day, dat's all. Vehy busy, not have time to wash wooden spoons in breach. We clean evaht'ing up. Dey come back Monday, recheck us. All be okay!"

"I'm sure it will be—"

"Pay hell wid customahs," she interrupted. "Nobody come eat heah. We d'ink maybe sue!"

"They'll be back," I said. "Look, here I am." I spread my arms as if acknowledging a crowd of admirers.

"Yeah, who you? You only buy cheapest stuff on menu."

"Not anymore, my dear. I happen to be temporarily flush. I'll take the Governor's Shrimp." It was just about the most expensive thing on the menu.

"Whah you get so much money? You rob a bank?"

I started to tell her bank robbery was kid stuff to a guy accused of two murders but decided she might not get the joke. I pulled a twenty out of my wallet and handed it to her. "Just get me some lunch, okay? I'm starving."

Five minutes later I was wading through a pile of papers and stuffing my face. It's amazing what you find when you start opening people's closets without asking them. In the years before discovering R. J. Reed, for instance, both Travis Webber and Karl Sykes had been sued in civil court over a long series of debts and charge-offs. Spearhead Press had been named in several civil suits as well, including one for copyright infringement and several lawsuits from authors claiming that they hadn't been paid royalties.

Four years ago Webber'd gone Chapter 7. That meant that two of the three people involved in the success of *Life's Little Maintenance Manual* had encountered financial problems severe enough to land them in bankruptcy court.

And up until the dough started rolling in from the book, they all must have had shitty credit histories. When I examined their credit reports, I saw none of them went back further than two years. I figured they must have gone back and settled up with their past creditors to get their files cleaned up. They couldn't get those bankruptcies off, though. Once you wind up in bankruptcy court, it's almost impossible to get that blemish removed.

I turned to all the information I'd gathered on Erica Benedict, Reed's editor at Spearhead Press. Truth is, Lonnie was right. Having this kind of information on someone made you feel kind of cheesy. I had her age, marital status, next of kin, address, unlisted phone number, credit history, the outstanding balance on her condo mortgage, her employment history, and a ballpark estimate of her yearly income. I had her college transcripts, a copy of her divorce decree from 1994, a copy of her DMV sheet—jeez, she likes to drive fast—and the fact that in 1985 she was arrested for misdemeanor possession and received a year's probation. She also forgot to pay her Visa bill on time last month. About the only thing I didn't have was her shoe size, and I could probably find that out if I looked hard enough.

I shook my head. None of this was any of my business, yet here it all was. I don't want to even consider the moral and ethical implications of what I'd done.

Yeah, don't want to, but I can't help it. I'll put if off for now, though.

I sipped my tea and finished the last of the Governor's Shrimp. My impending blood-sugar crash had been staved off. I felt tired but reasonably ready to go back out and tackle the world.

I checked my watch. Reed's funeral was in a couple of hours. I still hadn't decided how to handle that one. Chances were, Erica Benedict as well as Sykes and Webber and a ton of other people would be there.

The thought occurred to me that I hadn't yet checked my office answering machine today. At least do that, I thought, and see if Victoria Reed or anyone else had called. I took my tray over to the large wastebasket by the door of the restaurant, dumped my trash, then walked down the short hallway leading to the restrooms. Perched between the doors to the ladies' and gents' rooms was a pay phone. I pumped in a quarter, dialed my office number, and tapped in the code to play the messages back.

"Hello," that annoying computer voice said, "you have . . . twelve . . . messages."

"Crap," I muttered. I've got to get rid of that damn thing.

I scrambled for a pen and slip of paper as the messages began playing. The first was from Sergeant Fouch, who had apparently tried my office this morning before he got me at home. The next was from Victoria Reed, with a request that I call her.

"Good," I muttered, scribbling a note down.

Then there were ten messages from reporters: TV reporters, print reporters, radio reporters. Damn, I used to be one and now I hate them.

But why would they be calling me? I'm old news. Has there been something new with Reed's murder? Maybe they'd caught the murderer and I was off the hook.

The first one to call, of course, was Randy Tucker at the *Banner*. I dialed the main switchboard of the paper and got switched through.

"Yeah," he said.

"Harry Denton. I just got your message, along with a dozen others. What the hell's going on?"

"Christ, you haven't heard?"

"Heard what?" Suddenly, the taste of recycled Governor's Shrimp filled the back of my throat.

"There was a press conference this morning at the DA's office. They're getting a court order to exhume the body of your landlady!"

"Damn it!" I said. "I can't believe they're going through with this."

"You haven't heard the rest," he said.

"There's more?" I asked weakly.

"Your landlady's son was at the press conference. He's quite a preacher."

"Oh, no, what'd he say?"

"He says you killed his mother, Harry. He says you killed Mrs. Hawkins. They're pushing the police to arrest you."

I stood there a moment, staring at the wallpaper. The pattern

was alternating green and red swirls, sort of a Chinese-restaurant
version of Christmas wrapping paper.

"Any comment, Harry?"

This is insane, I thought.

"Harry?"

"No. No comment," I said slowly.

How many times had I heard criminals say that in my years
as a reporter? Now it was my turn.

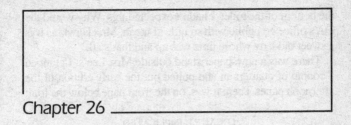

Chapter 26

"Damn it!" I yelled, slapping the side of the phone after I hung up.

Mrs. Lee was around the corner and in my face in a flash. "Whattsa mattah you? Hit a phone like dat! You crazy?"

I leaned down, got right back in her face. "I hate reporters," I growled.

She stared at me for about three heartbeats. Then she turned around and, flat-handed, slapped hell out of the phone herself.

"Damn repohtahs!" she yelled. "Eat, d'ink, and fuck off!"

I broke out laughing, a reckless, out-of-control guffaw that had me fighting to keep from blowing Governor's Shrimp out my nose. My eyes watered and I threw my arms around her, wrapping her in a great bear hug that lifted her off her tiny feet.

"You're great," I stammered. "God, I needed that more than anything in the world."

A loud, irritable string of Chinese emanated from the kitchen. Mrs. Lee turned to the wall dividing us from her husband.

"Oh, shu' up, you pain in de ass," she stage-whispered, grinning. Then she let loose with a clamorous string of Chinese that seemed to quiet him for a moment.

"I gotta go back to work," she said. "You get out heah 'foah you cause moah trouble."

"Okay, sweetheart," I said, still trying vainly to compose myself. "Take care of yourself."

"You, too, Harry. Don't letta bastahds weah you down."

Despite the badly needed howl, the fact remained that my own personal situation had just gotten another notch closer to the bottom of the toilet. I hadn't expected this. Why would the DA's office go public with so little? I mean, Mrs. Hawkins was a sweet old lady whose time was up and that's all.

There was a newspaper stand outside Mrs. Lee's. I pumped a couple of quarters in and pulled out the early edition of the afternoon paper. There it was, on the front page below the fold:

LOCAL P.I. IMPLICATED
IN SECOND SUSPICIOUS DEATH

Luckily, my mug did not grace the front page, but next to the article was a small single-column photo of Mrs. Hawkins. Below the photo a caption read: DEATH SPURS INVESTIGATION.

My chest hurt, like someone reaching through my shirt, grabbing my heart, and giving it a good hard twist.

Somewhere in the back of my mind, in a tiny little locked closet where no one ever went, I made a note to remember this. One of these days, I'd figure out how to pay this one back.

But not now. Not today. There was too much else to do.

I cranked up the Mustang, pulled out onto Gallatin Road, and headed toward town. I made a left on Douglas Avenue and cut over through several side streets, coming to my street from the intersection farthest from Mrs. Hawkins's house. I pulled over to the curb and stopped, the idling engine a low rumble.

There were two sedans parked in front of my house. Each of them carried the logo of a local television station. They'd headed me off at the pass. I could park here, sneak through the alley, and come at it from the backyard like before.

No, I'd gotten lucky the last time I tried that. The reporters hadn't been camped out front. This time was different. All they had to do was have a camera on the backyard as I came loping over it like a cat burglar and I really would have some serious problems. Talk about looking like you've got something to hide. . . .

I sighed. The next best hiding place was my office. I put the car in gear and slowly pulled away, hoping I wouldn't spot them in my rearview mirror chasing me.

Funny thing, I was starting to get a sense of what it's like to be on the run.

It sucks, big time.

I rounded the staircase at the landing and took the last half flight of stairs up to my second-floor office as casually as I could. I didn't figure any reporters would be patient enough to hang out in this fleabag of an office building for very long, but I was ready. If there was anyone in front of my door who even looked or smelled like a journalist, I was turning right instead of left and heading down to Slim and Ray's office. Just pretend I'm another aspiring singer looking for work.

Nothing—the hall was empty. I strode quickly down the hall, unlocked my door, and locked it behind me as quickly as possible. I reached over, took the phone off the hook, and gathered up my mail. As I sorted through it, I hit the button on my answering machine and half listened as one by one every damn print, radio, TV, and cyberjournalist in town tried to find me. If this is the price of fame, I thought, you can have it.

The mail was the usual: couple of bills, some junk, a notice from the state about the renewal of my license, and at the bottom of the stack a plain white envelope with my name typed on the front. No canceled stamp, no return address.

Curious, I slid the others onto my desk and sat down. My chair creaked and squealed as I leaned back and opened the envelope. Inside was a folded single sheet of paper, which when I unfolded it said in bold letters across the top:

NOTICE OF EVICTION

I was stunned, shocked, bewildered, and a half-dozen other adjectives courtesy of Mr. Roget that I won't bother to repeat here.

"Why?" I said out loud, holding the piece of paper out in front of me like it was contaminated. "I paid the rent."

The letter gave me ten days to get the hell out. Suddenly I was furious and found myself stomping down the hallway to the stairs, down to the first-floor office of the building manager, Mr. Morris.

Mr. Morris, with his slicked-back hair and his green cigar; Mr. Morris, who rented to anybody including the astrologer who ripped off the light fixtures when she skipped out on the rent; Mr. Morris, who was about to get a very large piece of my mind.

I had his stupid eviction letter crumpled in my right hand as I pounded on his door three times and opened it without waiting for an invite.

He jumped up from behind his desk as I burst into his office, which wasn't much bigger than mine. When he saw me, his bloodshot brown eyes bulged wide and he held his hands out in front of him defensively.

"What the hell's the meaning of this?" I shouted, thrusting the wad of paper toward him.

"Don't hurt me!" he squealed.

I stopped cold. *Don't hurt me? Don't hurt me?*

Who did he think I was, Jack-the-frigging-Ripper?

Then I looked down at his desk. The afternoon paper was unfolded and open to the jump page. He'd just finished reading how I was now a suspect in two murders.

Yeah, I guess he did think I was Jack-the-frigging-Ripper.

"Look," I said, suddenly completely calm. It all made sense now. "I'm not going to hurt you, Mr. Morris. I haven't hurt anybody."

"That's not what the paper says," he whined.

"Don't believe everything you read in the paper," I said. Snappy comeback, I thought. *Don't believe everything you read in the paper;* page 37 out of *Life's Little Maintenance Manual.*

"I don't care," he said. "I want you out of here."

"But I'm caught up on my rent," I said, trying to placate him. "I'm a steady tenant. I don't cause you any trouble. C'mon, this'll all blow over and everything'll be back to normal. You don't have that many paying tenants here. You can't afford to lose a good one."

He realized by now that I wasn't going to jump the desk and

strangle him like I allegedly did R. J. Reed. His bravado returned; his upper lip rose in a sneer under his mustache.

"Denton," he said. "You're an undesirable and I want you out of here."

My God, has it come to this? I'm an undesirable in *this* place? This House of Rodentia that would trade office space for food stamps?

I stared at him for a few moments and realized not only was I losing this battle, it wasn't even one worth fighting. I shrugged my shoulders and turned for the door.

"Ten days, Denton!" he called as I shut the door behind me. "Ten days and I change the locks!"

"Ten days and I change the locks!" I mimicked as I headed back up the stairs.

The door to the office where I'd spent a pretty good part of the last five years was cracked open, the inside light shining through into the dim hallway as I topped the stairs and rounded the corner. I didn't think anything about it, but then I remembered.

I had closed the door. I always close it. I hadn't locked it this time, but I had closed it. I'm sure of it.

The hallway was empty; empty and silent. I stopped and stood there, motionless, trying to control my breathing. To be as still and noiseless as possible.

Who the hell could it be? I thought. Reporters? Okay, reporters I could handle, although I'd need a place to take a shower afterward. What if it wasn't a reporter? Cops? Maybe with an arrest warrant?

I suddenly wished I hadn't listened to Howard Spellman when he advised against hiring a lawyer. Right then, I didn't care what it looked like; I wanted a lawyer.

My anxiety grew in direct correlation to my paranoia. I began to feel damp all over and a little shaky. I fought the urge to run but figured if there was someone in my office, I needed to be there.

I took a deep breath, steadied my nerves, and padded softly down the hall to my office door. I listened but could hear nothing from inside. Maybe the door had just swung back open after I slammed it so hard.

Maybe . . . maybe . . . I was so tired of *maybes*, I could scream. I jerked the door open and stood in the door frame.

A short, stumpy woman—four foot two, tops—in a brown skirt and jacket spun around, startled. Her hair was washed-out, brown mixed with gray. She wore thick glasses and had about fifty pounds on her she could've done without. An old-lady purse on a long strap hung at her side.

"Oh," she said quickly, squinting at me through the glasses. "I'm sorry. I didn't mean to barge in. I knocked. No one answered, the door was open. I—"

"It's okay," I said. "Who're you looking for?"

"Mr. Denton, if he's around."

I stepped in, closed the door behind me. "I'm Harry Denton," I said. "What can I do for you?"

"Oh, I'm so sorry to disturb you," she said nervously. "I hope I haven't interrupted you or anything. I just . . . I mean . . ."

"Calm down," I said. "It's okay. Why don't you start by telling me your name?"

"I'm Erica Benedict. I work for a company called Spearhead Press. I was the editor for—"

"Yes," I said, biting my lower lip. "I know who you are."

Chapter 27

Erica Benedict peered up at me through her thick lenses, a quizzical look on her face. She wasn't what I expected. The name Erica Benedict had a glamorous ring to it, like the pseudonym of a famous romance-novel writer or the villainess in a soap opera. She was a UCSC graduate with a 3.8 average as an English major, drove fast enough to have collected a slew of traffic tickets, and had been divorced barely four years. For some reason or other, I expected a high-flying, svelte, racy divorcée. And here was this chubby little nearsighted homunculus.

"You do?" she asked.

I stepped around her and pulled over my visitor's chair. "Please, sit down."

She hauled herself up onto the edge of the chair and squeezed back into it, her hips barely making it past the armrests. She fiddled with the purse in her lap, what there was of a lap between the mound of her stomach and the ends of her knees. I sat down in my own chair and studied her for just a second, trying to figure out what to make of her.

This was one I hadn't expected.

"So how do you know who I am?" she asked.

"I read the book. Reed thanked you in the acknowledgments."

I didn't mention that I also knew what her property settlement was from her California divorce, how many points she had on her driver's license, and oh, yes, that little incident with the Humboldt homegrown out in Oregon in the Eighties. Maybe all that smoke had stunted her growth and given her a monumental case of the munchies.

She shuffled a bit in the chair, as if trying to settle into it and finding it both too small and too hard for her.

"Victoria made him do that," she said. "I don't think he would have otherwise."

"Victoria's like that," I said. "She's very considerate and kind."

"She is, isn't she?" Erica Benedict said.

She fidgeted with the purse straps and looked down at the floor. I leaned back, my chair squealing with the motion. Her head jerked up at the noise.

I sat there. When she got ready to say something, I figured she would.

She cleared her throat. "Well," she said, "I guess you're wondering why I'm here."

"Just a bit." I raised my arm and checked my watch. "Especially with Reed's funeral in an hour."

"Are you going?" she asked, looking up at me.

"Haven't made up my mind. You?"

"Oh, yes. They closed the office after lunch. The whole company will be there."

"So you have to be."

"Yes. Certainly. I mean, why wouldn't I be?"

I shrugged. "You tell me?"

She sighed, unwound the purse straps from her hand, and let the bag slide to the floor. "I would anyway. He wasn't an editor's dream of the ideal author, but he didn't deserve what he got."

"No, he didn't. Nobody deserves that. What I can't figure out is why you're sitting in the office of the man accused of killing him."

"I don't think you killed him," she said.

"You're apparently in a small minority. Why don't you think I killed him?"

Her lips curled as her jaw tensed. "I've been reading the papers, talking to people in the office. There's been lots of talk, speculation. Everybody figures if you did kill him, it was only because Victoria hired you to do it. There was no other reason, was there?"

"No, there wasn't. And your coworkers' theories seem to be the morning line with the Williamson County Sheriff's Department. Not to mention the newspapers."

"I know Victoria," Erica insisted. "I can't believe she would have done this. We worked together back when she still had her job. I only got to edit R.J.'s book because she twisted Trav's arm."

"Trav?"

"Travis Webber, my boss at Spearhead. Travis was in charge of almost all of the editorial work. Karl Sykes was the administrator, the number cruncher."

I had the feeling I should be taking notes, just in case. But I didn't want to make her nervous. "I'm glad you don't think I killed Reed," I said. "And not just for my own hide." I hesitated a moment, then spoke low and calm, almost matter-of-fact.

"But I still don't understand why you're here."

"I should have gone to the police," she said. "But I don't want my name dragged into it. My work at Spearhead is pretty much all I've got. I mean, I—well, I live alone and don't have a lot of friends. And if anyone at the company found out I was even talking to you . . ."

"Don't worry. No one'll ever know you were here."

"I'm not even sure that what I know or what I think is important."

"If you told me what you know, maybe we could figure it out."

Her eyes darted around the room nervously. She couldn't look at me. "It's just all so hard, so weird. I've never known anyone who was murdered before. It's still not real. I mean, a few days ago he was in our offices and he and Karl were having this . . . this *screaming* match. . . ."

"Screaming match?" I said, trying to keep my voice in check.

"I was working late. Maybe nine o'clock. I was wading through manuscripts. God, you wouldn't believe the slush pile since R.J.'s book was published. All these terrible imitations, not even good enough to be cheap knockoffs."

"And it was late," I said.

"Yes, and Karl was in his office at the other end of the hall. Our editorial and management offices are all on the fifth floor. Production's on three, telemarketing and the mailroom are on two. We rent out some space on one. Anyway, I thought everyone else had gone home and I hear the elevator—"

Now that she'd gotten started, it all gushed out nonstop in a continuous stream of chatter.

"—and I figure it was the cleaning crew, you know. So I don't think much about it, but they always start at my end of the hall and they didn't, so I didn't think anything about it, you know, and just kept on reading. Anyway, I was about to fall asleep over this one particularly bad submission and decided to go make some tea. The break room is down the hall, you see, about halfway between my end of the hall and the executive offices, and I walk down and I notice there's no cleaning crew anywhere, but I hear these *voices*, you know, coming from inside the executive suite and they're, like, *yelling,* and I recognize Karl's voice first. He's . . . he's rabid, like I've never heard him before. And he's screaming about the company being ruined and 'if you think for a second I'm going to let some third-rate hack bring this company down, you're as crazy as everyone thinks you are' and all this kind of insanity."

She stopped to get her breath. Her face was splotchy, flushed red, and her chest heaved under the brown suit jacket.

I scooted forward on my chair an inch or two toward her. "So what happened then?"

"I ducked into the doorway of the break room. The lights were off, there was no one else there. And I could hear them clearly. They must have been in the reception area instead of Karl's office because it was like they were just on the other side of the door.

"So I hear this other voice and it takes me a second, but I realize it's R.J. Only it's not his voice I recognize, it's his laugh."

"He was laughing?" I asked.

"Yes, R.J. had a cruel, terrible laugh. I saw him make one of the secretaries cry one day. She didn't recognize him when he came in, so she asked his name before she'd let him go up-stairs. He went off on her, yelled that he was the guy who made it possible for her to get a paycheck every week and that if he wanted to, he could be the guy who stopped it. He laughed when she broke down sobbing. I was going out to lunch, saw the whole thing.

"Anyway, I heard him say that it was all a done deal and there was nothing that anybody could do about it. That be-tween him and Trav, they could vote the stock any way they wanted to."

"Stock? What stock?"

"I don't know for sure, but I assume it was stock in the company."

I rubbed my hand across my chin, the stubble scraping the palm and scratching an itch. What's that supposed to mean when your palm itches? You're coming into money, right?

"R.J. owned stock in Spearhead?" I asked, confused. That wasn't consistent with the information I'd learned in my re-search, but that didn't necessarily mean anything.

"I don't know," she answered. "I mean, there's no way really to tell. The company's private. Not traded . . ."

"Is there an ESOP?"

"Yes, but all the stock in the ESOP and 401(k) plans was Class B stock. Nonvoting, so that couldn't have been it."

"Hmmm, so how could R.J. have gotten voting stock in a privately held company?"

"I don't know," Erica said. "Maybe it was another company. Anyway, he and Karl went on yelling at each other and about two minutes later there was a big thump, like somebody falling."

"Falling? You mean one of them hit the other?"

"That's what I thought for a second, but then they kept yelling and I realized that Karl had probably kicked a chair or something. He's got a terrible temper."

"Did you pick up on what they were saying?"

She nodded. "Karl was screaming that he'd built the com-pany out of nothing and that the creditors had tried to take it away and the bankruptcy judge had tried to close them down and he'd not let them. Everybody was out to get him but he'd fix it. He'd show them. Crazy stuff. He'd be damned if he'd let it be taken away now. He was wild, almost out of control."

"And R.J.?"

"R.J. just laughed again, that low screw-you-you-little-insignificant-bug laugh of his. And Karl screamed at him to get out and R.J. said he would for now, but not to damage any more of the furniture because he—meaning R.J.—was sure going to enjoy it."

I put my lips together, let out a slow whistle. "So then what happened?"

"I ducked behind the door," she said. "The lights in the break room were off, like I said, and I just hid in the shadows. There was a clear view of the elevator. R.J. came through the double doors of the executive suite and punched the elevator button, like nothing had happened. He kept kind of giggling to himself, like he was real happy with what had happened."

"Yeah," I said. "The question is, what *did* happen?"

"I don't know the answer to that," she said. "And I don't know if any of this is really important. I only know that this was on Thursday night. Forty-eight hours later, R.J. was dead."

"And you haven't been to the police with this?"

"With what?" she asked. "That I was sneaking around eavesdropping on the president of the company I worked for? And that I sort of heard two people yelling at each other, but I only got muffled snatches of the conversation and don't really know what it means? I'm sure the police would handle that as delicately as they handle everything else. Only problem is, I'd be out of a job."

I looked at my watch. I was already trying to figure out how to pursue this one. I was also wondering if Erica Benedict was even telling me the truth. She seemed a stand-up kind of person, but I'd learned over the last few years not to make any grand assumptions.

"You're going to miss the funeral," I said.

She stood up, then leaned over, her back to me, and picked up the purse. The fabric of her skirt stretched tight across the back of her broad hips and I suddenly understood how a woman like that would find herself still in the office at nine o'clock at night. I hated myself for thinking that, but lately my self-image has taken a beating anyway.

"I don't know if any of this means anything," she said, standing up and turning back to me. "I almost hope it doesn't."

"Everything means something," I said. "It's just a matter of figuring out what."

"Are you going to R.J.'s funeral?"

I shook my head. "No, don't think so. Not a good idea. Besides, I have some other balls in the air right now."

"I don't know what I'll do for the rest of the day. I hate having time off. I really do love my work."

I smiled at her. "Speaking of your work," I said. "I've read *Life's Little Maintenance Manual* a couple of times now. I've always wondered—especially since I read your name in the acknowledgments—how one goes about editing a book that has so little in it to begin with. I mean, what's to edit?"

I realized that sounded insulting, even if I didn't mean it to be. She grinned, though, and shook her head wearily.

"You should have seen it before I got hold of it," she said, sighing. Then she turned for the door. "Yes, you should have seen it before I got hold of it."

Chapter 28

I briefly reconsidered the idea of heading off to Reed's funeral, then just as quickly dismissed it. I didn't mind running into the police and the news media; hell, by now I ought to be used to it. But his kids were going to be there and his relatives and friends, and there were bound to be those who would be, shall we say, distressed at my presence.

Shall we say, might take a notion to beat the crap out of me. . . . Do the words *lynch mob* have any bearing on this situation?

I quickly typed up my notes on the conversation with Erica Benedict and printed them, then stuck them in my file. In this business, sometimes you go on instinct even when past experience shows you that instinct can get you in a lot of trouble. This time my instincts told me that this was worth going after. It was like looking at a crowd of people in the fog. The wind shifts and one or two faces pop into focus for a moment, and then it shifts again and you see another face, but now the first two are clouded back over. But you take the memory of one face and tie it with the memory of another and eventually you figure out why the crowd has gathered.

Why would R. J. Reed even think of taking over Spearhead? Spearhead Press had made him rich, richer than any deal he might have dreamed of. He'd gone for the Big Lick and gotten it. The man had an ego, but wouldn't life as a famous best-selling author satisfy him? Why would he even want the headaches of running a publishing house? Take the money and run.

And how was he going to do it? Travis Webber and Karl

Sykes owned all the voting stock in Spearhead Press. Or at least I thought they did.

Once again, I thought, *shift happens.*

In the meantime, I remembered that there was yet another story in the afternoon paper describing a murder I'm supposed to have committed. Maybe I should read it, just to stay current with things. I once heard someone say there's no such thing as bad press.

I'm not at all sure about that.

The radio in the Mustang had a bad habit of periodically dying for no reason and then coming back to life when I least expected it. For the past day or so it had gone comatose on me and no amount of knob-twisting or dashboard-slapping would get sound out of it. I was on my way back across the river, en route to Lonnie's place to reconnect with his computer, when I got jammed up on some road construction on the Victory Memorial Bridge. It was nearly four o'clock and the traffic was thickening by the moment.

A Hispanic guy in an orange vest with a walkie-talkie lowered a pole with a stop sign on the end and the line of cars came to a halt. I drummed my fingers on the steering wheel. I hate to sit in traffic. Maybe it's having to pay for the wasted gasoline; hell, I don't know. I only know I've got one nerve left and this was getting on it.

Five minutes or so later the guy held the walkie-talkie to his ear, then raised the pole. We crept forward and as I got onto the bridge, I saw a large steel plate covering what I guessed was a hole. The car in front of me lurched as it went up on the thick plate, then bounced again as it came off the other side.

I had the car in first gear and eased slowly up on it. When I dropped off the other side, the radio popped loudly, then came back on with a blast.

"Jeez," I yelled, reaching for the volume knob before it did any permanent hearing damage.

"This is Sean O'Brien," the radio voice said, "for WMOT-FM news. Our top story this afternoon is the proposed shake-up at the Metro Nashville Medical Examiner's office. Sources within the mayor's office report that a deal is underway that would turn over the operation of the medical examiner's office to a private company."

"Holy cow," I whispered, turning the volume back up and hoping the radio would stay on.

"The mayor's office is reportedly in negotiations with a new company that was recently formed among several local forensic pathologists. That new company—ACA, or Autopsy Corporation of America—would take over a newly reorganized medical examiner's office on a contract basis. ACA officials, who refused to speak for attribution, claimed the company can run the medical examiner's office more efficiently and save the taxpayers money, while at the same time making a profit for company stockholders."

"Yeah, right," I muttered. "Republicans, no doubt . . ." My old boss at the newspaper had a wonderful term for it—*anal accounting*. You decide what numbers you need, then you pull them out of your ass.

"Dr. Henry Krohlmeyer, the embattled head of the Metro Medical Examiner's Office, was unavailable for comment and sources within the mayor's office would only confirm that discussions with ACA are underway. In the meantime, the Davidson County Grand Jury continues to look into allegations that the office is plagued by mismanagement."

I crossed the river into East Nashville, cut left for a block, then pulled into the parking lot of the Shell station on Main Street. I fished a quarter out of my pocket and dialed. When the answering machine came on, I tried to sound as calm as possible.

"Marsha, it's me. You there?" I waited a moment. "C'mon, damn it! Pick up!"

There was a click and then her voice, flat-lined, lifeless. "Yes."

"Hi, it's me."

"Hi, babe."

"You've seen the news. . . ."

"Heard it. Kay called." Marsha was sleepwalking, big-time.

"What is this Autopsy Corporation of America crap? They gonna hang out a sign that says 'Autopsies R Us'?"

She didn't react; I'd hoped for at least a chuckle.

I tried again. "Look, why don't I come on over?"

"No," she said. "Not necessary. I'm okay. Really."

"No, you're not. I can tell."

"I saw the afternoon paper. You're the one who ought to be not okay. Did you see that article?"

"I read it. It wasn't as bad as I thought it'd be. It only reported the family's allegations. The cops explicitly said there was no indication of foul play and they were just investigating."

"And you take that as a good sign?" A little life came into her voice.

"It could be worse."

"I'm the one that should be worried about you," she said. "Look, I've got to go. That fellow's coming to look at the Porsche in a few minutes."

"Why don't I just come over?"

"No," she said firmly. "I mean it."

"Okay," I agreed. "Call you later?"

"Sure. If you want to."

"Yeah, I want to."

"Bye." She hung up. I stood there holding the phone, staring off into the space where the abandoned Genesco factory used to be a few years ago before they tore it down and turned it into an urban park. Broken beer bottles and other assorted forms of trash littered the area.

"Yo, man, you done wid' dat?"

I turned. Tall black guy—baggy shorts, Bulls jersey, red bandanna—glared at me.

"Sure," I said, hanging up and backing out of the guy's way. I went back to the car and sat for a minute or so, trying to figure out what to do next. Nothing much came to me, but after a while I started the car and pulled away. Sitting parked in this part of town was a clear message that you were looking for trouble, and I already had plenty of that.

By the time I got home, the news media had given up and left. It was too close to their deadlines for the six o'clock news to get anything useful out of me. I pulled into my driveway, got out, opened the garage door, then parked the Mustang inside. Ordinarily, I'd have just left it in the driveway, but on this particular evening, I preferred to leave no evidence that I was home.

As I walked up the driveway to the steps leading up to my apartment, Crazy Gladys peered out through a slit in the Venetian blinds. I caught a glimpse of the movement in my peripheral vision, stopped, and turned slowly to glare at her. Just as my eyes caught hers, the blind closed and she was gone.

I shook my head, disgusted with Crazy Gladys and the world in general, then headed for the steps. I stopped at Mrs. Hawkins's back door and peered in. Her furniture was still there, which meant the rev and his wife hadn't been by. Given the events of the past few hours, I decided I was being entirely too accommodating to them. I made a mental note to have the locks rekeyed; then they'd have to work around my schedule to get their stuff out.

Serves 'em right, I thought. They can stand a little inconvenience, given that they're trying to have me sent away for a murder I didn't do and that wasn't committed in the first place.

I turned, walked down the driveway to the mailbox, and retrieved a small stack of envelopes. The electric and gas bills were there; I had two of them to cover now, oh, joy. And there were several catalogues for Mrs. Hawkins. Nothing else, which was fine with me.

In the back of my mind, I was still running around in circles trying to connect the dots between what I'd learned from Erica Benedict and from my research. The names—Sirius Corporation, Spearhead Partners II, LLP, and the mysterious Harvest Moon Corporation—danced around in my head. There had to be a way to tie them all together, and something told me that when all the dots were connected, the portrait of a killer would emerge. Nobody kills the goose that lays the golden egg without a reason, and R. J. Reed had laid the biggest golden egg any of them had ever seen. Somewhere in all this mess, there was an answer. But where was it? How could I find it?

I threw my coat on the kitchen table and walked into my bedroom. The shoes went in the corner and the shirt flew magically across the room and draped over the easy chair. I sprawled on the bed, popped a tape in the tape player, and punched the button.

The Jim Cullum Jazz Band's cover of Louis Armstrong's arrangement of "Potato Head Blues" filled the empty spaces about as well as anything else I'd ever found. The sweet double cornets wailed away while the clarinet wove its way in and out seamlessly. Every time I think there's no reason to keep pumping, I plug something like this in and think, Yeah, it's worth hanging around another day.

I stared at the ceiling and smiled, listening to the brass crescendo after the other solos. I think the thing I'll hate most about being dead—whenever that happens—is the silence. Darkness doesn't bother me, but an eternity without "Potato Head Blues" is unfathomable.

I unbuckled my belt and undid my pants, then raised my legs to pull them off me. When they were upside down in midair, the pockets emptied themselves. A wad of change, keys, burglar-alarm remotes, a single guitar pick—don't ask me where the hell that came from, except that everyone in Nashville seems to carry one—and little hunks of fuzz rained down on me. I muttered an appropriate epithet, then rolled onto my side to scrape the junk into a pile on the bed.

In the middle of the mess was a single silver key separate from the ones on my key ring. I picked it up and studied it for a second.

"Where the hell did you come from?" I asked out loud. No answer was forthcoming, so I lay back on the pillow and stared some more at the ceiling.

Lonnie's? No, that was the tubular Chicago Ace Lock key, and that one was on my key ring already.

Extra key to my office? The house?

"House," I whispered, and jerked upright in bed. It was a house key, all right, but not my house key.

It was the key to R. J. Reed's house out in Williamson County. I reached into my pants, grabbed my wallet. Inside, in the compartment next to two twenties, was a folded yellow

Post-it note. I unfolded the slip and read the series of numbers. They were the codes to the burglar alarm and the front gate.

I'd just been thinking about all the missing pieces, all the information I still needed.

R.J.'s office. They'd just finished burying him. He wouldn't care.

"You're out of your mind," I whispered.

But I was still under retainer to Victoria Reed, with the charge of finding the man who had murdered her husband. I needed information and the only place I could get to that might have that information was R. J. Reed's office. I was her employee; I'd explicitly been given permission to go on the property last Saturday night. She hadn't told me not to go back. I could stretch it and claim implicit permission.

Some stretch.

"This is insane," I said out loud. Then I reached for my pants.

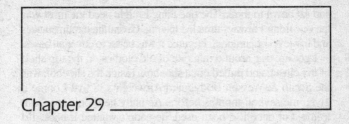

Chapter 29

What the hell, I was already a murderer. How much worse could it get? Once you're accused of killing little old ladies, burglary and trespassing just ain't that big a deal.

I'd gotten nailed the last time because I parked on the street down from the house. I wouldn't make that mistake again. I didn't have a whole lot of doubt as to what would happen to me if the police found me at R.J.'s again.

I poured a can of soup into a bowl, nuked it, and ate it without tasting it. I was going to give it a few hours, let the sun go down and the night take over completely. I didn't figure any of the family would be there. Who'd want to visit the place where your father was murdered on the day you buried him?

If I was wrong, if someone were there, I could just keep on driving. Otherwise, I was going to find out what I could.

One way or another.

I showered, shaved, brushed my teeth. I don't know why it seemed so important to be neat and pretty on this particular evening, except that I remember what every mug shot I've ever seen looks like. You can take the most devout preacher or the head of the largest corporation in the world or the president of the United States (*especially* the president of the United States) and put him in a mug shot photo and he'll look like a depraved animal.

Maybe I was trying to clean up for my own booking.

I gathered up my gear, which consisted of my 35mm Nikon with several lenses and strobe, notebook and pen, pocket tape recorder, a couple of flashlights, and my pocket case of lock picks. I laid everything out on the bed before packing them up and sat down to think. The one thing I might need the most was the one thing I always dreaded having. Given the circumstances and my level of paranoia, I figured it was better to cover all bases.

I got up, dug around in a pile of old clothes on the top shelf of my closet, and pulled out a shoebox. Inside the shoebox was the Smith & Wesson Bodyguard Airweight .38 that Lonnie'd given me several months before. Actually he'd only loaned it to me, but once it'd been used, he hadn't wanted it back. I'd once thought of throwing it away but decided to keep it. As what, I didn't know. A souvenir? Perhaps a talisman, a charm that had its own inimitable way of warding off evil.

I loaded the pistol, placed it in its hip holster, and packed it in my bag with the rest of my tools. I checked the clock; it was a little before nine.

It was too early to take off, but I was too fidgety to sit around here much longer. I fretted about it a bit, then decided to take a chance. I looped my arm through the strap on my goodie bag and headed down the stairs to the car.

She'd told me not to come by, but I had a bad habit of not doing what I was told.

A half hour later, I pulled off Hillsboro Road and into the parking lot of Marsha's condo development. The Porsche was gone; either Marsha got rid of it or she was out somewhere. I parked the car in an empty slot next to hers and got out. I almost hoped she'd be gone; I hated to see that car go. There was something about losing it that saddened me deeply. End of one era and beginning of another, I guess, and a damned unpleasant one at that.

Maybe I should have made her an offer. After all, I've got some extra cash. It would have only cost me about half my unexpected inheritance to buy the car from her. Probably would have cost the other half to keep it running, though. And pretty soon it'd just be a damned expensive lawn ornament.

I strode quickly up the walk and knocked on her door. In a moment, I saw the peephole darken, then lighten again as Marsha unhooked the security chain. She opened the door a crack, peeked out, and started to speak.

"I know," I interrupted her. "You told me not to come by. I did anyway."

Marsha opened the door all the way. She wore a loose maternity shift and a pair of Birkenstocks. Her skin was pale and splotchy without makeup, but she smiled wearily.

"I'm glad you did," she said. "I've been getting cabin fever."

"Can I come in?"

"Sure, c'mon." She turned, walked down the hall toward the living room. I followed her in and locked the door behind me.

"So you sold it," I said.

"Yeah, it's gone."

"I'm sorry you had to."

"Me, too. It's for the best, though."

We stepped down into the living room. She bent over and grabbed the remote off the coffee table, then muted the television, which was showing the tail end of an episode of *Married with Children* in reruns. Al Bundy chattered on in silence.

"Boy, have you sunk down on the cultural evolutionary ladder."

"I was just staring at it," she said, easing down onto the couch. "What are you doing out this late at night?"

I sat down next to her. "I'm on my way to run an errand. It was out this way and I just wanted to see you."

She smiled again, a nice one. "I'm glad. Been kind of lonely around here."

"Hear anything else from the office?"

"Not a word. Can I get you anything?"

"No, I'm fine."

"So what kind of errand are you on?"

I thought a moment. "Okay, there was an ulterior motive for coming out here. I did want to see you, but I also need a favor."

"Yeah?"

"You're better off not knowing where I'm going," I said, grinning despite myself. "I don't mean to get so cloak-and-daggerish, but trust me. It's better if you don't know."

"So what's the favor?"

"If things get hairy tonight, there's a pretty good chance I'll be in the Williamson County jail by tomorrow morning."

"What—"

I held up my hand. "Wait, let me finish. I don't think I'm doing anything wrong. But, damn it, people keep misinterpreting me."

She shook her head. "That's an interesting way of putting it. So what's the favor?"

"If you haven't heard from me by nine in the morning, call Lonnie. Tell him to bring some bail money. I'll try to get him, but sometimes he's tough to find and sometimes you don't always get your one phone call."

She looked down at her lap. "Harry, why are you doing this?"

"Doing what?" I asked.

"You are just amazing," she snapped. "Do you enjoy this, damn it?"

"What are you talking about?"

"Are you just not happy unless there's some kind of crisis going on in your life? What kind of pathology is this, Harry? What great big unfilled hole inside you compels you to get drawn into these kinds of situations?"

I felt my face redden and my collar suddenly felt tight. "Look, a lady walks into my office and needs my help and hires me to do a job and the next thing I know I find this dead guy and the cops think I did it! Now all I'm trying to do is get out of a mess I didn't have any part in creating."

She hauled herself up off the couch carefully, her center of gravity changing by the minute. She walked over to the window, stared outside for a moment. Then she turned and there was a coldness in her eyes I'd never seen before.

"You never have a part in creating these messes, do you?"

"What's that supposed to mean?"

"I mean you live for it, Harry. Sometimes I think it's the only thing that makes you feel alive." There was revulsion and disgust in her voice as she forced the attack.

"That's cruel, Marsha. And it's not true."

"It's truer than you're willing to admit. I can't live like this.

You're going to have to make your own phone calls. And if you're in jail, babe, don't call me."

"Marsha, I—"

I was interrupted by the chirping of the phone. Marsha picked up the cordless from the table next to the sofa and stared at the tiny built-in Caller ID screen.

"Who the hell?" she muttered. "Area code seven-oh-two . . . Oh, damn it, I know who it is."

She punched the button on the phone. "Hello?"

Her voice brightened, a chameleon-like shift that amazed me. "Hi, Aunt Marty! Thanks for calling me back. But listen, I've got company. Can you hold on just a second?"

Pause.

"No, it's all right," she said, glaring at me. "He was just leaving. Yes, that's it. No, honest, hold on."

She cupped her hand over the phone. "I'm sorry, but I've got to take this call. You can let yourself out, okay?"

I stared at her for a second, kind of numb all over, like this wasn't happening, like it didn't really sound like what it really sounded like.

"Is this the way you want to do it?"

Her eyes glistened and her lower lip trembled just enough to give her away, but not enough to change anything. She nodded.

"If that's the way it's gotta be," I said. "See you around." Then I turned and left.

I shut that side of my mind down as I wove through the traffic in Green Hills and then out of town. Night in the country, out of the city, is as thick and as black as axle grease. You get out far enough and there are no streetlights, and when it's late enough, most of the houses are dark as well. A thin sliver of moon was the brightest object in front of me, and as I turned right on Old Hillsboro Road, a silver shimmer reflected off the Harpeth to my left.

There'd been little traffic this time of night, and once I got off the main road, there was none. I curved slowly around the polo field, its lights off in the night as well, and drove slowly on toward the Reeds' place. A couple of mailboxes away from it,

I doused my headlights and coasted to the driveway. I stopped in front of the gate and sat there, the engine idling and only the dim running lights to illuminate the way.

The house was dark, pitch-black. And as far as I could see, the driveway was empty.

I rolled down the window and punched in four numbers on a small panel that stuck out from a pole. The gate slowly swung open in front of me. When there was room, I eased out on the clutch and started down the driveway. As I drove through, the gate began closing behind me.

The only house visible beside Reed's was the farmhouse to the right of his place. My eyes flicked back and forth between it and the thin ribbon of aggregate concrete that dipped and rolled toward the house. If a porchlight snapped on or a door opened, I was ready to throw the car in reverse and haul ass out of there.

My stomach knotted up on me. If this went sour, there'd be hell to pay. I could imagine that assistant DA licking his chops as I roasted on a spit in front of him.

Toward the middle of the driveway, the front yard took a real dip downward, taking me below a line of trees that blocked the view from the neighbor's house. I'd made it this far. If my luck would only hold out . . .

I goosed the Mustang quietly up the driveway to the house. To the right, on the far end of the parking area, an enclosed carport with room for four cars sat unoccupied. It was more like a garage without doors. Guess R.J. figured he had enough security already. I pulled onto the parking area and turned the car to back it into a slot.

Suddenly, the whole backyard was lit up like a baseball stadium. Motion-activated lights on the corners of the house and at the carport flashed on, spreading harsh white everywhere.

"Damn it," I mumbled. Nothing to do about it now. I was committed.

I backed the Mustang into the slot closest to the street and killed the engine. I stared hard through the windshield, studying the lit-up patio and swimming pool. Nothing moved. No sign of life. I hadn't recalled there being so much security light-ing last Saturday night.

Then I realized. There hadn't been.

I didn't know what that meant but shelved it away for later. The biggest fire I had to put out right now was getting in R.J.'s house before the bloody National Guard started parachuting in.

Most motion-activated lights are on a timer, and most of the time the timers are set short. If I sat here until they went out, I'd just set them all off again when I crossed the parking area. Bet-ter to go now, and then the neighbors would just figure a pass-ing raccoon or possum did it.

I grabbed my bag and slid out of the Mustang, then quietly shut the door. I went to the edge of the carport and peeked around.

Nothing. All silent, all still.

Sweat ran down my sides in rivers. Jeez, I thought, where's it all coming from? It's not that hot out here. Pretty cool, in fact. Shivers ran up and down my spine and I started itching in places where it wasn't polite to scratch.

I sighed nervously and realized my teeth were chattering. Okay, so the pressure's getting to me. Nothing to do about it now. I gritted my teeth, set my jaw, and walked calmly out into the light. My hearing was so acute, I could hear the wind rustling off the grass as I paced the twenty yards or so to the corner of the house. In the distance, a dog barked, which set off another one and then another and somewhere in the cacophony a cow bellowed mournfully.

Jesus, I thought, it's like Seventh Avenue at rush hour out here.

I got to the corner of the house and stepped into the tiny shadow cast by the soffit, just under the security lights. I stud-ied the area again, especially listening for sounds of noise in-side the house. As far as I could tell, the place was uninhabited, but it was also nearly eleven at night. Someone could be inside, asleep.

Maybe it was Victoria. And maybe she'd understand. And maybe she was standing at the door with a 9mm in her hand, waiting to blow away the first face that looked in her door.

I shook my head to clear it. Get a grip here, guy. And get inside the damn house before those lights go off.

I skirted the wall to a row of hedges, then around the hedges and onto the patio and to the back door, which led into the family room. The vertical blinds were closed, but I could see there was no light coming from inside.

The ornate black metal-and-glass door opened with a muted *whoosh* and I stuck the key in the doorknob. It was a simple cylinder lock, not terribly secure, but this was, after all, nearly a crime-free part of the county. Except for your occasional murder.

I stepped into the house and shut the door behind me. The air inside was dry, cool, the mechanized product of a high-efficiency cooling system. A tiny red light blinked away on a panel by the door. I punched in four more numbers, followed by the asterisk, and the light turned a steady green.

There was a light switch beneath the security panel. I thought for a moment, then took a chance. I clicked the switch down and the lights outside abruptly went dark.

"Great," I whispered. Then I remembered again that the security lights had been off the Saturday night Reed was murdered. He had been outside in the Jacuzzi, nude. Maybe he had preferred having the lights switched off so he wouldn't get any unpleasant surprises.

Then I laughed out loud, a soft dry crack of a laugh. Murder, I thought—the ultimate unpleasant surprise.

I pulled out the small flashlight and switched it on. Its narrow beam swept the room as I checked it out. The interior house lights were better left off.

That Saturday night I'd gone down the front of the house, peering into the windows, looking for Reed and Margot. I hadn't found them, but I had seen what looked like an office in the front of the house, near the side closest to the driveway.

I walked out of the family room into a large kitchen. A brick arch was built into the wall over a large restaurant-size Garland stove. A brass fixture hung from the ceiling over a center-island butcher block with expensive-looking pots and pans hanging suspended. It was a large country kitchen, warm and comfortable. No doubt the center of activity for some pretty swanky summer parties that now weren't going to happen.

Out of the kitchen and down the long hall, darkened rooms were off to either side. They were large, well furnished, but homey and warm. At the end of the hall, a locked door led into a room at the right while directly in front of me was the entrance to the master bedroom.

I stepped into the bedroom and ran the light all around. The Reeds had a large bed in the center of the room against the back wall with a huge cherry chifforobe facing it and antique cherry chests of drawers around the walls. A large Oriental rug covered most of the polished oak floors.

I opened the door to the chifforobe and peeked in. An immense black television perched on a shelf, with stereo system and VCR on shelves below.

Money, I thought, and lots of it. It was all top-of-the-line stuff. It may have taken them a while to learn how to earn it, but they had picked up the spending part fast.

I stepped into the bathroom, which was nearly as large as my bedroom. A huge sunken whirlpool dominated the master bath, with separate shower, his and hers sinks, and a closed-off phone-booth-size room for the dirty work.

"Nice," I muttered.

Next to the bathroom was a walk-in closet that was as big as my kitchen, jammed full of expensive clothes. I started to go through them, then realized I was starting to feel like a burglar as well as act like one. This wasn't what I was after.

I left the bedroom and returned to the locked door. I set the bag down on the floor, opened it, and took out my lock picks and the smaller penlight. Lonnie'd given me lessons in lock-picking—there's not much to it for most locks—and I'd practiced from time to time.

Now was an opportunity to see just how good a teacher Lonnie was.

I held the penlight in my mouth and focused it on the lock as I slipped the thin L-wrench inside the keyway and put just enough tension on the cylinder to press the pins against the shear line. Then I took a thin raker pick and slid it in next to the wrench. The idea is to rake the pick over the pins until they all hit the shear line; when they do, the tension wrench springs the lock open.

Sometimes you get lucky and you only have to pull the pick through a couple of times. Other times, you pull the damn thing in and out until you give up in frustration and try other picks, either a diamond or a ball pick or a different-size raker. This night I was lucky. Third time through and the cylinder spun around. I stood up and walked into R. J. Reed's private sanctum.

The flashlight beam shimmered off red leather and waxed oak. The rich smell of pipe tobacco seemed to fill the air, a kind of vanilla aroma mixed with the sharp edge of ash. I closed the door behind me and checked my watch: 10:55. The longer I hung around here, the greater the chances my karma would shift.

I've slept in beds that weren't as big as Reed's desk. It was heavy, constructed of dark wood, polished to a sheen with a sheet of plate glass a quarter-inch thick on top. Under the glass were proofs of his book covers, photos of Reed with celebrities and talk-show hosts, including an inscribed photo of Reed hugging Oprah and letters from other luminaries and famous people. In the corner, slipped just under the glass, was a small snapshot of Reed and his family, and next to it *The New York Times* bestseller list ripped from the paper the morning his book first made it.

A life under glass . . .

I sat down in Reed's high-backed leather office chair, opened the center drawer of the desk, and perused the contents quickly. It was the usual collection of pens and pencils, paper clips and old notes, business cards, ink cartridges, matches, a package of pipe cleaners. The routine assortment of junk and the detritus of a working life; nothing revealing or particularly useful. No bank books or checkbooks, no insurance papers or contracts.

I riffled the other drawers of the desk and found manuscripts, notebooks, a file of correspondence that I flipped through quickly. Again, nothing that would be useful, nothing that would give away secrets.

Not a clue as to why Reed had been murdered.

Frustrated, I ran the flashlight around the office again. There were floor-to-ceiling bookcases against one wall, with a credenza against the other that had a copy machine on top. I opened the drawers of the credenza; again, lots of files that took precious minutes to scan and provided nothing useful. What I was looking for were copies of his contracts with Spearhead Press, any information about the Sirius Corporation or the mysterious Harvest Moon Corporation. All I needed was a thread, something to grab on to that would lead me out of this fog and into something focused.

But there was nothing. In the corner of Reed's office was a closet door. As a last resort, I figured even a coat closet might have something to offer. I crossed the room and grabbed the doorknob.

It was locked.

"Now that's interesting," I whispered. "Why would anyone lock a closet?"

Determined to find out, I pulled out the picks again, set the flashlight on a shelf, and pointed the beam at the lock. This time it took a half-dozen tries before the lock gave way. I stood up, grabbed the flashlight, and opened the door.

It wasn't a coat closet. It was a large, rectangular walk-in closet. Two four-drawer filing cabinets were pushed against the back wall, with shelves full of office supplies, copy paper, and three-ring binders full of manuscripts lining the other two walls. The filing cabinets were locked, but I figured I could handle them. But down in the corner next to the door frame, about knee-high, was something that presented a somewhat larger challenge.

Reed had installed a safe.

Chapter 30 ⎯⎯⎯⎯⎯⎯⎯⎯⎯⎯

There's a world of difference between picking a fifteen-dollar lock you buy at a hardware store and cracking a safe. I stooped down and examined the damn thing. It wasn't much of a safe, just one of those fireproof jobs you can pick up these days at a Kmart or Home Depot for a hundred and fifty bucks, tops. But for me, it may as well have been Fort Knox.

I sat down on the floor of the closet and leaned against a filing cabinet. I was well and truly pronged, as the Brits say, and unless I figured a way out of this, then all the risk would have been for nothing.

"Bastard," I whispered. At least, I thought, I can try to pop the filing cabinets.

I grabbed the drawer handle on the cabinet closest to me and pulled myself up. I fixed the flashlight on a shelf and focused the beam, then commenced to fiddle with the tiny lock. The filing cabinet was harder to pick because the lock was smaller and there was less room to work. It took ten minutes to pop the sucker, and I had to use three different picks before I found one that worked. I had a cramp in my shoulders that ran all the way across the back of my neck and felt like somebody'd clamped about six pairs of Vise-Grips onto me. It was stuffy inside the closet as well; sweat ran off my forehead and dripped onto the floor beneath me.

The first filing cabinet contained all of Reed's back business correspondence, his travel schedules, diaries, and other business files. His royalty statements from Spearhead were in there as well, in addition to canceled checks, photocopies of his royalty checks, and several files that contained statements from his various stockbrokers. It's one thing to hear about somebody hitting it that big; it's quite another to see the figures in black and white. Seeing them convinced me more than ever that I am definitely in the wrong business.

"I got to write me one of them little books so I kin get rich, too," I muttered, flipping through the pages in astonishment.

This was all important stuff in R. J. Reed's life, but all useless in mine.

The lock on the second cabinet was a little more cooperative, thank you very much, and gave way in a couple of minutes. The bottom two drawers of that cabinet were empty; the top two contained copies of his press kit and what seemed to be file folder after file folder full of fan mail.

I couldn't believe Reed would save it all; maybe the guy had a soft, sentimental side after all. But for all the good it did me, he could've frigging been Mr. Rogers and Captain Kangaroo all rolled into one. I glanced down at my watch. It was nearly midnight. I'd been here an hour, with nothing to show for it but a headache and a large collection of my own fingerprints I'd left lying around.

I had to find the combination to that safe. Reed and I were about the same age, give or take a couple. Guys our age have usually stopped disillusioning themselves about their ability to remember everything. Half the time I can't remember what I had for lunch yesterday, let alone my checking-account number or my driver's license number or any of the other strings of numbers that life requires of Americans here at the close of the millennium.

No, if I had something that was important enough to lock away in a safe, I'd by God write the number down and put it someplace that I was sure I could remember.

Reed almost certainly would have done the same.

I stepped out of the supply closet just as a beam of light ran across the window facing the street. My breath caught in my throat and I jerked the flashlight down immediately, then snapped it off.

The light was coming from outside. It ran from my left to my right, disappeared for a few seconds, then came back.

I made my way cautiously across the office to the window and plastered myself to the wall next to the frame. The light ran back across the window again and disappeared. I hooked a finger around the thick heavy drapery and pulled it aside, then carefully peeked through a crack between the blinds and the window frame.

It was a Williamson County Sheriff's Department squad car parked in Reed's driveway at the street, just in front of the gate. The car had a spotlight mounted on the side of the driver's door and the officer inside was raking the house with a beam of light.

I held my breath, like that would do any good, and wondered how I'd get out of this one if he decided to come in and take a closer look. Then I remembered the Mustang was out of sight. He'd actually have to come down the driveway to see it.

If he'd just do a routine check, then leave . . .

"C'mon, man," I whispered. "Don't you need a doughnut or something?"

I stood there, sweat pouring off of me. It was that kind of gamy sweat that came from taut nerves rather than exertion, the kind that would take a ton of soap and water to kill off. The kind that would hang in the air inside Reed's office for a day or two. Just more evidence against me.

The spotlight outside clicked off, but the cop continued sitting there for a couple more minutes. I felt this sharp pain deep inside my gut and realized I had to go to the bathroom. I forced myself to stand there until he pulled away.

In the bathroom, I checked my watch again with the penlight. It was a few minutes after midnight. I guessed that I had at least an hour before the cop came back again. Something told me I didn't have the nerves for career burglary.

Back in Reed's office, I searched the obvious places. I not only checked all his desk drawers again, but I pulled them out and examined each surface for a piece of paper taped in out-of-the-way places.

Nothing.

I went through the credenza, opened the photocopier and searched inside it. I went through the filing cabinets again and flipped through his appointment books. I even tried to move the safe, thinking maybe I'd just haul the sucker with me. Luckily it was bolted to the floor. Even Reed's wife would think ripping off a safe was a little over-the-top.

It had to be somewhere, damn it. I'd spent nearly another hour trying to find the combination, all the while with my eyes and ears on alert for the patrol car. I didn't know how often the guy'd be back but knew he would. It was just a matter of time, and I didn't have a hell of a lot of that left. The batteries on the flashlight were even going.

Frustrated and increasingly fatigued, I sat down in Reed's chair, flicked off the dying flashlight, and stared into the darkness. This was useless, I told myself. Reed probably had the safe combination written down on a slip of paper in his wallet. And who would even know where to find a dead man's wallet?

I shook my head, trying to clear it and ease the spikes of tension in my neck. The headache was getting to me and I was cold and clammy all over.

"Okay, R.J.," I said out loud in a normal voice. The silence of the room seemed a broken spell now. In the very act of talking, I'd dissipated some of the tension.

"Where the hell is it? Where'd you put it, bud? Talk to me."

My eyes adjusted to the darkness and I could see the dim outline of the bookcase on the wall in front of R.J.'s desk. I imagined him sitting here after all those years of frustration and disappointment and failure. I imagined him soaking in all this adoration and wealth and trying to figure out how to make it last, how to get even more.

Erica Benedict said he'd laughed at Karl Sykes. He must have figured he had it sewn up, whatever it was he was trying to do. He must have figured it was a done deal and no one could stop him. And all as a result of one little book. . . .

Book.

Books.

"No," I said out loud. "You wouldn't . . ."

I stood up from behind the desk. No, surely he wouldn't. It'd be too much like the movies. I mean, come on, R.J., you're supposed to have this incredible imagination. Tell me you figured out something more clever than—

What did I have to lose?

I got up, switched the flashlight back on, its dim yellow light flickering weakly through the darkness. I didn't care; if I had to, I'd turn on the house lights.

I stepped over to the bookcase and started in the upper-left-hand corner. I pulled each book out, opened it toward the floor, fanned the pages, and carefully slid it back onto the shelf. I didn't pay much attention to the titles, but most of them were non-fiction: books about writing, business, investments, real estate. My movements were efficient, automatic, quick. I was midway through the third shelf when I pulled a black hardcover off the shelf, opened it, and my thumb caught on the pages.

Something didn't feel right. I jammed my thumb into the side of the book; the pages were stuck, maybe glued, together. I braced my hands and peeled the front cover off.

Reed had cut away the middle of the book's pages, creating a rough box-shaped empty space inside. A folded slip of paper sat alone within the secret space. I unfolded the scrap of paper. There were numbers inside: 26-8-54. I committed the numbers to memory and placed the paper back inside the book.

I turned the book over and in the dim light read the spine. The author was Brooke A. Wharton, and the title was *The Writer Got Screwed*. I grinned.

"You son of a bitch," I muttered. "I think I like you after all."

I stepped back into the supply closet, palms sweaty and cold, and sat cross-legged on the floor. I spun the tumbler to the left a few times and stopped at twenty-six, then back to the right past the first number, stopping at eight. Then back to fifty-four and twisted the handle . . .

The door opened.

I let out a deep sigh that seemed to have been trapped inside me for hours. My watch said 1:45. If the sheriff's department was on a two-hour schedule, I had barely minutes left.

The safe was jammed with file folders, but the flashlight was about dead, so it was hard to read. I flicked it off and pulled out the penlight, turned it on, and stuck it in my mouth. I jerked the stack of file folders out and squinted to focus on the tabs.

HARVEST MOON, the first one read.

If there was a bull's-eye anywhere in this house, something told me I'd just hit it.

Twenty minutes later, I was coasting down Reed's driveway. I'd thought of turning on his photocopier and copying the dozens of pages in the files, but there wasn't time. I threw the files in my shoulder bag, loaded up the rest of my gear, wiped the place down as best I could, and booked the hell out of there. I didn't know what was in the files and didn't know what I'd do with them once I did know. I only knew it was time to go.

The Mustang's engine idled roughly in the cold, damp night air. There wasn't time to let the car properly warm up. As I approached the end of the long drive, the electric eye caught the car and began opening the gate. I was through it in a heartbeat and gone to the left. I turned on the headlights with a shaking hand and tried to drive slowly and steadily. The last thing I needed was to get pulled over.

I made it past the polo field and back to the main highway. As I turned left on Hillsboro Road and headed back into Nashville, my breath came a little easier. And when that Williamson County Sheriff's Department patrol car passed me heading in the other direction, I didn't even flinch.

Chapter 31

Okay, so I find this dead guy and everybody thinks I killed him, and then the evening of the day he's buried, I break into his house and ransack his office.

Situational ethics aside, this was going to look real bad if anyone found out.

That was the problem, I realized, as I drove back through the darkened city streets in the middle of the night. So I'd found some contracts and some files that Reed clearly hadn't wanted to share with anyone else. If there were secrets to be exposed, insights to be had, clues to be pursued, how could I go after the truth without revealing my own ethical lapses?

Damn, nothing's ever easy.

Nashville at two-thirty A.M. isn't the same city most of us see during the day. The buildings take on a surrealistic cast, with the sulfurous glow of the streetlights and the stray ambient lights throwing a bizarre aura over everything. There's not much traffic—which in itself constitutes a totally different reality in Music City—and you rarely see anyone. There are places still open—all-night gas stations and convenience markets—but most of the people who work in them are hollow-eyed and suspicious or sleep-deprived to a state of numbness.

"We are de creatures awf de night," I sang as I pulled into the parking lot of a Shell station on Hillsboro Road. I stepped out of the car into a slight drizzle, the shallow puddles on the street reflecting the light in orange-hued rainbows. There was a pay phone mounted on the wall outside the cashier's booth. I stepped over to it, dropped in a quarter, dialed Lonnie's cell phone. If Lonnie was awake and around, the cell phone was turned on. If he'd gone down for the night, I'd get the recording.

He answered on the second ring. "Yeah."

"You're up," I said.

"No big deal for me. Pretty weird for you."

"One giant leap for mankind. Where the hell are you?"

"Southbound I-65, five miles north of Millersville. I'm in the wrecker."

"Got one, huh?"

"Yeah, picked one up in Kentucky. Big-assed Cadillac De Ville. It's on the hook."

"You going back to the lot?"

"Where else?"

"Meet you there in forty-five minutes, okay?"

"Done deal," Lonnie said. Then he hit the hang-up button. He was a man of few words while at work.

I made the turn off Gallatin Road just as a car full of rednecks in a late Sixties Chevy Malibu roared past and ran the light at Ben Allen Road right in front of a Metro squad car parked in the drugstore parking lot. Bad move, guys. Blue lights erupted like semaphore alerts, tires and sirens squealed, and the night's silence was broken with another *Dukes of Hazzard* car chase. Only this car chase wouldn't end at the commercial break or when the director yelled "Cut." The emergency room or the Metro jail; those are your options, boys. Feeling macho now?

Lonnie was lowering the Caddy off the towhook as I pulled in front of the gate. I got out, opened the gate, drove the Mustang in, and parked it, then closed and locked the gate behind me. Neither of us said a word to each other. The whooping of the Metro police car's siren faded to the north.

I pulled my bag out of the backseat and followed Lonnie into the trailer. Once inside, he flicked on the light and headed for the kitchen.

"Cold one?" he called.

"Yeah."

Two beer cans spewed as Lonnie popped them simultaneously. I sat down on the couch and pulled the files out of the bag, then spread them across the coffee table in front of me. I reached up, adjusted the gooseneck lamp, and tried to focus on the papers in front of me. Fatigue was catching up with me; it had been a while since I'd had much sleep. Come to think of it, I hadn't eaten much the last couple of days either. Wired, I guess.

Lonnie leaned down and slid a can of Foster's across the table to me. I picked it up, nodded thanks, and took a long gulp. It was so cold, it burned going down, that delicious tingly numbing burn that only comes from the first good swallow and that can never be duplicated until there's another first.

"So, what the fuck are you doing out so late?"

I leaned back against the couch. "Well, I guess I've been a bad boy."

"Hmm, funny thing. That's what Doc Marsha said when she called me tonight."

"What?" I sat forward on the couch. "She called you?"

"Yeah, and there were icicles in her voice, man. I had freezer burn on my jaw when I hung up the phone."

"I didn't think she'd do that," I said. "I mean . . . what did she say?"

"She said you came by her house just a little on the animated side. That you were going to pull some kind of shit that could land you in the Williamson County lockup, but that you wouldn't tell her what it was."

"I didn't want to get her in trouble. I just wanted her to call you if she didn't hear from me."

He smiled, took a long slug off the can, and belched loudly. "I don't think she wants to hear from you right now no matter where you are."

"She tell you that?"

"Let's just say I can read subtext. So what horrible crime are you supposed to have committed that I have to rescue your ass again?"

I pointed to the files. "I broke into Reed's country house and searched his office. Well, *break-in* is such an ugly term. Actually, I had a key."

"Was there anybody there?"

I shook my head.

"Harry, we got to have us a long talk here, buddy."

"What?"

"Well," he said, plopping his can of Foster's down on the table next to mine and sliding into a greasy easy chair, "let's just do a quick check on the old tote board here, okay? Your pregnant girlfriend's sounding like she's in the middle of dumping you, you're a suspect in one murder and about to become a suspect in another."

"Don't forget," I said, "I've been evicted from my office."

"Oh!" His right eyebrow shot up. "I didn't hear that latest development."

"Just happened today. Yesterday, I mean."

"So my gut feeling is that if we conduct a careful examination of every facet of your admittedly superficial and monotonic life, what we find is that virtually every aspect excites descriptions like—"

He brought his right index finger up to his cheek and smiled brightly.

"Hmm, does *down the toilet* work?"

"I still got my health," I said.

"Harry, how long are you going to have your health on prison food?"

I picked one of the file folders and opened it. "I'm not going to prison," I said absentmindedly.

He reached over, hooked an index finger over the edge of the folder, and pulled it down. I raised my eyes and stared at him.

"I'm not going to prison," I said firmly.

"Listen, asshole, this is me talking. Your bud, okay? Do you have any idea how much shit you'd be in if the Williamson County bozos had caught you out there?"

"They didn't."

"You got lucky."

I set the folder down. "What's going on with you? I came here to get some help and you're dishing shit to me."

"I am helping you, if you'd just listen."

"Some help—"

"Did you happen to catch the news tonight, big guy?"

"No. What happened?"

"Judge Bailey issued an order allowing the exhumation of your landlady's body. They're going to do this, Harry. They're going to autopsy her."

"So what?" I snapped. "She died of natural causes. I hate that they're exhuming her, but I can't do anything about it."

"That's not the problem, bud. The problem is, you ain't thinking so clear. This is a time in your life when you ought to be doing one of two things. You oughta: a) be sitting in your apartment watching television with your mouth shut; or b) sitting in your lawyer's office listening to him advise you to sit in your apartment with your mouth shut. Those are your two best options. . . ."

He hesitated for a moment, then picked up his beer can and leaned back in the chair. "And I don't see you taking either one of them. That disturbs me, Harry. It really does."

I glared at him. "At least I ain't walking around asking people who they'd rather fuck, Aunt Fritzi or Betty Boop."

His face went blank.

"I'm sorry, man," I said. "That was cold. I didn't mean it. I just . . . Hell, it's just been a rough few months, that's all."

He lifted his beer can and gulped. His Adam's apple bobbed as he swallowed the Foster's and his eyes went fuzzy for a second. It was the middle of the night, I thought, and sometimes in the middle of the night the mouth kicks in before the brain can stop it.

Lonnie refocused his eyes on me. "All right, no offense taken, man. I just don't want to see you get hurt anymore. That's all. I'm talking at you as a friend. Maybe I oughta stop talking at you and start listening to you. So what did you find in this guy's office?"

"I was hoping you could help me make some sense out of all of these," I said, relaxing a bit and hoping that maybe he was still in my corner. I took the stack of files and fanned them across the table like a deck of cards. There were eight different files, ranging from a few pages to nearly a half-inch thick. I hadn't had time to read any of them.

Lonnie leaned closer and examined them. "So you think there's something in here."

I shrugged. "The way I figure it, Reed was killed for a reason. And the reason had to have something to do with all that money."

"That's usually the reason murder is committed," he commented. "That or passion."

"If there's nothing in here, the worst that can happen is I gotta break back into the guy's house to put these back before anyone misses them."

Lonnie grinned. "You never learn, do you?" He reached across, grabbed the top file off the stack, and opened it.

I grabbed the next file and scooted over directly under the lamp.

"Hey," I said. "I'm glad you're not pissed at me. I can't afford to lose any more friends. There aren't that many left."

He peeked over the top of the file folder. "That's true," he said. "You can't."

My folder contained the original contract for *Life's Little Maintenance Manual*. The agreement was printed in small type, essentially boilerplate, and I imagined that it put as little of the risk as possible on the publisher. As Victoria had told me, R.J. received no advance. There were paragraphs that outlined his royalty percentages and described how that percentage would decline as the publisher offered bigger discounts to retailers. There were terms like "freight pass-through" and long descriptions of sub-rights splits. I couldn't imagine how anyone could understand the ins and outs of the contract without a lawyer, and truth is, I wasn't even going to try. That wasn't what I was looking for. I was looking for something that wasn't boilerplate, something out of the ordinary.

I found it in the next file, which contained the recently negotiated contract for the sequel, officially to be called *Life's Little Maintenance Manual, Volume II* and subtitled *More Nuggets of Wisdom from America's Dad*.

I suppressed a wave of nausea and read on. This time the contract was definitely not boilerplate. It was typed like a legal brief, had clearly been prepared by a lawyer. There were several variations or versions of the contract, with the final one at the bottom of the stack. There was also correspondence and notes of phone calls between Reed and the lawyer who negotiated the contract. I started reading the long contract, and as I read, I became more and more astonished by how different Reed's first deal was from his second.

Lonnie got up, still reading a stapled sheaf of papers, and disappeared into the kitchen. A moment later I heard two more tops popping followed by the spew of escaping carbon dioxide. I didn't look up as Lonnie set another can down in front of me.

I picked it up, took a long sip as I read, then turned to the next page.

Amazing, I thought. The negotiations were a long, complicated process full of hiccups and screwups that finally ended in an agreement that was signed the week before Reed was murdered. As I read through the stack of paper, what gradually became clear was that in order to keep Robert Jefferson Reed, America's favorite dad, on their list, Karl Sykes and Travis Webber had essentially given away a huge chunk of the company to him. Reed had demanded five million dollars as an advance. A bunch of letters between Sykes and the attorney ranged from conciliatory to threatening to an outright pissing contest. Bottom line: There was no way Spearhead could pay that much. They just couldn't come up with that kind of upfront cash. It would have taken a bond issue to raise that kind of dough, and industrial revenue bonds to create capital to pay an author's advance was a concept that Music City just wasn't quite ready for.

It took me over an hour and another can of Foster's to get through the file. Between three cans of Foster's and the weight of fatigue, I was good and punchy. I forced myself to focus, though, on what I'd learned. I tried to summarize it and see how it all fit into the larger puzzle, to see if it was the missing piece that would provide me with that rush of enlightenment I so needed.

"You know," I said, looking up through weary eyes at an intense Lonnie in the chair opposite me. "In order to keep R. J. Reed as an author, Sykes and Webber gave him enough stock in the company to make him the third-largest shareholder, behind the two founders."

Lonnie put the file in his lap and stared into space for a moment before speaking.

"That's interesting," he said finally, holding up one folder, "because these are the incorporation papers for a Cayman Islands corporation called Harvest Moon."

"Yeah, I found that on the Web," I said. "It's some kind of company that Webber and Reed were in together."

"And in this file," he said, holding up a second folder, "is the instrument of transfer for both Webber's and Reed's shares in Spearhead Partners II, LLP, to the Harvest Moon Corporation. It's dated a week from tomorrow."

I sat up confused. "What?"

"Don't you get it?" Lonnie asked. "Webber and Reed were going to take over the company. They were going to stiff-arm Karl Sykes the hell right out of the picture."

My jaw dropped. "And forty-eight hours before Reed was murdered," I said, "he and Sykes got into a huge fight. Sykes said he'd be damned if he'd let anybody take his company away from him."

Lonnie smiled. "Maybe he will be. . . ."

I grinned back at him. "By George, Watson," I said, mimicking a thick British accent, "I think we've got it."

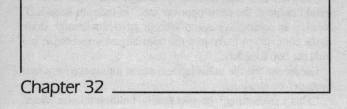

Chapter 32

The sun came up and we switched from Foster's to coffee.

"It's got to be Sykes," I said, closing the last of the file folders.

"Sure looking that way," Lonnie said. His eyes scanned the coffee table, now covered in files and papers. "Sykes and Webber had to give Reed a chunk of the company to keep him."

"Reed, meanwhile, had transferred copyright interest and ownership in his books to the Sirius Corporation."

"Which he probably created to get some tax breaks . . ." Lonnie speculated.

"Then the Sirius Corporation became a pipeline," I added. "A pass-through corporation to hide what he and Webber were planning. You got a legal pad or something? I've got to write this stuff down or I'm going to lose it."

He disappeared down the hall, then came back with a pad and pen. I took it from him and started making notes.

"First, the book becomes a megahit. The taxes are killing his ass, so Reed sets up Sirius, with himself, Victoria, and the kids as sole shareholders."

"But Victoria and the kids never hold enough to have any kind of control," Lonnie said.

"Of course. Reed's not giving up control of anything to anybody. Ain't his style. So he goes back to contract."

"The question is why he decided to stay with Spearhead in the first place. A big trade house in New York probably would have given him the five mil up front, no questions asked."

I tried to put myself in Reed's place, to think like he'd think, to maneuver like he'd maneuver.

"Yeah, but at a big publisher he'd be just another pain-in-the-ass, bestselling author," I said. "At Spearhead, though, he was king of the frigging hill. You look at Reed's history, what was he?"

"A player," Lonnie said, smiling.

"Exactly. It was the game that mattered. He wanted to win, but once he was a winner, it was off to the next game, the next deal. That was the shark ego at work. He had to keep moving or he'd die."

"So he decides to work his way into the power structure at Spearhead?"

"Yeah, and then once that's done, he's off to a bigger game. So the first thing he does is negotiate his way into partial ownership of the company."

"And then he allies himself with Webber," Lonnie said. "And between them the two of them own enough shares to take the company over."

"They set up Harvest Moon in the Caymans," I said, "to disguise their moves for as long as they can. Eventually, Sykes is going to find out."

"But by then it's too late."

I made a few notes. "At least that's the way it was supposed to work."

Lonnie picked up a file and opened it. "What I can't quite place is why, in Reed's will, Webber is named his literary executor."

I looked up. "You mean why not Victoria?"

"Yeah."

I leaned back, stared at the splotched ceiling of the trailer.

"Don't forget," I said, "Victoria and R.J. didn't exactly have the strongest marriage in the world. Maybe R.J. figured if she was going to divorce him anyway, it was better not to have her in control of his literary estate if anything happened to him."

"Still," he said, holding up another folder. "It seems odd that in the living will, the power of attorney is divided into two parts. Victoria has the POA over his business affairs, but Travis has the say-so over all his literary affairs. Seems confusing."

"You know," I said, "I did this article once, a feature on the

Du Pont plant out in Old Hickory. Rayon City, they call it. And in the research I read about this old guy—let me see if I can remember—Flanagan, yeah, that's it, Henry Flanagan. A financier, supposed to be a financial genius robber-baron type who worked for the Du Ponts, later went on to make a fortune in Florida real estate. Built the Florida East Coast Railway. Anyway, every evening at the end of the day, all Flanagan's top boys would gather in his office for a drink and ol' Hank would hold up his glass of bourbon and deliver the same toast every night. Know what it was?"

"No," Lonnie said. "But I got a feeling you're going to insist on telling me."

"Confusion to our enemies," I said, holding my coffee cup toward him and toasting. "I'll bet this was just R.J.'s way of keeping some shit in the game."

Lonnie tossed the file folder onto the coffee table. "Guy was a piece of work, wasn't he?"

"Yeah, and in a strange way, I think I would have . . . well, hell, I hesitate to say I would have liked him. You know what I mean."

"Yeah," Lonnie said. "He was never boring."

"The question now is, what do we do with all this?"

He shrugged. "I don't know. Take it to the cops?"

"Oh, yeah, that's a great idea! Uh, excuse me, officer, I just happened to be breaking into this house, see? And I found all these files and stuff that just happened to jump into my bag when I wasn't looking, and when I found 'em at home and read 'em, lo and friggin' behold, I figured out who the bad guy was."

"All right, smartass, let's hear your ideas."

I leaned into the couch and put my feet up on the table, weary and fuzzy-headed. Ideas, ideas . . .

If only I had any.

I thought maybe a few hours of sleep would clear my head, give me the chance to recharge and refocus. I felt like a window had been opened, and even if the truth was not visible through this window, at least some part of it might be. I had to grab on to whatever I had and start pulling, like a loose thread on a coat, and see what unravels.

Only problem was that as exhausted as I was, sleep wouldn't come. I lay in bed not tossing and turning, but perfectly still, on my back, my hands at my side, staring up at the ceiling and seeing little patterns in the swirls of dried, flaking paint. The edge of my vision was brittle, fragile, as if I'd crack into a million pieces if a stiff wind came from an unexpected direction. But still, no sleep.

There were no messages on the answering machine. For once, I'd gotten a break on that count. But it feels curiously lonely to come home to an empty answering machine. I felt out of touch, detached, alone. I almost wish there had been some, so I'd have something to concentrate on and keep my mind from spinning off in dozens of different directions at once.

So they think I killed Reed and they think I killed Mrs. Hawkins. And you're a burglar and a thief. And you need a shower, too.

And Marsha wants out.

Live with it, guy, because there's nothing you can do about it. I guess I can understand it; who wants to live the rest of his life on the fringes? That was certainly where I was headed if I wasn't already there. No security, no steady paycheck, no health insurance, no unemployment insurance; no 401(k), no SEP, no Keogh account, no IRA. None of the safety nets of life that middle-class American baby boomers nearing the turn of the millennium are so obsessed with. Thirty years ago we were on the front lines, smoking joints and sticking flowers down the barrels of National Guard rifles manned by clean-shaven boys our own age while chanting *Hey, hey, LBJ, how many kids did you kill today?,* something that strikes me today as both brave and unfathomably cruel, all at the same time. And now the obsessions in our lives are investments and cholesterol levels, marriages gone stale and retirement, who's going to pay for the kids' tuition and the parents' nursing-home bills.

"Stop this," I whispered. "Turn the brain off. Switch all circuits to 'off.' "

Not a chance.

I got up and turned on the television. *Good Morning, America* had just broken for a local news segment and the smiley-faced anchorette came on. She led off with another drug killing on Jefferson Street, then a six-car fatal smashup on Briley Parkway.

Slow news day, I thought.

Then the painfully bright-eyed, cheery lady dropped a bomb: "The district attorney's office announced late last night that the Davidson County Grand Jury probe into operations at the T. E. Simpkins Forensic Sciences Center has been dropped as a result of yesterday evening's resignation of Dr. Henry Krohlmeyer, Metro Nashville Medical Examiner."

Okay, I'm awake.

"The surprise resignation came after a late-night meeting in the mayor's office. According to mayoral spokesman Tammy McCallister, Dr. Krohlmeyer met with the district attorney and the mayor and an agreement was reached whereby Krohlmeyer would resign after first dismissing the entire staff at the medical examiner's office. In return, all allegations of wrongdoing at the *blah-blah-blah . . .*"

Dismissed. Canned. Terminated. Sent packing.

The entire staff fired. My God, Marsha's never been fired from a job in her life. This is going to crush her. I picked up the phone, dialed her number like a reflex.

Busy.

I set the handset back down. For all I knew, she didn't want to hear from me anyway. I stared at the wall as the voice on the TV droned on.

"Council members are expected to approve the agreement negotiated between the city and ACA, the Autopsy Corporation of America, at tomorrow night's meeting. Dr. Frank Wilson, president of ACA, said yesterday afternoon that the company was ready to take over operations of the medical examiner's office immediately."

Yeah, I'll bet he was. To pilfer one of their metaphors, the body won't even be cold yet.

The world was being remade right in front of me. This, I realized, was a whole different reality.

I showered, shaved, made a pot of coffee and another bowl of low-fat, low-taste health cereal. I also tried Marsha's number about ten more times, getting nothing but a series of busy signals.

Maybe she had the phone off the hook. Maybe she was on the line with her lawyer instructing him to sue the bloody hell out of those bastards.

I'd find her later. I'd do what I could to help; despite our differences, I cared deeply about her. Her welfare was important to me. Maybe in the end that's all we can expect love to be, because it seems that to expect anything more was to ultimately face disappointment.

For now, I had the feeling I knew who'd killed R. J. Reed, and as the morning went on, I gradually figured out how to prove it.

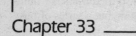

Chapter 33

I've never been one for going with the flow. My experience has been that going with the flow usually results in a trip over the waterfall. And the rocks below aren't much of a cushion.

But it occurred to me that in this case, going with the flow might not be such a bad idea. There are just about a million people in greater Nashville, and right now a good three-quarters of them think I killed R. J. Reed. A growing number no doubt figure I killed a sweet little old lady.

So be it. If it's low-life scum they want, then it's low-life scum they'll get.

"You're crazy," Lonnie said, rubbing the sleep out of his eyes as I gave him the abridged version. "It'll never work."

"Look, Sykes must figure he's gotten away with it now. If that picture changes, he'll get desperate."

"Yeah, desperate enough to shoot your ass."

"That's where you come in."

He pulled up his jeans and zipped them, then leaned over to pull on a dirty pair of boots. "Why don't you go to the cops with this? Make it easy on yourself."

"You know how much credibility I have with the Williamson County Sheriff's Department."

He grunted as he yanked the boot over his foot, then fell back on the bed, breathing hard. "Christ, Harry, I was up all night and just woke up from a whopping four hours of sleep. Give me a chance here."

"You get dressed and pull yourself together," I ordered. "I'll make a pot of coffee."

He squinted through crusty eyelashes and lifted his upper lip to expose the right canine. "You don't need any more coffee."

I walked into the trailer's tiny kitchen. There was barely enough room to turn around. I scrubbed out the coffeepot, dug around in cabinets until I found a can of Maxwell House, and set up the coffeemaker. I poured water into the machine, then stood there tapping my feet.

"C'mon, damn it," I muttered. "Let's go."

Lonnie was right; I didn't need any more coffee.

I heard water running in the bathroom and the sounds of spitting and gargling. I picked up the cordless phone and dialed Marsha's number. It rang four times. The machine picked up. I let the outgoing message run its course.

"Hi," I said, suddenly tongue-tied. "Uh, it's me. I just wanted to see if you were okay. I mean, I heard the news this morning and I'm really sorry."

The only thing I heard was a faint buzzing in the phone line. If she was there, she wasn't picking up. I held the phone out, hit the button to disconnect.

"What news?"

I turned. Lonnie was standing in the door frame, dressed, combed, and washed. He still had the three-day stubble, though, but on him it didn't look bad.

"They had a massacre down at the ME's office. Krohlmeyer resigned. Everybody else was fired."

"Doc Marsha fired?"

I nodded my head.

"Heavy-duty," he said. "Guess this means the vultures can circle and pick the bones clean."

"Yeah," I said.

"I wish we could privatize the politicians, then lay their asses off. You talk to her?"

"No, I've tried about a dozen times already. The line's either busy or I get the machine."

Lonnie poured a cup of coffee, raised it to his lips, and took a careful sip. "Think she's screening her calls?"

I glared at him. "Can we talk about something else?"

He raised a palm. "Okay, backing off, effendi. . . . Now, how are you going to pull this little gem of a scam off?"

I poured a cup of coffee, adding sugar and a dollop of milk that was just short of lumpy as I spoke.

"I figure I'll call Sykes, let him know what I've got. If he wants to buy it back, it'll cost him. We'll meet somewhere for the transfer. Can you wire me?"

"Sure, no problem. How much are you going to demand?"

I took a small sip of the coffee. It went down, hit my stomach with a *whomp*, and proceeded to go straight to my brain. Nothing like a caffeine rush on top of an exhaustion high to get the synapses firing.

"It'll have to be high enough to convince him I'm serious, but low enough that he won't decide it's easier to take a chance and—"

I hesitated.

"Shoot you before I can blow the bugle and come riding over the hill?" Lonnie asked.

"Something like that."

"What makes you think the guy'll even take your call? The last time you guys talked, it didn't exactly go too well."

I studied that one for a few seconds, then it hit me. "I'll use the files. I don't know how yet. But there's got to be a way to get his attention."

Lonnie swirled the remains of his coffee around in the cup. "So," he said, "when you going to do it?"

I started wondering if I could pull it off; all the coffee and Foster's and the cardboard health-food cereal suddenly coagulated into one solid bowling ball right in the pit of my gut.

"Oh, hell," I said after a moment. "No time like the present."

Lonnie reached over, grabbed the cordless off the counter, and handed it to me.

"Okay, big guy," he said. "Showtime."

"Phone book?" I asked.

He opened a drawer under the counter and pulled out a greasy yellow pages. I looked up Spearhead Press, dialed the number.

"Hello," the computerized voice said. "Welcome to Spearhead Press. . . ."

I rolled my eyes. "Voice mail," I whispered.

He laughed. "You don't have to whisper, dumbass. It can't hear you."

I listened to my menu options for what seemed like a day and a half, finally punched 0 for the operator. The switchboard rang about ten times before a human voice answered.

"Mr. Sykes's office," I said.

"Please hold."

I cupped a hand over the mouthpiece. "I hate telephones," I said.

"And Nashville drivers and politicians and idiots," Lonnie said. "You're becoming a curmudgeon in your old age."

"Damn straight," I said.

"Mr. Sykes's office," the young voice of Sykes's pretty receptionist said.

"Hi, Mr. Sykes, please."

"May I ask who's calling?"

I was afraid she'd ask that. "This is Harry Denton."

"Oh," she said. "Please hold."

I shifted my weight, leaned my hips against the counter, and drummed my fingers on the countertop. Finally she came back on.

"I'm sorry, Mr. Sykes is in a meeting."

"It's important," I said. "Is there any way to interrupt him for just a moment?"

"No, I'm sorry, that's quite impossible." The bright, cheerful, courteous facade was fragmenting.

"Now, look, I have to get a message to—"

"I'm sorry, sir," she interrupted, "but Mr. Sykes has said he will not speak to you under any circumstances and that it's quite inappropriate for you even to be calling him."

My face reddened. "You give him this message," I warned. "Or you're going to be in a lot of trouble. Not with me. With your boss. Understand?"

"Oh, all right," she said, disgusted. "What's the message?"

"Have him call me at this number immediately," I said. I looked at Lonnie, mouthed the word "Okay?" He nodded. I rattled off the number.

"And here's the message. Two words: Harvest Moon. You got that?"

"Yes," she said. "But I don't understand what it means."

"He will. You just give him the message."

"Yes, but I don't think he'll—"

I hit the disconnect button to cut her off. We'd see how good she was at following directions.

Lonnie was grinning when I turned to him. "You're faster on your feet than I gave you credit for."

I smiled back. That was high praise coming from him.

"I'm gonna take a crap," he said.

I reached for the coffeepot. "Thanks for sharing that with me. It was an—authentic—moment."

Thirty seconds later the phone rang.

"Yeah."

There was silence on the line for a few seconds, then a voice that was lower and more intense than the last time I heard it.

"What do you want?"

"Think of this as a sales call."

"So what are you selling?"

"I have some files you may be interested in. Some files you might not want other people to see."

"What makes you think I give a damn about what files you've got?"

"Maybe you don't give a damn," I said. "But the William-son County Sheriff's Department might."

The voice snorted, a guttural, mean sound of derision and scorn. "I care even less about them than I do about you."

"Bad decision," I said. "Because these files provide the one thing the cops need to figure out who killed Reed."

"Yes, and what is that?"

"Motive."

The phone was silent for what seemed a long time. Somebody told me once that in a sales call you make your presentation, then you shut the hell up. The next one to speak loses.

"What motive," Sykes asked finally, "can be found in a bunch of paperwork?"

I smiled. "Well, let's see. One file is labeled Sirius Corporation and another's labeled Harvest Moon."

"Meaningless names," he said. "Just words."

"Interesting comment from a man who makes his living publishing words."

"The words I publish mean something. Yours mean nothing."

"How about the file with the contract to Reed's next book, outlining how you and Webber gave him a piece of the company to keep him. Oh, and don't let me forget, there's the other file that contains a lengthy agreement describing how Reed and Webber were going to transfer their shares to the Harvest Moon Corporation by way of the Sirius Corporation."

"Why would anyone want to go to that much trouble?"

"To hide the fact that Reed and Webber were conspiring to take over the company and boot you out."

More silence. Then Sykes again: "You have an active imagination, my friend. There are several ways to handle that kind of imagination."

"Let me suggest the cheapest and easiest. The files are for sale. Thanks to the cops' ineptitude in deciding I killed Reed, not to mention a couple of other unfortunate circumstances, my reputation in this town is shot. I couldn't buy my way out of traffic court. I'm leaving Music City, leaving it for good, and I need a grubstake."

"So tell me, how big a grubstake are you looking at?"

"I have eight files, but only five of them provide a motive for Reed's murder. So let's say ten grand apiece, in small, unmarked nonsequential bills. And I'll throw in the other three as lagniappe."

"You're not only a murderer, you're a blackmailer as well," Sykes said.

"Ah, ah, ah—" I warned. "Sticks and stones . . ."

"Where can we"—he hesitated—"consummate this arrangement?"

Interesting turn of phrase, I thought. I wondered if he realized I didn't have any intention of getting consummated on this one.

"They say the murderer always returns to the scene of the crime," I said. "Why don't we meet in Reed's backyard, say at ten tonight? That way at least one of us will prove the adage true."

"My wife and I have a dinner party," he said. "But I guess I can arrange to leave early."

"Black tie?" I asked.

"What difference does that make?" he demanded.

"Just wondering if I should wear my tux."

"No, it will be quite casual."

"Good, you know the code for the gate?"

"I've been to R.J.'s many times," he said.

"Yeah, I'll bet. See you then. And Karl?"

"Yes."

"This is a solo gig. Make sure you come alone."

"I should say the same to you."

"Not to worry, babe," I said brightly, as if arranging a lunch date. "Ciao."

Sykes slammed the phone down so hard it hurt my ear. I turned. Lonnie stood in the doorway, yawning and scratching himself.

"We on?"

"Yeah," I said. "We're on."

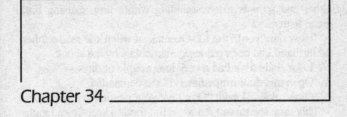

Chapter 34

The tension of faking my way through the phone call with Sykes dissipated as soon as I hung up, and in its place was a wave of fatigue that threatened to engulf and pull me under. I had to get home and lie down, even if sleep wouldn't come. I could turn the air-conditioning up and pull the shades and peel off these clothes and be still for a moment. Try to quiet the storms for a little while.

Ten minutes after leaving Lonnie's, I pulled into my driveway, only to find my path to the garage blocked by the Reverend Hawkins's big Lincoln.

"Blast," I muttered. "Just what I need."

I backed out and parked on the curb, then walked up the driveway, resisting the urge to carve my initials on his car door with my keys, and turned the corner.

Hawkins and his wife were standing on the back stoop, the wooden screen door open, twisting the knob and rattling the door. He was bent over, with her huddled behind him, frantically trying to get the door open.

I padded up undetected, then cleared my throat with a deep rumble that caused them both to jump and shake.

"You scared us to death!" she hissed.

"Can I help you?"

"We're trying to get into my mother's house," he blustered. "And the door's stuck."

"The door's not stuck, you moron," I said. "I had the locks rekeyed."

He turned bright red and it was like this huge bubble was inside him, trying to get out, and it was too big to come out either end so was just resounding within him, causing him great distress.

"How dare you!" the Ice Queen spat when she realized her fat husband had been rendered inarticulate by the shock.

"Look, lady, I've had a very long couple of days—"

"Open this door immediately!" she demanded.

"Okay, okay," I said. "Don't get your panties in a wad."

This time she turned red as well. I tried to keep from laughing, but I swear the two of them looked like some kind of mutant radioactive overgrown radishes wearing clothes, and tacky ones at that.

"How dare you," she sputtered again. "You have gone too far this time!"

"No, you two are the ones that have gone too far. How could you dig up that woman and subject her to an autopsy just to get your grubby, greedy little paws on something she didn't even want you to have?"

The Ice Queen backed off, frightened, her breath coming in short gasps. The reverend fell back, a gagging sound erupting from his throat.

"And when they slice open your mother like a field-dressed deer," I continued, pointing at him, "and lay her guts out on a steel table to examine them and they discover the truth, which is that she died quickly and peacefully from old age and I had nothing to do with it, then the two of you are going to be exposed as the small-minded, venal little shits that you are!"

They looked numb, almost in shock. I didn't expect any of what I'd said to change anything or make any difference to them, but it felt good to say it.

"Now if you'll move," I said, turning to the Reverend Hawkins, "I'll open the door to my house so you can get your stuff out. And I'd appreciate it if you'd make arrangements to take care of this as quickly as possible, because frankly, the sight of the two of you makes me want to barf."

His bulbous, bloodshot eyes twitched in their sockets, but he stepped out of the way and he kept his mouth shut. I drew from this the conclusion that at least he wasn't stupid. I unlocked the door, then turned my back on the two of them and started up the stairs. Behind me, the Reverend Hawkins did the only thing he could do under the circumstances; he started spouting Scripture at me. Religion, like politics, is one of the last refuges of the scoundrel.

"And if it seem evil unto you to serve the Lord, choose you this day whom ye shall serve—"

I sighed. Like I really need this crap.

"—but as for me and my house!" he yelled up the stairs. *"We will serve the Lord!"*

"Oh, shut up," I muttered. "It's not your house."

Somehow sleep came, and when it did I fell into that black pit that had become sleep for me over the past few months. I can remember dreams, can remember a time when sleep brought rest and I woke up renewed. Now it was like weight on me, more like coma than slumber. And then, hours later, when I began to drift up toward the surface, a dream came to me that was so vivid it was like a knife in the belly. In the dream, I relived the first time I ever made love with Marsha. It was a dream beyond the erotic. Sex dreams always seem to concentrate on a certain specific and somewhat narrow focus, a vision that converges on body parts and visual movement. This was different. In the dream, I smelled her, felt her, heard her, tasted her, saw her. In the dream every sense came alive in ways that I seldom experienced while awake. I remembered so vividly the sounds she made as I touched her, the way her lips pouched out and her eyes narrowed when she was aroused. The kittenish, almost mewling sounds that erupted from her throat as she came; sounds of pleasure and surrender.

At least I thought then that her sounds were of surrender, but knew now that Marsha never surrendered. There was a part of her inside, a core place that never surrendered no matter how intense the assault, how powerful the desire, how desperate the yearning. There was a part of her that was hidden and would remain forever hidden, and in the end she turned me away, perhaps because I had threatened that place inside her in ways that no one ever had before.

I awoke in pain, partially from my own pressured arousal and engorgement, and partially from the end of the dream wherein I realized for the first time that she was gone, that I had lost her. Marsha was somewhere else now, and I was no longer part of her world. I was her history.

The world had realigned itself and I hadn't even realized it. Nothing was the same. She had been part of the structure of my life and now that structure had collapsed. I would have to start again, somehow, and adjust to a new world.

Shift happens.

It was midafternoon when I woke up and I had to see her; not to hold on, not to beg in desperation, but to close out the accounts and say goodbye. I picked up the phone, still half asleep, then decided that wasn't the way to do it.

I ran hot water and plastered a steaming washcloth across my face. The heat soaked in to the bone and I rubbed until my skin felt raw. Outside, the reverend and his awful wife were gone. I checked the doors to the house to make sure they were locked, then started around the front to the car.

The tiny plastic strip of a miniblind moved in Crazy Gladys's window next door as I passed. I turned and faced the window as I walked by and gave her a slight smile. The blinds jerked as she pulled away from the window.

Forty minutes later I knocked on Marsha's door. With the Porsche gone, there was no way to tell if she was home. I stood there for a few moments after knocking, then started to leave. The door opened behind me as I stepped off the porch.

"Oh, hi," I said, turning. "Didn't know if you were home or not."

She wore a pair of denim maternity jeans with some kind of billowy top over them. Her hair was pulled back in a ponytail and she wore no makeup. There was a thin sheen of sweat on her forehead and a gray smudge on her cheek. And the seemingly permanent circles under her eyes were particularly vivid today.

And yet she was beautiful. I tried not to look at her.

"Yeah," she said quietly. "C'mon in."

"Look, if it's a bad time . . ."

"No, c'mon." She stood aside and held the door open for me. I stepped into the hallway of her condo and stopped, startled.

There were moving boxes everywhere, piled in the hall, stacked in the foyer.

I turned to her. "Looks like you've been busy."

"Been a crazy couple of days," she said. "C'mon back."

Marsha closed the door and threaded her way between the boxes down the hall to the living room. I followed her, stepping around the boxes as well. The built-in bookcases in her living room were empty, little dust lines the only evidence of the books that once filled the shelves.

She turned, faced me. "I meant to call you," she said.

"Did you? I tried to call you but couldn't get through."

"The phone's been tied up."

"And when it's not," I said, perhaps more coldly than I intended, "you aren't picking up."

She tucked her chin, looked away from me. "I'm sorry, Harry."

"So where you going?"

She sighed. "I'm leaving town. I can't stay here. Not now."

"You could have another job with a phone call," I said.

She looked up at me. "And spend the rest of my life here with everyone knowing what's happened? This is a small town. I won't have people whispering behind my back at cocktail parties. I have some pride left. Not much, but some."

"Oh, lack of pride's not your problem, babe. Not at all."

I crossed my arms and leaned against the door frame. "So where you going?"

"I'm going to live with my aunt Marty," she said. "At least until the baby's born."

"That was her that called when I was here, right?"

"We were working out the last of the details," Marsha said. "I knew two weeks ago I'd be moving. I knew it was all going to end at the office."

I stared at her and shook my head.

"I'm sorry," she said.

"Yeah, me, too. So where's Aunt Marty? Where are you moving?"

"She's well off. Real well off. She lives in L.A. most of the time, but she has a nice place outside Reno. She's going to let me stay there. The movers come tomorrow morning and this place goes up for sale."

My mouth went slack. "Reno?" I asked, aghast. "You're moving to Reno-fucking-Nevada?"

"Yes, Harry," she said coldly. "I'm moving to Reno-fucking-Nevada."

"Well, I mean, were you going to tell me about it? Or was I just going to get the goddamn change-of-address card? Were you at least going to send me a birth announcement?"

"God," she said. "I knew you were going to do this!"

"Do what?"

"Make it harder," she said.

"Oh, should I have made it easy, Marsha? Is that what you want? Well, let me make it easy for you now, okay? I love you and I thought we had something special and I thought the two of us having a kid together was going to be a miracle, but I guess I was wrong. So you pack your stuff up and pay the movers and you run like hell just as far away from me and this city and the terrible drivers and the bozo politicians and the rest of your problems as you can!"

Her lip trembled.

"You want out, Marsha? You're out. Officially. End of story, okay? Now if you'll excuse the hell out of me, I have an appointment with the guy who murdered the guy everybody thinks I murdered."

I turned, started for the hallway.

"Wait," she said behind me.

"What?" I asked, without facing her.

"I was going to call you. I was going to say goodbye, Harry. I just wanted to do it in my own way and in my own time."

I turned and looked at her. "Doesn't really matter much now, does it?"

"It does to me," she said. "I never wanted to do it this way."

"What way did you want to do it?"

"Harry, I'm just doing what I have to do. I hope you'll understand that one day."

"I hope I understand a lot of things someday."

"I have something for you," she said.

Confused, I looked at her. She seemed a stranger now. "What?" I asked.

She walked over to a pile of boxes, dug around in one, and pulled out a padded envelope.

"I was going to mail it to you after we said goodbye and I left. I wanted you to have it, but I didn't know if I could give it to you face-to-face. But I can, Harry. I can do this and I want you to have it."

She stepped over and held out the envelope to me. I took it and unfolded the end, then reached inside.

It was a license plate, her vanity plate from the Porsche she'd just sold.

DED FLKS, it read.

"I'll give you this much," I said. "You got a hell of a sense of humor."

"I know how much you enjoyed that car. How much fun we had in it. I hope it's okay to do this."

I stared at it for a moment, held the cold, sharp-edged metal in my hand.

"Yeah," I mumbled. "Yeah, it's okay."

"Take care of yourself," she said.

"Yeah, bye."

Then I turned into the hallway, walked out her door and into a world without her.

Chapter 35

For a few minutes, I was in free fall. There was an air of unreality—no surreality—about all this; as if Marsha would come running out the door, hair flying, arms wide, and scream that it was all a joke and wasn't it fun and wasn't it hilarious and let's do it again sometime, only now let's go in and climb into bed and go at it like it was rutting season and be in love and laugh and here, baby, let me help you with your shoes and would you like a drink and let me get the body oil because I could use a good shoulder rub before we get into the sweaty stuff, and maybe a long hot bubble bath afterward and we'll listen to the new Diane Schuur CD.

I even stood in the parking lot staring at her door for a few seconds.

Only it never opened.

Damn.

And I realized the only way I was going to get out of free fall was to grab hold of something and hang on to it, hang on for dear sweet old life, and hope that the roots held and my grip was strong and that age and mileage hadn't taken too great a toll. Because the rocks below were hard and unforgiving, and there was no help for a wounded man anywhere, no one to get him up to safety and no way to do it if there was anyone. No sir, if Harry survived this one, then it was because somewhere inside him, buried in the guts and the tears and the snot and the sweat was iron, and this time if he didn't find it, he was lost.

Truly lost.

So he did the only thing he knew to do. He went back to work.

"Okay, how sensitive is this thing?" I asked.

Lonnie peeled off another strip of clear plastic tape. "Very," he said. "Now shut up and be still."

The microphone was a tiny piece of plastic with a grid in the end, black and smaller than a cigarette filter. A thin black wire not much bigger than a thread ran out of it and down the center of my chest.

Lonnie placed the mike in the center of my sternum, in the middle of my chest on an invisible line connecting my nipples. I don't have a whole lot of upper body; weight lifting has never been my specialty, so there aren't two huge mounds of breast-like pectorals to hide anything in. I've only got a slight dusting of chest hair as well, which is a comfort given that eventually all this tape will have to be ripped off.

"Hold this," he instructed.

I held the end of the mike between my thumb and index finger and pressed it into my chest. Lonnie carefully placed the tape on the body of the mike, being careful not to cover the grid with tape, and then pressed it into my skin and ran it over the wire all the way down my chest, stopping at my waistline. I felt the uncomfortable pressure of his fingertips, of someone touching me, and the stickiness and clamminess of the tape.

There was still a foot or two of wire left, with a tiny plug on the end. Lonnie reached over on his desk and grabbed a small gray cylindrical case about the size of a transistor radio battery.

"This is the power pack and transmitter," he explained. "The mike plugs into it. This little toy will broadcast about five hundred yards if there's not a lot of metal obstruction around. Got about a two-hour charge. Plenty of time."

He sat down in a chair and leaned in close to me. "Okay," he said. "Drop 'em."

I unhooked my belt and dropped my jeans down to my knees.

"Oooh," he said, laughing, "love the lingerie."

"Just shut up and get on with it."

"Sensitive, aren't we?" He giggled. "I've never seen such colorful trow."

"Three pair for six-ninety-five at Target."

"Bet it drives the chicks wild."

"You bet your ass it does," I said. "What happens if Sykes decides to frisk me?"

Lonnie looked thoughtful and hummed. "Let's see," he said. "Wait, I've got it. There's one place I know he won't look."

He turned to his desk, opened the center drawer, and started digging around in the junk.

"Now where's that tube of K-Y jelly?" he intoned.

"Forget it," I said. "Don't even think it."

He shrugged, slammed the desk drawer shut. "Hey, you asked. . . ."

"I'm serious. What if the bastard decides to frisk me?"

Lonnie laughed again. "Here, turn around."

"Not a chance," I said.

"That's not what I meant. Look, people frisk just like in the movies unless they've been trained to do it right. He'll pat your armpits looking for a gun and he might run his hand down your chest looking for a wire, but I doubt it. The mike here's small enough that he has to know what he's doing to find it. Then he'll run his hands down your legs. So we tape the transmitter to the back of your leg, just below your butt, and run the wire through this provocative pair of panties—"

"Easy, bud—"

"Just kidding, macho man. The power pack'll be hidden just about where your wallet is. Guy's gotta really know what he's doing to find it, okay?"

"All right," I said, "if you're sure."

"Turn around," he instructed. "I only have one condition to all this."

"Yeah?"

"Can I rip the tape off when this is over?"

"God," I said, turning my butt to him. "You're a sick puppy, Lonnie."

*   *   *

There's a certain amount—and no small amount, either—of trust involved in this kind of operation. You have to trust your tools, that it's quality equipment you're working with, and you have to have even greater trust in the other people, or in my case, person, who makes up your team. You have to trust that everything's been planned as well as it can be, that all options, contingencies, and scenarios have been considered and planned for.

But mostly you have to trust yourself: that you know what you're doing, that your reflexes and your rapid decision-making skills are intact, and that when something unexpected happens—as it invariably will—you'll be ready.

This was the part I was having trouble with. Given what had happened to me over the past few months, and especially the past few days, something inside me had been shaken. I'd been in tight spots before, even back before taking up private investigating. As an investigative reporter, I once had an aristocratic Old Gentleman, who was a key behind-the-scenes player in a soon to be discredited gubernatorial administration, threaten to scrape together some pocket change and have me killed. He had offered me some of the clearest, purest, most devilishly deadly moonshine ever made in the Tennessee hills in the parking lot outside his son's wedding. We toasted the newlyweds and then he warned me not to print what I had learned, which was that the counsel to the governor was the guy you wanted to see in Nashville if you wanted to buy your way out of prison. Even reporters, he explained, could be silenced. For pocket change . . .

I printed it anyway, and I'm still breathing today and the governor went to prison and the Old Gentleman retired to his farm in Hamilton County. But I was younger then, and still in a place where that which didn't kill me made me stronger. Only problem was, so many things had nearly killed me.

How damn strong was I supposed to get?

I rounded the curve off Old Natchez Trace that went around the polo field and led to R. J. Reed's country house. It was nine fifty and as dark and black as the Old Gentleman's heart. The borrowed cell phone on the seat next to me chirped.

"Yeah?"

"In place," Lonnie said.

"Look, what if the guy just decides to shoot me?" I asked, suddenly wondering if this was such a good idea. We'd considered my wearing the Kevlar vest, then decided that not only would it interfere with the wire, it might also set Sykes off.

"I'd suggest ducking."

"Where are you?"

"You don't need to know that. It's better if you don't," he said. "That way, you won't be unconsciously looking around. Just pretend you're alone."

"Yeah," I said, approaching the gate to Reed's, "that's easy for you to say."

"Now tell me about this guy Sykes again."

"He's tall, thin, almost wizened, with a strange foreign accent. German maybe. Eastern European? Hell, I don't know. And he wears a goatee and has a burr haircut."

"And you know the drill, right? You're going to take the money, get him to confess if you can, and then we go straight to Lieutenant D'Angelo's house with the tape and the cash."

"Yeah," I said, rolling down the window and reaching out to tap in the security code on the keypad. "I got it, okay? Look, I'm entering the property now. You should see me pull behind the house in about thirty seconds."

"Cool," he said. "And Harry?"

"Yes," I said impatiently.

"Watch your ass."

"Right," I said. "I'd hate to ruin your favorite pair of underwear."

I clicked off the cell phone as the gate swung open in front of me and drove quickly down the long driveway. The Reeds' house was quiet, dark. I backed the Mustang into a slot, doused the lights, and killed the engine. Cicadas chirruped loudly and in the distance mournful bovine bellowing mixed in this time with the bass profundo of bullfrogs. My feet scraped across the drive as I walked over to the patio. I leaned against a chair and set the briefcase with Reed's files on the cement next to me. Lonnie and I figured we'd actually make the transfer; that way

D'Angelo could get a search warrant and find the files, clearly marked with my name in invisible ink. Just one more bit of proof, we figured.

I looked around, my eyes adjusting to the darkness. The only light came from the soft glow of some outdoor ground lights around the perimeter of the patio.

I tried to relax. I couldn't sit down for the time being, not with the transmitter taped to the back of my leg. I scanned the area once again to make sure I was alone, then reached down through my jeans and pressed the button to start the wire. The clock was running now: two hours.

"I hope you can hear me," I said quietly. "I hope this thing works."

I smiled; this was all going on tape and would be delivered to D'Angelo. Perhaps I should be careful, watch my language, not say the first thing that comes to mind, which is my usual practice in unguarded moments.

Minutes dragged by. I pressed the button on my cheap wrist-watch that made it glow a dim green: nine fifty-eight.

"He's still got a couple of minutes," I said. "Just for the taped record, it's nine fifty-eight P.M., May 16, and I'm in the backyard of R. J. Reed's house on Old Natchez Trace."

Then I hummed a few bars. Of what, I don't know. Just nervous humming.

I walked over and leaned against the redwood siding of the Jacuzzi, where, what seemed like months ago, I found R. J. Reed facedown. The lights in the pool were off, the motors silent. I'd heard that death by drowning involved several stages, from fear to panic to rabid desperation and clawing, climaxing with a final, almost sweet surrender to death, a relaxation of the body and a letting go.

It sounded like a rotten way to die, although truth be told, I can't imagine many ways that aren't.

Behind me, I heard the distant hum of electric motors and a slight metallic scraping sound.

"Show time," I said to the middle of my chest. "I believe that's the sound of a gate opening."

I crossed the patio, grabbed my briefcase, and stepped over

to the corner of the house, secreting myself between two tall shrubs. In a moment, the flicker of approaching headlights danced against the hill behind the house and glittered off the high chain-link fence surrounding the tennis court just in front of it. I heard the sound of tires on aggregate, a kind of muted crunching sound, and then a silver Mercedes sedan pulled into the parking area, turned to point the headlights at the patio, and stopped in front of the garage. The driver cut the engine but left the headlights on. The car door opened. My eyes struggled to adjust to the headlights' glare. I could barely make out the figure climbing out from behind the steering wheel of the car.

But I knew it wasn't Karl Sykes.

I shifted my weight and slipped in the dewy grass, causing the shrubs to rustle against each other.

"Denton?" a voice called out. It took me a second, but I figured it out.

It was Webber. Travis Webber.

Chapter 36

He stepped around in front of the car, the headlights back-
lighting him, the humid air seeming to condense around him as
fog. He was larger than I remembered from our first meeting,
his hulking form shielding a good portion of the car. His hair
was splayed out, as if improperly blow-dried then sealed with
spray. His arms hung at his sides, the white cuffs of his dress
shirt extending too far below the sleeves of his badly fitted
suit coat.

"It's not Sykes," I whispered. "It's Webber. I have no idea
what this means."

I lowered the briefcase to the ground and let go of it. Webber's head flicked in my direction at the movement. I walked
quickly across the lawn and stopped in front of him, maybe ten
yards away. He remained motionless; I tried to position myself
so that his body blocked the glare and I could see him. Still, I
had to squint to block out the painful light.

"What're you doing here?" I demanded, forcing a strained
anxiety into my voice. "I told Sykes to come alone. Where
is he?"

"Everything's cool, Denton," he said, his voice low and
calm. "Don't panic."

Good, I thought, let him think I've panicked. Blanche Du Bois
may have always depended on the kindness of strangers, but
I have always depended on the willingness of people to underes-
timate me. It has been the one constant throughout most of
my life.

"Don't talk to me about panic," I snapped, my voice tight.
"Where's Sykes?"

"He told me about your phone conversation this morning and about the deal you've made. But he was afraid to meet you. Afraid it was a double cross."

"There's no double cross," I said. "I'm here alone and you better be. Otherwise, the cops are going to know what really went on with the two of you and Reed."

"This is, of course, assuming you know what went on with the two of us and Reed."

He brought his hands together across his fat stomach and rubbed them, like a hungry man anticipating the carved turkey.

"It was pretty easy to figure out," I said, remembering that I was supposed to keep him talking. I wondered if I was close enough for the wire to pick it up, then decided that for the time being I was as close as I wanted to get. The night air felt clammy and sticky and the tape running down the middle of my chest and across the back of my leg started pulling uncomfortably.

"I mean," I continued, "as soon as all the paper was in one place."

"And where, little man, was all the paper in one place?"

I nodded toward the house. "In the safe in Reed's office."

"So you're a burglar as well as a blackmailer," he said.

"I notice you didn't say killer."

He chuckled, a low kind of rumble that started as a humming sound then erupted out of his massive chest. Even backlit, his face shrouded in darkness, I could see the reflected light on the surface of his eyes. It gave him almost a twinkle.

"Why don't we conclude this deal so that we can both get on with our lives?"

"Works for me," I said. "You bring the money?"

He tapped his coat pocket with his left hand. "Right here."

"Toss it over," I instructed.

"It seems to me that there's a decided mistrust at work here on both our parts. Why don't you show me the files before I hand you the money?"

"They're here."

"So you say," he said. "Show me the paper."

I stared at him a moment, trying to figure the next move. I

wanted that money, that proof that he was willing to buy my silence because he needed it. Whether to protect himself or his partner, I didn't know. Then I remembered how big R. J. Reed had been, and how big a man it would have taken to hold him—in the desperate panic stage of drowning—underwater until he passed into the light.

A cold knife went through me. Webber? But why? He had been Reed's partner in the conspiracy to take over the company.

"Okay," I said. "The files are over here."

I stepped backward a couple of steps, keeping my eye on him, then turned and walked over to the bushes. I fished the briefcase out of the shrubbery and brushed some leaves off it, then stood up.

He was still standing there, completely motionless. I brought the briefcase up so that he could see it.

Webber reached into his pocket and removed something. When he held it up, I could see its shape in the darkness. It looked like a thick envelope.

Thick with money . . .

I crossed over the patio and stood a few feet in front of him.

"I just have one question," I said.

"What?"

"I thought all along Sykes killed Reed. That's what the paperwork looked like; you and Reed were conspiring to take over the company and Reed was foolish enough or arrogant enough to brag about it to Sykes. So Sykes killed him."

The dim light reflected off his wet teeth as he smiled. "That's quite a supposition," he said. "Too bad it's completely wrong."

"So what's the truth?" I asked. "Who killed Reed and why?"

"What difference does it make to you? You're getting your money, and as you told Karl, you're leaving Nashville for good. That's still the plan, isn't it?"

"Yeah, but let's just say it offends my narcissistic sensibilities to be so wrong."

He stepped toward me, shifting out of the path of the left

headlight, which caught my eye and erupted into a blur of pure white that blocked everything from my vision.

"Reed was a narcissist," Webber spat, "and an arrogant fool. We took him from nothing, a loser, a failure, a man who couldn't even feed his children, and we made him famous. Made him rich."

"And did pretty well yourselves," I added, bringing up my right hand and shielding my eyes. I couldn't see him now; he was just a large black form to the left of the light.

"Not as well as everybody thought," Webber continued. "The company spent a fortune adding staff, buying the building, on promotion and publicity once the book started to take off. It was the biggest gamble any of us ever made."

"And it paid off," I said.

"Barely. Just barely. But Reed took it upon himself to decide he was better than the game, that the rules didn't apply to him. He came back with these outrageous demands, demands for part of the company, for millions in advances."

"And you gave it to him." Webber moved farther to my left and I realized he was a few steps closer. Then it hit me.

I was being circled.

"Yes, we did. We figured we had to keep him in order to finish the ride. If he'd gone to another house, we'd just have his backlist. Backlist is steady money, but it never sells like new product. Then, after we made the deal, we discovered that publishing fads come and go as quickly as any others. See how much that vintage Cabbage Patch doll is worth today, or go to any remainder table and see how many hardcover Robert James Wallers can be had for three-ninety-five."

I had to keep him talking. I shifted slightly to my left as he continued moving, trying to keep him in my field of vision.

"So Reed's numbers were dropping," I offered.

"Enough that we knew we'd overspent for the sequel to his nasty little book. Enough to know that with the company's debt load, there wasn't much chance we'd make it. And everything we'd both worked for all these years was in jeopardy."

"So you cooked up this little plan whereby you and Reed would conspire to take control of Spearhead Press via the Harvest Moon Corporation, but only after Reed had ceded the rights to his books, his royalties, his merchandising, to the Sirius Corporation."

"Which became part of the Harvest Moon Corporation when the pass-through of assets was completed," Webber said.

"Reed threw everything in one pot, thinking that you and he were in cahoots together. And all the while . . ."

"Karl was selling his shares in the Spearhead partnership to me, and I was converting them to shares in the Harvest Moon Corporation without Reed's knowledge. When that was complete, then I'd vote not with Reed but against him."

"And in the end you'd own the rights to the books and to the company and Reed would be out in the cold."

"Not really," Webber said, continuing to step around me. "He'd have several millions of our money as a consolation prize. Not bad for the few weeks it took him to write that awful piece of crap."

"Only he found out, didn't he? He figured it out."

Webber stopped. "Yes, he figured it out. And he went to Karl and threatened to sue, to have us all thrown in jail, the company denuded. We couldn't have that."

"So you and Sykes killed him."

Webber was silent. The only sounds were those of the woods and pastures. "No," Webber said after a few moments. "I killed him. Not Karl. Karl wanted to, but he didn't have what it took. He wasn't willing to go the limit. You always have to be willing to go the limit."

My chest locked up and I realized I was sweating like a field hand in July. He'd said it. That was it and it was on tape and we could all go home now.

"I actually didn't intend to," Webber said. "I came here to talk to him, to try to convince him not to take a course of action that would ruin us all. But he laughed at me, was his usual arrogant, overbearing self. He was in the hot tub over there and the sun was going down and there was no one else here. And I—"

"You couldn't help yourself," I said, forcing my voice into a false calmness. "He pushed you into it. Well, I say what's done is done, Trav. It can't be helped and it can't be changed. So why don't we conclude our business. I got a train to catch."

"There's no train service to Nashville," he said, low and menacing.

"Figure of speech, Trav," I said brightly. "Let's get this over with."

He moved to his right a few more feet and I turned to follow him. I was the one backlit by the headlights now and he was fully illuminated. His face shone with sweat in the humid night and his eyes darted back and forth.

And then I saw his hands clearly, for the first time, hanging loosely at his sides. They appeared white, ghostly, unreal, like the hands of a corpse. It was an unnatural color. My eyes focused on them and then he raised his right hand, the one with the envelope in it. That's when I realized where the color came from.

Gloves. White latex gloves.

"Yes," he said. "Let's get this over with."

I had this funny pain in my chest, like a quick clutching followed by a tremolo vibration. The blood seemed to rush to my face and I felt myself flushing.

Webber stepped forward. "Give me the briefcase," he said. I tossed the briefcase about fifteen feet in front of me and it landed at his feet.

"Now throw me the money," I said.

He leaned down, picked up the briefcase, opened it, and bent to let the light hit the folders. He studied them a second, then snapped the briefcase shut. He let it drop back to the ground, then swung his right arm back and let the envelope fly in a slow-pitch softball arc.

I held out my hands to catch it, and in the dim unfocused background behind the envelope in midair, he charged.

The envelope bounced off me as I yelped and tried to dive out of his way. But Webber moved with a speed and grace amazing for a man his size and he was on me before I took two steps.

His arms were outstretched and before I could block them, the surgical gloves were wrapped around my throat, choking off my air, forcing my eyes partially out of their sockets.

I locked my hands around his wrists, trying to pull his arms apart. But his forearms were as big as my upper arms, or bigger, and I didn't have a chance against him. I tried to think— *Think, damn it!*

Knee him in the crotch, let go of his wrists and punch him in the gut, do one of those karate chop things to his neck and bring him down like a charging rhino in a Tarzan movie. . . .

Nothing. My hands were locked around his wrists, my feet scrambling for ground with no luck. I couldn't get a footing and I realized he was dragging me. My back hit a piece of patio furniture and it clattered out of the way. I tried to yell, to scream for help.

Nothing came out. Nothing could; my throat was blocked off.

And then something hit me in my lower back, right above the belt line. I looked into Webber's face and his eyes were wide, vivid with fury, his jaw locked, his upper lip curled, exposing straight, white teeth.

Then he smiled.

I felt myself going up and over, my head suddenly below my feet as they kicked helplessly in the air.

Wet. Everything was wet.

My eyes burned as everything went first out of focus, then dark. My nostrils filled and Webber's hands relaxed. He was holding me under now, but I knew not to breathe, not to let go. My throat was locked tight, my jaw clenched. My feet thrashed in the water.

I felt my foot hit something solid—the wall of the tub. I planted, pushed as hard as I could.

My feet slipped, gave way.

Panic crashed in on me like a roof giving way. My brain flashed adrenaline-charged impulses to my arms, my hands, my feet.

Nothing. I felt myself moving in the water, but that's all. Helpless, hopeless thrashing, to no end except my own.

Lonnie? I thought. Where's Lon—

From the corners of my vision, little red sparkles started glittering, mixed in with flashes, sparks of blue and green. My lungs ached, my chest so tight the skin could split. I was going to explode into a million pieces, blood and tissue and bone fragments all over the place.

That would show the son of a bitch.

A red beam of light grew larger from the center of my vision, then hotter and redder and more intense, seeming to grow by the second. I felt myself relaxing, a strange kind of peace coming over me, and suddenly I was slipping and sliding, gently falling into the red that began to vibrate and hum. It was a warm red, pulsing and glowing and as I let myself go it began to change colors. My chest didn't hurt anymore and I couldn't feel the hands around my neck, and the water was so warm and comforting, like being in the womb, going back to the womb.

Sleeping.

The red went white, brilliant white, searing white, and then from its edges a long slow fade to black.

Motion.

Upward, yanking motion. Water against my face, rushing.

A thought flashed: *Heaven. Going up to heaven . . .*

The hands gone from around my neck. Noise, yelling, screaming, hands all over me. Pairs of hands on my chest, my arms, and then pressure on my gut.

The black zaps the white, the red diminishes to a pinpoint, and I can see again.

Not much, though. It's dark. I see concrete beneath my face. Its texture registers: hard, cold, sandpaperish. Then hands on me again, delicate hands, pulling my shirt, raising my head off the concrete. I'm dripping, soaked; my hair's down in my face. It tickles my nose.

"Harry!" a voice screams. Then a slap, a ringing, sharp, stinging slap to the left side of my face.

I shake my head; she comes into focus.

Sheba.

My gut heaves and there's an explosion of water, bile, goop coming out of me. It's awful, bitter, but it's followed by an enormous gulp of air.

"Be careful," a voice says from above. "Keep his head up. Don't let him aspirate."

I swivel my head, look up. Jerry the Drill stands above us,

staring down, a cool blank look on his face. I squint, trying to focus, trying to remember where I am, who I am, why this is happening. Why am I here?

"Lonnie!" Sheba screams. "Lonnie, stop!" She slams me against the side of the hot tub and jumps away. Beyond her, I focus on Lonnie, standing over this fat guy who's facedown on the ground, writhing and moaning.

With each kick . . .

Lonnie's dog-stomping this guy, like his clothes are on fire and Lonnie's trying to put him out. Sheba runs up behind him, jumps on his back, her weight pinning his arms and pulling him backward.

He stops, shakes her off, turns, sees me. I smile, raise a hand, wave weakly. Lonnie's face is stricken, tears running down his face. He looks down at the fat guy—and the name comes to me, Travis Webber—then turns and grabs Sheba, burying his face in her blonde mane, his shoulders heaving. She wraps her arms around him, pulling him to her, comforting him.

Jerry the Drill squats down in front of me. "How ya doin', big guy?"

I opened my mouth, tried to speak. Between Webber's ham-sized hands and puking my guts out, it hurt to talk. The sweetest hurt this boy's ever had.

"Okay," I croaked. Feeble, real feeble.

"Sorry it took us so long," he said, pointing off behind me. "We were up in the barn. When the fireworks began, we hauled ass down here ASAP."

I smiled, though it was the frail, debilitated smile of the stricken.

"Thanks," I whispered.

Lonnie appeared over his shoulder, his face still wet, hair down over his forehead. He pushed Jerry out of the way, stooped down in front of me.

"How ya doin'?"

I nodded my head. "You get it all?"

He nodded back. "We called 911 on the cell phone," he said. "Cops are on their way."

"Good," I said, reaching out for him to help me up. " 'Cause I'm getting too old for this."

Lonnie broke out laughing, wrapped both his arms around me, and yanked me to my feet.

It felt good to be standing again. I took a deep breath, all the way to the bottom of my chest, the cold night air burning through me like fury.

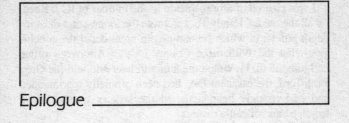

Epilogue

The next few days I did a pretty good Lauren Bacall imitation, my battered larynx delivering the deep, low rumble of the lifelong smoker. From jawline to collarbone, my neck was a rainbow of black, blue, green, and yellow beneath skin scraped raw and pink. It hurt like hell to move anything from my shoulders up, and in order to shift my field of vision, I had to move my entire upper body. Frankenstein with a sexy voice . . .

Between the tape, the paperwork, and the eyewitness accounts of the assault on me, the Williamson County District Attorney's office charged Travis Webber with a laundry list of offenses ranging from first-degree murder—which would almost certainly be bargained down to second-degree, if not voluntary manslaughter—to attempted murder and aggravated assault. They'll pile on a few other things before trial for leverage. He'll plea-bargain and be gone for a few years.

Sykes professed ignorance of any of this and is scrambling to avoid a charge of accessory after the fact. It's anybody's bet whether he'll succeed. As far as I know, *Life's Little Maintenance Manual, Volume II* will be published just in time for Christmas.

Victoria Reed paid my bill and wrote me a note of appreciation that included a couple of the more poignant nuggets of her dead husband's wisdom. I valued it just long enough to fold it into a paper airplane and launch it into the trash can. The insurance company, which had been balking at paying Reed's life insurance until she was cleared, came through in about ninety days. Between that and Reed's estate, I'd say Victoria Reed and her kids are set for life.

I was cleared of any suspicion in the murder of R. J. Reed. Of all the media, Randy Tucker wrote the longest and most in-depth article, in which he outlined in great detail the conclusions that the Williamson County District Attorney's office had jumped to. He called me a month later and told me Greg Bransford, the assistant DA, had been officially reprimanded and had recently been assigned the task of prosecuting a teenage band of cattle rustlers.

I took a couple of days off to recover, then borrowed Lonnie's pickup and cleared out my office on Seventh Avenue. It took only one pickup load and a couple of hours. A month later the building was sold for demolition as part of a plan to convert the entire block into satellite parking for the arena and the new football stadium.

So I guess it worked out okay in the end.

Mrs. Hawkins was disinterred and autopsied. Two weeks later the results came back. She died of old age. Her heart gave out and she went. I never heard a word of apology or otherwise from the Reverend Hawkins or the Ice Queen. I briefly thought of suing them or causing some other mischief in their life, but then, perhaps out of respect for his mother's memory, I decided to let it go.

That and the fact that I just didn't give a damn anymore.

Lonnie and Sheba moved in together and for a few weeks I didn't hear much from him. In the meantime, Mrs. Hawkins's part of the house had been cleared out and I began to ponder what to do with it. Truth was, I had all the room I needed up-stairs and even though she'd been kind enough to leave me a bathtub full of cash, I saw no need to spend it all buying a lot of furniture and stuff to furnish a place that was too big for me to begin with.

I decided to renovate her part of the house and rent it out. The house was paid for; all I had to cover was the property taxes and the upkeep. Anything else was gravy. She had three bedrooms downstairs, and fixed up I guessed I could get some-where between eight hundred and a grand a month. Not a ton of dough, mind you, but enough that if I went a few weeks without picking up some work, I wasn't going to starve. Working without a net was eventually going to get old.

Besides, it would give me something to do while I figured out what to do next. I liked investigative work, but in the past few months it had taken a real toll. Maybe I was ready for semiretirement. If nothing else, it would be nice to know I could pick and choose the cases I wanted to work.

I started by gutting the bathrooms and replacing the ancient fixtures. Then I installed a dishwasher and a new kitchen sink. I discovered, much to my surprise, that I was pretty good with my hands and that hard physical labor was gratifying in ways I'd never understood before. The reward was nearly instant, compared to the work I'd done most of my life, and it felt good to go to bed at night physically drained but emotionally charged. I lost some weight and started to firm up a bit. I kept a radio going in the background, tuned to the jazz station, and a cordless phone nearby that almost never rang. I spent a great deal of time alone and that was just fine.

Like many of the houses in this area, Mrs. Hawkins's house was built after the famous tornado in the early Thirties—1932, I think it was—wiped out most of the area. Construction methods back then were different from what they are now; cruder in some ways, more refined in others. Interior walls were constructed using traditional lath and plaster methods. I discovered after phoning around that plastering walls is almost a lost art. Everybody uses drywall now. For some reason or other, I wanted to stay with the old methods and after some inquiries I found a retired plasterer down on Sixteenth who was willing to teach me. I spent the rest of the summer replastering walls and mastering the art of flowcoats, then painting and trimming and replacing molding. Then I hired out for refinishing the oak floors. Better to pay for that; it's too easy to destroy a good floor if you don't know what you're doing. I landscaped the yard and cleaned up, then painted the garage while the floor guys did their work.

The summer months passed quickly and pleasantly and by Labor Day I had a house that was prime rental property. I went through an executive relocation firm and found a young couple with one kid and another on the way. He'd been transferred from L.A. and they were delighted to find a three-bedroom rental near downtown in a decent neighborhood for only $1250 a month. I suddenly understood the complaints by locals that the immigrants from L.A. and the northeast were driving property values up.

I was making lunch one afternoon and studying the classifieds to check office rental rates when the phone rang. Startled because my phone had become so silent I sometimes checked just to make sure it's working, I picked it up.

"Hello," I said. Original, huh?

"Hey, you."

It took me a second. It's not that I'd forgotten what she sounded like; it's just that I'd finally managed after all this time to go as long as forty-five seconds or a full minute without thinking of her.

"Marsha?"

"Yeah. How you doin', babe?"

So it's babe, is it? What the hell is going on?

"Okay," I said. "And you?"

"As big as the Goodyear blimp. I heard you were cleared of the murder charge."

"Yeah. Beat the rap one more time."

"Got your good name back, eh?"

I laughed. "I wouldn't go that far."

We both sat there for a few moments, awkward and clumsy. "So," I said finally, "what's new?"

"Well," Marsha said. "It looks like I'm having this baby in a couple weeks. I'm ready for it to be over."

"How are things working out at your aunt Marty's?"

"Fine. She's rarely here. I've got a young woman who comes a few hours every day to cook, clean, help me out. She's not much company, though, because her English is not too good and my Spanish is nonexistent."

"Gee, sorry to hear that."

"It's not so bad. After the past few months, I'm glad to be left alone for a while."

"Funny you should say that," I offered. "That's exactly how I feel."

"So what are you up to?"

"I spent the summer renovating Mrs. Hawkins's house. I've rented it out to a nice young couple and I'm still living upstairs. Truth is, I'm trying to figure out what to do next."

"Yeah, I know the feeling." She was quiet for a long time, and I decided it was her turn to speak first.

"So," she said, "you think about me much?"

What was she up to?

"Yeah, I do."

"I think about you a lot, too, Harry. I wish I'd done some things differently."

"Like what?"

"I made a lot of mistakes, that's all."

"Yeah, well . . . Shit happens."

She cleared her throat. "So," she said brightly, "would you like to know what we're going to have?"

"What *we're* going to have?"

"Okay, what I'm going to have, but what we made."

"And what did we make?"

"We made a little girl, Harry."

It was like a fist in my gut. I drew in a sharp breath and tried not to choke. There was this lump in the middle of my chest and pressure in my eyes and for a brief moment it was like I could feel Travis Webber's latex-gloved hands around my throat again.

"You there?" she asked.

I cleared my throat, tried to compose myself as best I could. *Damn her.*

"Wow," I muttered.

"Yeah," she continued, just as chipper as she could be. "I had my last ultrasound a week ago and you know how they always want to know if you want to know, whether it's a girl or boy, you know, and I'd always said don't tell me. But this time I just decided I couldn't wait anymore, so I said—"

"Marsha," I interrupted, "why are you telling me all this?"

She stopped, stunned. She seemed to hiccup into the phone and there was a long, staticky silence.

"Because," she said, her voice breaking, "I miss you and I'm scared and I need you and I want you here to see your baby being born."

"What?" I asked. My eyes welled and everything went out of focus.

"Is that too much to ask, Harry?" she said, clearly speaking through tears now. "Is that too damn much to ask?"

I leaned back in my kitchen chair and stared out the window. Is life weird or what? Here this woman takes me on the rowdiest roller-coaster ride of my life, announces that I am definitely not the guy she wants to spend the rest of her life with, keeps me in the dark when that life falls apart, then walks out on me. And now she's halfway across the country, weeping into the phone and pleading with me to come keep her company.

Modahn women, as Mrs. Lee would say.

What the hell, I thought. If the last six months hadn't killed me, a drive out West wouldn't. Besides, I could use a vacation.

"No," I said. "I guess not."

"Well, I think you're out of your frigging mind."

"Oh, shut up, Lonnie," Sheba said. "Give him a chance."

Lonnie walked back into the dining room of their condo with a fresh bottle of wine. They'd invited me to dinner the following Saturday night and I'd been shocked to see a wonderfully furnished, top-floor condo of a West End high-rise near Saint Thomas Hospital. The place was full of antiques and packed bookcases and original art by some of the finest local artists around: huge Polly Cook tile paintings, Myles Mailie murals in chaotic swirls, lots of Southwestern stuff in big comfortable rooms full of Stickley furniture. And the real shocker was that it had been Lonnie's all along; she'd moved in with him because his place was bigger and the address was more prestigious. This guy was full of surprises.

"No, seriously, love," Lonnie said. He wore a pair of pressed jeans and a tuxedo shirt and was clean shaven and well groomed and had a diamond stud in his left ear. Guy cleans up well.

"Here's this woman who dumps on my main man here. Who uses him essentially as an anonymous sperm donor, then discards him when she's done with him."

He turned to me. "Take my advice, Harry. Stay here. What the hell you going to do in Reno, Nevada, anyway? I've played poker with you, pal. You got no future in that."

"He's not staying there forever, right?" Sheba turned to me, almost imploring.

"No, of course not," I said, sipping a buttery California chardonnay Lonnie'd set out to accompany the fresh lobsters we'd just finished chowing down. "I'm going to go out for the birth, and then we'll negotiate. We'll figure out what to do next."

"Well, I mean, look, dude, it's your call. We'll watch the house and if there's any maintenance problems, you just tell the Steinbergs to call here and the old Lonmeister will get right on it. And we'll collect the rent checks and pay the utilities and you can take that management fee and stick it where the sun don't shine. But I still think you're nuts."

"Love is nuts." I smiled at him as he sat across from me at the table with an arm around Sheba's chair. "But it's one of the few things that makes getting out of bed every morning worthwhile."

"Aw, that's so sweet," Sheba cooed, turning to Lonnie and gazing into his eyes.

"Yeah, you're a regular poet," Lonnie said. "I'll just say the one thing that I seem to say to you a lot these days."

"Yeah? What's that?"

"Will you *please* watch your ass?"

Lonnie and I tuned up the Mustang the next morning, changed the plugs and the oil and lubed it up. Then I packed a bag, gave the Steinbergs instructions on how to find Lonnie and where to mail the rent checks, then bade farewell to their seven-year-old girl—who'd developed sort of a crush on me, I think.

Then I headed for the freeway. I-65 north to I-24, then on to St. Louis and points west. If I didn't dawdle, I could make Reno in three days, maybe four. Marsha and I'd have maybe a week to readjust before the baby came.

After that, who knew?

There's a place on I-65 north, right before you get to the I-265 junction and a few miles before you take the I-24 split, where you go under a bridge. When you come out, you're on a little rise and in the rearview mirror you get a portrait of downtown Nashville. It's the place where some photographer about three decades ago took a picture of the Nashville skyline and put it on the cover of a Bob Dylan album of the same name.

I'd forgotten about that picture, that place. I came out from under the bridge in a long line of traffic and glanced in my rearview mirror and there it was. And I thought of how much the Nashville skyline had changed since that time, since my days as a young man listening to "Lay Lady Lay" and wondering what love and life and women were really about.

I still haven't figured it out. And I'd had the crap beaten out of me a few times trying. But I realized, as I said goodbye to the Nashville skyline receding in my mirror, it was still worth the trouble to keep trying. As long as the secret handshake was still out there, it was worth going after. Some time away would do me good. I felt almost young again.

Go West, middle-aged old gentleman with the heart of a boy, go West.

Look for these award-winning mysteries by
STEVEN WOMACK
featuring Harry James Denton

DEAD FOLKS' BLUES
The Edgar Award–winning debut of P.I.
Harry James Denton

Harry is unpleasantly surprised when his old college flame walks into his office requesting his services. Needing money more than peace of mind, he agrees to investigate her rich husband—but by the time Harry catches up with him, he's dead.

TORCH TOWN BOOGIE
Nominated for the Shamus Award

The fiancé of Harry's ex-wife, Lanie, is found bludgeoned to death in the aftermath of an arson fire—and Lanie is the primary suspect. Harry must match wits with the firebug before Lanie's life goes up in flames.

WAY PAST DEAD
Nominated for the Shamus Award

When rising country singer Rebecca Gibson is murdered, all evidence points to her ex-husband, but on the night of her death their marriage seemed to be perfect. To solve this nasty case, Harry probes the seamier side of the country and western music business. . . .

CHAIN OF FOOLS
Nominated for the Shamus Award
and the Anthony Award

Harry James Denton's search for a rich runaway teen takes him to the very wild side of Nashville, and even a hardboiled P.I. like Harry isn't prepared for what awaits him there. He hopes he can save this lost girl before she destroys herself—or lets a ruthless murderer do it for her.

by STEVEN WOMACK